The Ove

If you bring forth what is within you, what you bring forth shall save
you.
If you do not bring forth what is within you, what you do not bring
forth will destroy you.

(from the Gnostic Gospels)

The quotation on page 254 is from
Part 5 of *The Hollow Men*
by T.S. Eliot

SYLVIA GROVES

The Overshadower

ASHGROVE PRESS, BATH

Published in Great Britain by
ASHGROVE PRESS LIMITED
Bath Road, Norton St Philip
Bath BA3 6LW

ISBN 1–85398–085–4

First published 1996

Typeset in 10.5/12 point Caslon by
Ann Buchan (Typesetters), Middlesex
Printed in the UK by
Redwood Books, Trowbridge, Wilts.

Contents

1: Passing Through

WHEN THE TIME comes, they take you through. Through the ritual of steel doors. Down the lime-green corridor to the isolation cell.

It's nearer to the glassy cage. The Death-Machine.

You've been living with that as a next-door-neighbour for six years. It's been nearer to you than your thoughts. Soon you get to meet, face to face. And you've heard dangerous men crying like new-borns; their voices echoing back to your cell along the green corridor. Until the steel doors close, and you can't hear them any more.

You've heard a man who always wore a wooden cross shouting 'Screw God! There ain't no God! I didn't ask to be born! Give me a drink of water, Man – just give me a drink of water! And you can dump my corpse in the garbage can, you sons of bitches, when it's done!'

You've heard their feet in that corridor so many times; or the feet of the guards, half-carrying, half-dragging them. They've gone past your cell room. But they won't be coming back. You've heard them being taken through. It makes you more familiar with the Final Moment. And more familiar with the nature of Men.

You can get yourself a choice preacher, if that's what turns you on; but if you don't care one way or the other, you get Father Sean McNally. He's their gift to you on the Last Day – your Day of Armageddon. Through him, the State of Mississippi tries to make amends.

Who'd have his job? No-one you ever knew. The State of Mississippi or the Almighty gave him a commission that lines stomachs with asbestos, and turns hearts into ticking things. Maybe he was a kid once. Who knows?

The last hour has come. And the corridor feels too short. Not enough steel doors. But it takes forever to walk down it. And as you walk you smell something weird; and realize it's the liquids of your body, flowing the wrong way. Fear does that to you. They flow the wrong way and become unrecognizable. You smell it. It smells acrid and sickening.

And you want to piss; though you just did. Just when you can't any more. Just when you realize you'll never be able to piss again. You can't feel your hands; and the Medic tells you it's hyperventilation. You're taking in too much oxygen: the stuff that makes life possible. He gives you a brown paper bag to blow into, and you laugh because it's odd that he should carry brown paper bags in his Death-Kit; and because it's the last paper bag in the world.

They're efficient, polite, kind in the Last Hour. They've got nothing to lose any more. They're about to send you to kingdom come, and you're a trapped rat. But here, even if you smoke, you can't have a cigarette. Not here. No smoking area. Dangerous equipment nearby.

The wheels of Beaurocracy turn ever on. Not even for Richard Brett do they do any different. Tonight, they have a streak of sadism because they keep you here for a while; in the waiting-place you don't want to be. But you've got no choice. This is it; the sum total of what you are, and of what you've ever been.

They have things to arrange. Calls to make. Checks on the efficiency of their Death-Cage. Tonight, beaurocracy can waste time; for the reason that there's more of it where this hour came from.

Not for you.

Some of the bastards in here didn't even do it. Only a few among the crowd; but some. Each one a Black face. But you did it. You know about that. You did it okay. A long time ago, now; but it was a deed still done.

Let us pray. McNally's come through with you, because you're on record as a Catholic. A fact dug from so long ago it's not even true any more. This is what you are. This is all you are:

NAME: BRETT. Richard Anthony.
NATIONALITY: Naturalized Citizen of the United States of America, State of Mississippi.

MALE CAUCASIAN.
AGE: Thirty nine.
HEIGHT: Six feet two inches.
COLOUR OF HAIR: Brown.
COLOUR OF EYES: Grey.
DISTINGUISHING FEATURES: None.
RELIGION: Catholic.
MURDER ONE. THREE COUNTS.

No doubt that's how it goes.

Let us pray. You didn't care if he came in with you or not; but he came. Into the White Room. His God is a beaurocratic God. To get to him, you have to have the I.D. You have to fill in all the forms. Do you require Extreme Unction?

Surely he shouldn't ask you? You've got no answer, but you notice that he doesn't seem to care. He prays, anyway. The room is too white for eyes that haven't slept; that will never sleep again. And it smells of bleach. Why?

Now I can hear McNally's voice but I can't hear the words.

How long is there till midnight?

They're shaving your chest – to put the E.C.G. terminals on you, they explain, There was one Medic, but now there are two. You wonder if there always were two; or if one came through the steel door, without you noticing. They tape stethoscopes to your bare chest. They are so polite – they even bother to explain. The E.C.G. terminals are there so that they can tell for certain when your heart stops beating, and their mission is accomplished.

One of the Medics is so fair, his eyelashes are white. He wears a little moustache; and he looks about twenty. When he asks you if it's comfortable, he doesn't look you in the eyes.

Some guys hope for a miracle. It carries them through. A last minute call from their attorney. Reprieve from the President. They sit here, smiling. I've heard about it. Not me. Miracles don't know me. For them, I don't exist.

Let us continue to pray.

Then you can put your shirt back on: if your arms still work. Every second of your waiting puts pressure on the air in the White Room. It feels like something's going to blow. Now you can hardly hear. There's a ringing sound; and you know it's from your own brain. They keep you waiting. Like desk-clerks keep you waiting. Like subway trains and Welfare officers keep you waiting. But it's so long ago. So long ago that I ever had to wait for them.

Then they come. The moment stops – so suddenly, it turns back on itself. And it's me they want. Me. This is it.

I hear Father McNally say he's coming with me. Under guard we walk on. He calls me son.

The pressure's coming back, and it's building up behind my eyes. And my mouth is too dry to swallow.

I'm moving with them. And why am I walking? Why am I going with them?

And it's cold. So cold, I can hear my teeth.

No, it's not you. It's not you they want. You want to turn, and fight. And kill again, just to get out. You cannot be doing this; going to a place where there's no more you. But the steel doors wouldn't let you out and the guards would bring you back, no matter how many times you ran. Then they'd give you a shot of something to make sure you walked in the wrong direction. They're not persuadable.

You see it. The Death-Cage. It's so neat, so clean, so scientific. But it's from another century. A futuristic Machine of the Inquisition. Steel, glass windows, pipes coming out of it, rivets. A wheel to seal the door. It's like a diver's bell. They're going to send you under the sea.

I can't go in that thing. Why am I doing what I'm told? Christ Jesus!

Through those windows they watch you die. They watch you die. I'm not going in it. It stops here, on this threshold. The whole world stops here. The buck stops right here.

Then I stop, because I can't go on. It's not sensible. Not possible. But I can feel hands on each side of me. I can feel the guards moving me through. After all, their politeness was a mask of unreality. I can feel the hard, muscular determination of them; but I can't feel where their hands are touching me, any more. I look; and see that they are still there. Father McNally makes the sign of the Cross.

Go to Hell.

The straps come down with a leather slapping noise. Curiously, I look down at them. They're just like the belt on a pair of jeans. No different. Just that. They wrap around, hook in, buckle up. Ankles. Arms. Head.

It's too cold in here; and too fast. The seat feels damp. Maybe this isn't my body in here. Maybe it's a mistake. The airlock doors hiss. It's you. It is you in here. They are all out there, now; moving away. You still have to wait. Wheels have to turn. You wait; and you wait. And the air feels thin, coming through your teeth that are biting down hard. The seat is so cold. Too cold to stay here. And there isn't enough air.

Not enough air.

I'm choking. Jesus Christ, I'm choking. Going to puke. But there's nothing in me any more. Something's getting so thin. Too thin.

A light took over . A terrible burning, so bright, so painful that I dared not look into it. I closed my eyes again, and felt a throbbing cutting into my head. The light was eating through me. I couldn't open my eyes. Couldn't look at the light.

But I had no eyes. I had no life. I'd gone through the Death-Machine.

But there was pain in my eyes, where the glare had touched them. And a torrent of voices came through from somewhere behind that glare. Words, in German. Words of languages I'd never heard. Music; tribal drum-beats. Crying and laughing, and loving voices bore down on me; passed through me, and moved away. And the light was all I saw; even through my blindness. A fresh wave of sounds came at me. Children, and creatures. Dogs howled, and I heard the screams of slaughtered cattle. And, rising up on the wave I heard a language I understood; and the voices crowded in. One after the other, they approached; then passed me. Their torments shattered whatever there was of me into fragments.

And I knew I was with them; with the screaming and the dying. With the laughing and the still-living.

I heard the low throb of a helicopter engine; and the shouting of a man. His voice was desperate; ragged as he barked orders.

Go through! Get over there! Now! And that's an order! Do it! Let's move it out! Let's move it . . . His voice passed into a distance, as others replaced it.

Mom . . . Mom . . . just look after them for me. It'll be okay now. It'll be okay. He never should have done that . . . it was too much, too much damn pressure . . . It's okay, Perretti . . . we'll get you out of there just as soon as we can . . . Okay? Now you just hang on . . . hang on . . . What'll I do? . . . When you . . . are far away . . . and I am blue. What'll I do? . . . Oh God! shut them up, please! I can't stand it! . . . I can't . . . can't stand it! . . . . . . In nomine Patrii . . . et Filii, et Spiritus Sancti. Amen.

Someone was shooting. Heavy artillery fire. Let's give 'em something hot now . . . hot hot . . . We're cooking 'em . . . and Charlie's roasting his ass! Okay, back to the chopper . . . back . . . back . . .

We've done what we can, but he's not going to come out of this. E.C.G. reading is flat . . . too late . . . too long . . . We've got to stop now . . . He never loved me, the son of a bitch . . . he never loved me . . . and when he finds me O.D'd and blue in the face that'll be fine because it's what I want . . . it's what I've always wanted! . . . Jesus! . . . Jesus! . . . where are you? . . . They told me you'd be here! . . . Oh Lord . . . oh Lord! . . . where are you? . . . Mamma! Where's my Mamma? Mamma, where are you? . . .Oh Jesus, Lord, don't leave me! . . .

As they circled in the vortex of acid brilliance, the voices shaped themselves into a wind; a jagged, wretched gale that lifted what was left of me and carried me with it through the centre of the light, until I knew that I would be crushed, pounded to dust.

And we were all sucked through.

The sounds stopped. Out of a sudden quietness came one voice. It laughed. 'Welcome,' it said. 'Welcome to the Levels.'

2: Meeting on the Levels

'WHERE THE HELL am I?'

But the voice didn't answer.

There was no more pain in my eyes. No more light. I looked around; saw no-one. I'd heard a man, laughing; speaking to me. But I realized that I was alone. In the grey twilight, all I could make out was a high dry-stone wall directly ahead of me. As I scanned its length, I saw that it stretched endlessly across a treeless moorland; a wide, bleak, undulating landscape. It could have been somewhere in England; perhaps Cumberland. The thought struck suddenly with a powerful jolt as I remembered that had been my birthplace. My birthplace, a million miles away. But the grass had been green, there, green. This was different; dead. The grass rustled with lifelessness as I sank down on to it and drew up my knees; clasping them in my trembling arms.

You're not dead. You're alive. You've come home.

I wasn't in a cell room. I wasn't in the Death-cage. I was sitting on some greyed-out bit of England. In front of me was a dry-stone wall. Around me there was nothing but total silence.

And someone had spoken. I knew for sure they had. I sprang to my feet. Anger surged up in me.

'You damn well hear me! I asked you where in hell's name I am, you supercilious bastard! You hear me! Now you damn well answer!'

But there was no response. My voice died away in the dull air. Anger faded. Panic came in on its heels as I struggled with what was happening,

Okay, you've died. You've been finished off. There was no way out of the airlock doors. They're sealed. You know that. No way out, and those guys mean business. They don't change their minds.

I looked at the wall. In places it had weathered and crumbled, and stones had fallen, leaving rough gaps, surrounded by lichen growth. I stepped up to it, touched it. My hand felt stone; just stone. Nothing else. But I knew this wasn't real. I was living it, feeling it; but it wasn't real. A large stone dropped away; rolling to my feet. Another one fell. And I jumped back; watched as a small gap formed in front of me. I could see through it to the other side; and there, the air seemed lighter. A colourless glow filtered across the landscape .

As I watched it spread and brighten slightly, I felt a quick flash of hope. The odd sensation rose, and then sank away. I searched for the light-source, but could see no sun. It seemed to have no origin. In the uncanny silence, as I bent to look through the gap, I suddenly knew there was something behind me. A presence which hadn't been there before. I stayed still; didn't move. Then, grasping the dregs of my strength, I whipped round to face it.

Behind me, a gaping chasm had opened up. The moorland had split apart, and was still splitting; snaking towards me. As it widened, moving in on me, it cracked the bleak terrain open. I stood, fixed with horror; watched the deep crack edge its way towards the wall. It moved quietly, menacingly. There was no vibration of the ground; no upheaval of the dry grass on each side of it as it reached out, crept steadily forward, drew closer and closer to me. And I could only watch, as its breadth kept widening.

Then, when the brink of it was only about six feet away from me, it stopped moving, as if in answer to a command I couldn't hear, and revealed its depths. As I gazed up and down the entire length of it, I saw that it stretched from one horizon to the other, following the line of the wall perfectly. Its depth seemed to suck me in, swallow me up. I began to back away but immediately felt the solidity of the wall behind me. I had six feet of space, and a great stretch of length; that was, if the chasm stayed as it was, and didn't move any more.

I couldn't stay where I was. That was certain. So I turned to the gap. I had no choice but to try to go through it. I bent, and tried to squeeze inside; but the space was tight against me, and didn't seem wide enough to let me through. I backed off a bit, lay down and tried to force my body into it, head-first. The stone pressed in on my shoulders, so I twisted sideways. Then the wall gripped; closed in on me. It began to contract; pushing and squeezing my body. And I had no control.

Fighting a choking panic, I struggled, trying to haul my body along a passageway which seemed to extend as it became a tunnel of moving, pulsing rock. And it was warmer than stone. It had a kind of life.

Then, with a great and sudden rush, I was thrown out of it, and fell floundering on the other side like something vomited up by the sea. A terrible howl echoed across the landscape; a howl half way between the sound of a beast, killing, and the sound of a man, weeping. And then I knew that the voice was mine, and that I was released. I lay, washed up, not able to move as a faint light glowed around me.

Then I remembered the strange voice; the one which had spoken to me. I tried to stand up, but found it difficult to co-ordinate; to find my balance. Struggling up, I looked around, but saw no-one.

'Okay!' I called out. My voice sounded small. 'Who are you? Someone's there . . . okay . . .?'

No answer came. I waited; but no-one spoke.

Then I saw my hands. *My hands.*

You're dead. You know you are. Nothing else makes sense. That's why it doesn't seem real.

They were outdoor hands; the way they'd always been. They weren't the hands of a man six years on Death Row, but were weathered, corded with veins, hard-working.

I saw my clothes. Ex-army combat pants, grey-blue work shirt, walking boots. It was clothing I used to wear; not State Pen. jeans and vest. The sight made me dizzy. I gazed out at the landscape, yellow-green and russet. It reached into the distance flatly in all directions. There were no features; no trees.

'Where am I . . .?' I whispered to myself; and began to move forward to nowhere.

'In the Land of the Ancestors.'

The voice came out of nothing. It was the same voice. But now it wasn't laughing. It halted me in my tracks. I spun round and saw a man, who sat with his back against the stone wall. His eyes were on mine. I'd checked that wall checked every inch of it. But he was there. He gave me an odd feeling.

'Jesus . . .! Is this really happening . . .?'

He grinned. 'I reckon,' he answered.

Unable to take in what I saw, I stared at him. He was all

colours and fringes and braids; like a Red Man, but not quite. He was something else.

'Who are you . . .?'

He'd sprung out of nowhere. So had the chasm. The stones had fallen at hardly a touch. The landscape was weird. It wasn't what it seemed to be.

'Yeah,' he said. 'Sure is confusing.' He grinned again, wider. But he didn't get up. I turned on him fast;

'Okay wise-guy! So you're a damn mind-reader! What do you want?'

'Man, you're in one hell of a bad mood, ain't you? You have some kind of tough time getting through?' He looked me up and down.

'What?' I took a step closer; 'A what?' I could feel the return of my energy, like blood to a numb limb. With it came my temper. There was something which instantly annoyed me about him; something a bit too cheerful and smiley, and I felt like giving him a hard time.

'Some guys it gets that way,' he continued; 'Specially the ones who ain't ready to go. They go hard. The ones who have to go fast. Know what I mean? When they're no way ready. But boy, you sure are lucky, when you get to thinking about it. Oh yeah. 'Cause there's some – and this is a bare-ass fact – there's some who never do get through, not under their own steam. And that's even tougher. They get stuck – kind of stuck – and they don't move nowhere, not till they're ready to go. No smart-ass, no sweet love, no angels gonna get them moving. That's heavy-duty bad news.'

I said nothing. I just looked at him. But that didn't seem to give him any problem, and he kept on talking.

'How was it for you, boy–?'

I'd had enough.

'Look, jerk' I said, eyeball-to-eyeball with him now. 'Why don't you shut up?'

'Hey, Man . . .'

'I said . . .' I spoke very quietly, very slowly. 'Shut it. Give it a rest. Put a sock in it. Silencio. Got it? I said, have you got my drift?' He nodded; still smiling.

'Good,' I finished. But I kept my eyes on him. I'd met his sort before. Lurkers, I called them. He was a lurker of the worst kind.

'You know what you are?' I said. 'You're a goddamn lurker, that's what. Do you know what one of those is? Well, let me tell you. Let me put you in the picture. They lurk − that's what they're best at − looking for someone, anyone, to give it to. They hang around at street-corners. They hang out under lamp-posts. Airport terminals and station platforms are their all-time favourite venues. Well, they're never quite bad enough to get locked up, and they make sure they stay that way, because to get grounded would really cramp their style. But they're head-cases, all right. And they're tricky for some guy just wanting to mind his own business.

Now they usually draw the line at anything physical − that's because they haven't got the guts − but verbal knockout is definitely their speciality. And it's always verbal of the really boring kind. And they can keep it up. Oh sure, they can keep it up all day and all night, given the right sort of encouragement. And some of them − the really seasoned lurkers − are so goddamn patronizing, know what I mean? So butter-wouldn't-melt-in-their mouths cheerful and considerate! And − oh shit! Every now and then, one of them picks on me! Well, I'm not having it! You hear me? Not here. Not now. Definitely not now!'

I took a last, long look at him; then turned my back. He didn't give me the impression he was dangerous, but I couldn't be certain. I decided to ignore him, and move out. If he jumped me from behind, he wouldn't have stood a chance, anyway. He was slight, and didn't look much of a physical type. I could have him flat out in seconds. So, I thought, he'd better not try anything, for his own sake. I started walking. Where to, I had no idea. But I'd only gone a few steps when I heard him start talking again.

'Weird out there. Uncharted territory, some of it. Can take a guy by surprise.'

Sure it was. I didn't answer. I just kept on going.

'Where you going? Got any place to go?' he called after me.

Just shut up, I thought, I don't need this.

'You're going riding, Man. You can do some wild stuff, now. Wild. Hey, how about that?' He called again. 'Fly like a bird, Man Fly! Yeah! Bird-Man! Go, go, go!'

Then the ground fell away under my feet. And I was high;

much higher than I wanted to be. Too many miles high; and too fast.

'Shi-i-i-it! Get me off! . . . Get me off this thing!'

Oh, God. I hated flying. It was the one thing that terrified me; that turned my guts to water. I didn't know where I was going. Or how fast. Or how far.

'No-o-o! Right now! For Christ's sake! Get me . . . off!'

'Okay,' I heard. 'Sure.' And I was down. I swayed about like a drunk.

'You see what I mean, Man? Stuff like your wildest dreams, hey?'

'You son-of-a-bitch! You crazy son-of-a-bitch! You did that!'

'Yeah. Guess I did. That was some rough ride . Sorry, Man. Just some party trick; to show you how your mind ain't your own. Had to do it. Had my reasons. Try not to get mad at me.'

'Try not to . . .! Damn you to hell!'

'Had to get you to ease up a bit. Stop for a bit; hang around, y'know. Had to give you some shock. I know it's the thing you hate most of all.' I could hardly speak. If I hadn't felt so bad, I would happily have ended his career, right that minute. I looked at him, speechlessly.

'Had to get you to listen, 'cause you've got an attitude. Only way to sand it down a bit.'

'I've got an attitude? What the hell is this? You psycho freak-ass! Now you tell me, right now, how you got into my mind like that, because I want to know! Do you hear me?'

He nodded; smiling. 'Sure. I hear you.'

He'd got into my thoughts. He'd made me not only think, but experience something. I'd lived it, for those few moments. He was dangerous. For all he looked like an out-of-date hippy – he was dangerous. I decided to be especially careful with him. I wouldn't make a break for it, yet; but save it for later. I'd wait, for something to distract his attention, then get out while the going was good. No doubt he'd used a kind of hypnotism. If he could do that, he could do . . . what? Anything?

'It wasn't, y'know,' he said, cutting through my thoughts. 'Hypnotism. No way. Hey, I know it was kind of hard-core mean of me; but I had to get you to stop and maybe listen a while.

There's a lot to . . .' I cut him off. 'Look. I don't know you, and I'm damn sure I don't want to know you. What are you, anyway? You come here off the last bus from the crazy-farm, or what? You're pathetic, you creep! And whatever it is that you want to try and make me listen to, well, I don't need it! Got that? Leave it out, pal. You've picked on the wrong one!'

He grinned again, sighed, and said 'Okay. I know how you feel.'

'Don't give me that! You know how I feel?'

'Yeah. I do. Kind of. I've seen a lot of stuff here. Seen guys dragged through, out of their heads, sometimes. Heard a lot of them screaming. Screaming to go back. Some of them take a long while to shape up. You're one of the lucky ones. Some have even attacked me.'

Well, I thought, I can't imagine why.

'Hey, you want to listen?' he went on. 'Give me a minute, hey?' Much as I wanted to go and leave him to it, I didn't trust him. There was nothing but wide open space ahead, and no cover; and if he decided to pull another stunt, I'd be at a loss. I didn't fancy that. So I stood where I was. He still hadn't moved from his original position: back against the wall, legs straight out on the ground in front of him.

Then I really looked at him. He was old; older than he had first appeared, as his build was slight and boyish. He wore rainbow-coloured leggings and a fringed sleeveless deerskin jerkin; like the kind of things hippy girls wear. His hair was quite grizzled, and hung in two long braids down the front; his forehead bound with a thick twisted leather thong headband. I guessed he could have been in his seventies, maybe, but his clothes created a different impression. And his brown, wrinkled face looked as if he had never grown hair on it. It was as smooth as a woman's. As I looked him up and down, he didn't say a word. He didn't move an inch. There was something else incongruous about him. His eyes – strangely young, strangely clear for a man of his years – were the palest ice-blue. Yet his face looked part Negro, part Native-American. There was a humorous cast in those eyes, which I found irritating. He was laughing at me.

'Right on!' he said. 'Bullseye! Momma was as Black as the Ace of Spades. Pa was a Cheyenne warrior! You got that one hot on the target!'

'Okay. Okay! You've got something to say? Well, say it! Say it, and then leave me alone.'

'Hey! You don't mix with my sort, your sort? Ain't that right? 'Cause something about me worries you, doesn't it Englishman? Maybe you figure I'm some kind of way-out queen, huh?'

'Now you just wait a minute. I never said . . .'

'Yeah, Man. You said it. I heard you psyching me out. Sure did!'

I sighed in exasperation; and the sound came back to me. It sounded feeble; petulant. It was obvious he was trying to manipulate me into a conversation; the way lurkers usually did. But I sensed he was more than that. I saw a peculiar strength about him; and it disturbed me in a way I couldn't understand. His eyes were still laughing.

'Could be you need to wise up on some information,' he went on. 'Right now you need to know a few things. Need to get your ass in gear; learn a few tricks. Could come in useful. Bad Lands if you don't. Hey, you got no idea. You're still green as a spring twig; still slippy as a new-born baby. You don't want to listen? Fine. You'll find out. There ain't no teacher like Experience. Say, I can't teach you nothing, Hard-Man, but I can show you this and that; help you along a bit. What d'ya say?'

'I don't damn well need you! Let's get that straight right now, shall we? I'm here. You're here. Big coincidence. End of story.'

'Tell you what,' he said. 'Tell you what, we'll flip on it.' And he took a coin, or what appeared to be a coin, out of the winding tendrils of his headband. He flicked it in the air, and caught it in his left hand, slapping it down on his right. He didn't take his eyes off me.

'Gates or birds?' he said.

'What?' I really didn't want to know. I didn't want any more involvement with him. I just needed time alone; time to think things through.

'Go on, call.'

'Do you never give up? For Christ's sake!'

'Gates or birds?'

'Birds!' I spat at him.

'Birds it is!' Eagerly, he lifted his hand to show me the coin. I had no interest in his crazy games. I never even looked.

He laughed, and shouted. 'Gates you stay! Birds you go! Go!' And he waved his arms about, wildly, gesturing at the landscape around us.

'You chose!' he laughed. 'Birds! You chose! Fly, Man!'

Then I started walking. I'd had a belly full of him. Whatever was out there, at least I'd be keeping my own company. I'd find my way around, given time. I didn't need lectures from a head-case.

'Birds!' he called out behind me, still laughing. 'Birds fly, Hard-Man! They fly! Go Johnny, gogogo!'

I turned; looked at him. He had got up from the ground, and he was jumping up and down, flapping his arms. He was making bird-calls; then running in circles, simulating flight, with his arms stretched out wide.

'You're crazy, old man! Really blown out! Anybody ever tell you that?' I shouted after him. Then I turned away and kept on walking.

'Hey! Name's Nelson, if you want to know!' he shouted to me. 'You might. You might want to know. Only need to give me a call!' And he mimed, as if he were using an ancient bell-telephone.

'Only need to give me a call! Any time you like, boy! Service with a smile! How about that? Nice to meet you!' He continued to flap his arms and run in a circle. He was making noises like a crow. Now and again, I glanced back; keeping my eye on him. As the distance between us increased, I realized he was preoccupied, and was most likely going to leave me alone. But then I heard his voice again. It carried clearly across the open space.

'Hey! Hard-Man dies! Bird-Man is born! You just remember this one thing! I know the way out of the Circle! Oh boy, I sure do! I know the combination!'

His voice had a strange ring. There wasn't a trace of insanity in it. It sounded steady; strong. His laughter came to me again; rippling through the air. Then he was quiet.

I turned round. He had gone; disappeared. There was a sudden, peculiar sensation of emptiness. Alone-ness, hollow and odd. The sensation took me by surprise. There was no-one around. No-one there. Not even him, the crazy guy. I was glad to be rid of him, but his absence left a gap in the air.

I shook off the feeling, and carried on moving. Now I could think, without hearing his constant chatter. And maybe I could find out exactly where I was.

I walked for a long time, with no idea of where I was going; and no sense of how long I'd been travelling cross-country. There was only an urgent need to keep on the move, no matter what.

I became aware that I felt neither hunger nor thirst. But a tiredness had worked its way into me; and a heaviness that clouded my mind. Then I felt the rise of a painful anger at the lonely, empty, total meaninglessness of what was happening to me. I couldn't even feel glad that I was free because it wasn't freedom. It was perpetual motion; and even escape from six years of a Death Row cell, and life after death, hadn't done me any good.

All around, the grassland was the same colour; yellow-green and russet. The light hadn't altered. The sky stayed the same; still, cloudless, pale yellow-green. It seemed unreal; lifeless, like a backdrop.

I guessed I'd walked most of a day, but there was no sign of the approach of night; no fading of that yellowish light. Neither were there any landmarks so I couldn't gauge my direction. The air was unnaturally still, without the faintest trace of a breeze; and an eerie silence pressed in on me. I could hear no sounds of a living moorland. Nothing but lifeless, unchanging colour, monotony and barrenness. Then I needed to feel thirst or hunger. Even though I had no food, the craving itself would have been a living thing, and would have broken the meaningless feeling.

Tiredness weighed heavier on me. I kept trying to fight it and keep on the move. There was no cover; and the animal in me wouldn't allow rest without shelter. But after a time, I found I couldn't will myself on any more. Weariness overwhelmed me; and the need for rest became greater than my apprehension. I sank down on to the barren turf. The last thing I was aware of was a high-pitched squeaking; with an organized rhythm, like

Morse Code. Faintly, I registered that sound as the first thing I'd heard in a long time. Then I couldn't focus any longer; and I fell away into an inner darkness.

3: *Circle of Artademes*

MUSIC WOKE ME; strange, unearthly music. It filtered through the blackness in my mind. My eyes felt heavy. I opened them, slowly and looked up into a wide canopy of blue-black sky. There were many voices, singing. The drifting, sweet notes soared and fell. But behind the sweetness was a trace of something strange and bitter.

I couldn't tell where the sounds came from. I turned my head to look for their source, and I saw a woman who stood on a spiral pinnacle of rock beside me. With each note, each chord, bright sparks and light-reflecting dust flew up around her. Above her head, they soundlessly exploded drifting down again to circle the rock on which she stood. More sparks: blue and green, violet and red, shot out to form spirals which curled upwards, and were lost from sight in the dark sky.

She stared at me. On her face was the faint trace of a smile. Fascinated, I wasn't able to move. Then I realized I didn't care. I didn't want to move. I had no desire for anything but to watch and listen, as the voices and the colours wove their shapes. And the woman, clothed in substance of silvery-black, like the skin of a fish, looked down and smiled. Around her head and shoulders, something gossamer-fine floated on a soundless breeze. Suddenly the voices stopped. Then I saw her ancient, angular face; its jutting bones thinly covered with dry parchment-like skin.

Filled with horror at the sight of her, I twisted violently; tried to get up. But I couldn't. I was bound. On each side of me my arms were stretched out, and my feet were held together, so that my body formed the shape of a cross on the ground. She smiled again, and the tightening of her skin pulled back the fibres of her mouth into a rictus grin; the smile of rigor mortis held in eternity. I fought to free myself, but could only move my head. I gazed in disbelief at my legs and arms, which were bound tightly with something invisible.

The song began again. Silver voices twisted together; rising in thin purity. But vaguely, as though from a distance, waves of dissonance rose with them. The desperate movement of my neck slowed, dragging, as I tried to look at the woman's face. The paleness of her skin, and the now softened angles of her bone-structure stood out against the background of starry indigo. She lifted her hands; lithe and supple as a dancer's, and I saw threads of shining substance leave the tips of her fingers, and fasten on my hands and wrists. They pierced the ground beneath me; weaving up and down with the rising chords I struggled as if in a dream; but the weight of those threads pulled at me as I tried to escape. Helpless, I could do nothing but stare up at that great dark sky decorated with star-patterns I had never seen before.

Then the woman raised her arms; and her voice rose up over the waves of sound. 'Blessed is the body of the Endless One! Blessed are the children of the Circle! Oh, blessed are the seeds of the wilderness; brought on winds to their harvest within the Wheel! Come forth, O Ancient Ones. Come forth, O Newly-Begotten Ones. Draw near!'

Something writhed in me: a warning. Again, I tried to struggle free, but my attempts were nightmarishly slow. Battling against the weight that sapped at my strength, I lifted my head.

I saw that I lay inside a circle of upright standing-stones; each of which was about the height of a man. As I watched, human figures moved out of the stones. Withered, old people and young children silently walked forward; each one clothed in smoky greyness that clung to their shape. They formed a ring, raising their arms to the sides so that their fingers barely touched. Their faces were lifeless, ghastly. Their eyes were dark and soulless. The woman spoke again.

'Long-awaited one, we greet you. Your homecoming fills us with joy, O Bright Flame of the Living. In the waning of our force we have waited for you, and our strength has grown dim without you. Did you doubt, O wandering one, that you would be returned to your Brotherhood? Seek no more, for you are found, gathered from the barren wastelands of the Lost, brought to the Circle, where you shall dwell with us. Wander no more.'

I strained uselessly at my bonds; and found that I could make no sound. My voice was dead.

Then the woman began to call on strange names, one by one. The words which she spoke were unfamiliar to me, but the very sound of them chilled me. As she chanted those names, her arms were stretched up high above her; her face was upturned, looking for something in the dark sky.

Desperately, I twisted my head again, looking from one to the other of the Undead creatures that surrounded me. They stood, as still as the stones out of which they had come. Around their heads, wild white hair floated, cloudlike.

The young ones, the children, terrified me the most. Not one of them could have been more than seven years old. But they were held in frozen greyness, like streams, dammed and stagnated.

Then I saw, in the circle of living dead, one stone without a figure in front of it. That empty place filled me with a greater dread, with a sense of raw horror. I knew it waited – for something, or someone – to fill it.

Then I realized what, or whom it waited for. That space, I suddenly knew, was for me. Through that gap in the circle, I could see beyond; and in the shadows I saw that there was yet another circle outside the first one. Behind that was another ring of stones. Circles within circles. How far they extended, I couldn't see; but it seemed there were a great many of them.

Then the woman's chanting stopped abruptly. She stood, tall and straight; her arms and face still lifted to the stars. As I watched, a circle of cloud formed high up in the deep blue, slowly drawing itself in, focussing into a whirling form. And as it did so, it gave off a low-pitched humming. The sound began to work into me, into the very core of me.

Unable to move, unable to make any sound, I gazed up at it. Somehow I could feel that this thing was alive and intelligent in a way I couldn't fathom. It started to spin; slowly at first, but gathering speed. High among the stars it turned; throwing out ball-lightning which disappeared into the darkness. Then gradually it drew down, and as it came nearer, I saw that it was formed not of cloud, but of spikes of barbed light. As spears of cold brilliance were cast out into the sky, I heard the woman's high keening; a sound not of fear or awe, but of sheer joy. It came down; drawing nearer and nearer to the place where I lay. Then it centred above me. Now its low hum was deafening; mind-numbing. But the woman's voice carried through it as she fell to her knees, half chanting, half speaking.

'O returned art thou! Returned from out of the farthest places! Returned to thy guardians, O great Wheel! Receive the offering we give to thee; this new life-flame! And we, Children of Artademes rejoice that through thy power we shall dwell forever in thee on the Day of Claiming!'

She stood, her back and neck arched upwards. And her face burned with a terrible luminescence. Rays burst out from her eyes, merging and binding with the spears of whiteness in the circle above her.

'Turn, O Wheel!' she commanded. 'Turn, O Eternal One! Turn and receive thy gift!'

And at that moment, a huge cross appeared in the inner part of the ring; a huge, equal-armed cross formed of a combination of cast-off shards of light and the rays from the woman's eyes. Quickly, it took form. Then it centred above my body; synchronizing itself exactly with my position, and somehow with the very speed of the vibration of my existence. Somewhere inside me, I felt cords pull tight. I felt them begin to snap, one by one. The wheel began to turn. I began to turn with it. Terrified, I tried to call out; to make any kind of sound. But no voice came from me. I struggled against the force of both the wheel and the bonds that tied me. But my efforts were useless. I had no hope of freeing myself.

As I turned, I caught sight of the lifeless faces of the gathering. One after another I saw them; and the woman. She was lit now by a cold glow of lurid fire.

The wheel increased in speed; I with it, until the stone circle and the hollow creatures around me passed by in a blur. I began to feel myself dissolving; as though the threads which held me together were being eaten away. Slowly, that wheel and I were becoming inseparable. But there was no dimming of my awareness. And I knew that whatever happened to me, I couldn't die.

Maybe I could be broken, tortured, made like them, the Undead. But I couldn't die.

I felt the force of the wheel moving with me; taking me with it. But in me something still struggled, as I recalled those faces, the faces of the gathering of dead souls. And I knew I wasn't meant to be one of them. All I'd been through, all that I was, couldn't be for that. I didn't want it. That wasn't going to be the sum total of what I was. It was a thing apart; foreign. And as I knew that, a last drop of strength inside me rose up and fought hard against the force which had claimed all those ancient and too-young sentinels of the stone circle. And I fought because of a terror; a terror like I'd never known before. The stones spun by like a wall of death. And I was held in it, held in the bowl of rock.

The Circle.

Something surfaced. What was it about the Circle? Somewhere in me was a recollection. Then it came. That crazy old man by the dry-stone wall. His odd blue eyes. His brown half-breed face. His last insane words returned to me. The Circle. Then I knew. He wasn't insane. This was. This pit of stone, and the Undead. The memory came back, sharply, clearly. And I heard his words again:

I know the way out of the Circle . . . I know the Combination.

'Hey!' A voice. His voice. I could hear his voice.

'Hey, Bird-Man! Over here!'

He was laughing. He was there, in the very centre of the swirling. I didn't know how, why. But he was there. I wasn't able to speak.

'Bad news, Bird-Man! I told you so!'

He seemed to be above the wheel; and though something about him wasn't a part of what was happening, I could see him – and he could see me. He was really there; yet not there.

'See all the circles . . . all the gaps? Okay! Line up the gaps, Bird-Man! Line 'em up. Make a path!'

I couldn't respond.

'I can hear you,' he said.

(I can't see them. Can't see the gaps. Can't see . . .)

'Concentrate!

I stared into the whirling maelstrom. I could see nothing but a blur.

'Missed that one. Try again.'

In the blur, I made out one dark spot. Then it was gone. That was it. Was it?

'You're scared! Okay! But don't listen to that fear, Man! Ride on it!'

(What about the others? Line them up . . . what about the other gaps?)

'Wait till they come round the circle. There's a place they all line up. Concentrate. Don't miss it.'

A dark spot flashed. I missed it.

'Aieee!!' Below me, I heard the woman shriek. Inside the light, the arrows became barbed; touched with green and blue. They shot round at deadly speed and began to point inwards and downwards.

'Don't listen to the woman, Bird-Man!'

(She can see us. She knows.)

'She can't see me. I'm the Invisible Man! Different level.'

Frantically, I sought the dark gaps again. I made out three. No sooner had I seen them than they were whipped away.

'Seven! Concentrate!'

(I can't do this. Too fast.)

'No choice! Shit or bust! Death or Glory, boy! Line em up!'

(Okay! I've got it! There!)

'Wait. Next time around. Stop thinking. Be! Get ready!'

(How do I get out?)

'Man, you missed it! What you thinking about?'

(How do I get out?)

'Hey, birds fly, Bird-Man! They fly!'

(No . . .!)

'Yeah! Go for it! Do it! That path's coming up soon! Get your ass ready!'

(I can't. I'm tied down! I can't . . . fly!)

'Think gaps! Then think flying! Only flying!'

The arrows within the wheel drew nearer; grazing me. I felt their jaggedness; not with my body, but with something else. I looked down again; concentrated. Seven flashed by. I counted. One and two and . . . Seven again. Five seconds between. I waited. Once more the path flashed by. The arrows grazed again; deeper, this time. A shooting pain drove through me. I felt I couldn't trust. Never mind. Never mind trust. Just do it. I missed two seconds, and waited. Think gaps. Think flying.

Oh God! . . . One and two and Three and four and . . .

Flying! Oh, dear Jesus, flying! Down a dark tunnel a dark airspace, not high, but deep.

4: Base Camp

'THAT WASN'T TOO bad.'

Then I saw the crazy half-breed, whatsisname. I couldn't remember his name. I was lying on a floor. We appeared to be in a cave. I felt dizzy; tried to move, but had to close my eyes. The sound of twigs popping and crackling in a fire came to me.

'Got through. Skin of your teeth, Man, but you got through.'

I found my voice. It came out cracked and dry. 'Where am I . . .?' I asked feebly.

'Here.'

'What kind of answer's that?' I whispered.

'Damn good one, everything considered,' he replied. 'It's the truth.'

I tried again to sit up. I had a bad case of vertigo. Moving didn't do it much good. He was quiet for what seemed a long time. I lay, listening to the sound of the fire crackling. There was something really beautiful about that sound; and about the easy quietness behind it. The noises echoed in the cave. Then he spoke to me again;

'Got into some Bad Lands sure enough, didn't you, Man? Thought you might. Shock does weird things to a guy.'

I grunted. A lot of questions needed answering. After all, it seemed he might have some answers. Carefully, I propped myself up on one elbow, and looked at him. Nelson; that was it. That was the half-breed's name. The dizziness gradually subsided and I took stock of my surroundings.

The cave was high and wide. The entrance let in light, of the colour and warmth of sunlight. Ivy hung down over the opening, splitting the glow into delicate rays. Moths flitted there; drawn either by that light, or by our little fire. I watched the fire. Its smoke disappeared straight up into the dark recesses above us, no doubt pulled in that direction by a smoke-hole. As a result, the air was clear and clean.

Then my attention moved to the cave walls and I noticed that they were decorated with cave-paintings etched in shades of brown and red, highlighted with streaks of white.

There were images of running bison, deer and a huge horned creature. Lichens and mosses, red and black, had crept over other parts of the walls, creating dramatic patterns of their own. I lay on a mat, thick and skilfully woven, of grasses and pliable green twigs which was much softer than it looked. It moulded itself to the shape of my body. The old man sat, cross-legged on a flat rock, across the fire from me. The light from the flames played over his wrinkled face, giving it the colour of polished terracotta. Under his long grey braids I saw that he wore great chunks of amber hung on rings through his ears. As the firelight caught them, they glowed. He was staring at me. His strange blue eyes were boring into me.

'Feeling better?' he suddenly asked.

'Yeah.'

'You were out; knocking out zeds. Couldn't wake you. No way.'

How long?' I was confused; and my sense of time was distorted.

'Don't matter,' he said. "Cause Time ain't the same dame you used to know. Oh no sir.'

'Oh Christ . . .' Then all the detail came back to me in a rush. I groaned and lay back on the mat. 'What the hell was it?' I asked. 'How did I get into that?'

'You didn't want to know me, did you? Wanted to go off on your own. Do some exploring. Have some adventures. Your choice. Birds, you fly. You always got a choice.'

'Now wait a minute. You just wait right there. You did all that stuff. Yeah, now I'm beginning to get the picture. You made that whole thing up; made up the whole thing somehow! Like the flying thing, maybe? Just so you could come and get me out. Just so I'd give in and play your game! Isn't that right?'

He laughed, shaking his head, so that his long braids swung from side to side. Then, in a flash, he fell serious, and fixed my eyes with his. 'That's the arrows,' he said. 'The woman's arrows. Didn't you feel them bite you? Bite out a bit more of your trust? That's what they were meant to do. She's hungry. Always been and always will be. You weren't so hot in the trust department to start with. That's why you went off on your own Maybe you got to learn to trust something, sometime. Hey, we got to talk; and you got to do some listening.'

'Okay, okay!' I lay there, looking up into the darkness at the ceiling of the cave. 'Okay! Tell me stuff! Go on, tell me. Explain it all to me You've been here longer than I have! Okay, you tell me what's going on! Because I'm pretty confused for a dead man! The way I see it, dead should be just that; dead! Time for a rest! Lights out! Not this stuff!'

'Hah! You reckon you're dead? Is that so? Are you?' he shouted; and his voice rang off the walls of the cave. You feel dead?'

I shook my head.

'Right,' he went on; 'You just moved house! Moved out! Gone on the Inside. On the Inside of things. But you figure you should have gone to *Heaven*, huh? Well, let me tell you that there ain't no easy way. You work your passage to that pie-in-the-sky, Man, and there ain't no such thing as time for a rest! But there's plenty of things on the Inside. More than you ever knew. And that's good news, 'cause it means it sure ain't boring. Now what'ya say? You still want to listen?' Then he lowered his voice, and he said; 'You ready? Ready to talk?'

'Yeah.'

'Okay. I lied to you.'

'What? When?'

'Lied to you about the woman.' And he laughed again. 'She could see me sure enough; she knew I was there. She knew I'd heard you. Once she caught sight of me I knew we'd have to haul ass, fast, and getting out was a close one. You could have lost your Immortal Soul, Bird-Man. She'd have eaten it like a piece of candy, and soon got hungry for another one. That's what she's like. She'd have taken the force in you for the Wheel; for the Circle of Artademes. She's bad news.'

'So what about those . . . people? Those . . . creatures? Oh, Christ, what about them? Are they people? I mean, real people?'

'Real, oh yeah. But not much use anymore. Except to her. They're sentinels of the Stones. Guardians of Artademes. They've been there a long time, filling the gaps one by one.'

'So where do they come from?'

'From the Plains. She gathers them from the Plains of the Lost. People who won't listen, maybe to love. Weak ones, who've just passed through. She sends a ray to find them. There's rays on those Plains all the time. Sometimes she gets lucky.'

'But no-one got them out! Why? If you got me out, why didn't someone get them out?'

'Hey, wait there a minute! I didn't get you out. You got you out. I gave you a few tips. And if you hadn't wanted to listen, you'd still be there. If your wits hadn't been tuned up, if you'd not cared, about going into the Wheel, if you'd been too freaked out to fly . . . well, you'd still be with 'em.'

'But those people! Dear God! They stay like that? Can't they be got out? I mean, who the hell is that woman, anyway? And that damn Wheel! And you're telling me that those zombies are there and it's tough shit? Well, that philosophy stinks! There's got to be a way to stop her! Jesus Christ! some of them are little kids!'

'Hey, Vigilante! Want a war with her, huh? Want to go get her; the Woman of Artademes? What'ya say, huh? You got an Immortal Soul to spare? Maybe got a few saved up, tucked away for a rainy day? Say, let's go blast her with White Light! Let's go blow her apart! Let's split her atom, Man! No way. Some things you can change. Some things you can't. She's part of the Law.'

'The law of goddamn what, for Christ's sake?' I was angry now; angry with him. I pulled myself upright on the mat.

'The Law of Spiders and Flies,' he said; 'Spiders got to eat; but you got to guard your own ass. Ain't nobody gonna fish you out if you want to be a fly. Here endeth the first lesson!'

My anger rose. I didn't want to hear any more; but he was giving it to me.

'Can't lay a finger on her. That's how it goes. Reckoning'll come to her. That's a fact. But it ain't got nothing to do with you and me. She ain't even from this Solar system. Now what'ya gonna do about that?'

'I can't listen to this!'

'Hey, come on, chill out! Like I said, some things you can't change. But some things you can. You got to know that before we go any further.'

'So she can't be stopped? That's what you're saying, is it? Just leave her to get on with it? Right!' Disgusted, I turned away from him. I was seething.

'Forget her,' he said. 'Best thing. Oh boy! You ain't started yet and you're in trouble! You forget about trying to change things you can't lay a finger on; or we spend forever in this cave. Nice and safe, here. How about it? We stay here and get boring. Oh, Man, I'm stuck with you and you're full of attitudes and head-trips. Or, maybe you shape up a bit, hey? You loosen up, and we get ourselves some action?'

'Action? Look, I don't need any action! I've had enough damn action, thank you! More than enough! More than I can stand! I got gassed to death after six damn years, and I end up here! I don't know why I did that – now I think about it! I'm sure it must have been a really bad move! Perhaps I should stack these cards and get another lot! Or maybe I should go back and do it again; right, this time, huh? Oh yeah, and maybe I missed Saint Peter. Maybe I blinked at the wrong time!'

'You still don't know why, do you? Still don't know why you got your ass into trouble back there. I'll tell you again, Bird-Man. Listen good this time.'

'Do me a favour, will you?' I said; 'Stop calling me Bird-Man, for Christ's sake!'

'You didn't trust me,' he went on, ignoring me; 'You thought I was crazy. You said, hey, I don't want to know this guy. He talks weird. He looks kinda weird. Someone who looks like that; talks weird like that can't tell me nothing. Could be I'm God and I know best so maybe I'll go out on my own and get hung up in some Bad Lands, 'cause he sure can't be much use to me, he's fizzed-out. You didn't listen. You were a Hard-Man. A hero that don't need no-one. An explorer. You still think you are. You didn't want to listen to truth. You wanted to hear lies. Truth comes small, and you wanted to hear Big You. But you know what? It's in there, Bird-Man.' And he jabbed me, hard, in the chest.

'It's in there. Your ears are in there, and you can hear that small thing. But you don't like it much 'cause you got to be small to hear it. But you hear the truth, alright. Remember what it felt like, when you were in that Wheel, when you thought about what I'd said, y'know, about knowing the way out. Remember it? That was it. That was the small thing. And it was that, not me, that got you out. Remember the thing that wouldn't let you rest on the Plains? That was it again. Why you listening now? Why? 'Cause it wants you to. When you come through from Old World, it's like you get what that small thing really wants. Only your thinking don't know it's what you want 'cause that small thing's in a place deep down inside of you where you don't often visit. Now, there's your strength, There's your power! And you really want to find it! Hey, maybe not just find it, but be it. Then you can forget your three-D hard man, and be a Bird-Man! Oh boy!'

He hit the rock he was sitting on, hard, with both hands. He did it again; and his face didn't look old. It looked strange; timeless. And as I saw his face in that moment, I felt a sudden shock. He sprang up and, in one move, jumped off the rock. There was excitement in his expression, and an intensity in his eyes. I was suddenly aware of my own dullness and slowness. In his face, I became aware of myself, reflected. And what I saw was an old, tired man; trapped in an ungainly shape. Then he grabbed me by the arm, fixed his eyes on mine, and grinning, said:

'You got guts, Bird-Man. Guts. I like that. Oh yeah, I do. In fact, I like you. We're gonna have some good times. What'ya say, hey?'

Something about him affected me. I found myself smiling. For the first time, smiling. Then I thought that for a crazy he wasn't all that bad. I just shrugged, and tried not to smile too much. I didn't want to give him the impression that I necessarily had to agree with him. Also, I wasn't sure I needed any more action, as he called it. And he looked more than ready for some. Then, without any warning, he pulled me quickly and quite roughly through the cave, to the entrance.

'Hey, come on!' he whispered excitedly; 'I got to show you something!'

His grip was strong and firm on my arm and I, taken by

surprise, stumbled and lurched after him to the cave mouth. What I saw then was one of the most incredible things I had ever seen.

The mouth of the cave opened on to a steeply wooded slope. In front of us a wide ledge of golden rock stretched out; its surface covered with brightly coloured rock plants growing in tiny cracks and fissures. I noticed that I could smell those unusual flowers. Their light, sweet scent drifted across to me. I realized that my senses, far from being dulled by death, were sharpened.

The cave itself was set into a mountain which soared upwards ruggedly behind us. High above, amongst blue-grey and sand-coloured boulders, bushes and creepers grew, cascading downwards. I turned again, and in amazement, scanned the landscape beyond the rock ledge. Far below, rolling hills, shallow valleys and woodlands reached out to the horizon, where the distant heights of a mountain range rose up, created with the brilliance of a glowing sun. Threads of silver light bathed the land beneath.

I looked up, to the sky. It shone with the fresh light of dawn; and there, hovering and gliding on the still air, I saw many different species of birds. Great eagles curved and banked; their wings lit by the rays of the sun. And high above, where the air was rosy and blue, a crescent moon shone; just visible.

I'm free, I thought. Jesus, I'm free. And this is where I am. I couldn't speak; and I was aware that Nelson was quiet. I was glad. If he'd started, then, I would have told him to shut up.

Then I saw him. He was lying, flat on his back at the very edge of the rock ledge. I watched as small birds hovered about him, and dragonflies settled on his hands. After some time in that position, never moving, he got up, turned to me, and said;

'This is my favourite place. Of all the Lands of the Levels; and I've been around. But this is it, Man. This is it.'

'Yeah,' I replied. 'It's fine.'

'Okay!' he said. 'This is where we make camp. How about that?' He laughed. His voice was loud, and it echoed as he shouted;

'Base Camp for the great Explorer! We can get tuned up for some action here! Do some work!'

'Hey . . .' I replied; 'What work? Nelson, what work?'

'How come you got the idea you're here for a rest? You get some impression you're here for your retirement huh? No way. Soon as you get your ass in gear, we got stuff to do. This ain't no old folks' day out, it ain't no retirement home, and it ain't no boy-scout camp. This is Base Camp!' Then he fell quiet, and his mood changed. He looked out towards the distant mountains and his expression had a far-away look.

'I fell in love here, once, Man.' He said; 'Guess that's the reason I like it so much here. I called her Moon-Rider, though that didn't always used to be her name. And she was the sweetest, bravest, kindest woman I ever did know. She was in some bad old way when she first came through. A darn sight worse than you. She'd been mainlining in Old World, and paying for it by turning tricks. She'd wanted to be a movie star; but guess that didn't work out. Well, she'd just about had enough of Old World, and she'd bought a one-way ticket out. There was just too much stuff cramming in on her spirit. But she found she had wings, boy! And then she learned fast! Moon-Rider. Yeah. Don't suppose that's what she's called now. Ain't no need of names, where she is.'

I looked at him. He just kept his eyes on the mountains in the distance.

'Where did she go; this woman? What happened to her?'

'Okay. Well, I worked with her as far as the Crossing-Place. That's as far as I work. I can't go beyond that. Say, you don't know what I mean. Not yet. Maybe this is too much stuff for you right now.'

'No. Go on, tell me. Go on. I want to know.'

'Okay. You want to hear? Okay, I'll tell you. I went with her through all the Levels. And things ain't like this all over the place. No way. They ain't necessarily like Base Camp. You'll see. Well, she worked. She worked at finding her real Truth, and boy, watching her do that was like watching Angels dancing! And she was learning stuff real fast. She was moving on, if you get my meaning. Moving on. I sure didn't want to lose her, but I didn't want to keep her where she didn't belong. Oh no sir.

So we got to the Crossing-Place. And if the Levels are on the Inside of things, then that Crossing-Place is like the Inside of the Inside. Then there's a place where, if it's your truth, you cross over. Like a river. But oh boy! It's a fine river. Like nothing you've ever seen; nothing you could even dream up. A lot more like light than water, but that still ain't putting it right. That river divides the Worlds. From then on, it's unknown Lands. Unknown, unborn, unknowable. But I do know what it's like there. I just do, and that's all there is to say about it. Something in me knows, like I've been there before . . . And oh, Man, it's the Big One! Well, it came to be her Truth to cross it. And I saw her go over, 'cause her spirit was called, and was needing to go. And I waited and waited by that river, watching into the light where I couldn't see her no more. And I waited, 'cause I knew that if a certain sound came . . . Hey, I can't explain that sound. It's just too much for explaining. Well, if it came, I could go, too.

And then what did I hear? I heard crying Souls from out of the Bad Lands on all the Levels. And that sure is weird 'cause usually you don't hear them, there. Then I knew. I knew it wasn't my Truth to go with her. I knew it was my Truth to come back; to do stuff.

But I know she's okay. Over that river there's nothing else but okay. And I'll tell you another thing. One day I'll go there and find her. One day'll come when it'll be time to go over. And I won't be back no more.' Then I began to understand what he'd done. He'd come back for this; for people. For Godforsaken people like me.

5: *Time, and Other Mythical Beasts*

SO WE STAYED at Base Camp for a while. There was no way to tell how long. It could have been days. It might just as easily have been years. There was no night. No daybreak. No change in the constant glow of the sky. That disturbed me. I asked him what it was all about, but I never got a decent answer. His replies were always eccentric; never straightforward. Although I was damn sure he hadn't forgotten what a day, or a week, or a year was, he showed no interest in my attempts to keep score by relating to such measurements. He only laughed at me, and said that Time was a Mythical Beast, which men hunted and thought they could trap. It was a shape-shifter, he said; and was neither straight, as in desk-diaries, nor round, as in clocks. The more men chased it and thought they knew it, the more it changed shape and eluded them. And, he said, I had better stop nagging him about Time, or he would take me hunting for it, so that perhaps we could waste some of it when we could be working.

Work. What work? It sometimes occurred to me that the work he kept on about was a Mythical Beast. All the work I ever saw him do was add to the cave paintings; drawing strange creatures, naked women, and abstract patterns with lumps of what appeared to be red clay and chalk.

For much of the time he wasn't bad company. I was, after all, a man recently bereaved of his physical existence who had touched the cloak of the Living Dead. His weirdness had grown on me, partly because I had seen weirder. But there were times when he irritated me beyond endurance. He baffled me too, and that made my irritation worse. He was baffling because for all he was unpredictable and had a peculiar wildness about him, there was something else; something more clear and sharp-edged than I had ever come across. That something was a steel blade: a finely-tuned instrument: the very tip of a flame. To my way of thinking, the one didn't go with the other; and I wondered how a man like that could still be as crazy and bizarre as he was. He had iron discipline and chaos happily married inside him.

There were times when he managed to annoy me so badly that I would feel the old urge to take off again on my own. His particular brand of humour was in bad taste most of the time, and perverse. He didn't seem to care about what I felt, or the position I was in. If I asked a straight question, he would confound me with meaningless riddles, delivered either in deadly seriousness or hilarity. If I tried to get him to tell me things I really needed to know, he would jibe and joke and ridicule me.

I had things on my mind. There had been too much happening for me to give them much thought. But now, in the quietness of the cave and the landscape which surrounded us, those thoughts came up to the surface. And I was haunted by them; plagued and driven by them.

The past. That life. Mine. And all Nelson did was paint on the cave wall, endlessly. And if I tried to speak to him about anything serious, he laughed, or even sang: blues numbers; rock numbers; country songs. Tormented by the dark circles of my life, I would run from his gravelly singing and go down the mountain as far as I could get; slipping and stumbling in a rage of frustration and irritation at the total lack of response from him.

I could never get further than a small rock ledge. There I would sit and brood; recalling recent events, the baffling nature of where I was, and the whole mean, uninspiring procession of things which I had learned to call my life. And it didn't stop. It went on and on, catching me up in its bleak downward spiral; showing me an endless succession of banal events, lovelessness, carelessness, in which I was the star player.

Then I would hear that old man's barking-mad howling laughter from above me. And the sound reminded me of a hyena. When I heard that, I would be driven even further into miserable contemplation of unchangeable things stamped forever on the history of one man, me. A meaningless, possibly useless existence. And what had I got at the end of it? Beautiful scenery, and a terrible loneliness. Oh, and dances with an idiot.

His attitude drove me to obsession with those unrewarding memories. His derision drove me, as sure as a gale drives everything in its path; and I found myself cruising the drab streets of my past, over and over, searching in circles for something. Perhaps meaning. I didn't know. But all I discovered was self-loathing and a worthless stream of non-events. It was a friendless, heartless existence that had brought me to stand alone, trusting no-one.

More and more often I sat alone on that high ledge overlooking a most incredible landscape; but I was hardly even aware of it, as all I could see were the images of my memory which became more and more grey and tedious. I became dully fascinated with those visions as I watched them parade in front of me like out-dated re-runs. Then, without warning I was swamped by a deep exhaustion; so that it was all I could do to lift myself from the narrow ledge of rock and try to make my way back to the cave.

I never saw him approach. He didn't say a word; but he was suddenly with me on the mountainside, before I had even climbed a few steps. Without any knowledge of the climb, I found myself back on the woven mat; drifting in and out of a strange unconsciousness. I finally succumbed to it. When I came back to awareness, he was there; drawing on the cave wall, and singing quietly to himself. Vaguely I recognized the tunes. They were hit songs from the nineteen-fifties.

I'd no idea how long I'd been out, but I sensed that I had slept for a long time. Still unfocussed, I couldn't get up, so I lay watching him for a while, and the flicker of dancing shadows cast by the firelight on his back.

He stopped his drawing and spoke. He knew I was awake, though I'd made no sound. He asked me if I'd had a good rest. I didn't reply. He came over to the fire; taking up his usual position cross-legged on the flat stone. And he gestured behind him to the drawings on the wall.

'Mythical Beasts,' he said. 'Once they lived, but now they're moving on.' I looked where he pointed and saw images of my life; not in red clay and chalk, but in full-colour. There, like a silent movie I saw events I had lived through and people I had known. And in contrast to the meanness and heaviness of the thoughts which had plagued me so long, those images showed the good things. The good things which I hadn't taken in. Then, as they faded away, I saw one figure, a boy, who stood out among the others. Seventeen years old and strong-looking, he seemed filled with an energy for living, and ambition. I recognized him as myself.

'Now they're moving on,' Nelson said. 'The good and the bad. All shape-changers leaving foot-tracks in the snow. Like Time. They're all gone, but they're all melted down, like metal-ore, into the moment. And that moment's now.'

I had to listen to him. I didn't have the energy to argue; and I let him talk. Whether he laughed or not seemed suddenly not to matter. I didn't know how he could have seen my life but he had seen it. He'd seen the people in it. He had drawn them on the wall. I was still finding it hard to focus. Gear-boxes and clutch-pedals seemed to be the topic of his rambling; though what they had to do with anything here was beyond me.

'This stuff, 'he said, 'is like driving a car. Know about that? Damn sure you do. Know what goes on in a gear-box?'

'I don't know what you're talking about. What is this?' Back to his craziness. Maybe it was simply that he and I weren't meant to be stuck in each other's company too long.

'Okay. What do you do when you want to go faster? You get some speed up, in clutch, through neutral, and into the next gear, right?'

'Sure. Driving lessons after death. So I've ended up in the Advance Driving School, first grade. Now everything's making sense.' I couldn't fight him. I felt too weird. 'Yeah,' I said. 'I know. Nelson, I've only just wakened up. What is this stuff?'

'It's you. See, you've got to change gear, but don't want to. You get some speed up and then want to slow down. You try to get back to the gear you were in before. You do that too often and it's bad news for your engine. Going to trash your synchromesh, Man.'

'My synchromesh.'

'O-kay! You get what I'm saying?'

'Dunno. Not really.' I didn't get what he was saying.

'Okay. Let's put it another way. You were in one gear in Old World. Always in that gear, you. Always thinking in the same old way. It got you around. But then you passed through. Now you can't stay in that gear. It ain't me that says so. And it sure ain't some old guy-in-the-sky that says so. It's the things that move, boy, that move in you. Things are always moving, always changing. Got to go with it, or you trash up your synchromesh. That's what we're doing here in Base Camp. This is the changing gear place, from one speed to another.'

It was slowly filtering through. I was beginning to see what he was trying to say.

'Okay, Nelson. I think I've got you. I've got to change speed or something. That it?'

'Haven't got to. You are. You are changing speed. You're going faster; faster on the inside than you were. Now you got to think in a different way. Then you start to feel your way to that next gear, 'cause you sure as hell can't stay in the old one. Hey, listen, this ain't fizzed-out stuff I'm laying on you. It's the way to ride the Levels, and if you ain't got no skill, you can't ride. No way. You need skill whatever you're doing. Skill to canoe white water. Skill to stay on a wild horse. Skill to ride a Harley Davidson, or make real love with a woman. Skill to be in your Truth. If you're gonna ride your Truth you got to learn how, or get tipped off it. You ride on your Truth here, you have some real wild time! You step out of it too long and there's some bad lands just waiting to make you welcome. Real bad, some of 'em, too. You think about Old World too much and it'll jam you in neutral too long. You got some Mythical Beasts sitting on your gear-stick, Man.'

'Is that all something to do with why I passed out?'

'You stalled the engine, doing some damn fool thing. You been chasing things that ain't none of your business no more.'

'None of my business? Just a minute! If you think that's none of my business, you can go to hell! You done years in the State Pen. old man? Have you? You done time on Death Row? Don't laugh so quick till you have!'

'Bullshit, Man! You don't live there no more! You moved out! There ain't nothing for you there no more! You just moved house! This is where you are, now! And I don't mean this place, neither, this cave, Base Camp! Your home is your Truth! That's where you got to try and live now!

Okay? Okay? Got that one? Old World can look after itself. You're gonna look after your own ass! You start dreaming old movies when you ought to be driving, and boy-oh-boy is there gonna be some road-block!'

I didn't have an answer. He was shouting at me. The crazy old wrinkled-butt was shouting at me, right in my ear, and I didn't have an answer. I just stared at the wall where he'd been drawing. The images were gone. Shadows flickered there; that was all. For a while he said nothing. Then in a gentler tone of voice, he said:

'Things are gonna cook up just fine. I know. That's all you need bother your head about. But it's time to move on now. If you hang on, dragging your wheels in the past too long, it starts kinda pulling you back. But there ain't no way back, though you'd start heading in that general direction anyhow. There's channels between the Levels and Old World, with currents you'd need real skill to ride. Now you get caught in one of those currents, and

Man, your ass is a dead dog! Oh there's some, with a hell of a lot more skill than you, who can move down 'em, go back. But there ain't many. And that is the gospel truth. And even those guys got to have some smart reason for going there. So best you keep facing the direction you're heading, and get up a lick of speed for your gears. How about that?'

Then he turned around, gave me a thumbs-up sign, grinned, and disappeared out of the cave, leaving me alone. I felt suddenly weighted. My legs felt like lead. I went to lie down again by the fire.

I slept; giving in to unconsciousness. But at the last moment, before I sank, an image sprang up before me. It was the image of a young man, seventeen years old; strong, bright, and full of hope. He didn't look at me, but I took a good look at him.

6: *Stairway to Cruising Speed*

WHEN I CAME to it was totally silent. I sat looking about the cave, but there was no sign of Nelson. I had no idea how long I'd been unconscious, but sensed that it had been a long time.

The fire was dead. When I touched the ashes they were stone-cold. Around the shallow fire-pit, the stones were almost icy. I got up. Even without the fire, enough light came through the entrance for me to see that Nelson was definitely not inside the cave. The interior felt empty and long-deserted.

I was quite alone.

I went outside to the wide rock ledge, and walked up to the very edge of it. That ledge was where Nelson often lay, hands clasped on his chest. I'd always wondered why he did that; knowing by experience that he had no need for rest or sleep, as I did. Yet he would often lie in a deep stillness that wasn't sleep of any kind. It was too controlled to be unconsciousness. He had never told me why. When I didn't see him, I called out. No answer came. My own voice was thrown back to me from the rocks. Beneath me the drop was sheer.

He had not gone down by that route. I investigated the stony path, along which I'd often stumbled and slipped in my black moods and my haste to get away from him. It looked more like a goat-track than a path, and it led first to the narrow ledge where I had often sat alone, then to a short slope of loose shale which angled down steeply for forty feet or so.

Carefully I let myself down, to see if the track continued beyond it. But as I began to make the short descent, the shale began to flow, tumbling around me. I lost control and slipped. A jagged flattened boulder broke my slide. I realized how lucky I was, for beneath me the rocks sheered away for hundreds of feet. Pressed against the boulder, I just sat, not daring to move too suddenly; remembering how I had nearly passed out on that narrow shelf just above me. If I had, I would surely have taken a fast trip to the bottom of the mountain. I wondered if it were possible to smash this apparently solid body of mine to pieces, and decided I was in no hurry to find out.

Carefully I inched my way up again, grasping handfuls of loose gravel which betrayed my grip and rolled past me to launch themselves into empty space. I gratefully hauled myself onto the ledge and rested for a while. Taking stock of this new World, I saw that there was plenty of danger here. It appeared that some of the terrain was almost identical to the way it would have been in Old World, as Nelson called it.

But some things were vastly different. That much I could grasp. Where one ended and the other began, I hadn't a clue. I looked around, and could see no sign of any track leading down the mountain, and no possible routes round the huge boulders to either side of me. There was no chance of Nelson having gone down the mountain to the valley below.

So I returned to the cave entrance, and turned my attention to the rocks which rose above and behind it. They were unclimbable. In places, massive boulders jutted out, creating impossible over-hangs. Baffled, I stared out over the valley. As I watched, a herd of deer moved slowly across a green clearing far below. Passing like leaves blown on a lazy breeze, they disappeared into wood-land. Where had they come from? Were they creatures of this World; native and born of strange stuff? Or were they passers-through, too, like me?

I gazed at the beauty of that scene. It could have been somewhere on Earth; some unspoilt, untrodden place, untouched by Mankind. Yet it was in some way different. Its atmosphere made it that way. But for all that, suddenly it didn't seem enough. I recalled something Nelson had said. Give a man peace, he had said, and the next thing you know, he has to fight for it. And that's because nothing ever stands still too long. No movement; no growth.

I had argued with him, and said his philosophy sounded dangerous. But he'd laughed, and said only a dancer could truly understand what movement and stillness meant to each other. The Bright Spirits which gave birth to the Universe, he said, were dancers. I hadn't grasped what he meant; not really. But now, standing on that wide ledge, I began to feel what he was getting at. In me was an urge for movement. The ledge seemed too narrow; the cave too tight. And Nelson had disappeared somewhere. I needed to know where. I waited; vaguely expecting him to come back as mysteriously as he had gone.

It occurred to me to try and re-light the fire, but there was no wood, and no means of making flame. So I abandoned the idea. During our time in the cave, that fire had never gone out. Not once. But I had never seen him attend it or put wood on it. When I thought about that, I realized that I had never seen any fuel in the cave. It surprised me that not for one moment, had I ever thought about it before.

I went up to the rock wall at the back of the cave where Nelson's drawings, now dimly-lit by filtered light, triggered a memory of those images of my life which had played there. Then, quite a way below the other figures he had drawn, there was something which seemed new. Close to the ground was a bow, sketched in white chalk, its whiteness stark in the shadows. The bowstring was pulled back; an arrow on the point of release from it. It drew my attention, more so than any of the other drawings.

Fascinated, I found myself looking in the direction in which the arrow pointed; and caught sight of a dark niche far at the rear of the cave. I approached it. Why had I never noticed that niche in all the time we had been there? I saw that it was quite small, maybe eight feet wide, and only about four or five feet high.

Barely enough light reached inside it from the cave entrance for me to be able to see properly. So, crouching low, I went in. It appeared to be empty.

I was about to come out again, when something at the far side caught my eye. In the semi-darkness, I could just make out the faint shapes of narrow rough stone steps. When I reached them, I discovered I could stand up straight, for there the rock ceiling opened up to form a stairwell. As my sight grew accustomed to the shadows, I saw that the steps, steep and irregular, disappeared up into blackness. Then I knew that Nelson must have left the cave by that route. I made up my mind to try it; but wished I had some sort of light to see by, as the light which came in from the cave entrance was minimal here, and after only a few feet I was going to find myself in total darkness. I hesitated for a moment, not knowing what I was letting myself in for. But Nelson had gone up them. I was sure of that.

With a quick glance back into the cave, I started to climb; knowing that if the stairway became impossible, or was blocked off anywhere, I could always come back.

Soon I was in pitch-darkness, and the steps became really hard going. I found myself counting each stone as I climbed, and counted over seventy. But as I kept on, the strain of the climb increased, and began to press on me in a strange way. There were no physical signs of strain; no hard breathing or pounding heart. But the pressure was one of *feeling*. From a place deep in me, a storm of things I didn't even know I could feel rose up in great waves. Tremendous flashes of happiness and hope rushed in, and so did dark, nameless fears. Anger was wild, dangerous, burning. I kept going; forcing myself against the storm. It didn't lessen; and battered me until my feet were moving mindlessly. I hung on; tossed like driftwood on a sea. With terrible speed I passed from one state to another. Cruel pain, sweetness, despair, soaring happiness, all burst through me as I was thrown from killing rage to the tears of a broken man. In the dark my hands groped blindly; grasping at the rough coldness of stone. Exhaustion began to drag me down.

Then the winds came. A howling gale roared from above, where the steps merged into a black unknown. I stumbled and fell to my knees; bent double by the force of the head-wind and unable to see. I couldn't struggle any more and had no more strength to go on. I could only think, go back . Half-crawling and clutching at the cold rock, I had only managed to go a short distance back when the stairway was violently shaken.

Under my hands I felt the walls change shape as all around me stone began to crumble and fall. The steps seemed to lift underneath my feet as rock and debris rained down and shock waves devastated the narrow passageway. My grip on the wall was loosened. I lost balance and plunged down; falling hard against a heaving wall of rock.

Then I heard a sound, deep in the mountain, like the distant roll of thunder. Showers of dust and fragments of stone fell on me. I covered my head with my arms, and half-buried, waited for the shocks to pass. When I reached out into the dark, there was nothing but boulders. All round me I found no opening. I searched desperately, but found nothing but solid rock; no space of any kind where the steps should have continued downwards. Horrified, I searched frantically; but now there were three walls around me instead of two. Panic started to choke me as I realized that the rockfall had completely blocked off the stairway.

I still tried to feel for an opening somewhere in the darkness. Anything would do, any gap. However narrow, it had to be there, and I had to go through it.

There was no longer any way to tell the difference between fallen boulders and steps. And I knew that I couldn't die in here. If I was trapped, I couldn't even wait for breath to give out, for the dark to close in; for it to end. Because it hadn't got an end. And that raw fear ate at me as I grasped blindly at the stones.

It was then that I saw a light; a tiny spark, diamond-brilliant and intense. It flashed, just once, and was gone. But I stopped moving, and stared into the dark, into the empty space where it had shone. And as I stared, it came again, winking blue-white. Attracted by it, I started forwards clumsily; scattering loose fragments underfoot. I spun round as it suddenly flared again and lit up the whole passageway. At that moment I saw that I wasn't trapped. Through the rubble, the stairway did continue upwards. As the flare faded and solid darkness returned, I knew, with a flood of relief like I'd never known, that there was a way out.

I climbed on and on for what seemed like a long time, meeting no more barriers. The steps, though uneven and steep, were free of rockfalls. And no more howling gales battered me. All around, everything seemed strangely quiet. I wondered where I was, but was sure, at least, I had to be somewhere deep in the belly of the mountain. Yet that didn't make sense. The climb had been so long and steep that I was convinced I'd travelled much further than the height of that mountain, as I'd seen it from the cave entrance.

Then the light came again, only inches from my face. Instantly, I halted and watched in amazement. As I gazed, it returned, hovered in the air just in front of me, and began to move away slowly.

And at that moment, I sensed the presence of something alive, something trying to communicate. I sensed the nearness of a mind. And I knew that it watched me. It gradually expanded and spread into a dim misty glow, lighting the steps above me. And in the centre of it, the form of a woman began to take shape. Her outline shining, she stood, half turned towards me. I couldn't see her face yet sensed that she smiled. Slowly, she stretched out her hand in my direction, and then began to move upwards. The light which surrounded her drifted and clung to me; drawing me with it, up, towards her. As I followed, there was no longer any trace of the exhaustion I had felt only moments before. Soon, I became aware that I could feel a cool breeze, blowing from somewhere ahead; and I realized there must be an opening not far away. What it was, or where, I hardly cared, and was overjoyed at the prospect of getting out, getting free.

Then she turned, she reached out a hand, and suddenly touched me, once, lightly on my forehead. In that touch, my mind was burned. Everything I had ever been was cut to the bone. A heat came from her fingers, shocking my whole body. She then withdrew her hand and the light about her pulled itself in, drawing into one pinprick star of whiteness, and was gone. I stared at the space where she had been. I couldn't move; but after a while, reached out to feel the air there. And when I did, my hand tingled with the force of something electric. I moved into the space; and power crackled through me. It brought a sudden sharp pain, then numbness. But at the same moment, a warmth rose in me which brought me strength. And I saw that I was no longer gazing into pitch-blackness. I could now make out the texture of the boulders; the shape of continuing, irregular steps. In a twilight, dimly, I could now see.

In front of me they levelled out, and merged into an uneven path leading to a stone archway. Beyond that, I could see a faint flickering, like the unsteady yellowish glimmer of guttering candles.

7: *Legend Weaver*

I BEGAN TO move towards the archway; then heard a voice and knew, although I couldn't see her any more, that it was her voice. Behind me it rang clearly on the rock stairway.

'You are being prepared. You have already experienced some preparation, but there will be more . . .'

I stiffened; not able to speak or move. But the words burned, like her touch.

'You are chosen, Warrior. Shall you overcome? The choice is yours. Shall you choose to fight; to carry the Flower of Promise? You are All, and All is within you.' Then she was silent; and the invisible thing which held me, broke. I spun round quickly, but couldn't see her; only swift glints of intense light.

'There is Work for you,' her voice continued. 'If it is proved you are the One who overcometh. If your Soul survives, the Work shall be passed into your hand.'

'Hey . . .!' I called out into the shifting light.

But her voice cut through my own.' You are All, and All is within you. Now take the Sword.'

A sound behind; and I turned quickly to face the archway. Something furtive and shuffling had disturbed stones as it moved. I felt myself tighten; gather thought to a pin-point of focus. The gloom was alive. I couldn't see what moved, but knew I wasn't alone. I watched. Waxy light danced with deep shadows over the rock walls. Then a whisper sprang out of the semi-dark.

'There is no way out here.' It trailed off to a coarse breath-like sound. I moved back quickly; pressed myself against the stone.

'No way forward without me . . .' There was something sickening about that voice.

'Yeah? And who says . . .?' My words came out weakly. I didn't like the sound of them. 'Go to Hell!'

'You, command?' A dry, harsh laugh came out of the glimmering ahead. One moment the voice had been close by; too close, circling me. The next moment it was a distance away. It unnerved me.

'You command me, unsteady one? You talk to me of Hell?' It laughed again, close to my face. I froze. 'Weak sparks of curses shall weave reality.'

'Who are you, damn you?'

'Who am I? Do you like legends? Brave tales of Old? I'm choosing one to suit you while you curse.'

Slowly I edged forward; aiming for the archway. The stone passage felt too tight; closing in on me. But the whisper came again;

'The threshold is my domain. For the moment. Then more. So much more . . .'

'Get out of my way!'

It laughed. I kept moving forward; but there was a stickiness in the air.

'Legends . . .' the voice said. 'I weave them. I create Worlds fit for heroes, cowards, or fools. The game is interesting. Join me.'

I looked up at the great stones of the archway above the yellowish light. For a moment I caught sight of the glint of steel; a broad-bladed sword suspended from the hilt by invisible threads. It turned slowly, flashed, and was gone.

'I challenge you. Have you no will to take my challenge? Dare to enter the World I weave.'

'Goddamn you!' I twisted round. But the voice had taken no form. I could only hear the dry sound of its breath; like air blowing through pipes. 'Get out of my way!'

Again its whispering circled me.' . . . The boy who would be King? Shall I create that one for you? Shall you claim the sword from the stone, and be more than a man? To be honoured; woven into the centuries of memory? A truly Deathless One? No. I do not think so. That suits you not at all. There is a degeneracy in you which I have encountered rarely. Besides, that is a sentimental tale. I will weave you a reality to please your blood-lust. That is more your style. And as you are, so shall you dance with my creation. I have it. Loki, the antithesis of godhood; the Evil One. Or was he? Fenris, the Wolf, monster-birth of his father's dark mating. His kindred, Hel, welcomer of thieves, liars, cowards . . .'

'No more!' My voice cracked. The stickiness of the air had increased. Pressing against its unseen resistance, I tried to get through to the other side of the archway. But something held me back. The invisible one laughed, amused.

'The Vikings,' it said. 'I will tell you when the game begins. You have put your coin in; that meagre coin of what you are. And when I choose to let the coin drop, we will start.'

I struggled to escape the sickening presence. But the more I struggled, the more its pressure mounted. Suddenly, unable to argue or resist, I felt panic, and fought hard to control it. Something was coming. I didn't know what. But I was going to need all the wit I'd ever had. That I did know.

'We shall weave together . . .' it continued; '. . . You with what you have. I with mine; with my realm of possibilities. Shall we dance?'

I stared through the arch into the yellow light, but couldn't see what lay beyond. I wanted to shout; to fight against it.

'. . . Ten . . . Nine . . .'

I began to hear other voices from the unknown space ahead of me. Straining to see, I could only make out vague dark shapes moving about.

'. . . Five . . . Four . . . Three . . .'

'Go to Hell!'

A peal of laughter was my answer. And through it, I heard; '. . . One . . . Zero!'

I was thrown forward, too suddenly. I stumbled, fell, regained my feet. New voices were all around me. I clutched at the air; still unable to see more than shifting light and dark. Then I was gripped hard, dragged, thrown back against a hard surface. My sight began to piece things together, bit by bit through a white flickering. I seemed to see an ancient Hall; high-raftered and decked with gleaming armour and weaponry. I seemed to hear the wild, angry cries of men who have nothing to lose. I heard words of a language I couldn't understand; harsh and guttural. Whatever, whoever, held me down, spat in my eyes.

In a flash, I was hit by a sudden recall. The Vikings. A fast line opened up to another landscape. My eyes had been spat in before. I'd been held hard against the wall on the corner of the block . . . The Vikings. That's what they'd called themselves. A gang of them; mostly sixteen, seventeen. I was nearly fourteen. They had territory, and I'd crossed it. No-one crossed it and came out the same. That was the law. Whether the law of those guys was right or wrong, that was it. The Vikings commanded respect. They were a legend. But there was a kid in my class who hadn't respected. They'd taken his Marianne, the girl he'd had a crush on all summer vacation. They'd got her high, and done things to her that she'd never talk about. All she ever did was cry. So the kid vowed revenge and crossed Viking territory. And after that, he spent three weeks in Intensive and a whole year learning how to use his arm and his guts again. And he never, ever, gave evidence. The cops just couldn't get it out of him. Someone had beaten him nearly brain-dead, and knifed him five times, and no-one knew who.

But I did. Fang. That was who. Once, while three Vikings held me down, he had pissed in my mouth. But I'd been just a kid then, from another place. A new kid on the block with a different way of talking. Now I was not far off as tall as a man, and much, much stronger. The Vikings' territory was taboo. They held four blocks of the disused wharf, and I had no business there. But it was a week from my fourteenth birthday, and I was going to make it my business.

The air smelt of ozone and pollution. The sun, red and misshapen, was going down through thin smog behind the dark buildings. Dust pricked the back of my throat, and my ears were singing with the sound of something I'd never done before. I crossed the iron bridge and turned the corner of the block into a river of sunset-light. Brilliance stung my eyes and I knew I was too obvious. So I took a different route; moving in close to the buildings, then down steps edged with metal.

The wharf seemed deserted. But the Vikings had a way with them. They could make themselves invisible. You didn't find them. Whenever they wanted, they found you. On my way down to the lower level, my feet suddenly clattered against the edge of the steps. I hesitated; heard my pulse strike up a rhythm. Turning once to scan behind me, I kept on the move. Now they would know I was here.

Half way down, the handrail had rusted, and a two-foot section of it hung nearly loose. I gripped it and tore; glad about my luck. Now I was armed. At the bottom of the steps was a broad walkway stacked on either side with tarred crates. I stuck to the central area; kept watch as I carried on along it. The end of the iron bar snagged on my 'T' shirt and ripped. It didn't matter. I grasped the rusty metal harder. My hands felt cold.

And then I knew exactly what I was going to do. I was going to kill him.

I looked up at the empty buildings. A brick tower reached up into the sky. *Vikings. Death-zone* was spray-painted in black up near the top of it. Slowly I kept on the move; listening, watching. From somewhere above me, there was a crunching sound. I turned the corner of the block into a narrow walkway where the setting sun didn't reach. The air was cool now on my bare arms. I got in close to the wall. There was a groaning, straining grind of heavy metal.

Almost instantly, the dead-weight of a loading chain slammed into the brickwork, inches from me. And just as suddenly, my arms were gripped from behind. Then I was dragged into the dark.

'Bye-bye dog-ass.' My face met the wall. Teeth clashed together and I tasted blood and crumbled brick.

'What's this?' I heard; and the piece of iron was torn out of my hand. It hit something with a crash. Then my arm was being twisted. Muscles and tendons burned.

'Upstairs—.' I was thrown, pushed, dragged. I saw flashes of dark and light as my feet were propelled up rotting wooden steps. There, at the top, four of them were standing. One was swinging a chain, fast, so that it wrapped round his arm and swung out again. It whistled as it cut through the air. Then I saw Fang. Across the great stretch of half-rotten floorboards, he sat on an upturned crate. The logo on his baseball cap read U.S.A. Rebels. He smiled.

'I've been hearing about you, kid,' he said. 'How you're bragging you're gonna make me eat shit. How I'm dead meat.' He drank from a can of Schlitz, looked at it casually, then crushed it, and flung it through the glassless window. I heard it hit the ground below.

'Nobody makes me eat shit,' he said; and stood up, moving towards me.

'What we gonna do with him?' one of them said, behind me. I kept my eyes on Fang. When he struck, he was like a snake. He came up close, smiled, and spat in my eyes. I flinched; trying to see. But I couldn't move my arms. Someone had a hard grip on them.

'Play ball with him on the bridge,' Fang replied. 'Little assholes like to play ball.'

Then one of them was spinning me round; winding me with tarry rope. I felt a wave of nausea and my mouth filled with cold acid. I gulped it back as they dragged me away, along a floor where my feet broke through wood as I stumbled. They pulled me out on to an iron fire-escape, and down to a lower level where a narrow bridge crossed the canal. Then I was kicked hard, and fell sprawling face-down across the planks of the bridge.

Beneath me, through a gap, I saw dirty green water with floating garbage. Fang gripped the back of my 'T' shirt and hauled me up. I felt the rope around me loosen, but I had no strength in my arms. I wanted to do something. To fight him; to kick him. But I couldn't. I felt my will beginning to drain away. He pushed me hard, and I was thrown against the wire links on the side of the bridge. I tried running, but another Viking grabbed me and threw me against the opposite side. Something cracked. A plank gave way under my feet and splashed into the water.

'I'm gonna get your ass, Fang,' I whispered. My lip had swelled up and I could hardly get the words out.

'Yeah. Sure.' Then there was music. Hard rock. Someone had switched on a blaster. The volume was turned up and the beat echoed back from empty buildings. There were no words any more, just the blows of wire against my body and the cracking of

planks as I was thrown from one side to the other. I tried again
to run, but slipped and stumbled, and was dragged back. Then I
saw a blade in Fang's hand. He tossed it up. It spun. He caught
it by the hilt and moved in slowly towards me. The music was
deafening. I backed away; sliding against the wire links of the
fence. But next to me was a wide gap where the bridge planks
had caved in. I was going to have to leap it, and didn't think I had
the strength.

'*Hey, Waisichu . . .!*' A whisper; cutting through the music.
Across the gap I saw him. An Indian kid. His eyes burned and
his hair blew in a breeze that I couldn't feel.

'Jump!' I felt a strangeness; the meeting of Worlds I couldn't
know. Something told me that I knew what was going to
happen, because last time that had happened. Then I was kicked
black and blue and left in the twilight walkway in the dust. But
something had changed. In what I knew was going to happen,
the Indian kid wasn't there.

'Jump, Waisichu . . .!' His whisper snapped me back. I looked
at him. Fang swung the blade, and I heard it cut through the air.
I jumped. My feet missed the opposite planks. I slipped and
clutched at the splintered wood; hanging on. Then I felt some
strength creeping back, and pulled myself up. The kid's hand
grabbed my wrist, roughly, powerfully and I was on my feet.
Fang leapt across. The blade sliced my jeans. I didn't have time
to look at the blood. He swung another cut. I flattened myself
against the link-fence.

'Run!' The Indian kid's hand whipped out; pushed me. Then
I was moving, running across the planks, down metal steps to the
lower walkway. Fang leapt the fence, swung down; landed ahead
of us. The kid threw something at me. I caught it. The iron bar.
I felt a great surge of strength.

'Okay. Now use it.'

'Trash him . . .'

'It is your Arrow. Your Arrow, your Sword.'

Fang sliced the air. The blade clashed with rusted iron. He
crouched. I waited. Then he sprang and I swung the bar at him.
He twisted and a jagged edge tore at his jacket; ripping leather.
As I swung again, he spun round and slipped. The blade flew out
of his hand; clattered to the stones below. He fell back onto a

crate. I jammed the bar against his neck. His teeth bared and his eyes bulged. I kicked him in the belly, and he bent sideways with pain. Then I lifted the bar slowly . . .

'No!' The kid's whisper broke through my rage. 'Revenge is not the name of your Arrow, Waisichu. A Revenge-Arrow is shot too many times. It always keeps returning. Run now. While you have power, keep on the Winds. It is not the little coward who runs when he has already won. He makes the enemy dog-sick. You have counted coup on him. Now run.' I dropped the bar. It rang at my feet. Then we ran; together between the dark buildings of the wharf. Ahead of us, the sky was streaked with smoky red.

'Who are you . . .?' I panted.

'Little Wolf-Shadow.'

8: Down and Out in Hades

WE RAN; ON and on. And night crept over the sky. I looked beside me, but Wolf-Shadow had gone. I'd never seen him go. Then I was running alone. The ground sloped down, and the city began to shimmer with a strange shade and light. The shade took over, and the buildings changed shape, gradually becoming forest. But the trees were made of iron, and the sky was sickly-coloured. At my feet the ground became harder; sharper. The rocks there were black and looked volcanic. My pace slowed. It seemed that something was dragging on me. Soon I came to a halt. The trees had thickened. I heard moaning sounds in their branches.

'Hey, Man—'

'. . . Nelson . . .?' I turned quickly. He moved up from behind me.

'He came down pretty hard on your case, didn't he? He wove you a legend and made you dance to an old tune.'

I felt a sudden flash of irritation.

'Okay,' he said. 'What's bugging you?' I kept quiet; felt cynicism take over as I answered him.

'Where were you?' Maybe he was just like all the rest had ever been, after all. When the chips were down, he wasn't there.

'That Legend-weaver got you wound up in a Mind-Field,' he replied. 'He sent you to Hell, boy. Vikings' Hell. Any Vikings you like. Your legend. His legend. Take your pick.'

I looked around us. The spiked iron trees seemed to be closing in. The atmosphere was oppressive.

'This . . .' I whispered; '. . . Is Hell?'

'If you believe in it,' he answered. I couldn't reply, and he carried on talking.

'Okay. Let me tell you a few legends. And I ain't telling you ten kinds of horse-shit. It's dangerous here. It ain't real, except in the mind of belief, but it's still dangerous. It catches you up in a Mind-field. You got to break through it with nobody's Truth but yours. There's one thing I can't figure out, though—'

'Nelson! Will you cut it!'

'You couldn't give a damn. Ain't that right?'

'Yeah! Right! I couldn't give a damn!'

'Well maybe you'd better, 'cause you're in a pile of trouble if you don't. You've just up and gone like a lamb to the slaughter. Some guy tells you to go to Hell, and you just up and go!'

'Yeah, well,' I broke in angrily. 'I didn't see you helping me much, did I?'

'Hey, what? I can't believe this! What am I now? Some scairdykid's nursemaid? You want me to do it all for you? You want me to build you a stairway to Heaven? What do you figure I am? You choose, boy. You choose. And I told you a while back, if you recall, about guarding your own ass! There ain't nothing gonna fish you out of places where it's your own business. There's some places you could get into, where, much as they might like to, nobody else can get! Oh boy! You got to see some things yet. Maybe get to meet some people who can't even hear you. You can't even talk to them. 'Cause they don't even know you're there. Now there's some real Big-shots around on the Levels. People who help; people who've got skill. Real skill. And even they can't get through to those guys I'm telling you about. Oh yeah. I can help. If you choose. But I can't be your own Truth for you.'

'Why did you walk out on me anyway, back at Base Camp? Hey? Why did you suddenly disappear like that? What reason? I'd like to bet there is no damn reason! If it hadn't been for that, I wouldn't have had to go up that godawful staircase! I wouldn't have been nearly blown to bits! I wouldn't have had to get my brains melted down and re-arranged—'

'Brains? Man! Where are you coming from? Brains sure ain't the place. What you got re-arranged was your gears!'

'Nelson, don't argue with me—'

'Gears re-arranged. Feelings re-arranged. You got up to cruising-speed. But you don't appreciate it. Not yet.'

'Feelings re-arranged? Okay! Have you got any idea what it feels like to get your feelings re-arranged, as you put it? They're not chrysanthemums, you jerk! If it hadn't been for you playing games, I never would have had to go through all that stuff! We wouldn't be here, right now! You dropped me in it! There's no getting away from that! Your goddamn tricks dropped me in it! And they could do that any time. And I can't say I trust you much!'

'I got something to tell you. Now you're in a real bad mood, but I'm gonna tell you anyway. See this place?' And he stretched out his arms; gesturing at the landscape. I looked again at endless iron branches knitting together above; pointing at the hideous sky like dead fingers.

'There ain't such a place as where we are,' he said. 'Unless you believe there is. Then you're walking in it. It's built by belief; by the Legend-weaver's Mind-field.'

'Bullshit! If you're so clever, then what are you here for? You tell me that.'

''Cause I'm following you. Hanging on in there. Waiting on your moves. Keeping an eye on you. Want to stick around.' I sat down. The hard cold ground was black and dry. It rustled as I sat on it. I could hear a distant rolling, grinding noise.

'Nelson . . . Listen.' We were both quiet. In the silence we made, the sounds became more prominent.

'Can you hear that?' I asked him.

'Yeah. I hear it.'

'What is it?'

'Yeah. I know. I know what it's supposed to be. Part of the legend of the Hell-World.'

'What, for God's sake?'

'Glaciers. The Glaciers of Elivagar. Between the Spaces.'

I listened. That groaning and creaking echoed across distances I couldn't imagine. The hollow sounds were picked up by the trees, which sang out in eerie harmony. I felt chilled. Then I felt something else creep into me, which seemed to come from the air It rolled inside, sickeningly, as the iron notes hummed in the thorned trees. It brought coldness with it.

'Nelson . . .' I whispered; 'I've got to get out of here . . .'

'And you figure that if you keep walking, you will? Yeah, well, that's real three-D thinking. Old World stuff. See this path?'

'I see it.' Already it had become difficult to speak. But my feet were moving faster; treading the cold dryness of that path as it wound through the trees. Now the thing which had moved into me was slowly sucking at me. I felt its pressure. Its demand. It was mounting, churning, pushing my feet onward towards the green churning in the distance.

'Know where it goes?' I heard him say; 'Hel-gate. That's where. And after that, to the River of Blades. Want to go there?' But I couldn't answer. A desolate wave washed over me. I had nothing to fight it with.

'I said, want to go there?' He was shouting. I could hear him. I couldn't answer. The forest was moving in on me. I didn't want to sink into it.

'. . . Nnn . . . no . . . I . . . I don't want to go there! No!' But my feet were treading, treading. The pressure mounted.

'Then don't! Choose your way!'

I felt frozen tears, suddenly, on my face. 'God! Sweet Jesus! . . . I can't . . .!'

'Okay! I'm going with you. Do what you have to.'

'. . . Can't . . . can't even . . . stand still . . .! What's happening?'

'Then keep going if you can't do different. We'll figure something out. I'm coming with you. Okay, I'm coming.'

I stumbled on the frozen lava-flow ground; and as I fell, glistening black curved blades broke through the path beneath me. They were huge, deadly looking, shaped like the thorns of roses. I couldn't avoid them. They pierced into me, and blood flowed from the wounds; blood of blackened dark red smoke twisting upwards in tendrils. In the green air the smoke took on shapes; curling into snake-forms. Bared fangs whipped back at me. Swaying necks measured my distance. Through clouds of green and crimson, their eyes, like lasers, set me. I heard a cry of terror. It was mine. I heard Nelson's voice shouting.

'Don't let their fangs touch you! Kill them!' Snapping, they wove around me. A gas-like stuff poured out of their mouths.

'. . . How? . . . Kill? . . . How . . .?'

'Bite off their heads! Man! Do it! Bite off their heads!'

'. . . No!'

'Listen to me!'

'. . . Poison . . .!'

'Your poison! Your creation!' A retching sound came out of my mouth. Then I felt myself grow huge; felt my neck elongate, twist. I heard the cracking of my jaws as I stretched out to grasp a snapping head and tear; crunching, through neck bones which, once broken, shot fire into my mouth.

I turned; sprang again to bite into another. As I spat it out another head rose up; backed slightly to aim a strike. I slammed into it, devoured it, tasted the blood. Tasted metal. Nine heads fell sizzling to the black basalt; sending up clouds of sulphurous smoke as they rolled between tree-roots. I felt a rush of torment and victory.

Then my wounds closed. A blue light washed over me and sank into the open holes where the thorns had torn me. And the light passed; slowly faded away.

'-Jesus . . .!' I heard Nelson whisper; 'Oh boy! Oh beautiful!'

I slowly raised my head, and saw her. The woman. She gazed at me. At her feet a tiny blue flower grew from a crack in the black stone. I watched as she stretched out a hand to touch a bare iron bough. At her touch, buds sprang out, unfurling green until the bough was in full leaf. Then she reached into the leaves and plucked a rose of deep red. Holding it out with both hands, she moved forward, to hand it to me. I took it from her. And as I touched that flower I saw that it was dew-covered.

A shock ran through my arm. White fire. A thorn on its stem drew one drop of blood from the palm of my hand. I raised my eyes; met hers, which burned with blue flame. I saw her form; Woman. And yet not Woman. Her hair flowed deep raven-black, crowned with bright radiance. Her pale-skinned face was fine-boned; marvellously beautiful like an ancient goddess. She seemed cloaked in pearly light, but beneath that I saw an almost inhuman majestic nakedness.

The blue flame burned me. My eyes couldn't stand its force. Stlll clutching the rose, I fell down to the cold rustling ground. She neither spoke, nor touched me. And when I dared to look again, she was gone. I opened my clenched hand; saw that the rose had disappeared. But where its sharp thorn had drawn blood, there was still blood. Then I looked at the tree; at the place where she had taken the rose. It glittered; covered in a white dust, like hoar-frost. Where she had stood, the black rock was frosted with sparkling fragments. As I reached out to touch it, a force shot through me. I was jolted to my feet. I scanned the desolate landscape; searching for sign of her, but she wasn't there.

'Oh, Man . . .!' He was crying. Tears were dripping from his chin. We stood; still and quiet. We didn't even hear the glaciers grinding their course in that unknown distance.

'The Gift of the Rose,' he said, simply. Then he turned to me and said.

'See the blood on your hand? see it?' I gazed at it. The woman had gone, but the blood was still flowing.

'Drink it,' he said. 'It's the power of the Great Ones. Drink it while it's still moving through you.'

'Nelson . . . What . . .? What does it mean . . .?'

'Drink it!' I drank.

'She knows your Truth.'

'Where is she? Where has she gone?'

'There is no going and coming with them. They are, for ever. They just are.'

I stood, looking out into the trees. I saw the serpents' heads; their skulls scattered on the ground. Fleshless now, they gleamed; dully luminous.

'You have to go through here.' Nelson said; 'It's a part of your Truth. The journey through all this. Reckon we'll find out why.'

I kept watching the path as it twisted under the iron branches. I didn't care how hideous it was any more. All I could think of was the woman. And why she had come. And where she'd gone.

He read my thoughts. 'Man, she's Spirit-Fire. Seeing her means you've touched that fire. That's the level she exists on. The only place she can be reached. The way to her is known as the Way of the Arrow. It's a Warrior's way. It's the Way of Death. But it takes more dying than you know, to find her. She came, and touched you. That's enough. The rose is an image. It's just an image; a kind of symbol. But real, it ain't. And she ain't real, like you figure she is.'

I hardly heard him. 'I'm going after her,' I said.

'Hey, no way! You got limitations. Best you know them.'

'No, Nelson! She came. Twice! She wants me to go after her! She's asking for me and I'm going!'

'Man, you're crazy!'

No! I'm not crazy! I mean it!'

'Twice she's come. Okay. So maybe she will again. Let it alone. Don't you go demanding of the Great Ones. Asking for too much is the Way of a Fool! Guess it's too much power running through you too fast. It's set you on fire and you've lost your sense! She's not what you think she is! Will you listen? She's pure spirit!'

'No! I've seen her with my own eyes! Woman!'

'Hell! She ain't! She takes shapes! Anything she likes any time she likes it! To you she looks like woman, but she ain't! Can't you see? The Great Ones can do that!'

And he grasped me firmly; held me by both arms. Then carefully he said:

'She'd burn you up. The Way of following her is too tight. The Way of the Arrow ain't your Truth. Let's go slow, huh? Bit by bit. She'd ask you to die, and die, and die again. She's Light, and humankind can't live in pure Light. She'd destroy you like no other damn thing could!'

His words rang through me, and I felt myself drawing back; affected by the fear and doubt in his voice. Touched by his warning.

But the taste of the blood burned inside me.

'You're talking crazy! Real crazy! stupid crazy! You're a fool!'

'I'm hearing you, old man,' I answered, 'Sure and clear. But you're full of crap! Don't give me that, you lying creep! You're dealing me cheap lies!'

'Hey, so it's come to that, huh? You hating me; calling me a liar, after all we've been through together? Well, let me tell you we're down-and-out that's for damn sure, while we're here. The two of us are in Hell, now, Man! And you've gone and taken crazy, and you're saying I'm full of lies. Well, you're a fool for sure, and there ain't no other word for it. I'm getting us both out of here, out of this weird shit real fast! You're bang on right when you say I can get us out of it. I can. And you're coming along like it or not, 'cause without you I ain't going nowhere. We're gonna haul ass out of this place, 'cause you know what's up ahead, you with the crazy ideas? Huh? River of Blades, that's what! The Gate of the Kingdom of the Nine Dark Worlds! The Hall of Elvidner! That's what! And boy-oh-boy, I ain't going there on some damn fool fancy of yours. There ain't no reason to keep dragging ass through this Viking's Hell, boy! And looking for some woman who's bad news ain't no good reason! It's her that got you here in the first place! She wants you to be in this situation! You getting that?'

'No!!'

Quick as a flash I spun round and gripped him; locking his neck in an armhold. I twisted; pushed.

'It's lies! You're full of goddamn lies!'

He was on the ground and I pinned his arms. 'Lies, old man!' I screamed;

'Did you taste the Blood? Did you? Did she touch you? Did you take that rose into your hand? Did you? I did! It burns and it's sweet!'

'Evil sometimes tastes sweet.' His pale blue eyes glittered and he bared his teeth.

'No! Damn you! I'm not going anywhere with you! You can feed me all the crap you like, but I'm not letting you take me any place! I'm going the way I decide! You got that? You can do what you damn well like Get out if you want to, but I'm going right on!'

'Why?" His voice was a whisper now. 'Why?'

'Because it feels right, that's why.' Then, suddenly, he laughed and his eyes filled with tears.

'Okay, Man. Okay. I know. Let me up. I gotta tell you something.' I felt my anger slowly fade. Amazed, I let go of him. Still laughing, he got to his feet.

'Okay, it's cool. I was just trying you out.'

'. . . You were . . . what?'

'Oh boy, I'm sorry. But I'm glad. I was trying you to see if you'd hold on to your Truth.'

'. . . So what you said . . .'

'Wasn't worth five cents. You saw it. Truth. It's real, oh yeah. More real than you've ever had. She's real, okay. And you got to keep treading this way and she knows it. 'Cause once you'd seen her she could have lifted you out. But she didn't. And the reason is 'cause the way to her is through everything, even this place. It forges steel and she knows that.'

'I don't know about all those things,' I answered. 'But I have to go with it, and if this is the way, so be it.' Then, in those moments, I saw something more strange in him than I'd realized before. I knew him, better.

9: *Hell or High Water*

SO WE KEPT going, through the Ironwood. At first, the taste of the blood still burned hot inside me, and our way seemed easy, effortless. I hardly noticed the desolation around us. But slowly, the fire died down, and though it left its mark on me, it cooled.

As we kept on, step after step, over the sharp dark stones of that track, the reality of our position hit me. I felt the weight of my decision. It was my decision, yet it seemed to have been made for me. Not by Nelson, or by her; but made for me, nevertheless.

Nelson said little. With every step we took I noticed that we appeared to be moving on a gradual but steady downward incline; deeper and deeper into something. But oddly, there was no corresponding rise of the landscape either behind us or around us, to give me an idea of how far we had descended.

I watched as a green fog crept in and the forest around us slowly became invisible. I tried to speak to Nelson, but he answered in monosyllables, and didn't lift his eyes from the ground. It seemed that he, too, was oppressed by the atmosphere; for as the path we trod drew downward, the air had become stagnant and dense, and I felt weighted with a terrible heaviness.

It became more and more difficult to move. An eerie silence surrounded us, replacing the moaning harmonies of the trees. It filled me with foreboding. I needed to talk to him. The route we were taking made me uneasy. With the dimming of the fire in me I'd begun to feel confused and unreal: as if I'd wakened from a nightmare only to find that it had pursued me out of the dreamscape. But my thoughts moved heavily as my body was dragged down by a sensation of increased gravity.

Thoughts moved like fish at the bottom of an ocean. They glinted at me, sluggishly, and passed on their way. Hindered by the sensation of weight, I slowly turned to look at Nelson. As he raised his head, I noticed a strange tiredness in his expression. But he lifted his hand slowly, oh so slowly, and gave me a thumbs-up signal. Then his gaze dropped back to the stones of the track.

Out of the silence of the fog came the sound of a beating of wings, leathery and dry. The sound passed, fading away into swirling green. On the edge of my vision I caught sight of vague shapes shifting among the trees. But when I turned to face them, they were gone. I heard airborne things flitting through the iron branches; moving quickly. Creatures of this element. But whenever I looked, they had disappeared.

As the ground sloped further, the air became ever darker and heavier; and it was difficult to see more than an arm's length to either side. I stopped once, as cold wings brushed my face. But I saw nothing.

From deep in the mists, harsh metallic cries like bird-calls rang and echoed among the trees. They, whatever they were, were calling to each other, I was sure. They were communicating. I sensed they were predatory, and that our presence excited them. A ripple of apprehension ran through me. I didn't know if they'd attack; or what we could do to fight them if they did. I didn't even know what they were. I glanced back at Nelson; but he was moving slowly, his eyes on the path. He didn't seem to notice the cries.

Then the fog swept in more thickly about us; and the steely, echoing calls faded into it. In the darkening air I could hardly make out Nelson's shape, or even the path, any more. I stretched out my arms, feeling to each side of me; and touched bristling iron.

The trees had closed in on us. As the fog drifted and thinned slightly in places, I could see that the iron branches had inter-twined above us, forming a thorned, tunnel-like passage through which we descended.

Something changed. There was suddenly a shifting of the atmosphere. I sensed it, but couldn't tell what it was. I experi-enced a quick, dizzying, falling sensation; but when it passed, I saw that we were still in the tunnel. Nothing appeared to have changed. But I knew that something had.

'Nelson . . .' I whispered. 'What was that? '

'Stop!' he snapped quickly.

I halted in my tracks; listened. The sound of keening and wailing came from somewhere deep inside the passage of thorns. It was a grief-stricken noise, moving towards us in waves. It seemed distant; but at the same time, too close. I heard sobbing; then a long scream, which cut off, abruptly. Horrified, I listened; sure it was the voice of a child.

'What in God's name is it? I've got to go and see '

'No!' Nelson gripped me by the arm.

'Hey, it's a child! Down there, Nelson . . . Sounds like a . . .'

'No!'

It came again. Words, a litany, drifting towards us. I strained to hear more clearly. The words faded out and the weeping returned, rising and falling on the air. Then I heard that the tortured voice was praying.

. . . *At the hour of our . . . at the hour of our . . . death! . . . Holy Mary . . .*

'It's a woman,' Nelson said. 'Stay where you are. Ain't a kid.'

. . . *Mother of God! . . . Pray for us . . . sinners now and at the . . . hour of our . . . death . . .*

'Where is she?' I whispered. Crying howled along the tunnel. Sometimes her words were clear, and sometimes they were lost in the pain-racked sobbing. The sound of her grief was agony to listen to.

. . . Oh Mary . . . Mary! . . . Mother . . . Pray for us . . .!

'Where is she? Tell me! Where the hell is she?'

'Okay!' he said. 'Whatever you do, don't move! Not forwards! Not backwards! Hear me?'

'Why? She's . . . *Why?* what is it?'

'We've got ourselves into a slip,that's what. Hear her? What she's saying? It don't fit into this scenario, that's why.'

A scream came again; long and painful.

Michael!! . . . Archangel!! . . . The Lord confided . . . in your care . . . all the Souls of those redeemed! . . . Burning! . . . Burning! . . . Oh Holy Mary! . . . Come to the help of . . . men whom God made . . . in his own image . . . and whom . . . he bought from the tyranny of . . . Satan!! . . .

'What do you mean, it doesn't . . .?'

'A slip, Man. A slipstream. I can ride it. Not so sure about you. Maybe you've got the skill. Maybe you ain't. It's real dangerous 'cause of where it leads to. It's okay if you don't move, for a bit. Stay where you are.'

I froze. 'Okay. How did we get in it?'

'What were you thinking?' Nelson said quickly.

'When?'

'In the tunnel. Just as it closed in.'

'I don't know . . . Not sure.'

'That's what did it. You thought something.'

'Don't know . . . Trapped . . . Can't stand being shut in. Wanted out. Wanted to get out. That's all.'

He was quiet for a moment. Then, still holding me by the shoulders, he whispered; 'That's it. You thought out. But there ain't no out. Not yet. So you got us in a slipstream. You went kind of sideways. Best way I can explain it.'

'What do you mean?'

'A parallel state. A parallel darkness.'

'Another Hell-World?'

'That's what it is. Yeah.'

'And there are . . . more?'

'As many as there are Minds; beliefs. Sure.' Again he fell quiet, thinking. I didn't know what was going through his mind. Then he spoke.

'You got changed on that stairway. White Fire moved you.

Then you got changed again by the Sword. Changed when you ate your own snake-darkness. Changed by the Woman, and the Blood of the Rose. You got more power now than you had. More power, more danger. I'll tell you the danger now: Warps.'

'Warps? What are they?'

'Bad news. First-degree Trouble. That's what. You just might, and I mean might, be able to ride out a slipstream the way you are; and I ain't so certain of that. But a Warp . . . I wouldn't give much for your chances.'

The cries carried to us again, wave after wave. Racking sobs. Holy Mary. Michael Archangel. Lakes of fire.

'Got to keep out of them,' he continued. 'They can lead to the Outer Reaches.'

'That woman . . .' I began.

'Far as she believes, she's rotting in Hell. There's someone with her. But they can't move her out. Not yet.'

'. . . Someone with her? What do you mean?'

'Seen it before. Oh, I've seen it. Real strong ones do that work. See, they've got to wait for the right time; keep a thread to the one who's stuck. Got to keep it alive, and warm, no matter what. And there ain't no time-limit. Got to be a hero to do that. A real hero, 'cause it's tougher to be a hero in prison than it is on the battlefield. Seen it over and over. There's so many of them; trapped by belief, or dogma, or guilt. And for each one of them, there's a Saviour; only they don't recognize it, 'cause sometimes the Saviour looks like a teenager, or a pretty girl, or an old woman. The ones who come to stand by them, to try and lift them out, don't look the way belief, or any man-made teaching says they should. That's why it takes so long. Only when they are cleaned out, and they see the truth, can they be moved. And that can take a long time.'

'But what happens to them, then . . . after?'

'They're taken to rest. A long rest. There's a big difference between rules and Laws. The rules of what Man has figured out, and thinks he knows are a long way from Laws. The Law with those guys who've been through the burning is Love. And learning. After that, they're small again. And their minds are clearer, like little kids. They learn to find joy in smaller things. And they learn to follow Laws; not run away from those Laws, to hide behind Mens' rules. And they find their own Truth, and their power, in time. And they learn to ride.'

I heard him. But behind his words, which seemed so easy, I heard the woman's screaming pain. She had to be one of those people he'd just been talking about; the ones no-one can get through to. The ones who don't hear. I wondered about the nature of belief. It's strong. It's powerful. It grips. I wondered how long she'd have to suffer; or even whether she needed to. Or if, perhaps, that was the only way for her. I wondered if what Nelson said were really true; and she would be released.

Then I knew. I didn't have to believe anything. I knew. It would happen. The way he said it would. The awareness rushed through me as an unfamiliar thing. It was simple; an essence. It didn't need to be thought about, proved. It just was. And something from under the stones beneath my feet ran through to my eyes. It rocked me; and the woman's voice faded into the distance. I heard a roaring sound, and Nelson's voice, vaguely, far away. He was calling to me; shouting to hold still. But I couldn't understand. His grip was on my shoulders; tighter and tighter. His voice was cutting through. But with it, I heard another voice.

... *I know!* ... *I know!* ... *The Being, Matchet!* ... *Who is among the Watchers in the House of Osiris!* ... *shooting rays of light* ... *from his eye* ... *but who himself is* ... *unseen!* ...

It was the voice of a man: desperate, terrified. Behind it, I could hear a steady rush of water; tumbling and roaring.

But over the pounding of the water, the man's voice rose up and rang.

... *O Thou!* ... *O Thou!* ... *Who art named Millions of Years!* ... *O Traverser of Millions of Years!* ... *O Thou Great Green Lake!* ...

Then my vision opened up, and I saw a great river, rushing on its way; pouring black, foaming water over a dead landscape. Upon the wate, pieces of steel glinted. Naked, shining blades were tossed up, to sink back again into the maelstrom.

... *Bring my Boat to me!* ... *Grant me to sail with Thee* ... *among the endless stars* ... *which never set!* ...

'Stay still! Real still!' Nelson's voice broke through. 'It's another one! Stay still!'

'Another ... slip? We're in another slip?' I shouted to him over the turmoil.

'Yeah! Keep steady! See the river? It's the Viking's riverl It don't fit with him! The belief-systems are all different. Each one's making its own space, its own Mind-Field! Two spaces interlocking means we're close to an Interspace! Don't think!'

'Don't think?'

'Don't think anything, 'cause it might move you! Don't move!'

I saw the man. He was dressed in rags which hung, web-like, from his shoulders. On his head he wore a headdress of gold, crowned with a serpent. He stood on the bank of the river; his arms raised high above him. His body had turned a greenish-blue. I smelt decay on the air; an overpowering scent; like rotting wood. Not rotting flesh; but wood.

Then, close by him, I caught sight of another figure; a young woman, who appeared to be no more than seventeen or eighteen. She was tall, but delicately formed. Her figure was more like a child's than a woman's. A corona of pale pinks and blues shone around her. She paid no attention to anything but the man; though he appeared not to see her. She made no attempt to touch him, or speak to him.

. . . For my heart was weighed . . . and Ammet . . . Ammet! . . . devoured me not! . . . and I await thee! . . . Hail! . . . Thou who art in thy Boat! . . .

I felt myself beginning to drift. The scene disturbed me. I wondered how long he had stood on the banks of that river, screaming to gods who didn't seem to hear him. And how long had the girl watched over him? I began to drift to dizzy space; but Nelson's voice cut through.

'Okay, Man! This is a tightrope! I told you, don't think! I mean don't think! Slip down between the Interspace and you're gone! Trapped like a fly in a double-glazed window! See him? He made the state he's in. He made it himself. It ends; and the end for him is not long off! But he's in paradise compared with what you'd be like in an Interspace!'

He snapped me back to myself; but I found it difficult to be still. I could hear the wailing of the woman as she sobbed and shrieked her Ave Marias. I could hear the man; praying hysterically. One superimposed on the other. And through the crashing of the river another sound came; a belching, snarling noise. I had no idea where from.

'Okay!' I shouted to Nelson over the chaos; 'Okay! What do we do? Is there some way through?'

'Yeah. But we can't afford to slip any more!'

'Interspaces! Nelson! Tell me what the hell an Interspace is!' I shouted. 'Warps! What's a Warp? What happens if we get in one?'

'We don't!' he shouted back. 'Get that real clear, right now! Okay! An Interspace is a trap in a Slipstream! In one of those, nothing can reach you! Nothing! Two choices in a Warp, if you're damn fool enough to fall in one. Burn-up, or The Outer Reaches! On a thousand-to-one-chance, and a special dispensation, and a hell of a lot of skill, you could ride through it and come out. But you could come out anywhere! Any Universe! And I ain't too sure of that! The odds are stacked you don't come through! We don't get into one! Ever! Got that?'

'Okay!' I didn't know. Not really. Nothing I'd ever known had prepared me for this existence. There was no knowledge except that which was grasped and torn out of each move I made. And the learning was fast. The fast, the quick, the alive, survived in a wild world where ignorance was danger; where a mistake had too high a price. Mine was a ride on the edge. Always on the very edge. And along with me, he clung to that edge; riding it out, laughing in its face. That old, gnarled, crazy death-rider knew these Worlds like the palm of his hand, and I didn't.

'Didn't hear that!' His shout cracked through my thoughts; a gunshot to wake me. 'Didn't hear you answer, Man!'

'Okay!'

'Got you! Now see ahead? See that fog coming in?' I looked where he pointed. A grey, viscous fog had moved in from somewhere; and hung, rolling and churning over the River of Blades. Through it, faint light-rays shone, catching the unsheathed shards of metal, illuminating them as they rose and fell crashing back to the water.

'I see it!' I shouted back. Again I heard a snarling through the fog; and a gnawing, bone-crunching sound of some creature in the jungle of minds. I heard the drip of its saliva. Whatever it was, was out there, above the water.

'Something in the fog', Nelson called out. 'See it?'

'Beast . . . of some kind . . . eating!"

'What do you see?'

'See?'

'*What do you see?*'

'Light . . . .Rays of light . . .'

'No. Look! Can you see something?' I couldn't; except oily clouds, dark grey. Light shining on swords cutting through the torrent. Beams like watery searchlights, crossing, drifting over, disappearing and re-appearing. That was all.

'Lights.' I said.

'No.' Then he sat down beside the river, and closed his eyes. He lay on the ground and folded his hands on his chest.

'Nelson . . . What are you . . .? Nelson!'

'You can't see? Fine. I can't see,' he answered.

'Nelson!'

'Can't do your seeing for you. Going to take a break,' he muttered. I only just caught what he said over the confusion of sounds.

'Nelson! Listen to me! Don't do this! Not now! I can't see anything! I don't know what you're getting at! Don't do this! Don't drop out on me now!'

He lay, stone-still.

'Nelson!' There was no response. I'd seen him do that before; but always in the peace of the rock ledge of Base Camp. And I knew that at at time like that, he was gone. There was no talking to him. I shouted; trying to force him to hear me. Then I realized that at the fringe of my trust, he was proving to be unworthy of it. Trust, once more, was proving to be dangerous. I stopped shouting; aware that there was no point. I didn't see how I could get through, with him or without him.

'You're right,' I heard. His voice seemed to sound inside my mind. 'You're right. Ain't no use trusting no-one. Trust yourself. What if I see wrong? Could do.'

'Nelson! You can hear me! I damn well know you can!'

'Sure do.'

'You know the way round this hell-hole! I don't!'

'Told you I'd help, if you want me to. But I won't hold you up like I was your wooden legs. Won't be your glass eye. No way. Look! See what you see. Don't do so much thinking, just looking.'

I stared at him. He was still lying, eyes closed, on his back. I heard his words, but didn't see him speak.

'Look again.' I gazed out over the river where the beams of light crossed at angles, dipped and lifted. Just lights. Weak, sickly lights. Then I caught sight of something else. A single glint of something shone, illuminated by the rays; and was gone from sight. I watched. It appeared again. A thread; thin and frail-looking. A spidersilk thread which extended across the river to be lost in the fog.

'That's our bridge,' he said, rising to his feet. 'We cross it.'

'That? Nelson, are you kidding?'

'We ain't got no choice. We ride the edge of the Interspace on it. Hell or High Water, Man! It'd be serious bad news to stay here. Glad you saw it.' He laughed. 'We cross it,' he said, again.

10: Interspace Freeway

'WHEN WE GET on that bridge,' Nelson said, 'we keep moving. You got that? We don't stop. We don't think. And we sure as hell don't listen to nothing – not one damn thing, no matter what it is. We don't do nothing but keep moving, and keep riding that line in front of us. You're one mistake away from empty space. Slip, and you're gone. And there ain't nothing I can do to save your ass!'

I looked at our bridge; a glistening thin thread. Only where it was caught in the rays of light was it visible. My body felt too wide, too heavy to tread it. The way looked impossible. And I wondered if he knew that bridge; if he'd ever crossed it. Still we sat by the tumbling river. He seemed to be waiting for me.

'Have you ever crossed over here?' I asked, 'before?'

'No.' He answered. 'I ain't.'

'So you don't know we're going to make it. You can't know.'

'You never know nothing till you've done it,' he said. 'Or got inside of it. Or loved it.'

We were going to get just one shot at that crossing. That was all. No second chance. No room for a mistake. I knew I wasn't ready. Looking at it made me feel worse. But every moment we delayed, the pressure mounted. I felt the presence of more Hell-worlds. New voices sprang out of the heavy fog. They overlapped; pushing and slipping against one another. The tortures of too many languages, too many beliefs. We seemed to be on a junction, a meeting-place of darknesses. Nelson's assurance that these worlds were created from illusion didn't help. They were real enough to form vortices; whirlpools into which other minds could be drawn. It was gruelling to keep trying to resist them. And I didn't know how much longer I could hold out. I didn't know how far away my breaking-point was. We had to cross; but I wasn't ready.

'Got to move out, soon,' he said.

'I know.'

'Ain't got a good deal of time.'

I turned; looked at him. 'Time?' I said. 'Hey, I didn't think you rode on those Mythical Beasts, old man.'

Suddenly, explosively, he laughed; and his laughter cracked open an empty space between the sounds. Then they returned; flowing back like water, to fill it. He laughed again, louder, and fell over on his back; his voice blending with the hundreds.

'Hah!' he cried; trying to get up. 'Fell into my own philosophy! Dug me a hole there, and damn fell in it! Hah!'

His laughter infected me. A humourless fragment of me said that I was hysterical, and that we were on the brink of Hell or Nothingness; and I didn't care at that moment. I laughed.

'Not round 'I said; but couldn't finish. He did it for me.

'As in clocks '

'Or straight . . .' I managed.

'As in desk-diaries! Man, you crack me up!' So we laughed, the two of us. To look at him made me worse. He couldn't get up from the ground. Then something jumped up in me; fast and without warning. Cold, concentrated, edged. It wouldn't let me waste time.

'Right,' I said. 'We move.'

'You ready?' he asked. He was on his feet in an instant. He leapt up, cat-like, all laughter gone.

'Ready as I'll ever be.'

'Over the bridge?'

'Over the bridge.' I said.

'Know how to find stillness? How to balance in that stillness? How to move in it? Got to fix that first.'

Something took over, and I felt stillness take me. Something wanted the best shot I'd got; and to survive. And in the stillness, a note began to ring and vibrate; forcing the voices aside. It made a pathway. I heard Nelson. He was on its track. I felt his hand on my shoulder.

'Remember what I'm saying to you. No listening. No stopping. No thinking. Interspace Freeway – here we come!'

I stepped out; moved first. I felt my feet lift on a line which shifted, as though in a wind. But there was no wind. Then that line speared me; impaled me on intention. And I saw the Woman in my mind's eye. I sensed that she remembered me. There was no progression through space; no treading any more. But I felt a sense of movement outside the idea of travelling; so fast that I touched Aeons and saw the patterns of constellations move and change in form and brightness. They widened, opened up, simplified, re-formed into new shapes. I saw Supernovae flare, whiten, and flicker out; snuffed like candle-flames.

New-born comets streaked out of the distant places of their birth, and tore past me on their pathways. I watched as they dimmed, melted into skeletal shells and, burnt-out, crumbled to particles of dust. Galaxies formed. Atoms drew together; turning and spiralling. They moved with precision, grace, deliberation. Their movements made any notion of randomness impossible. I saw. I was. Motionless in the centre. There was no thought; as to think implies a search. There was no impulse to search. In that centre, everything simply *was*, thoughtlessly.

But at the edges of sight, vast cracks opened up, where nothing was visible. Yawning pits of no-thing, no-time, they gaped emptily; flanking me to either side. In them, the dance became distorted. They gripped and bent Creation. Dimly, I remembered Nelson. And the words which I heard, I already knew. I had always known them. But he reminded me. Time-chasms. Pay them no attention. Keep the Line or you go into Burn-up. Know nothing but the thread. The thread; or you'll be torn apart. The thread. It stretched out forever. It seemed to be formed of my own substance. I was a spider, crossing my own bridge. Devouring and spinning it over again. Then whiteness crashed into me. White Death.

The first thing I saw was my own hands; pulsing. I held them up in front of me; seeing them throb with lines of force, colours of liquid brilliance. Veinless, bloodless, but webbed with light, my hands were intensely alive. Fires rayed out from the tips of my fingers. I drew my hands together, slowly. And the light silently exploded.

I heard my name. Richard Anthony Brett. It sounded rare, and strange, yet it became irrelevant. And as the words I heard died away, I knew they would never be heard again. Not in the same way. Not in all existence. The words transformed into a simple music in which each note shone with its own colour. It shaped a pattern in the space in front of me: an angular form, precise and in accordance with the interval between each note. I knew the music was myself, unclothed. The words of the name had been my clothing. That music was my name; through time and space.

I watched it shine, and hold, and fade, and pass away.

And I saw my nakedness; essential but transparent. And I knew that it was both a purposeful thing and a passing thing; known to the music of that Name.

And I knew I'd never dared to be. I'd never dared to stretch the bow-string taut enough. I'd never dared many things. I'd never dared to really live – or die .

With that realization, I saw the colours which surrounded me merge into a redness; a redness which re-formed, clinging to me, into the clothes in which I had come through to the Levels. And with those familiar clothes I was returned to a familiar mind-state; similar, though not quite the same as I had been before.

'Man! Where've you been?' I heard. 'Like where? I couldn't see you nowhere! You freaked me out! Hey! Can you see me? Right now?'

'Yeah,' I replied; 'Yeah, Nelson. I can see you.'

'Jesus! You had me worried back there! Worried something

serious! Thought you'd gone into Burn-up.'

I turned to look at him as he came up behind me. I couldn't tell where we were. There were no surroundings; instead, we seemed to be shrouded in air which had the appearance of a back-lit cloth. I could see no landmarks. No landscape. But I could see Nelson clearly. And as he came up to me, a strong blue and silver light hovered for an instant about his head and shoulders. No sooner had I seen it than it was gone. He approached, gave me a left-handed military salute, and sat down, cross-legged on the ground. I noticed the ground as I watched him sit down. It had the appearance of fine sand, but was gold, sparkling. It was gold dust. All around us.

'Not me,' I answered.

'Where'd you get to?' he asked. I sat down, too, on the gold dust. It was soft; springy. The absence of landscape didn't seem to matter. Around us a quietness hung. A peaceful refreshing quietness. We were out of the Ironwood. Out of Hell-frost.

'Can't say I'm sure,' I said.

'Well, we made it! Son-of-a-bitch, we made it! Odds were stacked high against, that's for sure! Boy-oh-boy, we got through!'

'Bird-Man,' I said, quietly.

'What?'

'Bird-Man. You can call me Bird-Man. Any time you like.'

'It's a deal.'

'Because he's dead. Richard Brett's dead, that's why. Sort of killed. Dead. R.I.P.'

'Hey, what you been up to back there? You punched out someone's lights?'

'Yeah,' I said. 'Someone I used to know. An old pal.'

'Hope that guy got a decent funeral.'

'He got the works, Nelson. The works.'

He saluted again, left-handed; and grinned.

'We rode the edge of a Warp, didn't we?' I said suddenly. 'That stuff, it was a Warp, wasn't it?'

At first he didn't reply; but just looked closely at me. Then he said;

'Sure. It was a Warp. And we rode the edge of it. Didn't want to freak you by saying. But yeah. It was. And, for what it's worth, you got my respect. Re-spect! 'Cause there was only one guy I knew who could ride out a Warp, and that was me. So now there's you. You got some neat machine charged up there! Some turbo-charged engine running!'

I laughed.

'We didn't have no choice,' he said. 'We'd have taken it if we'd had one.'

'Just glad to be on the other side of it, that's all,' I replied. Then I took a look around. I didn't know where we'd ended up.

'Where are we? Where is this place, Nelson?'

'Where are we? Having a rest, that's what.' He adjusted the twist of leather thonging round his head. It had slipped over his eyebrows. Objects fell out of it: small blue feathers, the coin, pieces of shell, or bone. He pulled at his rainbow leggings. They had gone baggy at the knees.

'Ask a silly question . . .' I said, looking at the gold-dust desert, all twenty or thirty feet of it before it merged into nothingness. He stood up; trying to straighten the bags in his knees. He seemed to be listening to something. I was sure it wasn't me.

'Fixing my image a bit,' he said. 'We got visitors coming.'

'What?'

'Hear that?'

I didn't. I couldn't hear a thing. But he did. He stood still and gazed around. There was nothing to see.

'Riders coming,' he said. 'Maybe we should go and meet 'em.'

'Hey, wait a minute . . .' I was on my feet. I didn't like that idea. 'Wait a minute, how can you be sure . . .?' Then I heard it, the sound of horses' hooves. It didn't make sense. In dust?

'Sshh!' he whispered. 'Let me listen . . .'

'Jesus Christ, Nelson!' I whispered back at him. 'We can't just go and meet them! We don't know who the hell they are!'

'Sshh! Can you hear anything?'

'Horses!'

'Anything else?'

'No.'

'It's okay, Man. Okay. I figure.'

'You . . . what?'

'I know where we are. It's okay. At least, I'm damn sure I know where we are . . .'

'You're what? Oh, *what*? I can't believe this, Nelson!'

'Sshh! Wait!'

The riders drew nearer; but I couldn't see them. From the sound of the hoof beats I guessed there were at least two of them; maybe more. They were coming slowly but surely closer. Then they appeared; suddenly materialized through the shrouded air. Three riders, mounted on grey horses. Two women and a man; dressed strangely, and richly adorned. The three of them rode abreast, watching us impassively. I noticed, as they approached through the sandy gold, that I could no longer hear the sound of horses' hooves.

11: *Riders of the Blue Sun*

THEY RODE UP and stopped a few feet away from us. One of the women spoke. Her voice was rich and striking. It left an echo on the air.

'Who goes there?'

I was about to answer, but suddenly felt the restraint of Nelson's hand on my arm. He signalled to me to keep quiet. Then, quickly, he stepped forward. The woman didn't move and her expression didn't change. She held the reins of her white beast firmly in both hands. Nelson stood straight, and without saying a word, raised both his arms directly in front of him, holding his palms upward and very flat. For a moment he stayed like that, then he stretched out his hands to each side of his body; keeping the palms up and inclining his head slowly downwards. Then he touched crossed hands to his forehead, lifted his head, and stood still again, eye-to-eye with her.

The woman dismounted, gracefully, easily; and as she moved I saw the same lights around her that I had seen about Nelson when we came through the Warp. They flickered, suddenly blue and silver over her shoulders and arms; and the next moment they were gone.

She stepped towards us; halting a few paces away. In the

momentary silence I took stock of her. She was a tall, powerfully built woman who towered over Nelson, and was even taller than me. She was dressed all in white; in a substance which looked like fine white linen. Her upper arms and upper breast were bare, but gold arm-guards covered the entire length of her forearms. Over her shoulders were wide straps of light metallic webbing which fastened to loose folds of whiteness at her breasts. A curved girdle of thin gold outlined the shape of her lean hips, and her legs were covered with breeches of the same white linen. Her hair; long, perfectly straight, and deep crimson-red, was bound at her forehead by a metal band with the many colours of titanium. The lower part of her hands were gloved. From each finger and her thumb, fragile-looking chains ran across her hand to fasten on to the arm-guards. For a long moment, we watched each other. Both Nelson and I kept still and quiet. Her steady gaze held us; then she formed the signs with her arms and hands, exactly as Nelson had done.

'We bid you welcome,' she said, simply. Then the other two riders dismounted and stood by their horses. She spoke again:

'We heard the sounds of your coming.' Her voice, still oddly resonant, sounded gentler. 'On the Web.' I wanted to say something, but Nelson's quick glance told me not to.

'If you wish to follow us,' she continued, 'we shall guide you through. If you wish to remain we shall not hinder you. What is your choice?'

I glanced at Nelson. He nodded. Once more, the lights played over the top half of the woman's body. I noticed the two riders nearby. They too were lit by blue and silver.

'You gave the Sign,' she said, 'of the Gateway of the Law. Your Degree is true. Your Lights correspond. I offer you safe refuge and welcome with our People for as long as you require it. State your choice. But do not delay, for the Web is moving, and we must return.'

Then Nelson spoke. 'There are two of us,' he said. 'Not one, but two. Two men, two ways. While that's the case, you're gonna need two answers. Ain't gonna speak for him.' He nodded in my direction. 'Whatever he chooses, that'll do fine.'

'His Lights also correspond,' the woman said. For a moment she remained still, watching us. Then after signalling to her companions she turned to join them. They re-mounted and, three abreast, raised their right hands to their shoulders in a salute, and began to move away.

'Where?' I asked, turning to Nelson, who stood watching me. 'Okay, suppose we go? Where to?'

'To their encampment on the Plain of Xentha,' he answered. 'To the Tribe of the Blue Sun; the Charos.'

'. . . And if we stay here?'

'We can't. Not for long, anyway. We'd have to move out. See that sand? Nice, ain't it? But, Man, it's weird. It shifts.'

'So it's move-out time, anyway. That's what you're saying?' Okay. Let's do it. Let's go. What are we waiting for?'

He grinned. 'They're okay,' he said. 'Well, to guys like us they are.'

'What do you mean?'

'Tell you later. If we're going, we got to go now.'

We followed their tracks, which were easy to make out in the gold-dust. The three riders were out of sight, but the sound of their horses' hooves carried to us, and we moved towards the sound.

As we went, I tried to ask him about those people, the Charos; about the meaning of the signs they had exchanged. But every time I tried, he motioned to me to keep quiet. He knew them. That was obvious. And they knew him. But I needed to know more. Then he turned to me and whispered;

'Stay cool, and don't say nothing till we get there, huh? I'll tell you stuff later, okay? Pretty good reason or I wouldn't be nagging your ass.'

So I fell silent, and we both kept on walking. Once, I glanced behind, and saw that the dust flowed like water over our tracks, until the hollows of our footprints were erased. It wasn't long before we caught sight of the riders. They loomed ahead of us in the shrouded atmosphere, and I heard the light low sound of a horn-call. I remembered the small curved golden horn which had hung on the bridle of the woman's horse. Then I knew that they were aware of our decision, and were acknowledging our presence.

We kept on; slowly moving in their tracks, while behind us all record of our passing disappeared. As we drew up close to them I noticed that we were no longer treading on dust, but on a causeway formed of huge geometric blocks of quartz or glass. Then I realized why we had heard the horses' footsteps in the desert. The riders must have approached us along this causeway. The further we progressed, the greater the elevation became between the road we followed and the surrounding desert, until I saw that we were quite high above it. Beneath us, the dust shifted and rolled gently, like tides of a golden sea.

And so we continued, in silence and slowly, until the land below us became indistinguishable. In time, we passed through a tall archway of trees, the trunks of which soared up, dead-straight, on either side of our path. Above us their curving branches interlocked, like the Gothic arches of a great cathedral. But unlike creations of stone, those arches were in full leaf, and bore fruit; peculiar tear-drop shaped fruits of green and gold which hung down from the highest branches. For a long time we travelled through that bower. And the arching symmetry of its shape; and the purposeful silence in which we moved, filled me with a strange impression. I felt ancient; treading a mysterious and sacred path.

Eventually the distance between the trees began to widen, and the ground on each side took on a gentle but spreading curve; forming a shallow rounded valley, through which the causeway ran. Overhead, the branches no longer wove together; and a pale turquoise sky was clearly visible between them. It was a daylight sky; sunless. But I saw that it glittered with stars. The regular form of the trees slowly broke up until we were no longer flanked by them; but instead we were surrounded by the gradual slopes of the valley.

We had continued on that course for some distance when the riders ahead of us came to an abrupt halt. I saw that where they stopped two rounded outcrops of rock jutted out on each side, closing the valley into a bottleneck. Beyond that point I couldn't see clearly. It seemed that the land on the other side of those rocks was covered with a bluish, flowing mist. The woman raised her arm high, as a signal for us to stop. As she did so, her gold arm-guard flashed briefly, with light reflected from an unseen source.

We stopped, and I glanced at Nelson; but his gaze was dead ahead. Yet as I looked away again, I thought I saw him wink at me. The riders dismounted and, leading their horses, began to move forward slowly on foot. When they passed between the two outcrops of rock, I heard the sound of the horn again. Its note, fine and clear, pierced the air three times, and echoed all around us, gradually dying away. Then they moved through into the mist on the other side. We followed quickly, so as not to lose sight of them; but as we passed through I found that the blue mist, which had seemed quite dense from our vantage-point in the valley, was barely knee-high. I could see the three ahead of us quite clearly; and beyond the mist wove drifting tendrils over a wide flat plain.

Across the plain, in the distance, thin spires rose up above buildings which were faceted in some way, for flashes of reflected light, either from the stars or from the sky itself, rayed out from flat surfaces beneath the spires. From somewhere among the buildings an answering horn-call sounded; a single high note, drawn-out and echoing across the open space. When I heard it I became aware that those buildings were inhabited, and that our approach had been noted. That, I thought, had to be the encampment Nelson had said we were heading for. The dwelling-place of the Charos.

I wanted to say something, but thought better of it. Nelson seemed to be ignoring me, and not one of the riders had addressed me directly. So, in silence we crossed the wide plain towards the buildings, which, as we drew nearer, took on more distinctive, individual shapes.

The structures, I noticed, were all perfectly geometric; formed of a clear crystalline substance. Varied angularities fitted together with a mathematical precision which I couldn't understand; because five-sided figures stood, fitting easily with pyramidal shapes, cubes, hexagons and more complex forms. It seemed impossible. The architectural marvel was not held together with girders, or metal frames; but with what appeared to be lines of light, crossing and criss-crossing the planes and angles. Then I saw that what I had mistakenly assumed were spires, when I had seen them from a distance, were in fact tight spirals of light which soared up high above the buildings. I watched. At close range, I could clearly see an upward and a downward force; the upward force moving in a clockwise direction, and the downward force within the other's spiral, turning anticlockwise. How, or from where they originated, I couldn't tell. Nor could I guess what their purpose was; but I was certain they hadn't been constructed for decoration.

We stopped at a gateway; a latticework of light, made up of equally-spaced diagonal rays. The woman, leading her horse, approached it and the latticework changed form, flashing through numerous patterns until it settled on one; a frame of hexagonal shapes with a large gap in the centre. Through this, she passed to the other side. After her the other two riders, first the man, then the woman, came up to the gate.

For the first time, I noticed their appearance. They were both beautiful; though in a very odd way. High-cheekboned and very fair-skinned, they were extremely tall, and both had an unusual atmosphere of strength and serenity about them. They were dressed in a similar way to the woman who had spoken to us, but they wore a different type of head-dress; a plain gold band around the brow. As each of them approached the gateway its pattern changed to allow them passage. For the man, it formed interlocking triangles; for the woman, a grille. They passed through.

Then it was our turn. Nelson flashed me a wide grin and stepped back, bowing low and sweeping his arm in front of him in a gesture of exaggerated politeness. He meant me to go first. I hesitated, then approached the framework of lights. A bright double grille displayed as I stood in front of it; and it moved into a pattern of six and eight-pointed stars. That was obviously my key. I went through. Nelson followed behind me; and we came out into a small courtyard. The two riders had disappeared; but the woman waited for us. She gestured for us to follow her. And as she turned, she smiled faintly at us for the first time.

I glanced around. I could see no sign of her horse, and no sign of anyone else. The courtyard was cobbled; not with stones, but with flat-topped clear crystals. Trees surrounded the paved area; smaller, though of the same type which had flanked the causeway on our journey. These too bore gold and green fruits; and the sweeping arch of their branches were the only curves I had seen in that angular place. She led us through the courtyard to a pyramid a short distance away. Again she formed the signs with her hands; then spoke to us.

'You may communicate now,' she said; 'I regret any restriction upon you, and thank you for your compliance and respect. This is your dwelling-area for as long as you have need of it. You are at liberty to come and go as you wish, and you are welcome among us. I must leave you now, but if you require my attention in any matter, ask.' Then she turned and walked back through the courtyard, where she passed between the trees and was gone.

12: *The Charos*

It was quiet in the pyramid; quiet and somehow blue.

Then I realized the quietness wasn't total, but was relieved by a constant sound. As my sight grew accustomed to the odd light, I saw what made that sound. From about half way up the wall of the pyramid, a shallow and very narrow watercourse ran. It was no more than a hand's breadth wide. I looked at the water, and was filled with a lightness of feeling.

'Five-star accommodation.' Nelson's voice took me by surprise.

'No furniture,' I said, gazing round at the interior. Except for the stream, the pyramid was totally bare. 'Hey, how about room service?'

He laughed. 'Man! Who needs that stuff when you got an en-suite bathroom?' he said. 'We don't sleep, so who needs beds? We don't eat, and I can't see us getting round to writing no letters, so who needs tables? Who needs chairs when you can sit on your ass?'

'We don't drink,' I added; 'But we've got a stream.'

'Sure is! That's a stream.'

'Water? . . . Is it . . .?' I touched it carefully. Coolness ran between my fingers. It was water, pure and simple. 'What's it for?'

'Magnetism,' he said. I was about to ask him what he meant.
I remembered school science classes. Magnetism was Physics.
How could there be physics without a physical world? I opened
my mouth to argue with him about his 'magnetism', and closed
it again. Things, I thought, ain't what they used to be. And there
had been too much water, under too many bridges. Nelson was
looking at me oddly.

'All you have to do is know it, feel it,' he said. 'Don't go trying
to figure it out on some Old World sense-scale, 'cause that Old
World stuff is just gonna give you a bad case of road-blocks here.
Anyhow, science ain't got no idea about what's here. Hey, maybe
that's just as well, or there'd be flags up all over the place, all
starched and stapled to look like a moon-breeze is blowing!'

I was only half listening to him. I touched the water again. It
was smooth, cool, beautiful. I scooped some up and drank, just
for the hell of it. I didn't need to drink, but I did it anyway. It felt
good.

'Yeah, they learned to go to the moon, back there,' he went on.
Maybe one day they'll learn to go to Mars, or Venus, or whatever. But almost no-one wants to know about Inner Space, even
though it's only a few years before they get there, anyway! Then
they ain't got no choice but to know about it!'

'I never believed in it . . .' I said, absently. '. . . Inner Space.
Didn't know it was there, I guess. Didn't think about it.'

'Not ever?' Nelson asked.

'No.'

'Oh, but you did.' Then I remembered. Some memories were
misting at the edges now, but that one sprang up suddenly;
accessed without difficulty and in fine detail. The little kid in the
Hall of Mirrors, a long time ago, somewhere in England. He'd
seen something really terrible that nobody else seemed able to
see. And he was going to sink fast into the Mirror-World; and it
was a cold, scared, alone-in-the-whole-world feeling. On the
other side of the mirrors where long, thin, fat, wide people were
laughing, was a thing that wanted him. It wanted to drag him
inside the corridors of reflections. And he didn't want to go,
because he knew that if he did, there wouldn't be any way back.
He couldn't tell anyone about it; and with the instinct of child-
hood, he knew that he would be better off not to even try. So he

ran away, fast, and threw up, and left it for good; or so he thought.

'. . . Inner Space . . .? Is that what it was? Is that all . . .? I whispered.

'No,' Nelson said. 'No. Truth. Your Truth. That's what was so terrible.' He seemed to see the recall which passed through me. 'Humankind can't stand too much of that stuff.'

'Truth?'

'Yeah. You ain't no scientist, so what you getting hung up on science now for? You ain't no scientist! You're a killer, Man, among other things.'

'Oh right! Oh sure! That's what I am, is it? A killer?'

He laughed. 'You want me to tell you what you are, after what you've been through? Should be plain as day! Oh boy! They know; the Charos. They know what you are, or you wouldn't be here!'

Then he stopped talking, and a silence fell over us; broken only by the sound of running water. I heard the tall woman's words, over again. His Lights also correspond . . . You may communicate now . . . I looked around me. The walls of the pyramid shone with crystal clarity reflected in the water of the stream.

'Who is she?'

'Chieftain,' he replied. 'Chieftain of the Order.'

'And these people; the Charos?'

'From the Blue Sun. In the constellation of Lyra.'

Anything could happen, here. My mind-blow threshold was extending. It had no choice. I thought about the space-probes set up in deserts and places; about how they were searching for electronic patterns from outer space which might indicate other forms of intelligent life. I'd read about it in *Time* magazine. But they were searching in only one Universe. They'd missed the Blue Sun, it seemed. They weren't tuning in to Inner Space.

'Okay,' I said. 'Which planet?'

'It's known as Xentha.' I could hardly take it in.

'You can't be telling me we're on that planet, Nelson! I just don't believe this!'

He laughed again. He always laughed at mind-blowing things. I thought about his Moon-Rider woman. He hadn't laughed at that.

'Well, prepare to push that three-D thinking somewhere it's gonna hurt! Prepare to have those Space-Time-Continuum prejudices blown to pieces! No.'

'No?'

'Well, not quite.'

'What do you mean, *not quite* ? Nelson, are we there, or are we not there? In the constellation of Lyra! Jesus Christ!'

'It's an outpost. Their encampment on the Levels. An operations base.'

'Operations base?' What operations?'

'Defence mostly. They're a highly-trained Warrior breed. Annihilators. That's what they are.' Something in me ran cold. I'd not seen that in her eyes. Not a killing streak, but a steadiness of purpose, a kind of balance. Perhaps in those eyes there had been a mark of something inhuman. And her Lights; they had been the same as Nelson's. Same silver and blue. Annihilators. What did he mean? He was watching me closely.

'That . . . sign, Nelson. The signal you gave them; that was our insurance, right? What did she call it? . . . The Gateway of the Law, that's it. So that was our insurance for staying in one piece? Okay, how do they annihilate the already-dead? Yeah, stupid question. They re-arrange your particles! Put you into melt-down!'

'Talking wouldn't have been enough,' he said; 'Even the light-frequencies wouldn't have been enough; not on their own. But the sign, that's different. Put the sign and the Lights together, and you've got a pattern. That's your I.D. They had to know me by that. They made a small concession in your case. Just goes to show, it's not what you know, but who you know! That's what takes you on the up-and-up, it sure is!'

'Thanks.' I wondered how close I'd come to melt-down.

'Well, I've got a star-prize question for you Nelson,' I said. 'Somehow I think it's time I got clued-up. What do they annihilate? Hopefully not us, if we start singing out of key!' He seemed to think that was funny, too. I didn't. I'd seen enough of things so far on the Levels to know that at any time, anything could show me its flip-side, its wild card. I'd been just about to settle in and take a breathing-space with the compliments of the Charos; but suddenly I didn't feel so relaxed about it.

'They've got a mission,' Nelson said, 'to defend the Levels.'

'To hold the outpost? Is that it? Against what? Some kind of invaders?'

'No, no. More than that. Listen and I'll wise you up. They've been here a long time. Longer than you can imagine. On the Levels, they take form, 'cause something about the substance here makes them able to do that. On Xentha, they've got no shape like you could dream up. They're force-rays; multi-dimensional. Guess that's the best way to put it.'

'Okay, so they come here to defend the Levels. They take on shapes here. Why? Why do they take shape at all?'

''Cause it's easier, like I said, to build form in the substance here. And they come in Human form to be closer to the thing they got to defend.' He stopped talking for a moment; absorbed in some thought. He bent to the stream and played with the water. Then he spoke again.

'There's something going on. And to even *see* the Charos means it's getting worse.' He wasn't laughing. So many things made him laugh. Not this; whatever he knew that I didn't.

'What are you getting at?' I looked closely at him. He was staring at the water as it ran between his fingers. I felt apprehensive, and his hedging round the point was annoying me.

'Quit talking in riddles if you've got something to say. I don't get it.' I watched his hand. For the first time I noticed he wore a ring on the third finger of his left hand; a large silver-coloured five-pointed star with a green glass bauble set in the centre. It looked like a Christmas cracker trinket, or kid's stuff won at a fairground stall. I couldn't imagine why I hadn't seen it before. He noticed me staring at his hand, and he smiled.

'She gave it me for good luck. My woman. Now I don't reckon there's such a thing as luck, but I took it anyway, on account of how I felt about her. It was the first thing she made here, and it took a lot of making for somebody still learning. Said she'd had one just like this when she was a little kid, and it brought her luck. Who knows? Maybe it did, too. She survived one of the 'Frisco earthquakes.'

'One of the . . .? How many . . .?'

But he interrupted me. 'Take a look,' he said, taking the ring off his finger and tossing it to me. I caught it.

'Go ahead. A close look.' I examined it. It was nothing special. The silver-coloured metal had the weight of very light alloy. In a way it didn't even seem like metal, and I wondered if perhaps it was coated plastic. I looked closer. I could make out the slightly-raised moulding mark, as if it had been made in two halves and joined.

'Look at the stone,' he called out. 'What d'you reckon it is?' I thought for a moment. The ring was almost worthless. But I could see it wasn't that way for him. It meant something to him. The stone was stuck on with bubbly glue which had oozed out around the edges.

'Probably glass,' I replied, and added 'She made this? Here? For you? Nice.'

'Yeah,' he said. 'And can you figure out what she made it with?'

'Metal? Plastic? It's moulded. Looks like . . .'

'Mind. She made it out of mind. Memory. Concentration. Force of wanting to. Could be the original there. But that one's down a storm-drain somewhere in California. This is a replica. An exact copy.' He held out his hand, and beckoned for it. I tossed the ring back to him. Before he put it on his finger again, he studied it.

'But it's not made out of metal, or plastic, or glass,' he went on. 'But from Will, and knowing the essential pattern, the key of the original. Look, Man! Every little detail all in place! Even the little bits of glue!'

'But . . .'

'Just wait. You hold on there a minute. Got to finish my tale. What you see here; this ring, built on the Levels. It's real enough, ain't it? Sure. It looks the same as the original. So that if you had both here, you couldn't tell them apart. Now you try to imagine for a moment. If someone can build this, there ain't no limit to what can be built. The substance of the Levels. That's what makes it possible to do that. So if you've ever heard anyone telling you that you can't take it with you, then I'm telling you that's hog-dung, Man. 'Cause in a way, you can.'

'Come on, Nelson. What's this all about? You were telling me about the Charos. So what?'

'Okay. I'm coming to that. So what she did, she created something on the Levels that is a total replica of something that existed in Old World; from its data. Now that means if you've got the skill, anything can be copied. A ring, a crown of gold, your own back garden. You name it. Even Human Beings. They're harder, but it can be done. Like I said, you'd need skill and access to the data. And that data I'm talking about is an individual code. It's got its Inner Space, like everything else. Everything comes from Inner places, shaped in the Inner World first, before it becomes physical reality in Old World. You picking this up?'

'Oh, Christ, Nelson. There's no way I'm understanding this!'

'Well you just listen a bit harder there! 'Cause you got to wise-up on this one. You might be a killer. And you've done some damnfool stuff. But there's one thing I sure do know about you, and that is you ain't dumb! So you listen real tight! There is something here on the Levels that builds and copies in just the way I'm telling you about. That's what it does, and boy! Is it some heavy-duty bad news!'

I stared at him; not comprehending. He ignored my puzzlement and carried on 'Control. That's what it's after. Power. Possession. But even more than that. It has to survive at all costs. To spread and grow, and spread even more. To spread till there ain't no dance no more. Just it . . . just them!'

'The Charos! You can't mean . . .?'

'Oh no, Man. Not them. But now we're getting to why the Charos are here. Their mission. They're here to challenge the replica-builders . . . Gehina, the sons of bitches are known as. The Raiders, I call 'em. The Raiders of Gehina.'

He stopped talking for a minute, and his words sank into me. Where they touched, they chilled, with some ancient, obscene feeling.

'They're rising,' he said. 'Gehina is rising. They're on the increase like never before . . .'

'The Raiders of Gehina . . .' I repeated.

'Okay. Now let me tell you something. As long as the Raiders have moved on the Levels, the Charos have ridden against them. That's what they're here for. The whole reason for their existence is to guard Humankind, from here. To keep the Balance, and stop Gehina taking over completely.'

'I'm getting it . . . I think. People, right? These . . . Raiders are after people?'

'Yeah. They're after people.'

'But why?'

'Well, can you imagine an energy, a force, an intention that don't work properly unless it finds shape, form? Well, that's why. The Raiders were drawn to the Levels by nothing but opportunity. They came to find ways to grow, to spread. Don't everything that exists want to do the same? Humankind provided the opportunity. The Raiders came here hunting 'cause they found a good hunting-ground. Close to Humankind, in the Inner Space that shapes life in Old World they found real good opportunity to do their thing, and they learned to copy Human form . . .'

'Nelson, wait. They copy Humans? So what are they building? Armies of clones?'

'No. They get inside the one they're copying. Inside. Now what I've got to tell you, I know you ain't gonna like, 'cause it's serious trouble. They do it the same way this ring was built. They access the pattern of someone living in Old World, through Inner Space. Then they build a replica of that person here on the Levels. Only that replica, though it looks every bit like the person, ain't. 'Cause it's got Gehina's soul. Gehina's intention. And through it, the Raiders have got control over the original! Not only that, they've got access to a walking data-bank; of people, places, bits of city, whole communities, and all the rest. And the replicas they build here on the Levels are the Raiders' way of sending their intentions, their force, everything they are, back to Old World. The replicas are their transmitters!'

'Jesus Christ!'

'You're getting it. And you don't like it, hey?'

'That's happening . . . now? What you've just said is happening to the World back there? And doesn't anyone know? No-one there even knows?'

'Sure. Some guys know. But not many. And there ain't no-one listening when they start telling. They're crazies, cranks, freaks. But see, back in Old World, they don't generally figure on the Levels being here. And it's from here that the Raiders are moving in on them. How could anything be moving in on them from someplace that don't even exist? Some know. Sure. Some have got vision. Some are strong; real strong in their Truth. They're close to the dancing Universe. In their souls, they know the Balance. They make that Balance real in their lives. They hear the River of Life. They ain't always sweetie-pie pretty people, but they're on course, following the natural Plan. They're in their Truth. Now that's real important, 'cause that's their immunity. The closer you are to that living Truth, the harder it is for the Raiders to take you.'

'I don't want to . . . hear this!'

'Well there's more. You want to hear what happens in Old World when Gehina moves in on you? Remember Hitler? Manson? Huh? Do you? Oh boy! They're just the icing on the cake!'

'No! It's not possible! It's some sort of crap you're feeding me! 'B'-movie stuff like that! Body-snatchers from the fourth dimension! Who are you kidding?'

'I ain't. I ain't into wasting my breath.'

'I've got to get out of here . . .!'

'There's more. Man, there's more . . .'

'I don't need any more!'

'Well, you'd better, boy! You don't know how close you got to them!'

'What?'

'Sure. Your ass was sweet meat! You're getting better.'

'Armageddon . . .'

He stared at me. 'What?' he said.

'You're talking Armageddon, Nelson.' He didn't reply.

'Shit! I turned away from him; 'I've got to get out of here! . . . now!'

13: *Masks of Titanium and Fire*

I TOOK A walk. After what I'd heard, I felt claustrophobic and restless. I needed to move; needed time alone. Time to think. Nelson had given me plenty to think about. I didn't want to be in there with him any longer. He said there was more, but I didn't want to have to find out any more. I got outside quickly and took a look around. The courtyard was deserted; and there, the light wasn't blue-tinged as it had been in the pyramid, but was faintly gold; a glowing, slanted light of early evening. The atmosphere was still; silent. I looked back and saw the perfect geometric walls of the pyramid, shot through with-rays of coloured light. They gave the illusion of transparency; but as I stared, trying to see through them, I could see nothing of the interior. At my feet the little stream flowed. It moved from behind me; from the pyramid's entrance, and crossed the crystal pebbles for a short distance before it disappeared. From that point I presumed it continued underground.

The tranquillity of the scene was in stark contrast to the information Nelson had just given me. I found that information hard to believe but he had said it with such conviction. It was too much; too obscene. The obscenity churned in me; rolling over and over in my thoughts, as I walked. Gehina. The Raiders of Gehina. Formless Beings breeding, multiplying. Using Humankind to take on shapes. They get inside things. What did he mean? Then, when they gained too much, they were cut back; weakened. Not defeated, but allowed to grow again. And they were never totally, finally, destroyed. So he had said.

Why? If the Charos were able to control them, why didn't they terminate them? But instead, the Raiders were rising, breaking some demarcation line.

Hitler. Manson. All the rest. Just the icing on the cake. I thought of the millions of Holocaust victims, and the countless other victims of atrocity through recorded history and beyond. And what about the ones who had been left off the record? Raiders? did that? And the Annihilators; ancient enemies set against them, let them exist? It was too much. Too much to take.

I felt something draining me, sapping at my strength. I felt the rise of sickened anger; then a numbness. I walked; through the deserted cloisters of trees and crystal walkways, not knowing where I was going, and not caring. My thoughts suddenly shut down; then they returned like a cold wave against me. If it were true, the Charos were playing cat-and-mouse with darkness.

Yet it didn't quite make sense. What Nelson had told me implied that the deep evil of Mankind was due to the influence of those forces; Gehina, he had called them. Without them, it'd be a rose-garden? That wasn't possible. It was just naive fantasy.

Then I thought about Nelson. I didn't really know him. Not really. Although I was sure he wasn't one of the Charos, he had to have something to do with them. The signs they exchanged showed that. So did he, too, play games with darkness? Or was he playing games with me? He played games with everything else. What he had told me didn't add up; didn't make sense. Something had to be going on between Nelson and the Charos. They had welcomed us almost too readily. They had given us hospitality. But I found their politeness suspicious. I recalled the last words of the woman who had brought us here.

You are at liberty to come and go as you wish. But I was sure that was a lie.

Suddenly I felt trapped. The deserted alleyways of trees and the cloistered peacefulness became menacing. It masked an unseen thing. What, I couldn't imagine. But something. The glowing, gold air felt tight around me. And then, with a surge of panic, I remembered the Woman of Artademes. The Wheel. The Undead. The way her transparent threads had wound about me. Had she been one of them?

Nelson got you out. He got you out of that one. It doesn't mean a thing. Evil sometimes tastes sweet. Something was conspiring; binding tighter. I'd almost trusted him. Nearly. I'd been close to it.

You've got to get out of here. But I couldn't move. The gentle evening-glow bathed me. The crystal pathways glistened. There was nothing to stop me, but I couldn't move. I struggled; raised my hands. I could feel invisible solidity. Around me, the air had hardened.

They've trapped you. You've touched the Truth of them, and they've trapped you. Whatever held me would not give way. I tried to push against it. There's no-one here. But they can see you. What do they want you for?

They're watching. You know it. It was invisible. I could see through it. Claustrophobia engulfed me, as I realized I couldn't move.

You created it. You yourself. You trapped yourself. No. It's them. I didn't create it. I didn't create the Charos. Or their enemies. Or the Darkness.

You can make what you can imagine. Or copy. With enough concentration. Enough wanting to. You name it, you can make it.

The area I had to move in was narrowing. There was less than an arm's stretch to either side of me. I touched the hard edges of my entrapment. They were glassy. Clearer than glass, though harder. With a desperate anger, I swung my fist against it. But it didn't give.

You name it, you can make it. An axe. I saw it in the mind's eye. I grasped it there, and focused; remembering it. The image held; then faltered and began to slip away. I grabbed it back; saw the hickory shaft, gently curved and smooth from use. I saw the iron head, slightly chipped on the blade from sometimes splitting logs on stone. I shouldn't have done. But I'd always done what I shouldn't have done. It took form slowly, but it had no weight. The head wasn't connected to the shaft. It shimmered and faded. Again, I built it in memory; remembering where I had hammered the hickory into the iron. And it returned. I saw the initials I'd carved on the tip of the wood, one bored and stormy night in winter. R.B. in a triangle. Then, in one great surge, it came through, fully formed. I felt its weight; its solidity in my hand. With it, my anger came back. Resistance to the trap.

They've found your fears. They've accessed the dark-zone in you. How? It doesn't matter. But they've done it. They've got their methods. But what matters is they're not going to win. I struggled to swing the axe. The space was tight. I swung sidelong at the invisible walls. The axe rebounded; and in front of me, I saw a long crack.

No. You made this . . . You made the glass . . . And the axe to break it . . . Listen! I swung a second time. I heard my voice cry out.

What do they want you for?

No! You brought your prison with you! And the glass shattered, silently.

I lifted the axe in both hands; raised it high above my head, and brought it down, full-force, on the cobbles and glittering geometric shapes. It sank in, splitting nothing. It rested with its blade wedged in the ground of the courtyard. A golden fruit fell from above, and broke open in front of me. Its seeds were shed. They rolled like tiny black beads from a broken necklace. I watched them. A silence hung; and a change came in the air. Around me, the atmosphere suddenly seemed charged. I saw the shaft of the axe dimly gleaming. A sound came from it; a humming.

'There lies a part of your Power. Often mis-used.'

I spun round quickly; searching for the source of the voice. I couldn't see who had spoken; and couldn't tell if the voice were male or female.

'Shall you recognize that Power? Or shall you build traps to imprison it?'

I turned again; and it seemed that a wave washed over me, weakening me. But in the weakness, I felt less afraid. I saw her through a haze. Saw her moving towards me across the crystals of the courtyard. I saw her eyes. Blue Flame. As she spoke again, her voice rang from all around me.

'It would be wiser to trust the kindred,' she said. 'It is well you do.'

She reached for the axe; lifted it effortlessly from the ground in which it was embedded. It was on fire. A burning brand. Inside the glowing, I could only just make out its shape. She held it out towards me; but I shrank away.

'You created it,' she said; 'It is yours.' I dared not touch it. I dared not take it from her. It would have destroyed me; burned me up. She smiled, and lifted the axe high. It disappeared into the surrounding air. Her brow shone with white fire.

'I bring you a warning. The Balance is known. The Alpha and the Omega are seen. Judge not in your blindness the way of that Balance. Return to the Way that is yours, and do not wander. I bring you the warning of your Power and of your Beginning.'

I couldn't speak. Her eyes burned into me. She knew. There was knowledge in those terrible eyes. She knew me. And in those eyes was a love. But it was a love that knew how to kill. A killing Love. I felt joy. I felt terror. Because it was the strongest thing I'd ever known. A greater and more dangerous thing than I was even capable of imagining. And as I saw that, in that timeless moment, I wanted her. More than I had ever wanted anything. But it wasn't a Human wanting. It was something else. Something terrifying. She touched a thing in me that even I couldn't touch. And I couldn't speak.

She smiled again; and began to withdraw from me. I heard the sound of a horn-call, close by. Through my dazed awareness, I realized that someone was coming. The Charos. The woman drew back. And a blazing flare went up, suddenly, where she stood. She disappeared into it.

'Do not move,' I heard, from behind me. 'Do not move, or attempt to communicate. Stay still.' Immediately, I froze. Reflexively, I began to lift my hands away from my body.

'Do not move!'

A woman's voice. I began to turn my head to look behind me, and thought better of it. She walked slowly round me; stood in front of me. Her gaze; cold violet, bored into mine, then appraised my whole body. She was tall: my own height. And she was clothed as a warrior. Her hair, dead-straight and dark crimson, flowed behind her shoulders, clasped at the brow with a circlet of plain gold. Her skin was white; unusually white. And she was incredibly beautiful.

'Turn,' she said. 'One hundred and eighty degrees. Slowly.'

I turned, and stopped with my back to her; aware that I was vulnerable. Yet I had noticed that she didn't seem to be armed. I wondered what her intention was.

'Turn again. Resume original position.'

I slowly, carefully, turned to face her.

'Where is it?' she asked. Her voice was steady; commanding. 'You may answer.'

'Where is . . .?'

'Where is it?'

In those eyes, still deathly-cold, I saw nothing relent. No emotion. Only a singleness of purpose. And I sensed a razor-sharp skill.

'What?' I said, at a loss to answer her. 'Where is what?'

'The replica,' she replied. 'That which was built in sector twenty seven delta. The Creation.'

'The . . . replica?'

'Move forward,' she said. 'Move towards the Gate.'

I did as she asked, and slowly crossed the courtyard towards the gateway through which we had first entered the encampment. She walked behind me.

'Keep moving. Approach the Gate, and halt.'

I stopped, two or three paces in front of the latticework of lights. The woman drew up beside me. Immediately a pattern flashed across the lattice. A honeycomb appeared. Straight away, another form was superimposed on it. Six-pointed stars meshed precisely inside the six-sided pattern. Her code-form and mine, joined together. As the shapes appeared, she spoke, quietly to herself. I couldn't grasp what she said, as it sounded like some complex mathematical formula beyond my comprehension. The axe, I thought; the replica. She must mean the axe.

'Move away from the Gate,' she said. And I stepped back, sensing a subtle change in her attitude towards me. The tone of her voice had slightly altered. But her expression had not. Her eyes locked into mine. I dared to communicate.

'It's not here. It's been destroyed.'

For a moment she said nothing. Then she spoke.

'Total Matrix-Data disintegration?' I didn't know what she was talking about.

'Yes.' I replied.

Again, she fell quiet. I kept my eyes fixed on hers. Then, surprisingly, she dropped her gaze. For a fleeting moment before she looked away, I saw something cross her face. Perhaps it was a kind of shyness. It was a thing I vaguely recognized, but couldn't quite name. Or perhaps I imagined it.

'Follow me.' She said. I didn't intend to argue with her. Annihilators, Nelson had said. Trained killers. How did they kill? He hadn't said. But I got the picture. They were dangerous. I followed her, aware that her back was turned to me, as she walked a few paces in front. But I knew that it would be inadvisable for me to try to make a break for it. I didn't want to put her to the test. We moved through the courtyard, and she led me down one of the cloister-like arcades of trees on our right. I had no idea where she was leading me, and I had little choice but to follow her.

Then what had happened began to click into place. She knew about the axe. She must have seen it, and knew that something had been copied in that courtyard. That was it. I'd made a replica. And that was what they were up against. Their whole reason for being. The whole purpose of their work. Like Nelson had said. I'd given them a red alert. They're fast, I thought. Professional. And they never let go. They're on continual stand-by. I recalled what Nelson had told me. And it was beginning to make some kind of sense. Maybe that's how bad it is, I thought; it's a war. And we're on the front line. For all the trees and cloisters this encampment is a front-line position.

I remembered my code-pattern of six-pointed stars; and understood why she had ordered me to stand in front of the gate. To check me out. To find out if I was really me. If the code hadn't keyed in, that would have been it. Bye-bye, weird world. I was now on melt-down, minus precious moments, thanks to the six-pointed stars. And I remembered how perfectly they had meshed with the honeycomb. Did she notice? She'd noticed the axe.

She led me down the arcade of trees; never turning to me, never speaking to me. I wondered why I was following her so readily; then decided to go along with it, for the moment. If an opportunity arose for me to take off, I intended to. I watched the back of her; watched the flowing lines of her cloak as she moved ahead of me. I saw the flash of the gold band around her strange red hair. I looked for her Lights; the silver-blue Lights which seemed to be the Charos' hallmark. They weren't there. I focused my concentration, and looked again. Nothing. Then I sensed a sudden change. It made me uneasy, and I stopped. Immediately, she did the same. She turned slowly, to face me. A trace of a frown flickered across her eyes. She opened her mouth, as if to speak. And at that moment, a great radiance flared around her; its core just above her head. It lit the trees of the arcade with dazzling whiteness; then it began to descend, drawing down to her body. I watched as her features became indistinct; no longer definite, but liquid. I saw the expression of her face flow and change; moulded by the light into new shapes. And as I watched, they took on different form, gradually, line by line. And I saw the face of the Woman of the Rose.

'In the end is the Beginning,' she said. 'The Alpha and the Omega are one. When the serpent devours its tail, it is born anew.'

In amazement, I gazed into the light; feeling the agony of its brilliance, but needing to look at her. I watched as the body of the Charos warrior alternated with the Other One, she whom Nelson had called The Great One.

She takes shapes . . . I heard again . . . *anything she likes, when she likes* . . . *To you she looks like Woman* . . . *but she ain't.*

And I saw her hair, one moment red, like the Charos warrior, the next, blue-black; surrounded not by a circlet of gold, but by a ring of white flame. And as I met her eyes, they were incandescent; reaching into me for something that I was. That thing moved and turned in me like the promise of a creature not yet born but half-formed.

. . . *She'd burn you up* . . . I heard him in my memory. *She'd ask you to die, and die, and die again!* . . . *She'd destroy you like nothing else can!*

Her voice came again, through the light.

'Do you dare to meet the Beginning? Do you dare to receive that which is yours? Do you choose it?' I couldn't answer her. But the unformed thing inside me leapt up. And she saw it, because she smiled.

Then I saw the Charos woman return; saw the ring of white fire slowly cool to gold about her hair. Around us, the trees were no longer rayed with brilliance. And the light contracted. It circled the warrior, and entered her. But it was the Woman of the Rose who spoke, when she turned to me and said:

'Come, then. Follow me.'

And we continued, under the arch of trees. I watched the back of her. I watched the flowing lines of her white cloak as she walked with sure and graceful steps; never turning to see if I was there. Never speaking.

14: *Mouse in a Maze*

I LOOKED AT her. Just the Charos woman. No more than that.

We had walked a long way, through a warren of tree-lined arcades, and I had no recollection of how many turns we had made. There was a sense of having moved down the endless alleyways for a great stretch of time, but I had no distinct memory of the journey. I felt like a sleepwalker, suddenly awakened. And my recall of what had happened in the courtyard was drifting, slipping gradually away, like a sleepwalker's dream. With every step we took, the sensation of unreality deepened. I was following her; and I didn't really know why. She had asked me to. That was all I could remember. I stared at her back; looking for her Lights. They were there, silver-blue. They flashed briefly, and were gone.

'Where are we going?'

She didn't answer. Her pace neither slackened nor increased.

'Why don't you say something? Talk to me?'

There was no response. I wasn't even certain that she heard. As I looked at her, an image of the Other One came to me. Then it disappeared; and again, I saw only the woman in front of me. It had been an illusion. That was all. And I was being taken somewhere. I wasn't sure I wanted to go. I was waking up, fast.

'Right,' I said. 'Let me put it another way. All I want is for you to talk to me. Explain. This is giving me the creeps. Like where are we going? Where are you taking me? Like what happened back there? Something did. I know. I remember. Like what?'

Something had happened. A strange thing. Then, through my mind-haze, the recollection came back. The Other One was in her. She went inside her. That's what happened. Inside. *They get inside the thing they're copying.* Oh, dear Christ, that was it! I was getting it. I had to get away. I had to get back to the pyramid. No. Out of here, for good. But before that, I had to play it cool. Or I wouldn't be going anywhere. Her Lights caught my attention. They danced delicately, silver and blue over her head and shoulders. Nelson's Lights. Charos Lights.

I didn't know what was going on, any more. I was here. I

existed. I had survived death. That was all I dared to know. And I had to get out. There was nothing to trust but my own wits. A sinking feeling gripped me as I saw her Lights move and change; responding to some impulse I couldn't see. To what? My thoughts? It was possible. I didn't know if it was too late, but I reined in those thoughts; recalling the thoughtless state of the Warp-ride.

Two rays, pale amethyst in colour, rose from a place between her shoulders. They grew upwards, twisting together, and met above her head where they gradually shaped themselves into a circle; and within it, a flower of pale lilac began to take form. It was beautiful; so beautiful. But I dared not gaze at it, because it was a trick. The form began to break up and fade; returning to the rays which drew themselves in again, to her body.

I'd had enough. I wasn't going any further. She could do what she liked, but I wasn't going with her. I stopped, abruptly; trying not to forewarn her. On my left was an intersecting alley. I slipped into it. Then I had to move fast; think fast. Ahead of me, a long dead-straight tree-lined arcade stretched out, perfectly identical to the one I'd just left. Quickly I scanned its length; aware that if I kept straight on, and she came looking, I wouldn't get far. Soon she was going to notice that I'd gone, anyway. So I took the first right turn.

Then I realized I'd made a mistake; but it was too late to do anything about it. To get back to the courtyard and the Gate I was going to have to double back. By my calculation, the path I was now following ran parallel to the main arcade along which she had led me; and I knew that if I kept to it, I would be heading in the wrong direction. But there wasn't much choice. I wanted to put as much distance between myself and the woman as I could, as quickly as possible.

I kept on, and took the next left turn, intending to keep bearing left. I hoped to circle round to meet the pathway we had originally been on, and eventually find my way back.

I ran. No left turn came. I couldn't believe my bad luck. But I kept on the move. Sooner or later there had to be one. As I went, I searched for a way through the intersecting lower branches of the trees. But there, I was confronted with a criss-cross pattern of some substance which seemed organic, but was unnaturally regular and geometric. I stopped; touched it. It was stone-hard and didn't give. It shone with a metallic gleam. So I kept running. I passed turnings off to my right. But none to the left of me.

Eventually, I slowed my pace and stopped, aware that I was getting deeper into the maze of pathways, and further off my course. I listened, but heard nothing; no-one. The alleys were deserted. Reluctantly, I turned, to go back the way I'd come; knowing all I had to do was follow the arcade back again and take the right turn at the junction at the far end. Then, if I kept going, I would find the first path I had run on to.

But no right turn came. And a deep feeling of unease crept into me. The right turn should have been there; and it wasn't. It didn't make sense. I was retracing my steps, and there had to be a turning because I had only just come along it. I pushed on; but my hope of finding the junction grew weaker with every step. It wasn't there. Now there were left turns; as many as I wanted. But they all led the wrong way.

Then I knew. I was in a maze. And the maze was changeable; unstable. Changed by what, or whom, I didn't know. But it had moved in some way while I had been in it. It had slipped. I fought a rising feeling of panic. I had to think; just stop and think. There had to be a way through. There had to be. Unless there was a Mind behind it. Unless they were watching; playing. The Charos woman hadn't come looking for me. Why not?

I stood very still; and heard not the slightest movement or sound. I watched the long Gothic arches ahead of me; their quietness now sinister, their perfect balance and elegance now treacherous. They reached out into an impossible distance. That wasn't the way I had come. The left turns were still there; waiting for me. They hadn't moved, or closed off. In the stillness I was acutely aware of my inertia.

I started forward once more, and took the first turning. Ahead of me stretched an identical alleyway to the one I'd just left. As I scanned the length of it, I realized that I was already hopelessly lost and without any sense of direction. Nelson came to mind; and the Charos. And the Woman of the Rose. Could I trust Nelson? I couldn't be sure. And the Other One; the Great One, he had called her. Who was she? But I had seen her enter the Charos warrior, enter her. I had seen the one who brought me a flower in Hell take her over; become a part of her. I no longer knew one thing from another. And now the maze was moving. And something, I knew, was making it move; a thing unseen which was aware of my thoughts, my intentions. It had moved the maze accordingly. So it had to be very close to me. Inside me?

Road-blocks . . . They're only road-blocks . . . Don't force them . . . Don't go against them . . . Accept their variables. Go left. Go right. What the Hell? Don't think about it.

Road-blocks. Nelson had said something about road-blocks. But I couldn't recall what.

Maybe you made them. If you did, the way through is not to care too much. Laugh, like Nelson . . . He even laughs at Armageddon . . . You know he does. You've got to be mindless . . . but you've got to be like a blade . . . Dangerous stuff.

I ran. The words came again, from a place in me. My words.

If you think, it wins. In a curved Universe, all roads lead to the place you want them to. You'll find what you need to find.

Left turn; and a long passageway. Another left turn. I was circling. I'd made a wrong move somewhere.

Okay . . . What's a wrong move? . . . A tangent against a perfect circle? . . . You don't really know . . . You'll get there; where you're going. What is there to lose? . . . You're a mouse in a maze. Don't forget, mouse, fools stand, sometimes, where wise men fall.

Myself; that's what there was to lose. That which was me. Another left turn, and I took it. There was no choice.

I slowed my pace; glancing up into the high arches of trees. I followed the long, dead-straight arcade. A right turn came. I took it, forgetfully.

Instantly, the trees began to scintillate; slipping, in my vision into double and treble images. They vibrated, giving out no sound. Then, as they joined once more into a single image, they became transparent; and the network of strange substance between them seemed to open up its silver pattern.

There, through the spaces I saw moving visions. There, warriors of the Charos rode on a flowing battlefield, and were struck down. They rose again to wander on a wide plain; their tortured forms drifting on a tide of smoky air.

I saw faces, twisted in agony; unseeing.

I saw men and women become creatures: god-like shapes:

stones and stars. An eagle swooped, and as one, they were eaten.

Around me, a white circle opened up and the trees bowed outwards; spreading out their branches to a brilliant sky. At my feet, a circular pool of luminescence appeared.

And I heard the sound of a horn. It was a long, drawn-out call, followed by a second, and a third. I heard the approach of riders, moving fast; the drumming of the horses' hooves. They passed me like a breath; invisible.

The horn-blast drew closer, and broke through the circle. Around me, I felt the immediate constriction of another Will.

She was there. The Charos warrior. Tall and strong; eye to eye with me. Her burnished hair fell unruffled from beneath the thin band of gold. Beside her, two warriors stood. Both male. They left her side and moved forward to flank me.

'You must come with us,' she said. I nodded. 'You will not be harmed.'

I understood. I'd been returned to the trap.

15: The Dome

I looked up. I was standing on a wide floor of sheet crystal. Above me, countless facets, hexagonal and triangular glinted in a high domed roof. From every plane, every angle, liquid colour rayed down. I had no recollection of arriving; no memory of my journey with the three warriors through the maze. The Dome. I knew where I was because someone told me. The voice; a male voice, broke through my dream-like state.

'You are now in the Dome. Remain still. You will receive further orders. We ask that you feel no fear. We intend you no harm.'

I slowly turned, to see him a few steps behind me. He radiated an easy, confident authority; unchallengeable.

'I'd like to say something . . .' I began; but he cut in.

'You will be free to communicate,' he replied. 'But in due course, and not with me. Our words would be idle.'

He was powerfully built; young-looking. Much taller than me, he was naked to the waist but for a narrow breastplate inlaid with jagged clear crystals. His clear eyes were amber; his jaw-length hair the same colour.

Unexpectedly, he smiled. 'Ethamar asks for your presence,' he said.

I began to speak again, but he cut across my words.

'The point on which you stand is fixed. Do not leave your position. I inform you for your own protection.'

It took me a moment to grasp what he had told me. As his words registered, I quickly looked down; but the great slab of crystal on which we stood had not shifted, or changed in any way. I turned again to look at him; not sure what he meant. He was slowly moving backwards; away from me.

'Ethamar waits,' he said. 'I do not doubt that you and I shall meet again.'

Then I was rising; or falling. I didn't know which. And the speed of my movement seemed to stretch me dangerously thin. My awareness drifted, faltered and returned. I stood in the same position. In the Dome. The man had gone. I looked up, and saw the woman who had ridden to us in the desert of gold. The Chieftain. A short distance away across the crystal floor, she stood watching me.

I tried to gauge her mood. Then it occurred to me that perhaps these people had no such frailties. They possessed intention, skill, and an emotionless steadiness. I'd seen no evidence of anything else.

'You judge me,' she said, unexpectedly. 'As you also judge my people. Do you not? With Mind, for Mind is all you know. Thus, is the glass darkened; reality obscured. Thus must I be what I do not seem to be.'

I didn't know what she meant by that. 'Look . . .' I said. My voice sounded as if it came from far away. 'Look, whatever's going on, I don't know half of anything about, okay? I don't have a clue. I don't even know how I got here, to this place. All I'm trying to do is get . . . get back to the pyramid. Right?'

I expected her to order me to be silent. She didn't. I paused. I didn't want to betray my intention to leave the encampment; or I might soon find that I couldn't go anywhere.

'Okay,' I continued. 'I did something – back in that courtyard – that's taboo, right? The axe. The replica? Sure, I get the message. No more making things. No more building things. It gives you the heeby-jeebies. Got it. Anyway, then I didn't do as I was told; didn't just follow along like a good boy. Instead I made a break for it, and, well, you know the rest better than I do. Not a crime, as far as I can make out. The pyramid; that's all I was trying to do. Get back there.'

She moved slightly. As she did so, white streaks of light left ghosts of her previous positions behind her.

'I hear you,' she said.

I worked to focus my sight. The after-images disappeared. She continued.

'It is necessary to be direct with you. That is why you have been brought here. I, and my people are no danger to you; but that, you cannot accept. You behave dangerously as a result. You operate from Mind. That is your nature, your stage of evolution. I do not condemn you for acting according to your nature, but in the midst of swift change, Mind alone becomes unstable, treacherous. You may endanger our purpose if you continue. That is why I have elected to meet with you here, in the Dome. To communicate with you in the hope that you have the intelligence to understand us. An explanation, if you wish to call it that. Explanations are rare, but I see your Lights, and your Degree, which you in blindness cannot see. Mind, unbridled, creates blindness. And in blindness you wander, and stumble.' She moved again, towards me; and stopped. A calm strength radiated from her. In the set of her face, and in her eyes I saw coolness. But I sensed her mood and it wasn't threatening.

'At present there is a great urgency in our work,.' she continued. 'And my people prepare for an escalation of conflict, which is imminent. In this, they need my co-operation. Yet I am here. Because of you. Honour and respect that.'

'Okay,' I answered. 'Explanations. If you're giving out explanations, tell me what happened when I came into the Dome. I travelled. Where? I'm still here.'

'I see.' She replied; 'Our security disturbs you. Have you any idea why that should be so?'

I didn't answer, and she continued to speak. 'The Dome is bi-axial. It is the central core of our operations. The innermost position in our encampment.'

'The brain.'

'If you wish to call it that.'

'Uh-huh. Central H.Q.'

She looked closely at me. The faintest flicker of a smile crossed her face. She nodded.

'So what happened?' I said. 'When I came in?'

'It is bi-axial for security reasons. For protection. You travelled from one axis to the other; that is all. But you passed through under guard. Had you not done so, you would have lost the axis-shift. You would have been rejected.'

I tried to grasp the concept of what she was saying. She noticed my attempts, and smiled faintly, again.

'Mind. The Human Condition. It is your servant, but taken too often as your Master. As a servant, it is faithful, but it makes a poor Master.'

Then she moved away from me, and slowly paced the floor of the Dome. I remained where I was, in the centre.

'You know something of our purpose here. I am aware that you do. But I see that you require further information.'

I didn't reply. She continued;

'You know of our mission. He who travels with you has already informed you of that.'

I couldn't imagine how she had knowledge of the conversation in the pyramid between Nelson and me. Automatically, my guard went up again.

'But perhaps you have not been informed of the crucial stage that our work has reached. Security is tight in the encampment. It is required to be. But at present it is at its tightest. We are aware that in the Lands outside Xentha a change has occurred. A change in the balance of forces. My people prepare to redress the balance. The time of war is near at hand. Many times we have ridden to battle, down the Aeons. Many thousands of times, unknown and unheeded by your races. Such is our purpose. But this time, the balance has swung further; further than ever recorded. For this, we cannot account. But we await the call to move forward.'

'The Raiders. That's what you're talking about, isn't it? The Raiders of Gehina.' She took a moment to answer.

'Yes,' she replied. 'The Powers of Gehina.'

'Avenging Angels. You, the Charos. That's what you like to think you are.'

'If you wish to call it that,' she answered. I laughed.

'Well, I'm glad I didn't make it back to the pyramid now. I'm glad I'm here instead. Because there's something bugging me; giving me a real hard time, in fact, and this seems like a good time to open it up. Good chance for a pow-wow with the Avenging Angel Herself! Because I've been thinking; doing a lot of thinking about the inscrutable Charos versus the so-called Raiders of Gehina. And something doesn't add up.'

I expected her to silence me. But as before, she didn't. She remained still; listening. Her attitude took me by surprise, but I'd got steam up, and I intended to say what I liked.

'So they're out there, massing forces. And soon you're going to get them, right? That's what you're saying, isn't it? Only you won't pull them up by the roots. If it's all true, and those big bad guys are taking over, then don't you think it's about time you did that? Oh no. You'll just chop some of the weak bits off them. And you know what happens when you do that? Well, you should, if you don't. Let me tell you. They just grow up all the better for it, that's what. A bit stronger and healthier next time. Oh, I get it! I get it, all right! You need them. That's what you're all about, isn't it? Because without them, you're nothing. Without them, you're extinct. You're no-one! Maybe you need those Raiders, or whatever they're called, to *be*. Don't you? Your wars are just sham!' Still she made no attempt to defend herself.

She said nothing, but let me go on.

'You ride to war, oh yeah! But you never finish the job! Have you got the forces, the power, to do the job properly? You've got to have! But you sit in your crystal towers, untouchable! Protected by your security, your technology, waiting! Just waiting! For what you call the right time for war! So if those Raiders are doing what I've been told they do, all the time you're waiting, for them to overstep some imaginary line, they're working! Have you thought about that? Do you even care?

'That world I came out of is writhing with stuff you don't

know anything about, I bet! Some of that stuff gets noticed, but most of it doesn't! That world is full of goddamned living dead! And the worst of it is so many of them wear nice neat suits and ties, and talk a kind of authoritative babble that sounds like sense! And you'd never guess! You'd never guess they were goddamn possessed! And in the meantime, people; yeah, people, die in a million possible ways, and go through living hell, and go without food, and all the rest of it! Every second! Oh, and that's in only one of how many parallel Worlds . . .? The Raiders! They reap! You bet they do. And when the bugle blows, you knock a few of them down! Till the next time! And you, The Avenging Angels; do you even care that they rise up again? I don't think so!'

My anger drained me. I couldn't say any more. I looked her in the eyes; but her face showed no concern. No feeling. Her gaze, clear and strong, was set on mine. I was certain my words were wasted. She stood; quietly and still. It seemed that she were waiting for me to speak again. But I couldn't. A silence surrounded us. Then presently, I heard her say:

'You do not understand. You cannot understand. I regret that. Your mind rejects; because these matters concern principles which are beyond your comprehension. Your absolute identification with Mind prevents you from knowing of that *Will* which moves through all that is Manifest. That Will is beyond life, and the state which you have come to call death. Its centre is beyond the Manifest; and your Human logic cannot encompass it.

'We, the Charos, serve that Will; and its Word, its Law. We do not question it; we serve it. We are capable of harnessing Mind, and using it as an instrument; but we are not blind servants of it, as you are. We are Warriors of the Primal Word. You have spoken; words which you believe to be true and just. Yet you have neither the authority nor the wisdom to be judge. And no servant of the Law could question the Will which we serve. Drink from the first drop of water on the mountain's highest peak; even before it flows to become a stream. Do not drink of the silted water from the wide river on the plain. For the water from the lowland place shall make you sick, and weak. But the first drop shall bring you Understanding and Power. Yet I see

your Degree. Marked on your Lights is your Degree of Possibil-
ity. That is your right; if you choose it. But you are, yourself, a
battleground, where Mind struggles for supremacy. If you choose
that which is your right, then you shall die; and rise up again in
the Law.'

She turned from me, then, and continued to pace the crystal
floor. I was filled with a gnawing frustration as I watched her;
and a contempt for her attitude. Whatever she had just said
meant nothing to me.

'You're right,' I said, eventually. 'I don't understand. You're
damn right I don't! You talk as if you were God Almighty's
deputy! You're right I don't understand, because all you've given
me is some clever words and saccharined Cosmic bullshit! And
all that garbage isn't really what it's all about, is it? Life and
death, those mere, piddling little things, you seem to think are
some kind of illusion! That's what everything's really all about,
and you know it!'

'Again you judge us,' she said, calmly. 'Why are you so filled
with hatred and suspicion? Do you fear that we cannot feel? We
are not devoid of emotion, Richard Brett; but we are not hag-
ridden by emotion as Humankind is. We see the spread of a
threatening force on the Levels; and we see how factors operat-
ing on the Levels directly influence that World from which you
recently came. We are fully aware of the suffering and degrada-
tion there; that which you speak of with such feeling. And we are
aware of more than you are; for we have access to many Worlds,
which you do not, as yet, realize exist. Yet our mission is not to
weep, or rage, but to ride out to war. And were we not Keepers
of the Balance, then a dark night would fall over Mankind. And
that, you cannot see; for you mistrust us. Perhaps you suspect us
of conspiracy with darkness. We have attempted to monitor your
thought-processes when we were alerted to your dangerous
condition. You are intelligent, Richard Brett; but we have seen
your fear, and your illusion of separateness. You believe that
Gehina infiltrates this encampment. Let me inform you that it
does not.'

'My name! How the hell do you know that?'

'It was sounded on the Web,' she replied. 'The Web which
extends outwards across the Plain of Xentha and beyond.'

'Jesus H. Christ! Big brother is watching you!'

'All vibrations of a certain frequency are picked up on the Web, and relayed to us. The Web issues from the Spiral Tower, and extends through certain sectors of the Levels. It is an early-warning system for the activities of Gehina's forces; but it receives other frequencies. Such is our vigilance. That is how I came to know your name. The fact that I do disturbs you, does it not? The World from which you entered the Levels is largely in a state of unawareness, where Human-kind sleepwalks, endangering itself and the many other species of that World. And that is the reason for Gehina's power. There would be no need of the warriors of the Charos if the instincts of awareness and alertness were alive in Human-kind, as they once were. But in Aeons to come, from necessity, what is left of your race shall awaken; and the work of the Charos will be no longer required. Until then, when the call is sounded, we ride to war; and your misunderstanding – of which I am regretful – cannot alter that. The Word speaks, and we obey.'

'You make it sound so easy, don't you? You've got it all wrapped up and figured out! You're so damn arrogant! Well, I've heard more than enough!'

'We have given you hospitality because we received the signs from your companion, and because we recognized your patterns and your Lights. We have offered you safe refuge in our encamp-ment at a time of imminent war. Already the upheaval is occurring; and the plague of Gehina deepens and spreads rap-idly. We await that precise moment when we shall be called forth. War will be soon, and you are protected here. Yet because of unharnessed Mind and emotion, you cannot see that. The enemy, Richard Brett, does not always dwell without. Does it? Often it dwells within.'

Then she fell silent, and turned away from me. She seemed to be listening to something. Faintly, I heard the sound of a triple horn-call.

'My presence is needed elsewhere,' she said. 'You will be escorted back to the pyramid, under guard, as your undisciplined actions could prove dangerous. I will not jeopardize our work for your sake, Richard Brett. I advise you to be no longer a servant of Mind, but its master. Yet, no doubt you are unwilling to do that.'

Three warriors approached me. I hadn't seen them enter the Dome. They motioned to me to follow them. I didn't resist. There was no point.

16: *Degrees of Freedom*

'Man, I could've told you that would happen!'

Nelson. I looked up into the blue-tinted air of the pyramid. He was sitting by the stream in exactly the same position he'd been in when I had walked out. I'd been talking to him; sleep-talking. But I couldn't remember coming back. Slowly, I got up from where I lay by the water. I felt as though I'd been under anaesthetic. I knew that he had asked me where I'd been. I remembered answering him.

'I could've told you!'

'Okay! Okay! So what?' My focus was returning, and Nelson's voice was getting on my nerves.

'How could you lay all that stuff on her like that?'

'Like what? I said what I felt like saying! What I believe!'

'Oh boy! I recall you saw what happens to believers! Believing ain't knowing. Maybe you ought to keep that mouth of yours shut till you do. You know who she is? Huh?'

'Don't give me that stuff! Just leave it out! I spoke to her like that because she needed it! I don't give a damn who she is! No-one's going to pull rank on me!'

'Well, she knows more than you do, that's for sure! She knows her job. State you're in, you got no hope of seeing that. And don't you start laying your trips on me, 'cause it'd bore me to Hell and back!'

'Bore you? Oh yeah! I wouldn't want to do that! No-one really wants to know, do they? No-one wants to damn well know!'

'It's really got to you, ain't it? Knowing about those Raiders has really made you mad! You're like a wild ox! No wonder you got to the Levels so quick! You're a walking, talking, son-of-a-bitch one-man firecracker display! And all those things you've seen ain't changed you one bit! Some things move on, but Hard-Man don't! You still run into things like you were running a one-man war! Oh boy! These things ain't easy!'

'What do you mean, "these things ain't easy"? If those Raiders are doing what you say they're doing, then that sure isn't easy, either! *If* that's the case, which I'm not convinced it is!'

'Hey, whoa there! I told you right at the beginning about trying to change everything! Now your machine's got no brakes, and that's no way to be riding! Okay, so she talked to you. Then she told you, didn't she?'

'Oh yeah, she talked to me.'

'Then, far as I can see, she told you about the Charos; about the work they're here to do. You got it from the horse's mouth.'

'Hey! You know what, Nelson? I've just noticed! I'm taking all this in! Just being fed what you and her have been telling me. You've been telling me all about the Raiders! So has she! And you know what it sounds like? It sounds like the other Cosmic bull she was giving me, that's what! Maybe Raiders just happen to make good bogey-man-legend!'

'Yeah, Man, but. . .'

'But *what*? Out there, before we came here, do you remember bumping into any Raiders? The Woman of Artademes, was she one?'

'No, but. . .'

'Right. Think about it. You told me all this. Did you get it from the Charos?'

'Hey, wait there! I know what you're getting at, but that ain't the case!'

'You got it from them!'

'I've not been feeding you bullshit. Now would I?'

'I saw some weird stuff in that courtyard. Weird. I don't know what's with these Charos, or what they're up to, but I'd like to bet this Raiders thing is a wind-up. They're after something else!'

'Oh boy! I don't believe I got stuck with you!'

'So high-drama, isn't it? Well, perhaps I'm waking up! People will tell you any old garbage sometimes, to get you to do what they want you to do! Don't you know that? Well, maybe I won't be fed that stuff any more! Won't just swallow it all any more! Come to think of it, it doesn't really make all that much sense! Listen to it, will you? A bunch of invisible and who-knows-who bad guys, trying to take over the world by some kind of smart forgery! Oh, and I forgot about all the other Worlds! They're having a crack at those, too, just for luck! The more I think about it, the more crazy it sounds!'

'Look! I'm telling you straight! I got no hooks in you! What makes you think I have? I ain't trying to bend your mind! You're just saying it can't happen 'cause it freaks you out! It's too much to take in! You ever heard of possession by demons?'

'Oh, Christ! This gets worse! Yeah, I have! That's crap, too! Crap dished out by dumb sheep to scare us with things that go bump in the night! Notice how the way out of that one is to toe the line with religion! Do as they tell you! Don't forget to say grace, but only do it if there's someone watching you!'

'It ain't no such thing.'

'Okay, then it's Voodoo-magic. What your black Mamma weaned you on! Except the witch-doctor makes a fine living, thank you, and maybe even drives a Cadillac, paid for by your fear! You want to know what it really is? Keep the stinking peasants down, that's what! Keep them real scared, and you've got them where you want them!'

'No, it ain't. It's what the Raiders are doing, just called something else. It always was them, always is, no matter what name it goes under; only people had to find ways to explain them, so they gave them names. But it only ever was them. See, it's like a disease. And it's spreading faster and faster. People used to let their demons in by ones and twos, but not now! Gehina's moving in, not by ones and twos, but by hundreds, thousands! You ever wondered why things were getting so damn sick? How the things you used to hear of happening now and again started happening every day? You know, mothers beating up on their own babies . . . little kids getting raped, by kids not much bigger? Ten-year olds who ain't even old enough to read the long words in their own news reports doing time for murder? Governments slowly killing the people who put them into power? Crazy wars, maimings, in the name of some holy reasons? Waste and greed, garbage and poison! All that stuff and more! You ever stopped to think about it? Huh?

'Oh they don't all spit fire and puke slime and curse fit to take the shine off your shoes! No, Man! That's in the story-books. No. In Old World they seem kinda normal. Making money, making babies, flying all over the place in aeroplanes, running multi-nationals, driving delivery trucks. But what's in charge, what's providing the energy for all that, ain't human. It don't move in the same direction. Oh sure, it's spreading. And the way it spreads is interesting. People who get taken, they have a real strong effect on the others. Bit by bit, they infect them; most often through something it's hard to live without.

'Love, respect, things like that. *I don't love you, I don't respect you till you're just like me* ... get it? Like what's the point of hanging on to your Truth, if no-one loves you for it? And people are generally damn scared of standing alone. And the taken ones trample over the Earth and the living creatures. They don't see magic no more; magic of air, trees, ice, stone, magic of life. And most of all, 'cause this is all coming from the Inside of things, from the Levels, that they don't even know is real, they've got no defence. Every damn thing that grows in Old World, that ever did, or ever will, comes from here, first. Now am I getting through to you?'

'Okay! I can hear you! But why? Why should the Raiders do all that? What for? It'd have to be some damn good reason!'

'Sure there's a reason. The survival of their kind. That's one reason. The Raiders just being themselves; existing, the only way they know how.'

'So those Raiders make all the pain? The wars? The hunger? Everything? Is that what you're saying? That without them, it'd be a garden? Well, that won't go down with me, because I know damn well it's not a garden! Life isn't like that!'

'No way. I'm saying no such thing. But the Truth of things is balanced, that's the difference. You figure pain is evil? Ain't always the case, though that seems hard to take. An awful lot of time, pain's a message, information that can't be ignored no more 'cause it digs at your ribs. Though often, by the time you get it, you've already made the mistake of not listening to things you should have done. You figure war is evil? Tell that to the immune system that makes war for a living and keeps the balance, keeps the body alive. But that don't necessarily mean war's always the best answer. There's a time for war, and there's a time for peace. Okay, what about the Big One? Death? Ain't that evil? Well, without death, there can't be life. There's more dying than you know in being born. And at the same time, death, as you found out, is no way what you figure it is.

'Now all those things have got their place in the Dance. But the Raiders, they don't know no Dance. They don't know nothing but themselves. Just them. Is it sinking in?'

'So what about the Charos? What are they doing while all this is happening? *If* all this is happening! Why don't they wipe the damn Raiders out, and have done with it? If they're such Annihilators, like you said, what's the problem?'

'They wipe out the replicas where they find them. That's what they've always done. They ride to war, seek them out, destroy them. Time after time, their work has struggled to keep the Balance. Maybe the Chieftain told you about the Law of the Balance; that Law you most likely think is just so much bullshit. Well it keeps the order of things. There has to be some shadow in that balance; some, but it mustn't take over. The Charos are Law-keepers. But now, Gehina's got some sort of an edge. No matter what the Charos do, the Raiders keep growing. I don't know why. And I don't reckon even the Chieftain does.'

'It still doesn't add up! It doesn't figure! Something doesn't! Look, you've got what you're telling me from the Charos. Isn't that the case? From her, the Chieftain! Now there's something about them that I don't trust. And I sure as hell don't trust *her*!'

'Jeez! You never get it! What can I say to you? Hey? You figure people are out to bend your mind? Me? The Charos? Man, you're on one way-out paranoid trip! You don't believe what I'm saying to you about the Raiders?'

'Well, Nelson, as you're so fond of saying, no. I don't believe! No, I don't! Not from you, because you're unreliable! And not from the Chieftain, either! I'm telling you I saw some weird thing back there in that courtyard, and that woman, the Chieftain, is denying it! But I saw someone *taken over* back there, Nelson! Now whether that was Raiders, or what the hell it was,

I don't know! But some damn thing's moving in on me, and I'm not sitting around and letting it, that's all!'

'Boy! One minute you're saying the Raiders are lies, the next, you're running away from them! What's it to be? Hey?'

'I don't know! I don't damn well know anything any more! But the Charos give me the creeps. I don't trust them. And the Other One; the Great One, you called her, well she doesn't figure any more! Not in my reckoning! I don't trust anything here!'

'Well you're gonna love what's outside.'

'Outside . . .? Where?'

'Outside the pyramid. Take a look.'

I went to the entrance and looked out into the courtyard. There, positioned a few feet away from the little stream, she stood; the Charos Warrior. She saw me, but said nothing as her violet eyes met mine and her Lights flickered briefly. Immediately I turned and went back in.

'Nelson! What the hell is she doing out there?'

'Guard duty . . .'

'Guard duty? Guarding what?'

'You, I guess.'

'Okay, Nelson. See what I mean? She'll have heard every damn word! This is too much! Do you recall what they said when we were brought here? "You are at liberty to come and go as you wish". That's what! And her, outside, makes a mockery of it! See what I'm getting at? Do you think for one minute I could go where I want right now?'

'Sounds like you made some big waves, Man, that's for sure. So they're keeping their eyes on you. Can't say I blame them. They must reckon on you being too dangerous for them to let you out of their sight.'

'Right! That's it! I'm getting out of here!'

'Out of . . . where?'

'Out of this place. This encampment. Fast.'

'Aw! That's crazy! You won't listen, but you go out of here, now, the state you're in, and you're a sitting duck!'

'What for? Legendary bad guys?'

'Hey! Come on!'

'Is she going to try and stop me?'

'Man! Think about it!'

'I've done enough thinking! They're making a prisoner of me! That's what they're doing! But I'm not having it! Let her try and stop me! That would show them up for what they are! I'm getting right out!'

'Things are bad out there!'

'Yeah? Who says so?'

'Won't you wise up? Listen to me? I ain't giving you no bull . . .!'

'I'm going, and that's that! I've had enough!'

'Well, I'm coming with you.'

'You're not!'

'I sure damn well am.'

17: *Over the Wire*

'It would be inadvisable. Dangerous.' She made no move to detain me; nor did she appear to be armed. We stared each other out, by the little stream.

'Oh yeah,' I said. 'What do you know about it?'

'I do not wish you to be harmed,' she replied.

I didn't answer. I turned away from her, and looked back. Nelson was behind me.

'She's right,' he said. I made no reply to him; and turned back to her. She was watching me carefully.

'Okay. Are you going to try to stop me?'

'No. That would not be within my right,' she answered. 'My instructions are to guard you inside the encampment; to prevent you acting in a way which might trigger our internal security, or provide us with false data.'

'So you're not going to attempt to stop me going out. Good.'

'Man, she's advising you not to. Why don't you listen?'

'Because I've had it with these weirdos, Nelson. That's why. Look at her! Listen to her! She's unreal! She's a damn robot! I was fine till I came in here; doing fine, thank you. Give it a bit longer and I'd be thinking like them. I'd be a damn robot, too! The power of persuasion, Nelson, that's why. Christ knows what they want us for, but my instincts tell me that they want us for something!'

'That just ain't true.'

'Oh no?' I began to walk away from the pyramid.

'I'm going. Right now,' I said. 'You can do what you like.' Quickly I crossed the courtyard. At the Gate, I looked back. Nelson and the Charos woman were right behind me. My pattern flashed over the light-grille; and it was almost instantly superimposed by hers.

'Brett,' she said. 'That is your name, is it not? You are free to make your own choice.' Her voice had a gentle quality. I glanced at her quickly. Around her head, the blue and silver Lights shimmered.

As I turned back to the Gate, I heard her say:

'I ask only that you shall be protected.'

I moved through. The pattern on the Gate opened to let me pass. A momentary blackness fell over my awareness; then I saw the Spiral Tower, and the glistening angularity of the causeway at my feet. A great silence hung over everything, and the twisting light-forms of the Tower moved noiselessly. I gazed up, into the turquoise sky filled with stars.

'Hang it! Darn-nation! Son-of-a-bitch!'

I looked down. Nelson lay sprawled face down on the causeway.

'Damn Gate!' he said. 'Got tangled up there! Either that, or I tripped on some damn thing! I'd sure appreciate a hand up here.'

'Look, Nelson. I didn't ask you to do this. You bear that in mind. You want to follow me? Well, that's your own business.'

'Receiving you loud and clear,' he said, and stretched out a hand. I hauled him to his feet.

'Hey, Man, where do you reckon we're going?'

'Haven't got a clue. I'll tell you when we get there. Let's just get moving, shall we?'

In front of us, the Plain of Xentha stretched out, wide and pale amber; no longer wreathed in mist-tendrils, but open and clear. It extended all around, as far as I could see, from horizon to horizon. It seemed to be entirely formed of rock; a type of wind-eroded pale sandstone with occasional shallow fissures in its surface. There was no other way but to cross it on foot. It didn't seem to matter which direction we took. So I started out and, saying nothing, Nelson followed.

When we had gone a fair distance, I stopped to look back at the crystalline structures of the encampment. Their facets glinted in star-light, and I could clearly make out the Spiral Tower as a long finger of brilliance, rising above the buildings. The Chieftain had mentioned a Web which issued from that spire of light. I could see no such thing. As I scanned across the Plain, the horizon seemed no nearer. Whatever might lie beyond, I couldn't imagine. It occurred to me to go back; to try to find the causeway again. But I decided not to re-trace my steps. Then I remembered that the causeway had only led to the valley and, soon after that, to the flowing desert where the sands of gold shifted and changed. I realized there was no way we could return there. So the causeway was off the agenda, anyway.

'Got to admit it, . . .' Nelson suddenly said. 'You ain't got a clue where we're going.'

I stopped; looked at him. 'I don't think that comment's very helpful, Nelson.'

'Ain't such a smart idea to drift around without a clue to where you're going. The deeper in you get, the less that's a good idea. Things just ain't the same, nowadays.'

'Well, maybe instead of criticising me you could make yourself useful. I'm pretty damn sure you know a decent route we could take. Don't you? Maybe you could tell me where we're going!'

He laughed. 'Oh no, Man. I'm into following you. I'm along for the ride. I'm waiting on your powers of leadership, here. That's what I'm doing. And I don't rightly know where we're heading, either.'

'Okay. If you're going to be awkward, we'll keep going. Straight ahead. Got any objections? And you can take it or leave it.'

'Take it or leave it. Uh-huh. Take it or leave it . . .' he mimicked.

I ignored him and we kept on. I made sure we marched. He was annoying me again. As we crossed the Plain, a thought occurred to me. We didn't necessarily have to put up with what we'd got. Ahead of us was a flat, cracked-rock landscape; but it didn't have to be that way. I remembered the axe. Here, I could build, if I needed to: a pathway, a roadway. Maybe even transport. A vehicle? It would be hard, memorising the detail. But maybe I could do it. All in good time. Hardly had the thought crossed my mind, than Nelson said:

'You do what you're figuring on, Man, and we'll have the Charos down on us like a pack of ten-ton trucks!'

He was right. I knew it.

'Things are changing fast,' he went on. 'Getting tighter than they used to be. Time was, when you could do as you liked. That was fun. Now you got to stay in the frame. Ain't the old times no more. You got to learn to travel light now. You got your Truth, and that's it. You can't build nothing no more. See, if you do, it vibrates on the Web, jams up the surveillance system. And the Charos sure don't like that right now; not while they're trying to get information on the Raiders. If you want to end up in the cooler, you go ahead. You'd end up back with the Charos, and you wouldn't be able to go nowhere. If you want to keep getting yourself some action, travel light. Damn Raiders! They cramp your style, some. That's a fact!'

I'd had enough of the Raiders of Gehina. I'd had enough of hearing about them. 'Maps, Nelson. Maps.' I stopped in my tracks.

'What you talking about?'

'Maps. That's what. We need them. Maps of the Levels. Are there any such things?'

'Oh boy. Now you're getting ambitious . . .'

'Are there? It can't all be uncharted. My bet is that it isn't.'

'Now hang on there. You're getting into real complicated stuff . . .'

'What do you mean? Maps, that's all I'm saying. You didn't say there aren't any such things, and that interests me.'

'Hey, what do you figure you are? Some Cosmic boy-scout? You reckoning on working round the place with a map and compass? You're wild, Man, wild!'

'So there are such things, aren't there? There are maps. I just know it. So do you. Am I right?'

'Okay. Right. But they ain't maps like you imagine maps to be . . . They're way-out.'

'Charts, then. Showing different areas of the Levels.'

'Kind of. They show particular zones, landmarks, things like that. But to explain how, to you! Jesus, that ain't gonna be easy!'

'Well if we could get access to them, it'd help. At least we'd know where we were going. That would be a plus. So how do we get them, Nelson? Come on . . .'

'Oh boy!' he sighed. 'You always did go too fast for your gears!'

'Where are they, then; these maps?'

'In the Hall of Records.'

'Okay. We make for the Hall of Records. Let's move it.'

He didn't make a move, but stared at me with a doubtful expression on his face. 'It's gonna be a bitch,' he said.

'You know the way. So give, Nelson. Let's go.'

'The idea's wild! You know that? You ever heard that saying; fools rush in where Angels fear to tread? Hey? You ever heard that? Well, that's you. Tickets to the Hall of Records don't come free inside crunchy breakfast packs! They're rarer than a five-legged Moose!'

'Nelson, have you got anything against going there?'

'No. I got nothing against going there. It's just a damn fool idea, that's what.'

'Listen. We get the maps, we know where we are. What's wrong with that?'

He whistled, and scratched his head. ''Cause there's a lot of people who'd like to get into the Hall of Records, that's what. There's guys always trying to get hold of information from there. Out-of-body trippers from Old World. Psychic psychos who're into power. Helpers and healers. People who got an idea they might have been someone real special in a past life: Cleopatra, or Abraham Lincoln, or Napoleon, y'know. Then there's witches, wizards, weirdos, freaks, Gurus, all over the place. You name it, they're all at it. Most of 'em don't get there, that's a fact. But they manage to dream up some way-out library-in-the-sky; then they hang around it for a while, tripping out on some information they've made up themselves. That is, till the Charos come checking them out. Then they get some cosmic boot up the ass that delivers them back home faster than a prairie twister, and makes damn sure they don't feel much like making a habit out of it.'

'Well, Nelson. Whatever a bunch of crazies wants to do is nothing to do with me. I say we try and find it.'

'Hah! What makes you reckon you're any better than them? What's going to buy you a ticket?'

'You said yourself that wandering around isn't such a good idea. We can't keep doing that, for sure.' I looked back, across the Plain. I could no longer see the encampment of Xentha. A haze rose up in the far distance over the stone

'You know the way, don't you?' I said to him.

'To the Hall of Records?' He gave me a peculiar look, and laughed. 'Kind of. But you're going to need all your gears and more besides. There's multiple Warps to cross. We have to move into a whole new zone. Like flying through the eye of a needle, Bird-Man. But I know the way, yeah.'

'Okay. We'll go for it.'

'It's gonna be a bitch,' he muttered, and started walking.

18: To Kill a Prickly Pear

He turned abruptly left and, appearing to know exactly where he was going, he took off, striding across the Plain. I followed; but it was hard to keep pace with him.

'Ain't no teacher like Experience,' he was muttering as he went. I noticed that as we progressed, the fissures in the ground were becoming more defined; and there seemed to be more of them than there had been. They were deepening, and taking on a jagged appearance. One after another we stepped over them; but as they increased in size, we were forced to leap across them. But not once did Nelson slow his pace. Soon we came to a gully; far too wide to cross. On inspection, it proved to be horribly deep.

'What do we do now?' I asked. 'Fly?' I looked down the entire length of it. It reminded me too much of the snaking chasm I had encountered on my first arrival on to the Levels. It stretched out as far as I could see, on either side.

'To fly would be the decent thing to do. Only we ain't gonna do the decent thing, are we, Man? Oh no. We climb.'

'We what? We climb down into the thing?'

'Yep. Bearing in mind how you hate flying so much, thought we'd do something different. Ain't told you this, but flying's restricted, anyhow. Ain't possible to fly every place you are, here. You got any objections?'

The way he put it made it obvious that I wasn't supposed to have any. Warily, I looked down. It looked like a killer whale's jaws.

'That's a goddamn crack in the Cosmos, Nelson! I don't like that idea. Maybe we could go round it?'

'I go first, okay?' he said; and didn't waste any time. He slipped over the edge. I closed my eyes.

'You coming?' His voice echoed from somewhere below.

'*Jesus Christ!*'

'You want the maps, Bird-Man!' he called out, sounding even further away. It was Hobson's choice. I let myself down into the chasm, backwards, and grasped hold of the rock edge while my feet groped for footholds. Beneath me, my legs swung about in a frenzy, finding no purchase on what seemed to be a sheer wall. I wondered how Nelson could have got so far, so fast. Eventually, my right foot met rock, and I dared to put some weight on it. But I had little inclination to let go of my hold on the lip of the chasm. I hated heights, hated them; almost as much as I did flying. This, after all, was more of a depth than a height. But it was still a long way down. Same difference.

'Let go the edge,' I heard. 'Find a hand-hold. There's one to your right. About a foot or so down. Down . . . down . . . keep going. Okay! You got it! Grip it!'

I gripped, and let go with my left hand. 'Nelson . . .' I said, weakly. 'I'm dead, right?'

'No.'

'Am I immortal?'

'No.' My left foot found something solid. I was grateful.

'So it's possible to come to a sticky end . . .?'

'What a damn fool question,' he replied from below. 'Ain't supposed to be discussing philosophy. You're supposed to be trying to find a way to stop yourself falling twenty seven thousand feet.'

'Twenty seven thou . . . . .! Oh no! Oh Jeeees . . .!'

My left foot slipped; dangled in mid-air. I almost lost the right hand grip. Immediately I brought my left hand down to steady it; and held on with all the energy I'd got.

'Left foot up . . . up a bit . . . Okay.'

I recovered the foothold. Through a blur, Nelson's voice came up to me.

'Used to go down to Yosemite sometimes,' I heard him say. 'Used to enjoy that. Mostly on a weekend. Or whenever we weren't working in the meat-house. 'Course, we had all the gear. The ropes, belays, the lot. Pity we ain't got the gear right now. Make it a damn sight easier, though not so exciting, hey? Used to get ourselves some action, oh boy! We sure did! Up with the buzzards! Ten dollars each, and we hired all the gear we needed . . .'

My foot was jammed into the tiny crack as far as it would go in. Then I froze. My hands locked in a vice-grip on the overhead spur; and I became suddenly, uncontrollably, racked with violent tremors which flickered and tumbled through me. At that moment, I knew that there were two types of fear; the quick, and the slow. Quick fear is easier. Slow fear is different. It sickens.

'That was the old times, though. Fifty dollars won't get you far on gear like that, now, I guess. I'm throwing in the camping gear, too, for that. And five saddle-bags, 'cause we didn't have our own. Didn't all own our own horses, and Dozer always used to ride bareback. And that was for the whole weekend. Fifty dollars. Or eighty for the whole week, if we ever had cause to stay up there a whole week. Oh boy, that was fun. Takes me back to think about it. Hell, I'm talking like seventy years back, here, or maybe more. More. It's got to be. Guess I've lost count . . .'

I glanced down between my legs. Nelson was way below me now; descending lizard-like over the rock face. He kept on talking, and his voice was thrown back by the opposite wall. He wasn't looking at me. He wasn't helping me.

The frozen inertia snapped out of me like a whiplash; and

desperately looked up, wondering if it would be possible to climb back up again. Then the spur I was clinging to moved; only slightly, but with a sharp crack. I was losing it.

'. . . . . Time not being what you figure it is . . .' I heard him say. '. . . Guess it could be a hundred years or more. Thinking about that old Dame, Time, now, which I don't often get to doing, I can tell you that you've been here for more than forty years. Now that puts my figuring right out, so I guess I'd better let go of it.'

I groped frantically across the cliff-face with my left hand; searching for anything to grip. But there was nothing big enough to rely on; and quickly I brought my left hand back to the small spur. As I shifted position, it cracked again. I reached down with my right hand, and found a tiny ledge to take my hold. No sooner had I got my fingers locked on to it than the rock above suddenly crumbled and fell away; plummeting past me into the chasm beneath. Vaguely I was aware that I didn't hear it fall to ground below.

Then my left foot lost purchase and slipped. I hung on; fingertips frantically gripping the ledge. In front of me, so close, I saw green stone, striated with quartz. At the border of unreality, the slow fear was creeping back, beating a deathly, threatening rhythm.

'Ain't no use climbing down further . . .' I heard. But through the fear, I had trouble recognizing what his words meant.

'Fair sheer after the ledge here. Smooth as a baby's ass. Ain't got no belay pins, so it's off the menu . . .'

But this time, the fear didn't freeze me. It danced, teasingly, will-o-the wisp-like around me. It was waiting for me to lose my grip. Its face leered at me from each stone, each foothold in my struggle to stay on the rock. He was talking; but I didn't know what about. I chanced a look down, and saw that he was no longer climbing. He stood on a small ledge not far below. The ledge appeared to be no more than two or three feet wide; but it promised safety.

Slowly, I worked my way down towards it; each move suspended in an eternity. Then, hanging on to a fingerhold crack, I lowered myself down. But my feet didn't reach it. The distance was deceptive. I knew that if I overshot, or stumbled as I landed on it, I would end up down below. I let go, dropped, and my feet touched rock. I felt my whole body sway for a sickening moment. Then I recovered my balance. Nelson laughed. He was sitting with his legs dangling over the edge.

'For a beginner, you ain't so bad.' I couldn't answer him. Then he stood up; looked down into the depths, and said:

'This place ain't big enough for the two of us.' And with that, he leapt off. Into empty space. He didn't fly, he dropped like a stone. I watched him go; down and down. I watched him disappear. A tremendous silence followed; a dreadful nothing of quietness. I began to tremble; backed up against the rock wall.

'Jump off!' I heard, from a far distance. 'You don't believe nothing! Fine. No-one says you have to. But let's see if you got any faith, Man!'

Then I remembered this. I remembered the whole scene. It was a nightmare. My nightmare. And it had returned, again and again, until I'd learned the knack of waking myself out of it, always drenched with sweat and shivering. Now it was here again, like a memory of the future. But Time was a Mythical Beast. An old dame. Wasn't she? And this time around, I couldn't escape, drenched and cold. All I was was here, on this ledge. In the dream, a hound had bitten at my legs; had pushed me into leaping. Then I had fallen, and woken up. Nelson's voice. He was down there. He was laughing again. *Let's see if you've got any faith, Man!* echoed from the rock face of the abyss. To leap . . . was unthinkable. To stay . . . was to be trapped.

He had jumped, and I'd watched him drop away into the darkness. But he was somewhere down there, laughing. I could hear him. He hadn't been smashed to pieces. It could be twenty seven thousand feet; and it might not be. This was a whole new world, after all; run by laws which turned things inside-out. Whenever I had expected anything, I'd always been dealt the unexpected.

I had crossed a bridge as insubstantial as a spider's thread; so fine, it could hardly be seen. I had traversed the unknowableness of a Warp; and come out the other side. Why not this? Then I remembered the nightmare again, and the voice which had always taunted me in it. A disembodied voice, which had half-sung, half-chanted. And the words of the poem it had sung, came back to me.

> Here we go round the prickly pear
> Here we go round the prickly pear
> Here we go round the prickly pear
> At five o' clock in the morning . . .

Let's see if you've got any faith, Man. The voice. It was singing a knell of future past. The song of the old dame, Time. It was biting me.

> This is the way the world ends
> This is the way the world ends
> This is the way the world ends
> Not with a bang, but a whimper . . .

I jumped. No time. No distance. The ground was springy, under my feet. The old dame had a soft belly. Nelson cursed. I stumbled, and regained my feet.

'Don't go thinking I've got Faith, crazy old man. I've just learned how to dance with insanity.'

He didn't argue. Involuntarily, I sank to the soft ground; and he suggested that we stay put for a while. But I didn't want to stay. I wanted to move out. This place had brought back too many memories. So we moved on; and we travelled down the narrow gully, overshadowed by soaring rock faces which hemmed us in on both sides. Incredulously I gazed up; unable to see the top of the great crevasse. As the shock of what I had experienced wore off, I became very annoyed with Nelson. He read my mood, and gave me a peculiar look.

'You've got a hell of a nerve . . .' I said, suddenly; 'Do you wonder that I can't trust a word you say?' He kept walking.

'Okay,' was his reply. 'It wasn't twenty seven thousand feet. Okay. It was infinite distance. It was the height of your fear; the depth of your bad dream. What you complaining about? You killed it. You found a new gear. And boy! You're going to need it!'

'So what's all the Raiders stuff, then? Same thing? Bad dreams? Or bad psychology lessons? Or a pack of lies? Who's to know?'

He didn't answer straight away. He kept moving at a fair pace. I had to work hard to keep up with him; but I kept heckling. He wasn't simply going to laugh this one off. Every word was magnified by the rocks, and echoed all around us.

'You figure the Universe is down on your case, don't you?' he said. 'Well, maybe it ain't. You ever thought of that? But you know what I figure? I figure every time that machine of yours gets a bit more power, it makes you sore-headed. Now why is that? Every time you break through something, and find a bit more of your Truth, you get real mad about it. You know what I reckon? I reckon it's 'cause being boring is what you really want to be all about. You always were as prickly as a porcupine on heat, but you don't fool me. You're your own worst enemy. And it ain't easy travelling with some guy who's his own worst enemy. You make me miss my woman. Too bad.'

'Thanks for the lecture!'

'Well you can get mad if you like. Ain't no skin off my nose. But I'm telling you you stopped being boring when you took the Sword. And you stopped being boring when you took the Rose. So it ain't no use fighting it. You'd better get shaped-up and tuned-up. That gear you just found ain't gonna be enough, nor any of 'em are, if you keep fighting your Truth.' He suddenly stopped, looked directly at me, and said:

'I've seen your cards. I know what hand you're holding. How you play 'em, now that's your business. And I've seen guys who lost every damn thing they owned, on a Royal Flush, 'cause they didn't know how to play them cards real steady. You pack 'em, you chicken out, you lose. You get my meaning? Yeah, I figure you do.' Then he was on the move again.

19: *Lightfall*

WE CARRIED ON; working our way down the gully. Neither of us said much. I was thinking about what he'd said; that he'd seen my cards. I didn't know what he meant by that, but his words gave me a strange feeling, and I didn't like it. Also, I thought about what he'd said as we were climbing; about my having been on the Levels for forty years at least. There was no way of telling if it were true, or if he were spinning me a line. I decided not to mention it. The answer I was sure I'd have got wouldn't have done me much good.

We had covered some distance when I noticed that ahead of us on the left there appeared to be some kind of shadowy recess in the cliff-face. As we drew nearer to it, I saw that it reached back into the rocks, forming a tunnel; rough-hewn and dark. At the entrance to it, we stopped; and Nelson looked at me.

'You ever done any caving?' .

'No. I haven't.'

'Didn't figure you had. Oh boy! You ain't lived! You ain't been climbing. You ain't been caving. What did you ever do for fun? Play dominoes? But you sure are in luck, 'cause you're getting to do all the things you never got chance to. Now how about that?'

'Yeah,' I replied. 'It's a real treat. This is a regular adventure playground, Nelson.' I stepped into the mouth of the tunnel, and peered inside. There, the dark wasn't absolute. I could just make out the shapes of the rough rocks on each side.

'The maps are that way, aren't they?' I pointed into the semi-darkness. 'The Hall of Records?'

'Uh-huh.'

'Typical. Under damn ground! What next?'

Something amused him. I gave him a sidelong glance, and moved into the tunnel. Inside, the ground was slate-smooth; easy to walk on. Its regularity, in contrast to the roughness of the walls and roof, took me by surprise. It seemed almost man-made. He followed me in.

'No tricks,' I said. 'No stunts. No damn lies, okay? We just go through, you and I, and see what's down there. Right?' I turned; caught him in mid-shrug.

'Now, Man. Would I? Now would I?'

I didn't reply to that. I turned my attention back to the tunnel and kept on moving. As we got deeper in, I noticed that the dimness around us remained constant. Again, like the many lights of these Levels, its diffuse glow seemed to have no source. I couldn't understand it; but it was sufficient for us to see where we were going, and that was all that mattered. I'd expected total blackness. Trial by underground rat-hole. Another of my expectations hadn't worked out; and that one was fine by me.

We made good speed, but we didn't make much conversation. Nelson tried it once, and I told him to shut up. Every sound we made was picked up and tossed around until the echoes were unbearable. A whisper sounded like a thousand ghosts. Normal voice-level sounded like bedlam. Then the tunnel gradually began to narrow. There wasn't much headroom any more, and it became difficult to make any progress.

'We go down,' Nelson said. Ahead of us was a hole. I stopped. It looked like a rat-hole, after all.

'Don't spook out on me, Man. This ain't that deep.'

'How do you know? You been here before?' But he just laughed and started down it.

'I'll go first. It's a pussy-cat,' he said.

Apprehensively, I looked down. It didn't look too bad. Jutting boulders lined the shaft which angled downwards quite gently. And the light was decent. I followed him down. The rocks were dry, easy to grip. I instantly felt a sense of exhilaration, but couldn't think why. I was a long way underground in a mostly uncharted world. Then I though of something else. Everywhere I went, there were rocks. Stones, boulders, crevasses. Rocks. All the way along. It was weird.

'Rocks, Nelson. Why? Everywhere we go it's the same. Stones.'

'Yeah. Nice, ain't they?'

'But why? Why rocks?'

'Well, I guess it's 'cause you got to ride a rocky road. Somehow, you make your road out of what you are, here. Hah! Maybe rocks and you got some special feeling for each other now! That's okay!

Hard-Man gets rocks! So what? At least they're hard. You can walk on 'em; climb over 'em. Some guys get mud. Some guys get worse. Think about it; wading through a pile of . . .'

'Ssshh! Wait . . .' I whispered. 'Listen!'

Drifting towards us, I could hear the most incredible sounds. Faint, atonal music rose up from somewhere below us. Silvery sounds, flute-like, dived down low, and hovered trilling, before leaping up, and crossing strange intervals to scale impossible heights. I could hear pan pipes, and children's voices, singing, laughing, chattering. The sounds rose and fell, dying away, only to begin again. Clinging to a boulder I stopped, and listened. The music suddenly blended into a recognizable sound. Water, running, cascading water.

I realized that the echoes in the shaft must have changed the noise in some way, and fragmented it. I began to climb down again. Once more the notes began; fading in and out.

'Nelson . . . There it is again! Listen!'

'Yeah, I hear it.'

We reached the bottom of the shaft, and I saw that we appeared to be in a dead-end. But I could still hear the strange sounds coming from somewhere beneath us. Then Nelson flung himself flat on the ground, and began to scratch around amongst the loose pebbles, obviously looking for something. 'It's here,' he said.

'What is?'

'The way through. Reckon you can fit?'

I got down to take a look. A low passage led off on one side of the base of the shaft. It was no more than a couple of feet high, if that; and not very wide. Inside, it wasn't dark, but was lit oddly, by a yellowish-white phosphorescence. I reached in and touched the ground, expecting dampness. But the stone was warm to my touch, and dry. 'That's the way through?'

'Yeah.'

'It looks tight.' I experienced a flash of claustrophobia. It touched me and moved on. There was no indication of how long the passage was; or whether it narrowed even more further along. I could hear the strange water-music drifting along it. 'I'll have a crack at it,' I said; and I got down on the ground, flat on my belly. 'Only if I get stuck, call Drain-Busters.'

Nelson let out an explosive laugh which ricocheted from rock to rock; tumbling about in the shaft above us. The noise was almost painful.

'Nelson! Give me a break!'

'Sorry, Man.' The space was tight; but I belly-wriggled through. Again I was reminded of the first crevasse; and the stone wall through which I'd been birthed onto the Levels. When I tried to remember before that, my mind revolted. I reined in my thoughts, and pushed on through the tiny passage. Behind me, I heard Nelson. He was whistling *Red River Rock*. The water-music wove weird harmonies into the tune.

Suddenly, I remembered a breeze-block wall. Steel bars over the door to a corridor. Loud *Red River Rock* on a gravelly voice; echoing along. A drum-beat on a toilet seat. It was Duke's last day, and he was rocking. He had the mental age of a ten-year-old, and no attorney any more. But he had rhythm. I shuddered; couldn't go on.

'Why are you whistling that?'

He stopped; fell quiet. 'What?'

'*Red River Rock*! Why?'

'It's a wicked tune! '

'Shit!'

'Man, I'm stuck up your ass! You got a case of road-blocks, or what? This view ain't nothing to write home about.'

'Don't push me! Just don't – that's all!'

'Hey! What's got you?'

'Duke. That's what. All of them. Death Row . . .'

'You got a flashback! Okay! You got a flashback! It happens. Don't let it freak you. Keep moving. They get out, they all do. They get out and they go riding. You know that's a fact. Now let's go.'

'I can't . . . I can't go! I wiped men out! Three of them! One of them got out of the patrol vehicle, and I blew him away! I just blew him away! I was there, watching his brains leak on to the highway . . . and then there were two more of them . . . out of nowhere. And they weren't that fast . . . *they looked at him*! And while they were looking, I took them out too. It must have been ten seconds, the whole thing . . . ten damn seconds! . . . I can't! I can't go anywhere!'

'Okay!' His voice was like a thunderclap around me. 'Okay! It's bad news! You wasted three cops! You're a murderer, Man! You done all that stuff, and you paid the price, some of it. You got moved out of town. But you ain't finished your paying. No, not yet. And that scares you. If you destroy, you pay by creating. If you hate, you pay by loving. That's how it goes. Now you're going to move! You're going to keep going, right now, moving forward! You get the message? Move it out! Or you get something shoved up your ass that you ain't gonna appreciate!'

I trembled as the surge of recall pounded me. And through the waves of guilt, the music played. Pan pipes and flutes, and voices in a waterfall. In Nelson's voice I heard no forgiveness; only acceptance of what I was. But that was enough. I crawled on; aware that tears were running down my face as I levered myself through the narrow space.

Then, without warning, the ground gave way. The crawl-space opened out too suddenly, and I was scrambling head-first; tumbling forward over fragments of loose stone. I felt myself rolling, out of control; then found I was on my knees in a huge underground chamber. Nelson came tumbling too, behind me. As he slid down the long slope, shale and pebbles scattered. He found his feet, and skiied down the last few yards on his heels.

'Oh boy!' he shouted, and staggering to regain his footing, he slapped me hard on the back. 'Boy oh boy! Ain't this something else!'

I gazed around us; up above us. And in what I saw, the weight of my memory was taken away. Great columns of glittering white rock soared up through the massive chamber in wide, vaulted curves to support the roof of the cave, high above. From those huge, asymmetric arches, stalactites of emerald hung, glinting and smouldering with green fire.

'Nelson!' I whispered. 'Look at that! Those stalactites! . . . They've got to be . . . emeralds! Solid damn emerald!'

'It is,' he replied. 'Sure enough, it is. Hundreds of tons of it. Oh boy! Ain't it pretty?'

We were surrounded by the music; and the rocks of the chamber seemed living; responding to the sounds. Lights, many-coloured, hovered around the stones, dancing in every line and crevice; joining together, then shooting out lines of brilliance to traverse the great vaults and alight on other surfaces.

'It's alive! The whole place!' I whispered; 'It's moving to that music! What the hell is it?'

'It's the rocks.' he said. 'They make the sound. The Spirit of the stones.'

'The Spirit of the . . . stones?' I repeated. But behind that, I heard something else: a crashing, white-water sound.

'Look! I gripped him by the arm. 'At the wall, over there!' Between the glittering sweep of the arches I saw a monumental cascade, which rushed downwards at such speed that it appeared to be held, motionless against the cavern wall. I had to turn away from it. Its dazzling brilliance was overpowering.

'I can't . . . can't look at it for long.'

'That's 'cause it ain't no waterfall. It's light. Liquid light.'

I guarded my eyes with my hand, and turned to him. He was staring into it. His eyes were on fire. Afraid of what I saw, I gazed at him. Where the pupils of his eyes should have been, was brilliance. He kept staring. I shook him, and he laughed.

'Real power,' he said. 'Raw force. The Spirit of an Element.'

'I can't . . .'

'I know that. Only those who die for love, and fools, can look into it.' Then he turned away. For a moment his eyes still burned, before they returned to their own strange colour.

'Is this it, then? The Hall of Records?'

'No way.' And he pointed to the Lightfall. 'It's through there. That's the route.'

'Through it?'

'Behind it.'

I was speechless. I couldn't even bear to look at it, and I was going to have to pass through it. I didn't know how.

'You go through blind,' he said.

'But . . .'

'You let go to it. You let go, and don't try to see; and you pass through. Try to use your vision, and it'll be taken away from you.' He moved forward to the place where the cascade met the cavern floor. Shielding my eyes with both hands, I tried to make out what he was doing; but I was forced again to turn away. He returned, holding two small fragments of emerald in the palm of his hand. They were rounded and quite flat.

'Close your eyes.' Then he placed the stones firmly in my eye-sockets, against my closed eyelids.

'Walk.' I felt him guiding me across the uneven floor, until my feet jarred against rock and I stumbled. But the emeralds stayed fixed.

'Seven steps up!' he shouted, against the deafening rush of the torrent. 'We're going round the back of it!'

'Okay!' I replied, but my voice was lost. As we moved through, I felt the magnetic pull of the Lightfall on my body. Its force was tremendous. But somewhere, behind that, I detected some great difference; a change. I knew something was wrong.

'We're nearly through!' I heard him shout.

'No! Wait! Something's changed!'

'Oh boy!'

'What is it?'

'Ain't like it should be . . .' The sensation was familiar. I began to recognize it.

'Nelson, it's . . .'

'Okay! Now you've done this one before! Get your ass tuned up! You hear me?'

'It's a Warp! Isn't it?'

'Yeah. It's a bitching Warp – now don't lose it! Remember how to ride it! Remember and hold it! Hold out!'

I remembered that stillness from the last time; but that was the last time. A state of no-thing. Oh God; it was happening so fast. How did I do it? Through a veil of near-panic, I grasped at what I remembered. To be still; but how to travel in the stillness. On a thin thread. I could no longer hear Nelson. I could no longer hear the roar of the Fall. I could only hear a noise, like a tuning-signal, burning a line.

Then a wind came; a dry, hot wind, howling. Feather-light, I was picked up and carried. Stillness. Remember the still-ness. Don't think. I heard the creaking yawn of Time-chasms, opening. They wouldn't take me if I held the thread. I'd done it before. Their sound echoed from the Outer Reaches; from the pre-Universal core of Chaos. Their twist in the fabric of the Worlds formed a centrifuge, impelling motion against the grain of evolution. Their gaping jaws drew in the Lost, to eject them far, far beyond the created Existence. To what end? It was impossible to imagine. I knew the Warps, now; knew something else about them. Their essence. But to think was dangerous. And that was all I dared to know. So I fixed on nothing but the Thread; my line. And I heard Nelson calling me. We must have got through. Both of us. I remained still; stretched out my arms. I touched nothing. Afraid to move, I stood, cruciform. And the emeralds fell from my eyes. Stone again. We stood in a wide underground passage, which was dimly-lit. I felt a flood of relief. We'd made it across.

'You can ride 'em! Oh yeah! Really ride 'em!' he shouted. 'First time could've been a fluke! Second time shows you got some skill! You're on the up-and-up!'

'You didn't know it was there, did you?'

'The Warp?' He became thoughtful then, and said: 'No, I didn't. I've been through a Lightfall like that so many times. But I've never known one so close by a Warp. But then again, I guess these surprises keep us in our dancing-shoes, ain't that likely?'

'So why? Why was it there? Why did we run into a Warp?'

He frowned. 'Dunno. You most often find Warps close to multiple Interspaces. Places where one magnetism sets up friction against another magnetism. You know – they sort of crowd in on one another; set up vortices with gaps. Somehow it always seems to be connected with Warps.'

'Conflict?'

'Yeah. One thing pushing against another.'

'Okay. I get it. But in the cavern, what was there to create that kind of set-up?' He didn't reply at once. He just looked carefully at me.

'Not a thing. But I figure we'd better keep awake. 'Cause something set it up, that's for sure, and I reckon it won't be long till we find out what.'

I looked around in the passage, and listened. We seemed to be quite alone. It was just another tunnel.

'Okay, we move out,' he said. 'Let's keep on the move. And don't you forget what I said right now. You keep your ass wide awake, and your eyes coming through the back of your head. You got me?'

I nodded; and we moved on. There was no sign of anything untoward in the passageway, but I could tell by Nelson's attitude that things were by no means fine. He was very quiet, and seemed to be concentrating. I sensed that, underneath his calm exterior, he was a cat on hot bricks. It worried me, because I was sure it took a lot to make him that way. Even in the iron forest of Hell, he'd remained steady. We hadn't gone far, when the tunnel began to brighten and lose its greyness. But the light was uninspiring. Slowly, a creeping, lurid glow began to take over, filling the air around us with a muddy-orange light. We stopped; and I glanced at him.

'What the hell's that?'

'Okay. Go slow, and let's check it out.' Carefully, we moved forward, keeping close to the rocks at the side of the passage.

'I don't believe this!' he whispered. He was just ahead of me, and he motioned me to stay back.

'What is it?'

'Man, it's weird. It's street lights. Neon.'

'Street lights? Here? Nelson, are you kidding?' I moved quickly up the rock tunnel, and drew up next to him.

He threw out an arm to stop me going any further. 'Now you keep low. And keep your damn voice down!' He whispered through his teeth: 'I seen enough street lights to know when I see 'em. And where you get street lights you sure as hell get streets. And where you get streets, you get people. And people are the last thing we need right now.'

Then I saw it. A city. But this wasn't a night life city of traffic, cab horns, streaking head lamp beams, police sirens. It was a shadowy, foreboding slum of low warehouse blocks side-lit in neon; glowering under an oppressive night sky. Desolate and decaying, the blackened buildings sprawled; their windows ragged and smashed. Jagged edges of glass caught the sallow light, and glinted. Between the warehouse blocks, semi-lit narrow streets angled back; stretching into thick gloom. And behind them, skyscraper blocks rose up; unlit and ghastly in the wan air. Some were intact, but others were broken and crumbling high up, where they reached into the heavy sky. They reminded me of jutting, rotten teeth in the jaws of a dead and decaying beast. The place seemed predatory and coiled; ready to spring up out of its death to pounce and devour.

My gaze snapped back to the warehouses. I scanned their facades, and the dark alleys which intersected them. And there I saw no signs of life. No gangs of kids loitering round ghetto-blasters. No all-night drinkers. No mini-skirted hookers. There were no people.

20: Streetwalk in Neon

WE WATCHED FOR a while. But the buildings had an air of total desolation. No-one appeared.

'We're going in,' he said. As he started forward, I grabbed his arm.

'Hang on, we don't know what's in there! Whatever it is might not be obvious, but for Christ's sake, Nelson! . . .'

'There ain't nobody at home. Got a sneaking feeling I know why, but I ain't sure, yet.'

I didn't like the atmosphere one bit. It filled me with a deep sense of loathing. It reeked. 'Let's leave it out,' I said. 'We could go back, through the Lightfall cavern. There's got to be another route.'

'I ain't doing no action replay on that Warp, Man. I can take 'em if I have to, but I ain't dancing backwards with 'em. And I want to take a look around, here. I got a feeling, as I said.'

'A feeling? Goddammit, Nelson! I've got a feeling, too! It says leave this garbage bin out! That's what it says!'

'Okay. You figure there's someone hanging out in there? Is that it? Well, let's knock on the door and see. Just to make it official.'

Before I had chance to try to stop him, he let out a wild, animal-like call; half way between a triple howl and the bark of a coyote. The noise bounced off the lowering warehouses, and died away. It was unanswered. No movement or sound came from amongst the buildings.

'No-one at home. Like I told you.' It seemed he was right. That cry would have wakened anything.

'Okay,' I said eventually. 'Okay – we go in. Only let's keep a good lookout. And Nelson . . .?'

'Yeah?'

'When we're in there, do me a favour. Don't make that noise again. It gives me the creeps.'

'Okay. We play cool cats.'

'Let's take it very steady, Nelson. I don't like this place; not a bit. I don't trust it.'

We left the cover of the tunnel, and crossed into the shadows under the warehouse blocks. I noticed that the street looked slick: rain-wet, with bleary reflections of dull orange. Overhead, a streetlight dimmed. The unexpected change stopped me in my tracks.

'Man, what a spook-show!' Nelson said. The neon flickered and dimmed even further; then scintillated and went out. Around us, an unnatural stillness hung. I looked at the oily-black walls; then glanced back the way we had come. Precisely where the tunnel should have been, stood yet another warehouse. One that hadn't been there before. Running alongside it, was another street. I said nothing. There was no point. It was typical, I thought; no way back now. We were stuck to our course. We'd decided to go in, and that's what we'd got. I began to realize the weight of a decision, here. To change your mind was obviously not one of the rules of the game.

'Warehouses are empty . . .' I heard him say.

I turned around again.

'Ain't been used for storing stuff . . .' he went on. 'They ain't no more than scenery.'

Scenery? Some of the shattered windows were waist-high. I leaned in; felt a shiver run through me. I could see little but blackness. But it felt empty.

'Scenery. Of course. They shoot *Dracula meets Zombies from the Spacewoman's Tomb Two* here next week. You forgot that, Nelson.'

He laughed. The empty buildings picked up his voice and laughed back at us.

'Man, you're so cool!' Then he beckoned me to follow him.

'Let's check out down here,' he said, and slipped into one of the alleyways. I went in after him. Ahead of us, the narrow deserted street stretched miserably for a short distance; flanked by the oppressive darkness of the buildings. I looked up. Power cables ran from pole to pole alongside the yellow lamps. They ran to junction-boxes high up on the black walls, where the greasy-looking stone blocks were decaying. I glanced into the empty buildings as we passed by; but saw no lights inside. I wondered what purpose the power-lines served. We moved up the street to a 'T' junction, and turned left. Then, as we rounded the corner, we both stopped dead. Reflexively, I grabbed Nelson's arm, swinging him into the zone of deep shadow which lay between the walls and the street lamps.

'What's that doing there?' I hissed at him. A pick-up truck stood, slewed across the road. It appeared somehow sinister; forbidding. It shone; glossy and inky-blue in the deceptive glow.

'Hey, Man! It's only a pick-up . . .'

'Yeah. But whose? Whose is it?'

'Hey, you see anybody?' he whispered. 'Go on, take a good look. There ain't nobody there . . .'

'Now you understand this, Nelson. We're in here – just the two of us – and we're not armed. Now should anything take a dislike to us, well, that's too bad, because all we've got is our wits, and not much muscle . . . We've got no means of defence. Have we?'

'Hah! Who says?'

'For God's sake!'

'Hey, what're you expecting? Shoot out in Dodge City, or what? The driver of that truck ain't coming back. No sir. You can count on it.'

'How do you know? And keep your voice down!'

'Hah! Don't say you're really starting to *feel* stuff, Man? Don't say you're getting to feel the difference between what's bad news and what ain't? Oh boy! Hah! What'ya say, then? This bad news, or what?'

'Damn right!'

'It's what? What is it? Let me hear you!'

'Bad news! This dump is bad news.'

'Man! This place is a piece of bad dog's ass!'

I stared at the truck. It loomed there, silently. I noticed that it had no licence-plate. Whatever it was doing there, I knew it had to have been driven by someone, sometime. Someone drove it there. Someone skidded it across the street. Someone got out of it, and walked away. Someone. I needed a closer look. I needed to know if that someone was still in there; sitting in wait. Watching us. I let go of my grip on Nelson's arm.

'So what about the Charos?' I heard him say. 'You got any new thoughts about them? Now you're starting to *feel*? Like maybe they ain't such bad news, after all? Seems like Human-kind don't know what anything is, till there's something to compare with.'

As I heard his words, and they sank in, the memory of her face flashed back at me. That warrior's face: cool, steady, beautiful. But behind her beauty lay the discipline and skill of the Annihi-lator. Then I remembered her violet gaze; and the way her eyes had shown something to me. An odd thing in a killer; almost a kind of innocence. In my memory-image, the Woman of the Rose blended with her and became her.

'Yeah.' I said. But I wasn't convinced. I wasn't sure.

He laughed; moved out of the shadows, towards the truck. 'Buick, sixty-nine,' he said as he approached it; 'Nineteen sixty nine. Nice. Broken windshield. No wipers. Hey, now why do you reckon it ain't got wipers? Maybe 'cause it weren't ever meant to have. See there? There ain't no fittings for 'em.'

'Maybe it doesn't rain here.'

'No licence-plate, neither.'

'I noticed.'

'There's a lot of bits and pieces that this truck don't have. It don't have bits where it oughta have. Now, you figure anything strange about that?' He ran a hand over the body work. Its smooth perfection caught the acidic glow of neon. He bent closer to inspect it, and I saw his gnarled face reflected in sepia monochrome.

'So what?' I said. 'An abandoned pick-up, bits missing. So what? It happens all the time. It's been mugged. Kids collect licence plates.'

'Kids? Hah! You forgotten where you are or something? You're

on the Levels, Man! It's a whole new ball-game!' Then he
yanked the driver's side door open. I caught a quick glimpse of
the truck's interior before he slammed it shut again. The noise
shocked the empty streets. There was nothing inside. Nothing
waiting in there for us. No-one. I sighed, relieved.

'Kids didn't strip this,' he said, and patted the door hard. 'Let's
go.'

'Hey, Nelson, wait a . . .' But he was moving away along the
dim street. I caught up with him.

'We could use it . . .' I called out. 'Were the keys in it? If it's
fuelled up, maybe we could use it . . .'

'Keys! Hah! you got one hell of a lot to learn!' was all he said.

'Yeah, well I don't know what you're talking about.' He
stopped, turned, looked at me for a moment. Then, as he carried
on walking, he said: 'I ain't dead certain yet. Soon as I am, you'll
be the first to know.'

'Certain? Certain of what?'

'You feel it, don't you? Sure, your instincts do. But then some
other thing gets a grip on you and you forget your instincts. You
felt that truck; you felt what it was. Then all of a sudden you want
to get in and drive it! I don't get you sometimes. It's like you want
to get in your own way. Now that's how most guys operate. Bird-
men do different.'

'Look, Nelson. You're talking in riddles. All I know is that if
we've got a whole lot of these streets to go through; if we've got
a whole city, damn it! before we even come close to where we're
supposed to be going, then that truck back there could come in
pretty handy!' He didn't seem to be listening. I looked back at the
truck. Nelson was already a few paces ahead of me.

'I don't want to walk,' I shouted after him. 'There's something
hanging over this city, and I don't want to be walking if or when
it decides to drop on us, okay? We could cover a lot of ground in
that pickup. If there's no keys, I'm going to hot-wire it . . .' And
I started back for the Buick.

'Even if it goes, it ain't going far . . .' he called. 'You take a real
good look at it.'

I stopped, my hand on the driver's door handle. The vehicle
gave me an unspeakably bad feeling. I jerked the door open and
got in. There were keys in the ignition. I hesitated; then turned

the key. The engine immediately started up. I couldn't believe my luck.

'Nelson!' I shouted, over the noise of the engine. 'We've got it! We've got action!'

'Sure we have,' he said quietly. He was suddenly right beside me, leaning on the open door. 'Man, why don't you trust your instincts? What do you want this for? Speed? So that you'll feel safe? Well let me tell you that the road to Hell is paved with fallen Speed-Queens. It's about time I let you in on my theory.'

'Your theory?' I shouted.' Like what?'

'Like this is a Raiders' machine.' I felt a sudden chill.

'A what?' I whispered.

'Like this is a Raiders' city. Turn off the engine.' Without arguing, I turned the key. The engine cut out.

'Okay,' he said, and pointed down the neon-lit street. 'See down there? Just past the warehouses?' I looked where he indicated. There, the buildings were different; higher. On the wet-looking walls, I could see reflections of lights of another colour. Red and blue flashing reflections.

'That's a Black ghetto down there. Or it should be. Not a nice place, even if your face is the right colour. Past that is Roosevelt Street, then highway forty-nine. That goes right round the city, turns off north. Those lights you see there are from a kind of night-club. Man, it's a heavy dive! Pushers use it. Sammy's; that's what it's called. Addicts' Palace. I just know this place I know it real well. Yeah. I know it all right, but smell the place! Man, it stinks of Raiders' breath! My theory ain't a theory no more. It's a certainty . . . I know what this place is. It's a transmitter. But what I want to know is why the Charos haven't dealt with it. That question needs an answer.'

Then he looked at me closely. 'You still want to drive this machine?'

'Let's walk,' I replied, and got out.

'I need to go down there, and check out the scene, see if it all fits. You coming? And don't worry. Don't reckon there's a thing gonna drop on us but crumbling masonry. It looks like the whole place is abandoned. Turn around and take a look at the truck.' I heard a metallic cracking sound; and quickly turned round.

Pieces of the body work at the back and sides of the truck were lifting; peeling upwards. I watched them move; watched the edges of the metal panelling curling into contortions like strange fungus. Lumps crumbled off; slowly dropping to the ground. In other places which were untouched by the creeping undulating rot, the paint work was still immaculate.

'See what I mean?' Nelson said. 'It wouldn't get us far, anyhow.'

'What's happening to it?' I whispered, horribly fascinated by what I was seeing.

'It's rotting. But don't let that fool you. That don't mean a thing. It can change shape all it likes but it's still transmitting. Likely we're affecting it.'

'Us? How?'

''Cause we're treading on Raiders' ground. We're making waves.'

We turned away from the truck. As we moved down towards the blue and red lights, another neon lamp fizzled and died above us. At our feet, where its sickly glow had been was now a pool of oily blackness.

'They're going,' I said, looking up. 'One by one. The lights are dying. Maybe you're right, and it is because we're here. Everywhere we go, the lights go out. . . . And when they all go out . . . what then?'

'Then it's gonna get dark.'

We drew nearer to the ghetto. The road narrowed and turned to the left. Grotesque crumbling apartment-blocks rose up, side by side with the dark warehouses. Against the walls of the tenements fire-escape staircases hung precariously. In places they were detached from their moorings and leaned outwards, creaking and swaying. Narrow, unlit alleys cut between the seedy blocks; their entrances marked by sewer-grids. Fire hydrants stood sentinel-like in the deserted streets. Garbage bins, overflowing, poured their contents on to the greasy sidewalks.

At the corner of one of the alleyways, red cursive neon-tube script flashed: SAMMY'S. Blue stars lit up as the name flashed off; disappeared as the name flashed on. Cheap sin-city glitz. One of the stars was dead, and I heard an intermittent crackling hiss. Something was shorting.

'Yeah. This is it,' he said. 'Hey, don't go near the walls, okay? Let's move; check out Roosevelt Street.'

'The truck . . .' I said as we walked. '. . . It's like it was being eaten by acid . . .' I kept seeing the pick-up, erupting with growths; peeling and decaying.

'Truth burns,' he replied; 'You take it seriously now? Do you? You can feel it in the bones of your soul, Man! What they're like. Their creation speaks to you. Their work tells you about them. You hear it? You still reckon the Raiders of Gehina are a lie?'

I didn't answer. I didn't have a chance. Behind us a fire-escape fell with a shrill and deafening crash. I spun round and saw it, only about fifty yards behind us, in the place we had only just been walking. I watched as it bounced once, and broken steel rods were flung outwards. They seemed to fly in slow motion.

'Jesus! Nelson! We've got to get out of here! It's falling down around us!'

'Yeah . . . Roosevelt Street. Okay,' he answered. 'I've got all the proof I need.'

'Did you hear me?'

'I heard you. Sure. There's still one thing I can't figure out . . .' I followed his gaze. The street sign was bolted to one of the neon lamps at the junction. The 'T' of the name was broken. '. . . I can't figure out one thing . . .'

'Nelson! Come on! Let's keep on the move! Let's try and get out of here!'

'It's an experiment. Most likely . . .'

'What is? What do you mean?' But he moved ahead of me into Roosevelt Street; scanning up at the buildings as he went. He was saying something, but under his breath, and I couldn't hear his words. I stood; looked at the walls around me where stones and bricks were moving. Trickles of dust and debris cascaded from twisted window-frames. I was unsure of where to go. But we had to get out, and soon. I turned; searched for him in the gloom, then saw his figure a short distance away, passing beneath neon-tube advertising lights. Elsa's bar. Girls, live show. Jamaican food. Marlborough. I sensed a movement, behind me. Not stones, not bricks; but the rustling of feet in garbage and broken glass.

'Hey, Man . . .' A whisper, broken and cracked-throat; a female sound.

'Nelson . . .?'

'Here . . .' I spun round quickly; caught the whites of her eyes in the light. Her grey green form slipped out of the dark of the alleyway. Teeth glistened as her tongue flicked over her lips.

'Hey, mister Charlie . . .' Her back slid against the wall as she edged nearer. And the neon played highlights over her damp black skin.

'Candy Man's on time. Knew you was comin'.' A dustfall touched her back-combed white hair; flowed in a dry streak down her face. She didn't brush it away. Her hands stayed on the wall behind her. Her eyes kept mine .

'Ain't got cold cash, but the little crystals you got for me are makin' me hungry. You owe me from the last time . . .' Her hand streaked out; locked round my arm. I twisted; tried to pull out of her grip. But it was strong; manic. I tried to turn, to catch sight of Nelson.

'We cut a deal, Mister Connection.'

'What the hell?'

But her dry voice whispered back: 'I ain't goin' down on you white trash no more for promises! Promises keep you sweatin'. Sweatin's not where I'm at!'

'Nelson!' I called out, trying to wrench myself out of her grip. More debris fell from somewhere to the right of me.

'Mister Charlie, you got somethin' that I want. Somethin' that I paid for.' Her eyes came close to mine. They were whited-out, reflecting neon.

'You deal the Crack, white trash, or the next time when I'm suckin' you get to feel some teeth, right when it's gettin' sweet . . .'

'God-in-Heaven . . .!' I pulled with all my strength; broke away from her grasp, But her teeth sank into my hand as I tried to back off. I saw a small, light-reflecting blade in her fingers. I ripped my hand out of her bite.

'We cut a deal!'

'No! No way! It's not me! You've got the wrong guy!'

'I never get it wrong, Candy Man.' I flashed a glance at the blade. Then she was aiming a low slash, and I threw myself past her; collided with the wall. Above me, glass shattered. It fell, sprinkling the black street with fragments. She twisted side-ways; stepping towards me.

'Man! Don't argue with her!' Nelson's hand gripped my shoul-der; pulled. The woman lunged at us.

'Just get moving! Now!' he screamed. I stumbled – felt her hand clawing at my leg. Then I was up, and we were running, between the flashing, hissing lights, down to the intersection.

'There was no-one here!' I shouted; 'No-one! You said there was no-one!'

'Yeah! Well there was! Just move!' We rounded the corner, and I slowed; almost stopped running. Facing us, on an opposite wall a tattered black-and-white poster hung. The face of a Vietnam-ese woman smiled out. Her eyes seemed to look straight at me. Doves flew around her; settling on her outstretched arms. *The war is over!* The poster said. *A celebration. Sheep Meadow. Central Park. 12.30. p.m. May 11, 1975.* I felt his hand, hard on my back, pushing me on.

'It was a good hunting-ground for them, then!' he shouted to me as we ran. 'The war is over! Huh! I don't reckon so!'

21: *Destiny Dreams*

AT THE NEXT intersection we stopped running. There was no sign of the woman.

'What the hell is she?' I gasped. 'One of them . . . has to be . . .'

'Like I was telling you,' he replied. 'That's a transmitter.'

'How long do you think we've got?' I asked him. He was staring down towards highway forty-nine into a far distance. His eyes were narrowed and tightened with concentration.

'They don't know it's here . . .' was his answer. '. . . The Charos. And they haven't been able to touch it . . . Oh, Man!' His voice was almost a whisper: 'Maybe they don't know it's even here . . .'

'Nelson! How long? Before it caves in, with us in it?'

'Not long,' he replied, suddenly re-focusing on me.

'Well, don't you think we'd better get ourselves out of here? Look, what's bothering you about the Charos? The city's destroying itself anyway, without them! It's falling down, for God's sake! The only thing that matters is we get the hell out! Nelson, come on! Let's go!'

I grabbed his arm and pulled him. He seemed to be in a dream. 'Let's move out! We could at least try going back the way we came! The tunnel, the entrance to the Lightfall cavern! It's got to still be there somewhere! We're going to have to try and find it and take a chance on that Warp a second time! Anything's better than getting deeper into this place!'

'In Old World there's a bit of city like this . . .' he said. 'It's like this in every detail. Only back there are people; people living, or trying to live. Driving about, sleeping, arguing, fighting, eating, bringing up ghetto kids, working in strip-joints, mainlining . . .'

I turned to look at him. His eyes were misted with tears. 'And they don't know this is here, either.'

'Yeah, I know,' I said to him. 'Okay. Well let's get out! Let's leave this hell-hole to rot! Let's go!'

'Hey, you don't get it. Can't expect you to, I reckon. The Levels are created of a kind of stuff that takes imprints. Like a fluid, flexible kind of light. Best way I can put it. Where the Raiders build, they build a pattern of real darkness, real hopelessness. What they build is marked by them; tainted by them. Okay, if they don't reinforce the pattern, it rots and changes shape. But the pattern ain't destroyed. Oh no. It stays. Its potential stays, like a seed under the ground in winter. The Matrix-data needs to be destroyed. Unless that happens, it ain't disintegrated; not properly. And only the Charos can do that.'

'Well the Charos aren't here! We are! And there's not a damn thing we can do about it! I want to get out of this city, Nelson! Right now!'

'Man, this is a big one. It's one hell of a bad headache . . .'

As he was speaking, I heard a loud staccato crack, like gunshot, from above us. Quickly, I looked up, to see the wall of one of the buildings begin to split apart.

'Nelson! That was the apartment block! . . . It's . . .' Mesmerised, I watched as a jagged crack began to snake its way slowly down the wall of the tenement. Silently, it crept downwards. And not a stone fell. Not one brick shifted out of place. He looked at it.

'It's going to fall on us . . .' I whispered in disbelief. 'It's going to come . . . right down on . . .'

He grabbed me and pushed. I stumbled under the sudden onslaught of his surprising strength. The force running through him shocked me.

'Move ass!' I heard; and I fell headlong. Then I was half-turning; looking back, horrified as the building split in half. As the wall opened up, black unlit sky showed between the two halves. There was nothing inside it. No tumbling furniture, no water leaks, no sparking of ruptured power cables, no scrambling bodies. Only emptiness and black sky. Grey walls, dark windows were coming closer; reaching out for me. I felt Nelson lunge at me again. He seemed to lift me off the ground and propel me forward. His assault was brutal, fast, efficient.

'We can't . . .' I heard myself say, '. . . be crushed! Can we . . .? Dead men can't die . . . dead men can't . . .' In time-less stroboscopic flashes I heard the grind of iron on stone; saw the whiteness of his teeth as they grimaced with effort. I saw steel-hard determination in his eyes. A braid of hair whipped across my cheek. It stung. If it stings, I thought, we can be crushed. But I was already sure of that. I already knew we could be.

A deep darkness fell; and in it, a groping downwards, hand over hand. I was slipping; clinging to a metal-runged ladder. From nearby, Nelson's voice rang metallically.

'Sons of bitches! The war ain't over you shitheads! It ain't over, oh no sir! It ain't goddamn over!' Debris rained down; small stones. A heavy object hit my shoulder, and I tasted dust. I felt the wound of the blow as a sudden ignition of anger.

I'd wanted her. I'd chosen to follow her. And this was where she'd led me. The Woman of the Rose. Her mystery and her miracle of a flower in Hell had brought me down pathways of constant struggle. Her blue flame had led me from one Hell into another, and another. And he with me. I couldn't understand why. But I knew she was a death-bringer. And I felt fear; of that death which kills a dead man. I had touched her, and now she was gone; almost as though she had never been. The power of knowing her seemed to have been worn thin by conflict and experience; the field of action. The field had snatched her miracle away; and left me with only one part of her. The death-bringer. I felt afraid; rejected by the best thing I'd ever known. Disappointed with the scent of the Rose. And I felt weary and sick at heart.

'Sorry about this,' I heard him say; 'but we ain't got no choice right now. Know how you feel about rat-holes, and being underground and all, but it's a whole lot better than hanging out up there.'

The air was darkened and still thick with dust. I could make out the iron-brown rungs of the ladder; could see where they were bolted to brickwork. I could see little else.

'Where are we . . .?' I managed to whisper, gritting my teeth against the swell of painful emotion.

'Sewers,' he replied. 'Part of the scenery, on account of how a city ain't a city without 'em. But we're right in luck, 'cause if you notice that there ain't no stink, that's 'cause there ain't no stink. And boy! am I glad about that! I got a sensitive nature.'

'The whole thing fell, Nelson . . .! Did you see that? It cracked wide open, and just came down, so slow! Christ! so slow, then so damn fast . . . and there wasn't a damn thing inside it! . . . Empty . . .'

'Yeah. But it ain't the empty building that gets you. It's the goddamn empty feeling.'

'It's up there . . . over the hole. Tons of it . . .'

'And we're down here.'

'Oh shit, Nelson. Oh God! If this place caves in too . . .'

'Don't reckon it will. Not so quick.'

'Just how do you know that?'

'Okay, come on then. Keep on the move. I can't believe you! You're a mass of phobias! If it ain't being in the sky, it's being down a hole! If it ain't that, it's climbing down a rock! If it ain't one thing, it's another! Hey! I'm down here too, you know! And you hear me squealing like a pup? You sure don't, 'cause I'm saving my breath!'

I heard him drop down from the ladder; heard his feet ring as they landed on stonework beneath. It was a very earthly sound. I looked down and saw him through a twilight which seemed less dark as my vision adjusted to it. He was stretching up, holding out a hand to me. He was grinning.

'We can move faster down here,' he said.

'To where?' The hand was still there. Something in me held back as I was automatically about to grasp it. Then I reached down; leaned my hand firmly on his, and jumped. The distance was short; only the height of a man. But as I left the last rung of the ladder, and before my feet touched ground, I found myself in the body of a young child. Above me rose the forest. Redwood giants soared up into an opal morning sky. And the Grandfather's brown, long-nailed fingers pointed at an eagle, balanced on an air-current high above the trees.

'The Quest,' the Grandfather said. 'The Quest for Vision.' And in a second, his forefinger sliced downwards through the air, aiming at the foot of a Redwood. There, I saw a small green snake slowly uncurling. I glanced quickly at the Grandfather. His body had changed shape; to lichen covered stone. I was shocked; terrified by what I saw. I felt my guts melt and churn, because I knew he wasn't there any more. He'd left me alone in the forest. Then my sight was torn from his statue, to the eagle. It was dropping as fast as the wind through the branches of the Redwood above me. I lunged forward; grasped the snake. And the eagle swooped. Talons caught my hair, and tore. I felt warm moisture in my eyes. My sight blurred and reddened. The beat of the great bird's wings blew a wind against my face as it rose again.

'Now you are crowned with the eagle's hunger and his need,' the Grandfather said. 'But now he knows your power. Yours is the power of the snake. She will lend strength to you in worlds of the great forests, for you have washed her life with yours.' I turned; and through a blood-red haze I saw that the Grandfather smiled. And I saw his living body under the Redwood trees; flesh now, not stone. And the lichens no longer covered him. The green snake writhed in my hand.

'. . . No! Nooo! . . .' The child's terrified voice swept through spaces between the giant trees, and resonated from their ancient solidity. I looked down. The Grandfather's hand was in mine.

Behind his face, an underground shaft stretched back. The sewer. The crumbling city of replicas. Nelson's face. I returned; and snatched my hand out of his. The after-shock of my cry still lingered in the suffocating atmosphere of the tunnel.

He smiled; and in the half-light I saw the flash of his teeth.

'What the . . . hell . . .?' I whispered.

'You seen one of the Quests, Man.'

'It was you! The Grandfather . . . you!'

'Maybe. But that don't really matter. What matters is your Quest. Your Quest, like it or not.'

'What . . .? What does it mean . . .?'

'Got to use your vision. Can't do your seeing for you. Remember?'

'But you know it. You were there. It was like . . . the past: something happened in the past . . . and you were there. You knew what it was, then . . .'

'Past! Horseshit! It is, was, and ever shall be! It ain't round – and it ain't straight – you recall? You challenge the powers, for the purpose of a greater power. You always wanted that! You always tried to do it! But now, maybe it's coming to you tuned-in!'

'I don't understand.'

'Let's move.' He moved on into the twilight; leaving me a few paces behind. There was no way I was going to be able to get him to talk about it any more. He made that obvious.

'Our best shot would be to keep going,' he said. I took his cue. Underground again was bad enough; but there was a distinct danger that the whole place might start to cave in on us at any moment, and I didn't want to hang around. The sewer-tunnel was almost perfectly cylindrical; its curvature broken on each side by narrow concrete walkways. Single-file, we moved along it. The central section was dry. And Nelson was right. There was no stink. No people, no shit, I thought.

'Where are we heading? Have you got any idea?'

'North,' he replied; then added: 'they did a good job here. Everything just like it should be. They built the whole place like a fair old team of city planners, huh? They didn't miss a detail.'

As we moved along the main shaft we passed tributary

pipelines; storm-drain outlets high up on the curving walls. In the dimness I could see that they were dry. I was fascinated. Then a sudden chilling sensation filled me. I knew them. I knew what they were like. The architects of this replica-city would stop at nothing. And this tiny portion of their creation was hardly anything. It was a small fragment of what they were; and had been abandoned, cast off, thrown on the junk-heap. It was no longer required; old-hat. And even that would have been big enough to destroy us; to bury us under tons of decay.

The Raiders of Gehina had moved on, to bigger and better things. But the ghost of their perfect work choked me with a sense of dread. Now I could feel them. I knew what they were like. I felt overwhelmed, insignificant, And afraid.

'Why north?' I managed to ask; though I felt almost too choked to speak. He gave me a long look as he turned round to me.

'You know them through their creations. It's the only way to know them,' he said. 'North, 'cause that's the quickest way out.'

'And you happen to know what north is, down here?'

'Sure do. It's along this main pipeline. No left, no right. Keep to the big one. Soon as we get to the end of this, that'll be it. No more city. They won't have sprawled it out, you know, put all the out-of-town highways in, the gas stations, the Burger Kings. They'll have kept their edges sharp. What's necessary; that's all. They'll have built tight.'

'So what's on the other side of it?'

'Dunno. Room to move, I'm hoping, without getting hit by bricks.'

'Okay, Nelson. Let's go.' And I pushed ahead, moving as quickly as I could along the narrow walkway. We pressed on and didn't talk. And a great quietness fell; devoid even of the sound of our footsteps. The atmosphere clung about us in a brooding, unnatural silence; in which all I heard was my thoughts. *They're real. The Raiders are real, and they're bad news. And they're growing somewhere. Invisible; except through their creations. Seeds of Being from another Universe; another frame.* And they wanted us. They desired us; regardless of what shape, what sex, what colour, what level of intelligence. On every level they wanted us. They were hungry for the creatures of the

Worlds; every last one, indiscriminately. For what? What made us so desirable? And Truth was our only immunity. What Truth? I couldn't grasp the nature of that Truth which was the anti-venom.

We passed a cross-junction, where a large pipeline running east-west intersected ours. It gaped; empty and black. And I passed it by. I kept on moving; leading on in the silence. What was at the end of this? Christ Jesus I'd had enough of pathways and passageways. Nelson's hand fell hard on my shoulder, and his voice shocked me.

'Hold it!' I stopped dead.

'Take a look up ahead,' he said.

I looked where he pointed. At a spot about thirty feet along the tunnel, the air shimmered. Beyond that haze, there seemed to be nothing. The pipeline disappeared.

'Now, you feel anything?' he whispered. It was becoming familiar. A subtle change; a side-slipping of the mind, hardly noticeable at first, so that it could almost be missed. Until the Time-fields took you – up and away.

'Yeah. I feel something,' I replied. 'It's up . . . there! Another one. Another Warp. I know.'

'Oh boy,' he said quietly; drawing up alongside me. There was barely room enough for the two of us, side by side. 'You're riding, Man! You're really riding!'

I spun away from him and pounded my fist hard into the curve of the wall; then rested my head on my fist. The sound of the blow rang through the tunnel.

'Something biting your ass?' Nelson hissed in my ear.

'Yeah!' I lifted my head to shout at him; 'There is! Stuff! that's what! Warps and sheer drops! Rat-holes! Raiders . . . damn bastards! Running, moving on, going through fire and goddamn water! Stuff! Always stuff, non-stop! That's what's biting my ass, since you ask!'

'And you've changed your mind, huh? About what you got?' he whispered, his face close to mine. 'It ain't good enough for you? You want a ticket for a flight out? Okay. Go play wild with that Warp. Go on. Go ahead, boy. Fast exit. Terminal space-out!'

I didn't answer. I had no answer.

'Choice is . . .' he said, 'we ride it or we go back. Or we go sideways. And as you know, sideways means deeper into the city. Anyhow, in which case we'd be going sideways every time a bitch crossed our path. That ain't a Bird-Man's way.'

'Okay! What the hell do you keep going on about that Bird-Man thing for, Nelson? Who is this Bird-Man guy? Some working-class hero? Or a perfect God-Man? Well, it's not me! I'm not that, Nelson! Not any kind of hero! Dream on, old man. I'm not your Bird-Man!'

'No. He ain't no hero. He just does what he has to; when he has to. Without squealing. He does it. He don't cringe like a dog that's just pissed on the carpet! He sees rocks on the road, he climbs over 'em! He flies! He sees a job needs doing, he does it! That's all"

'You know what you sound like?' I answered, turning so that our faces were only inches apart.' You sound like a kitsch ad. for Mr. Super Cleen! You know! Dissolves lime scale! Knocks those germs dead!'

Then Nelson laughed. He exploded. He kept laughing and nearly pulled us both off the ledge. He always managed to do something noisy in tunnels and confined spaces. But before I had a chance to worry about the echoes, I was laughing, too. And the noise was intolerable. When we'd laughed enough, we looked at the Warp.

'We've done it before . . .' I said to him. 'Haven't we? Okay. Why not another one?'

'There's always a risk,' he replied. 'Don't imagine there ain't.'

'They look so . . . unfriendly.'

'Yeah,' he answered.

We rode it. And came through into a whole new world; a lakeside landscape with stars in a night sky. They twinkled, reflected in the dark of the water. Small waves lapped on shingle. There was no more city. We'd broken out; crossed the boundary. Then we hit another one; another Warp. It seemed to roll in towards us, over the calm water.

22: *The Edge of Gehina*

I MADE IT through first. There was no sign of Nelson.

I was quite alone in a shallow trench of soft sandstone. Warps, it seemed, spat you out wherever they had a whim to. It was a lucky dip of landscapes; or so it appeared. Or the Outer Reaches. I listened; and heard a faint, rhythmic drumming which vibrated through the ground. The sounds built up; growing stronger with each moment. I got the impression that whatever caused it was drawing nearer.

I eased myself up to a better position to see over the lip of the trench. And as I did so, I remembered something. The life-expectancy of a First Lieutenant in the Trenches of the First World War. It wasn't long; twenty four hours? Or two days? I couldn't recall the detail. But it was bad. He was first out; first over the top. First to the shells and bayonets. Leader of men was something I didn't want to know.

I saw a wide golden-amber plain; fringed in the far distance by angular blue mountains. It appeared to be the Plain of Xentha; but I couldn't be sure. In the middle distance, crossing the plain, was a lengthening cloud of yellow dust. I watched as the cloud-streak angled across the wide ground and turned, moving in a great arc.

Gradually it approached me, and I tried to identify the drumming sound. Then one long drawn-out horn-blast carried across the plain. And I knew, by the sound of that note, what moved in the cloud. Shapes emerged from the dust-flurries, and glints of gold and steel. I heard the metallic bell-like ring of fine chains; and saw pale horses loom out of the clouded air. Riders of the Blue Sun. They passed me by as if I were invisible to them; and they rode close enough for me to be swayed by the wind of their passing. As their horses' hooves pounded the ground, I saw the gold gleam of breastplates and the flash of arm-guards. The heads and necks of their mounts were covered with a silvery liquid substance; a fine gauze, which shone like sunlight on water. And from eye-holes in their head-shields, light from the eyes of the beasts rayed out. I stumbled and rolled to the floor of the trench; covering my head with my arms as the dust of the plain swirled around me.

'They're riding out,' I heard. 'Already.' I turned my head, and saw Nelson through the sandy air. He stood in the trench next to me.

'It's begun,' he said. The riders moved away. The dust settled.

'You got through,' I whispered. My voice was lost.

'Oh Man! Goddammit, Man . . .!' He crossed to the lip of the trench, and stared out across the plain.

'I've figured it out.' He looked distraught.

'What, Nelson? What?'

'The Raiders' edge. Knew they had to have one, and they've got one. Sons of bitches! They're hiding; holing up. They're going to ground. And I know their style. They'll just leave enough of them and their creations on show; let the Charos mow them down, let them think the balance is struck. And all the while they're hiding; where the Charos can't get. Where they can't even see!'

'What do you mean?'

'The Warps. That's what I mean. Didn't see it at first, and I'm an old campaigner. Oh boy, the Warps. That's why the city's there. That's what the experiment is. And they saw that it worked, and worked real well. And they moved on to bigger things.' He shook his head. He was covered from head to foot with the fine dust of the plain.

'The Warps? What do you mean about the Warps?' I got up; stumbled across loose fragments of sandstone towards him. He turned and met me with his pale blue gaze.

'Three of them,' he said. 'A Warp intersection. An intersection! With the city in the middle. You getting the picture? The Charos would've got to that, if they could . . .'

'But they can't, can they?' I interrupted him.

'You're getting it.'

'They can't get in? They can't operate inside those Warps?.'

'That's right. But that ain't all. Maybe they don't even know about it!'

'So it's a dead-zone for them; areas inside Warp-complexes like the one round the city. Is that what you're saying? The Charos don't even know they exist?'

'Maybe, he replied. 'Looks like it. I didn't think they'd grown like that; got themselves dug in like that. No wonder. No wonder things are getting so damned bad.'

'Hey, but just wait a minute, Nelson. You're telling me that the Charos can't handle Warps? With all their intelligence and experience they can't handle what *we* can cope with? Surely, if you and I can ride Warps out okay, then they could? That sounds too weird.'

He just stared at me. He didn't say a word. After a while, he spoke. 'You really didn't like their style, did you? You thought there was some kind of conspiracy. Like something was going to do you wrong. Ain't that so? 'Cause they were like nothing you'd known before; alien? You even thought that about me. Maybe you still do, huh?' I shrugged.

Till you felt the city . . .' he went on. '. . . Till you felt what the dark's like. Real alien. Real bad news.'

Just a minute, I . . .'

'And I'll tell you another thing, shall I? I ain't got a clue why it is that you and I ride on those Warps like they were some ten-cent fairground ride! Not a damned clue! All I know for sure is, we can, that's all. Compared with the Charos, you're a low-down dog. And I ain't no better. Hound-dogs. That's us. They're so far ahead of Humankind, if you want to look at things that way, I guess about fifty thousand years.'

'And they still go to war.'

He laughed; but his laughter had a strange note to it. He began to brush the dust off himself. 'And they still go to war, yeah,' he said. 'We've got to let them know. That was the first spearhead, those riders. There'll be more. And they're at a loss.'

Knowledge of the enemy . . .' I said.

'It comes in handy.'

'Call them out.'

'Huh?'

'The Charos. Call them out,' I said again. 'Strike the right frequency, and they'll come.'

'You do that and you get destroyed. Right now you would. You start playing on that waveband, and you won't get no questions asked. You get mashed up. We've got to get back to Xentha; back to the encampment, and go through the I.D.'

'So we've got to change course?' He nodded.

'. . . Can't be far . . .' I said quietly; and scanned the plain, searching for signs of the crystalline structures. But I couldn't see them. There was no spire; no distant flash of reflected starlight. I looked up at the sky. It was ultramarine; starless; different. Once more I scanned across the plain; trying to analyse what the difference was. But it evaded me.

'But surely this is . . . isn't this the Plain?' He was studying me. I turned to catch the cool focus of his eyes on me.

'Yeah. But no. It's an outer sheath. A level of the Plain; but not the same as the level where the encampment is.'

'I don't get it.'

'That's 'cause you like to think in weights and measures, Distance ain't necessarily straight lines on the Levels. It's most often spirals. One ring set inside another, with connections.' His words confused me, and had a dizzying effect.

'To get to the encampment we got to climb; in the spiral,' he went on.

'We've got to change course, right? We were aiming to get those maps, Nelson, or whatever you want to call them. Now we've got to go back to the encampment. Oh great.'

'You'd most likely argue with me, but something about the Charos, and the encampment fazes you. Ain't that the truth? It does something to you; freaks you out. Now why, do you reckon? This ain't the eve of war. This is the bugle-call; and the safest place for sure is the encampment of Xentha. But you were pretty damn well souped-up there; paranoid as hell. And you don't want to go back.' I had no inclination to answer him.

'Sounds like you're caught between the devil and the deep blue sea, don't it? Hah! Know which I'd choose! But I ain't you!' He hauled himself out of the trench in one fast, graceful movement. He stood, above me.

'What do you figure on doing?' he asked. I thought about the city, and the Warps. And then I thought about the Charos warrior; her violet eyes and the nameless strangeness of her. And of how she'd been, only for a moment, but in reality, the same as the Woman of the Rose.

'Okay,' I answered. 'Forget the maps. We'll go back to Xentha. Only . . .'

'What?' Nelson asked.

'I'm not staying,' I said.

We moved across the plain, heading in the direction of the distant mountains. It was the quickest way, Nelson said, to climb up through the spiral, and reach the inner ring of Xentha. As we walked, I noticed fissures in the otherwise flat rock of the plain; almost exactly as there had been on our outward journey. Many were as deep, or less deep, than the trench we had found ourselves in. But as we progressed, I realized that they were gradually deepening. Then it became impossible to keep to a straight course. We were forced to detour round them, when they became too wide or too deep to leap across or climb through. We kept the range of mountains as our target, but we often had to weave our way so far to the left or the right, that I began to feel that we would never reach them. Often, when there was no hope of crossing a fissure, we had no alternative but to follow it along its length and move far off our intended route; eventually finding that the fissure would peter out into a gap shallow enough to cross.

We travelled on such a twisted, erratic course, that I began to feel a gnawing frustration, and weariness. Our conversation dwindled almost to nothing as we negotiated our way; and I sensed that Nelson, though he didn't display any outward sign of frustration, was filled with tension, and as ready to get to the still-hazy blue mountains as I was. We seemed to have been walking for ever, and our goal looked just as far away from us, when I suddenly looked back, imagining that I could gauge the distance we had travelled. On the far horizon, behind us, I caught sight of a dust-flurry. It moved across; slowly elongating. I heard no sound. I watched; and Nelson turned round.

'Another wave,' he said. 'Knew there would be.'

'Charos?' I asked. He nodded and turned back to our course, moving ahead of me. Now they were real. The forces of the Charos and the forces of the Raiders; meeting in an age-old struggle that I couldn't fully grasp. A struggle to keep a balance; a terrible ecology. They were weaving the threads of the Worlds into patterns of dark and light. But now they weren't characters in a movie that I didn't even want a part in. They weren't colourful words in some Doctrine of the Apocalypse; or pictures painted by a schizophrenic. They were real; and they were now. They were riding. I looked up, and realized that we were drawing closer to the mountains. Their sharp grey-blueness was beginning to blot out the sky. Then Nelson turned to me and said;

'Why'd you do it? Huh?' Immediately I knew what he meant.

'Do what?' I said quickly. He stopped. Behind him there was one more crack in the surface of the plain. One more detour.

'What you did,' he answered. 'Must've been a reason.'

'Okay. I don't have to explain myself. Not to you. Not to anyone!'

'They were gonna shoot you? Is that it?' I fell silent. A quick, defensive anger sprang up in me.

'Don't you know?' I answered sarcastically; 'You know most things!'

'I do. Oh yeah. But do you?'

'Okay! I did it because that's what I wanted to do! Got that? That was exactly what I most needed to do! What the hell are you making out to be? Some State Pen. social worker?'

'He had two kids; one of 'em did. And a sweet woman no more'n twenty-one. And a little spotted dog.'

'It's done!' I screamed at him. 'It's damn well done! And there's not one thing I can do to undo it!

Right? Guilt? Is that what you're talking about? Is that what you're after? I've been there, Nelson! I've done that one!'

'That was just one of 'em. What about the other two?'

'You want to try and make me feel guilty? Here? Now? All you can think about is how to make me feel guilty?' The blue rock across the gap ahead rang with the sound of my voice.

'They go out, Nelson! Just like me! They go out; you said that yourself! Shut up! For Christ's sake, shut up! What are you digging it all up for, now?'

'Okay,' he said, and turned back to our course. We followed the fissure, and climbed through it in a heavy silence. I felt shattered and afraid; though about what I wasn't clear. On the other side of the gap the mountains met us; sweeping up straight off the plain, with no foothills, no interim stage between the extremes of flatness and steepness. They cast no shadow on to the sandstone where we stood. Yet they seemed, themselves, to be in shadow. Only a short walk away, the first sheer sweep of rock loomed in front of us. I scanned it for signs of a way up, for any cracks, lumps, or footholds. But the smooth rock-face seemed devoid of them. We climb up, he had said, through the spiral. I needed to know the next move, but I didn't want to speak to him.

He moved past me to the foot of the slate-blue rock. Then sat, cross-legged, and stared back at me. At that moment, at the edge of vision, I caught sight of a movement; and instantly I spun round to my right. In the middle distance a lone figure was walking towards us, keeping parallel with the mountain range. The figure moved slowly, as if out for a stroll. But its silhouette against the sky kept on coming; still too far away for me to be able to make out if it were male or female. But I felt something within me crawl. It drew closer, oddly concealed by a light which seemed to shine out of it. And I saw by the way it moved that it was a man. Nelson turned to face the stranger; but he didn't speak and didn't get up. Instead, he looked across at me.

Then the details came into focus. White male; approximately five-ten. Yellow hair. Too skinny. Sleeves rolled up. Mirror-lens shades. No cap. Of course not. The cap had rolled into the dust at the edge of the road as he'd come down. I remembered now. The whole scene flashed back. He was wearing the uniform of the Mississippi State Highway Patrol. I felt myself back away.

'He was just a traffic-cop!' I heard Nelson say. 'Wasn't he? Hey, Hard-Man! He wasn't the Mob! He wasn't the C.I.A.! He was just a traffic-cop!'

I was moving back; between the slab of rock and the fissure. But there was nowhere to go. Weismann. Allan Weismann. How could I ever forget that name? I wore three names around my neck. Weismann was one of them. My mind locked, as if it had been clamped in a steel trap. In desperation, I glanced at Nelson. But he still sat cross-legged, his back against the blue-rock face; staring at me intensely. And my voice was trapped. I could make no sound. Weismann kept coming; walking slowly. He passed Nelson; not appearing to see him. His mirrored eyes were set on me. In the glass of his shades, I saw reflections of the mountains. He opened his mouth. A voice came out; cracked and metallic, and out of synchronisation with the movement of his lips.

'How're you doing?' he said. 'Long walk it's been. One hell of a long walk. Unfamiliar places, y'know? It's cold out there. Cold in the desert.' Three or four feet in front of me, he halted. I caught glimpses of myself in the convex lenses; glimpses of a rabbit caught in the headlamp beams. Roadkill. Under his masked gaze that's all I was. Roadkill; like he had been. The shades were hypnotic. Fascinating. I tore my sight away from them; in a reflex, checked to see if he was armed. He wasn't. His holster was empty and hung loosely on his belt. I'd given him two shots. A lung shot, low on the left. And a head shot. His left temple had been blown to a pulp of blood and bone. But there wasn't a mark on him. Not any more.

'Weismann,' I managed to whisper. That was all I could say. His mouth opened again. A fragment of time later, words followed; tinny, hollow-sounding words.

'Mind if I tag along?'

'You hear that?' I heard Nelson say. 'Voice ain't right. No way.'

What he said came across empty space. I didn't know who was speaking to me. I didn't know Nelson existed. I was back at the junction where the patrol car had pulled me in. And I saw the cop reach for his gun. He'd just turned half away from me; radioed something. Then he was turning back, and he was reaching for his gun! It caught the late afternoon sun; flashed blue-grey. Gunmetal grey. No! It wasn't a gun! But it was too late because I was moving, moving fast. *And it was a gun. It was . . .* One shot would have been murder. Two made it murder One. Then there were Deane and Butterfield. Murder One; three counts.

'Take a look at his eyes . . .' Nelson said. 'His eyes! That voice ain't right!'

It was hard to recognise the sounds Nelson made; but slowly they became familiar. I began to return, as an underwater air-bubble moves to the surface.

'The . . . eyes . . .' I whispered. 'Shades . . . can't see.' Then Nelson was standing beside me.

'Take them off.' He said.

'. . . Take them . . . off Weismann's face?'

'He ain't right, Man.'

'. . . Ghost . . .'

'Ain't so. Take a look at the eyes!'

I heard a howling, coming in from a distance. Drawing nearer; rising, falling. And a wind tore in across the plain. It bore down, moaning; lifting dust in wild swirls around the three of us. In its sudden violence I swayed, trying to turn my head out of the gritty gale, but needing to hold Weismann's masked stare. Unflinching, he still faced me, as the sandstorm darkened the air and the wind battered us. Minute sparkling lights danced in the dust-flurries and rushed past, whirling on the air-currents. Instinctively, I lifted my arm to protect my face; and the power of the gale forced me at last to half-turn. As I did so, for a brief moment I caught a glimpse of Nelson. He stood, straight and still as the dust-devils blew around him; obscuring and revealing his shape. He faced across the plain into the storm. The skin of his face was stretched tight by the wind's force and his braided hair blew behind him.

Then, with an icy strength and the speed of a cobra's strike, Weismann's hand clamped my raised arm. Coldness ran through me – coldness like I'd never known. I spun back, half into the storm. Feeling my strength slowly ebbing, I set my eyes on him.

'We're going back,' he said. 'Back awhile. Okay? Time travelling, you and I. You're mine.'

The storm's volume increased. Somewhere on it I heard: *You ain't going nowhere, Man. Not Yet.*

But I couldn't shift Weismann's grip; and in the mirrors on his face I saw a pixie-faced girl-woman with short cropped blonde hair. She was smiling. She was holding a baby. Someone was taking a photograph. Between Weismann and me, tiny starbursts danced. And the woman was gone.

Instantly I twisted my arm, hard. *Take a look at the eyes.* I tore at the shades on his face; tore them off. The eyes were there. But they weren't Weismann's. They weren't even the eyes of a dead man. They weren't human. They were filmed over with blackness; a dreadful, bottomless blackness. Something glowed in the dark just beneath the surface; a living, craving thing. But it wasn't Weismann.

Horrified I moved backwards, keeping my sight locked on the

thing in front of me. Its mouth moved again, as if to speak. But
a creaking hollow sound issued from its lips; a sound that I
couldn't recognize as speech. Then the air lit up, dazzlingly
bright. In the whiteness I saw Weismann's skeleton through the
uniform he wore – through his body. I was flung back against the
rocks. And in front of me a pale horse reared up through the
searing light. The plain melted into quicksilver and flowed;
concentrating into a whirlpool which sucked Weismann into it.
A tongue of fire in the centre of the whirling mass obliterated
him. At my feet, the ground began to crack, buckling upwards
into grotesque shapes. Then it froze. And the wind died. The
blinding flare faded. And seated on the pearl-grey mount was
the rider. And I knew her as the warrior of the Charos. And as
the Woman of the Rose.

23: Thainé

SHE GENTLY PULLED the bridle of her horse, and turned
towards us. Then she moved slowly across the racked and twisted
surface of the plain. As she approached, a faint breeze lifted her
hair, blowing it out like a crimson veil behind her. On her brow
the golden band glowed with a pale luminescence. I noticed that
she wore a sharply-faceted, colourless jewel at the base of her
neck, and that it, too, glowed dimly. But as I watched it, its
emanations faded and the jewel became inert. She stopped, only
a short distance in front of Nelson and me, and without speaking, watched us. Nelson moved forward; formed the signs. And
she dismounted, answering his salute with hers. Then, leading
her horse by the silver threads of its bridle, she came towards me.
Unable to move, I stood against the slab of blue rock, as her eyes
sought mine. I was still shocked by the encounter with Weismann,
and by what I had seen happen to him. I felt depleted and weak.
His grasping hand on my arm had drawn out some vital thing
from me.

'The outer Rings of the Plain are treacherous, now,' she said. 'As is the way with places of fortification. They have their interfaces.'

She watched me for a moment, carefully. Then she spoke again. 'Are you travelling to Inner Xentha?' I couldn't give her an answer. It seemed that a part of me had split off, and hadn't yet returned. Nelson answered.

'That's where we're heading.'

She left her horse. It stood patiently, head up, and the light breeze caught its war-mantle, casting the silver gauze-like substance with a mercurial lustre. Then she drew close to me, and without hesitation laid her hands on my shoulders. I saw her straightened gold-clad forearms elongate; stretching away into an impossible distance. Her figure, marvellous and strongly-built, drifted in front of my sight like a fever-dream; far away and unreal. But in a moment, energy returned to me. And the parts of me which had seemed separate, flooded together and were bonded. I saw her again, across the arm's length distance between us; and felt the sudden impact of her reality as a jolt which wakened me. Then she took her hands away; stepped back.

'As Xentha is your destination,' she said, slowly drawing her gaze away from mine, 'I will take you in through the Rings.' A heightened sensation of energy came to me; and with it came a strength, and clarity of thought. Something in her brief contact had moved from her, into me.

'Okay,' I heard Nelson say; 'That's fine. Lady, we're all yours! What d'you say, Man? You ready to hit the trail?' I nodded as I watched her cross to her horse and gather the delicate reins in her semi-gloved hand.

'In the mountain there is a track,' she said as she led the creature towards the great slab of rock. 'Not easy to find, but it is the most direct route. There is not room enough for three abreast. I shall lead, and you must follow closely.'

She moved away from us and, keeping parallel with the rock face, walked about fifty paces and stopped. I was about to do the same when I felt the sudden but gentle restraint of Nelson's arm across my chest.

'No. Wait,' he whispered. I saw her reach out towards the rock, touch it lightly, and step back one pace. Immediately a high-pitched note sounded on the air. It gradually rose in pitch until it became inaudible. She moved forward. Then, as I watched, I saw her disappear. Alarmed, I started forward and stumbled. I was overcome with dizziness, and almost fell. Nelson grabbed my arm; steadied me.

'Man, leave her be.' I regained my balance, and strained to look at the place where, only a moment ago, she had stood.

'She's coming right back. You feel kind of weird, huh?'

'Yeah.' I replied.

'Ain't surprised,' Nelson answered. 'He was one of them. He'd been taken.'

'Who? Weismann?'

'The same. Raiders had hold of him. Only by the skin of your teeth and friends in high places that you didn't get to join him.'

In front of us, a movement caught my eye. She re-appeared, seeming to walk straight out of the mountainside. Nelson said nothing, but indicated that we should join her. We crossed over to where she was preparing to mount her horse.

'We must go,' she said. 'The way is open now. But it will close off very soon.'

I looked at the rock face, from which she had just emerged, and saw a double image. The rock was there; and yet was not there. In it was an opening about five or six feet wide. But as I concentrated on it, it merged into the surrounding stone and was gone.

'Come,' the woman said; mounted her beast, and rode slowly into the opening until she was lost from view. Without delay, Nelson followed her into the space and he, too, disappeared. I was left suddenly alone on the plain. I had no desire to stay there. I tried to pass through the rock; hesitated. I couldn't. The more I tried to distinguish space from solidity, the more impossible it became. Then I realized that to get through, I had to allow my concentration to lapse. That was the method of passing. So exactly opposite to the method of traversing a Warp. I grasped the knack; glimpsed the woman and Nelson ahead of me, moving on an upward-sloping pathway inside the mountain.

I walked forward; passed through, and found myself on a narrow path of geometric shapes, not unlike the causeway on which we had first entered Xentha. We followed her. The way sloped up quite steeply for a short distance, then turned abruptly at a sharp angle. Around us the great mass of the mountain closed in, hemming us on both sides with rock strata and huge slabs of blue stone. Yet overhead, above the sheer planes of massive rock formation, was only sky. A strange sky. For some reason beyond my understanding, the stars in its rich blue were magnified, and they shone as great glowing orbs of light. It appeared that the very depth and narrowness of the cutting through which we travelled was acting in some way telescopically. I could clearly see crescents and gibbous forms of planets in their orbits around the stars; and, circling the planets, moons of very pale, pastel colour. For a long time we followed the track as it zig-zagged upwards inside the mountain. We climbed slowly and quietly until Nelson, breaking the silence, spoke to the rider.

'Something's changed out there. The whole picture's different. They've got an advantage. A big one. I got to talk to you about it.'

'A matter of strategy?' she replied.

'I suppose it is, yeah.' She was quiet for a moment, and her pause seemed to anticipate the nature of what I knew Nelson was about to say. His approach was cautious.

'So the shape has changed,' she eventually said. 'You have discovered a vital development?'

'An unexpected one,' he answered. 'A city. Raiders' work. Still standing, inside a Warp-complex. We had an effect on it, and it started crumbling, breaking down. But it's still there.'

'Creatures?' she slowed her pace, but didn't turn round. He hesitated for a moment before he said: 'One; that we saw.'

She suddenly held up her hand and, still without turning, spoke again. I noticed that her voice was tinged with something very much like sadness.

'I understand the implication of your discovery; it concerns me. But I must ask you for no more personal discourse about this at present. It is a matter for Inner Xentha, and for Ethamar and her council of the Alta. I am not at liberty to discuss the business of strategy, until we are united in conference.'

Then she gently pulled her horse to a halt; turned back to us. And I saw her eyes: they betrayed her concern. 'Ethamar must be informed before any discussion takes place,' she said quietly. 'Immediately upon our arrival at the encampment, I shall see that you are both escorted to the Dome.'

She turned again and rode on. Nelson nodded agreement, and said no more about it. I looked at the back of her as she ascended the zig-zag path ahead of us. I saw her straight-backed beauty seated on the pale grey beast. I saw the power, and the discipline in her; the discipline that masked a deeper quality, which I didn't have a word for. Something in that beauty filled me with a terrible yearning, and a kind of fear. I wanted to run; to turn back down the track and run on the broken plain until there was no more of me. But I wanted to follow her.

Soon the path began to widen, and we passed through the last of the cutting out on to a high, wide plateau. There, the path of geometric patterns crossed the surrounding landscape, rising higher as it went. It became, once more, the causeway to Xentha. We travelled, following it, climbing with its ascent as it soared free of the land beneath it. I saw that we passed over a slowly heaving sea of mist; and that here the sky had become a pale turquoise, studded with the brilliant pin-point lights of stars. Then, in the far distance, I caught first sight of the encampment. The thin spires of Inner Xentha pointed up out of the blue mist, and I saw glints of reflected starlight from its crystalline buildings. She turned to me, smiled, and said:

'My name is Thainé.'

'What does that mean?' I replied, drawing abreast with her as she rode.

'The seventh Tide,' she replied. 'Seventh of the twenty-four. Tide of the morning.' She said no more. Nor did I. But I walked beside her. And we continued, to the dwelling-place of the Charos.

24: Dogs of Fortune

AS WE DREW nearer to the encampment she suddenly pulled away from me and rode on ahead. I heard her short, triple horn-call; and then almost immediately its answering signal from somewhere within the faceted structures. The notes which heralded our approach and its sanction, hung thread-like over the Plain. Nelson came up alongside me. He gave me an odd look and a slap on the back; but didn't say a word.

'What happened to him?' I said to Nelson. During our journey, while I had walked with her as she rode, the incident with Weismann had seemed far away. But now I recalled the scene; and its meaning chilled me. He sighed, stared for a moment at me, and replied:

'Okay. That thing was no way Weismann. You got that? It was a replica. A Creature. You got that? If the Raiders are on your case, it don't make no difference if you're in Old World, or here.'

'Yeah, okay. A copy – a Creature. But where is he? The real one? Where the hell is he?'

'Dunno,' he replied.

'You don't know? Nelson, you must know.'

'Can't say I do.'

'So what happens to those people the Raiders take? They've got to end up somewhere.'

'They're taken over. Guess they're slowly mutated out of existence. Told you those Raiders ain't got shapes unless they fix up copies to live in. Then, when the transfer is complete, the original just ain't there any more. It's gone. Where to, I dunno. Just gone. Bye-bye, baby.'

'Yeah, alright, but why Weismann? Why him, right there, right then?'

'"Cause using him, they might have got another one. You. They got him from you; used your guilt to build the shape. Once they got hold of the data, you did the rest.'

What he said horrified me. They had been in me. They'd not just been near, but inside me; inside my mind. Then I remembered something else.

'Oh yeah?' 'I said, taking a good look at him. 'I seem to recall you gave me a hand in building up that guilt, Nelson. Right before it happened. Now don't you think that's weird? Somehow, I do!'

'Oh boy . . .,' he sighed. 'I know what's coming now. You're gonna get sarcastic on me. Or paranoid as usual. Or something like that. And you ain't gonna appreciate what I'm saying next. But listen, anyway, if you can shut that mouth up for a while. I knew it was dangerous to cross that plain; the way things are growing. Didn't say a word to you about it, 'cause it wouldn't have done you no good. But I had a damn clear idea that the hunters were gonna make a play for one of us; and the one they'd find easier was you. With all that guilt and stuff in you, you were a sweet target. So I had to punch a little hole in your can of worms. Take some of the pressure off. You had a better deal that way. And you'd better believe it, 'cause I'm giving it to you straight. If they'd taken you by surprise, things might have worked out different. You want to know why they didn't try to move in on me? Hey? That's 'cause my cards are all face up. That's the goddamn reason. Not 'cause I'm holding aces.'

'Your cards are all face up, huh? Oh yeah!'

Then he laughed. 'Trusting sure ain't your strong point, is it? Well, that's a bitch. But it's your bitch, not mine.'

His glance said you're stuck with me, boy, like it or not; and he walked on in front, whistling a tune. It was a Bob Dylan song, but I couldn't recall the title. Then he broke off whistling, and called back to me over his shoulder:

'Did you see his eyes, hey? That's how you tell 'em, here on the Levels. All blacked-out and gone like that. Now in Old World they get by 'cause they ain't so obvious, those Creatures. The only way of telling what they are there, is by them having no soul. But it ain't always easy to tell, unless you ride your Truth real tight, whether a guy's got no soul no more or not. Sure, they've got a kind of weird, cold look about them, even in Old World. But it ain't everyone that notices. Here, they're marked. It's the eyes that show you; mostly, anyhow. It's other things, too. But the eyes are a dead give-away.' He increased his pace slightly, until he was quite a way ahead.

'Wait a minute!' I called after him; but he kept his back to me, waved a hand in the air, and kept on whistling. Then my attention was distracted from him, as ahead of us I saw the great Gate of Xentha begin to open, widening as a silvery haze enveloped its geometric pattern. Out of the strange light which rayed from it, a number of mounted warriors appeared, riding away at terrific speed. Their gold war-dress glinted in the starlight as they passed us. Then they were gone, across the Plain.

I turned quickly, watching as they passed. I tried to count the riders, but they moved with such speed that I couldn't number them. As I watched, I saw them melt away into the air, and disappear from sight. And I knew they must have gone through the first Ring. Nelson came to a halt. He was quiet, gazing at Thainé. She rode up to the Gate, which had instantly re-formed behind the riders. Then she turned, and motioned us forward.

'Goddamn.' Nelson said as I caught up with him. 'Ain't nothing I can do, right now.'

I knew what he was getting at. The riders had disturbed him. 'A war-party?' I asked. 'Another one?'

'Yeah,' he replied. 'Let's just do what we came to do, huh?'

I looked towards Thainé; saw her key in her code, and move through the Gate until she was lost from view. We followed, entering the courtyard behind her. On the other side of the Gate, riders were gathered. They stood, poised and silent, in an arrow-head formation. As we entered I saw the foremost warrior salute Thainé. She returned his salute; then addressed Nelson and me.

'Follow me,' she said. 'I will take you into the Dome.' She dismounted, letting her horse free. It glanced at her, then moved slowly away across the crystal paving.

'They're preparing to ride out, aren't they?' I said to Nelson as we followed Thainé through the labyrinth. He nodded.

'And they've not been briefed . . .' I added. 'They don't have a clue what's going on out there. Can we delay them? Hold them back a bit, till they've heard what the situation is?'

'Hey, Man. Wheels within wheels. They turn, no matter where you are. And there ain't that much waiting about you can do, when the storm's coming. And the storm's here! It's come. They'll ride. They'll ride, anyway, to where they're needed. They ain't gonna slow down the action. No way they can.'

Thainé said nothing. She led us along the gothic pathways of tree-lined arcades, until they opened out into the shining facets of the Dome. The interior was deserted; cast with a deep blue light. But I knew that we weren't there yet. We had to pass through the axis-shift. She touched me, lightly on the shoulder. Taken unaware by her touch, I half turned. And she withdrew her hand.

'Ethamar knows that you have returned,' she said. 'She has been informed and expects your presence. Remain still. As you are already aware of the procedure for entering the Inner Dome, the effect on your consciousness will be minimal. Please do not move. The axis-shift is now activated.'

I experienced a momentary dizziness, and realized that I could no longer see either Thainé or Nelson. A white-noise sound blotted out my hearing. The colour of the air changed. It lost its blueness and became clear; sharply defining the facets of the domed ceiling above and around us. And I saw the tall, impressive form of the Chieftain standing before me; and became aware that Nelson and Thainé stood next to me. Ethamar bowed her head slightly towards us before she spoke. There were no preliminaries. She went straight to the point.

'You have news for me?' She said. Nelson nodded, glanced at me, and stepped forward.

'We have,' he replied. 'What do you know about Warp complexes?'

'We are aware of their existence.'

'Well, there's a city out there. Right in the middle of one. A city the Raiders built. And it's still there.'

Ethamar was quiet for a moment. She glanced at Thainé.

'Lightfall sector; Beta thirty five,' Thainé said.

'I understand' was all Ethamar said. Then she addressed Nelson again: 'Tell me what you know. This is of the utmost importance.'

I stepped forward. 'Wait a minute . . .' I broke in. 'Hold it there. You're saying that you know the Warp-complexes exist, but you know nothing about what's going on inside them?'

Ethamar looked directly at me, and simply nodded agreement. But then I felt Nelson's grip on my arm. I knew he was trying to shut me up, and I half turned, feeling a flash of irritation.

'Hey, Man. Leave it out, huh?'

'You know they're there' I went on, ignoring him,' but you can't get inside them. Isn't that right? Those Warps are a big mystery to you; to the Charos? Right? That's crazy! Surely you don't expect us to believe that?'

'Why should we be all-knowing? All-seeing? We are not gods; though from your attitude, it appears that you think we are – or devils, Richard Brett,' Ethamar replied. 'We are neither. Yes, we are aware of the existence of the Warps and the Warp-complexes. But the information you bring is vital to us. It is vital that we know more. We need to know the details of your discovery. Please do not fight me, for we both stand on the same ground, and I am not your enemy. I looked at her; saw that a kind of sadness crossed her face, and that her eyes, holding mine, had no trace of arrogance or coldness in them. And she had let me speak. She hadn't tried to stop me. Like the last time I'd spoken with her in the Dome. She'd done the same then. She baffled me. 'We went in, through the Warps,' Nelson continued. 'Into the city. It's Raiders' work alright. A replica down to the last detail. And I reckon it's a testing-area. An experiment.'

Calmly, she listened; her pale face set with concentration on his every word. Then she interrupted him.

'You went into the city through the Warps?'

'Yeah.' Nelson replied. 'There were three. The first one crossed the edge of the Lightfall. On the way out we came across two more . . .'

'Both of you? You found them no restriction?' she said, and frowned slightly. Nelson laughed.

'Can't exactly say that,' he said. 'But we completed the traverse, yeah.'

Ethamar paced the floor of the Dome; moving away from us. Then she looked up; staring high into the glittering facets of its ceiling. She was deep in thought, and seemed to be searching for something above, in the crystal shapes Then she lowered her eyes, and turned to us.

'Then you have skills that we have not,' she said. 'And you have knowledge that we have not. And you have broken the Law.' As she spoke, she glanced from Nelson to me. My guard went up, and I was about to speak, but she continued:

'The Law of the Attraction of the Perimeter,' she said. 'The Law of Centrifugal Force. You have traversed it.'

Nelson looked at me and shrugged.

'Many warriors were lost to the Warps,' Ethamar went on. 'Lost to the Outer Reaches in our training program. Since then, we have always known the Warps to be impregnable; uncrossable. We have assumed, quite erroneously, it seems, that nothing could survive them.'

'Well the Raiders can,' Nelson said. 'They're using them. I know what the city means. They've moved out now, but they're somewhere else. Somewhere, in a Warp-complex, they've got a stronghold. That's for sure.'

'The Web . . .' Ethamar said, coming nearer to us. 'There must be a malfunction on the Web.'

'No. It ain't that,' Nelson replied. 'The Warps are blocking transmission. Simple. The signals can't come through. They're a dead-zone.'

She nodded. Distantly, I heard a triple horn-call. The Chieftain stopped talking for a moment, listened, then concentrated once more on Nelson.

'You see,' he continued, 'that's why they built there. So they've got the best advantage they could have. And they can do what they like 'cause the Charos can't get at them; don't even know they're in there.'

'Yes,' she replied. 'I understand.'

I felt an odd sensation, and quickly turned round. I saw that Thainé was no longer behind me. She had gone.

'They will have a centre,' I heard Ethamar suddenly say. 'As we, the Charos, have. A centre where their forces are massed. A heart.'

'Okay,' Nelson said. 'It'll be a big one . . .'

'Their centre will have to be weakened,' she added; 'or the balance cannot be struck.'

'I know where it's got to be,' Nelson said quickly. 'By the Crossing-place. There's a massive Warp-complex there. It's the highest zone of the Levels; the place where the Worlds meet.'

'Sounds like that's got to be it. It figures.' Then Ethamar looked away from Nelson, to me. 'Will you go in?' she said. 'The two of you; will you guide an attack-force? Take them through?'

Her words shocked me. Nelson said nothing, but I caught his gaze. And the expression on his face was inscrutable.

'What?' I asked. A silence followed.

'Man, you heard the lady,' he said.

'Will we go in? Nelson, *what*? You and me?'

'You can both pass through the Warps,' she continued. 'But our warriors do not have that knowledge. With your help and your skills, a force could perhaps be guided through . . .'

'No! No way!' I moved forward, passing between the Chieftain and Nelson, and began to pace the crystal floor. 'No!" I said again, spinning round quickly and pointing a finger at her. 'You can forget that one! This is your war, not mine! I didn't damn well start it, and I'm not playing Soldiers of Fortune! Okay?' I stopped pacing, and in shocked disbelief, looked at Nelson. He stared, eye to-eye with me, and shrugged again.

'They ain't gonna get through without us.'

'What?' I felt my anger rise. 'Tell me again, in case I've got it wrong! She's asking us to go, where? She's asking us to lead an army of Charos warriors, through God knows how many Warp-crossings – into . . . into what? Into the heart of the Raiders of Gehina? Oh no! Count me out!'

Nelson made a move towards me; began to say something. But I barred his approach with the flat of my hand and turned away. 'You said yourself that it's not hundred per cent sure, crossing a Warp! You said it, Nelson!' I went on, pacing again as I shouted. '*There's always a risk. Don't imagine there ain't!* That's what you said! Well I'm not risking my butt for someone else's war! I don't know what you feel like doing, but I know what I want! And it's to stay as far away from those twisted sisters as I can get!'

'Man, she only asked. Jesus Christ! There ain't no harm in that!'

'She asked! Oh yeah. That's all she's got to do! Ask! It's making real good sense, now; the whole thing! I told you they wanted us for something, didn't I? Well, that's it! Cannon-fodder! That's what! Maybe some kind of decoy-ducks? Hey?'

'I am sorry,' Ethamar said suddenly. She didn't try to approach me. I spun round; saw the expression on her face. It was grave, and her eyes, set on mine, were solemn and tense. 'I am sorry. It is not my intention, nor would it ever be my intention, to coerce you. I know the risks. But you have a skill and a knowledge that we do not possess. In that knowledge, that skill you hold the counter-weight. You hold the future . . .'

'Okay!' I cut in. 'Tell her, Nelson! Tell her how it's done; the traverse! Give her the dance-steps! Then that should be it! Then they can boogaloo all they like, and we don't have a thing to do with it!

'Information!' he said. 'You figure information is the same as knowing? Data! Sure, give her the data. God-damn, Man! A billion guys think like that! Data is knowing! Well it ain't! Data, boy, is data! And knowing's something else! We give them the knowing; that means we go in there and do it with them! Knowing is getting in the thing. Loving it, getting inside it. And doing it!'

'No way! No damn way! You're the one who's always giving it some about Truth! My Truth, and all that stuff! Well, this is it! This is my Truth! I'm not risking my ass!'

'Told you you're a killer, too. Told you a while back. And there's still some stuff you got to kill. Some stuff that needs wasting. And you ain't finished paying.'

'Don't give me that! I've paid my ferryman, Nelson! What she's asking for is a lot more! She wants blood, plus interest! Only she can't do it, because I'm not in the guilt market any more. I've seen my ghost! I've had him grip hold of my arm, and try to hook me down to Hell! And I'll tell you what I've learned from Weismann. I've learned that I'm no way going where he's gone! They're not moving in on me! You got that? I am not fighting in this goddamn war, no matter what the blackmail price!'

The Chieftain spoke. 'I cannot force the issue. The decision rests with you. I have asked for your help, and my entreaty has been refused. I can ask no more.'

'Okay,' I replied. 'Fine. Now can I go? Or is there another price to pay for saying no? Like no exit from Central H.Q. till I've seen the light? Or terminal maze-games, till I've done what you want? I want out of here, right now!'

'You are free to go,' she answered. 'I am saddened by your decision, for as a result, Gehina shall hold the balance of power. But I am bound by Cosmic Law to continue to extend the hand of hospitality to both of you. And I shall do so, to the best of my ability. I ask nothing more of you, but only that you stand aside now, and do nothing which may hinder or jeopardize our operations. The war goes on. And we will wage it with whatever means we have at our disposal. To the last.'

She looked at Nelson. 'I have to thank you,' she said to him, 'for the information you brought to us. We could not have known . . .' Then she glanced down, turned, and slowly began to walk away to the far side of the Dome.

'I will activate the axis-shift for you,' she said. 'Whenever you are ready. And if you wish to return to the pyramid, you are welcome to do so.'

25: Bye, Bye Baby

WE PASSED THROUGH, into the blue air of the Outer Dome. Except for the two of us, it was deserted. Ethamar had gone. Then I realized that Nelson must have taken us through the axis-shift. It took me a moment to get my bearings; then I started forward down one of the tree-lined passageways, leaving him behind. He'd been ready to do what the Chieftain wanted. I knew that. And his point of view and mine were obviously not going to find a meeting-ground. I wanted to hear no more about it, because whatever pressure he felt like putting on wasn't going to change my mind one bit. The whole idea was a bad one. They could fight their war any way they liked, but leave me out of it. They'd had enough practice. And I'd seen enough of the way the Raiders operated to last me for ever.

'You've kinda got the makings of a survivor,' I heard Nelson say, behind me. 'It don't make sense, all the things you made happen, back in Old World. When I come to try and figure it out, it don't make no sense. You sure know when to haul ass out of trouble there. Ain't a totally useless kinda quality . . .'

'Is that supposed to be some kind of smart-ass comment, Nelson, hey?' I said, spinning round angrily to him. He caught up with me.

'There've been sons of God, dammit, Nelson, who have risked their butts for the saving of the World! And I am not one of them! That is for certain! If that's what I'm supposed to be, if that's what you and her think I ought to be, it stinks!' I turned right at the junction of identical arcades. Nelson stood a while at the corner, watching me. I saw him indicate left with his thumb. I backtracked and stormed past him.

'You make me miss my woman,' he said quietly. 'You sure as hell do. She'd have done it, and wouldn't have made no noise about it, neither. She knew how to ride wild. She knew how to ride into the wind, Man! And she was beautiful all the time, but when she rode like that, she was beautiful for sure!'

'Get off my back!'

'We got the skill . . .' he said. 'The skill, but only half the inclination. And that's a damn shame.' We walked on, under the arches of tall trees. I didn't even want to speak to him any more, and he kept quiet for a while. Then, out of the heavy silence between us, he said:

'You bring out what's in you, it saves you. You hold that thing back, and fight it, and pretend it ain't even there, and it destroys you. You were built to ride wild!'

I didn't reply. And he didn't say any more. We just worked our way through the labyrinth. I was aware he knew where he was going, and I had no choice but to follow him. I could never have found my way through alone, and I knew it. But I didn't want to be walking along with him. His very presence was like a mirror, reflecting something back to me which I didn't want to see. I was a selfish son of a bitch. I had two options; either that, or join the army. I decided to choose the former. The Warps, the Raiders, the Charos, were all far more than I had bargained for. And I wanted to be a million miles away from the whole scene; and from the pressure I had felt from Nelson and her. I didn't like what was going on out there. The city had been bad enough; but the bad news had really struck home with Weismann. I never wanted to see eyes like that again, or feel the vice-grip of a hand that intended to take everything I was, and mutate it into its own image. Bye-bye, baby. But I wasn't the hero. The Bird-Man. I wasn't the storm-rider. They could keep that.

'I'll stay just as long as it takes the storm to blow over,' I said angrily, turning to Nelson as we negotiated our way through the passageways. 'Then I'm on the trail again. I'm out.'

'What makes you think it will blow over?'

'Things do.' I answered. I caught the expression on his face.

'Ain't nothing like a wind with something riding on it that intends to kick some ass! Ain't nothing like it for giving it some encouragement to blow over!'

'Quit the pressure! Okay? I'm not doing it! No way!'

'Yeah,' he said. And we both moved on under the trees, saying nothing, until at last we reached the courtyard. As we entered I saw twelve mounted warriors waiting in silence. The riders had formed into an arrowhead group; their horses controlled, but obviously eager for movement. The creatures' heads, decked in silver war-gear, tossed impatiently up and down, nosing the air, waiting for the horn-call that would send them out through the Gate. At the head of the formation Thainé sat, high on her pale grey horse. She turned as we came towards them from the trees. For a moment she watched us; then she left her position and rode slowly in our direction.

As she drew up, facing us, Nelson stopped. He looked up at her and said nothing. I caught her gaze as she glanced from him, to me. And her eyes were bare; they opened into a depth which repelled me with its honesty. I turned away from what her eyes made me feel, and kept moving through the courtyard, heading for the other side. She called me by my name, and I heard the light tread of her beast on the crystal paving as she followed. Then she overtook me, and turned until we were face to face.. I halted; looking up.

'We ride out soon,' she said. 'I need to know your decision. Are you to ride with us?' I made no reply; but side-stepped round her and walked forward in the direction of the pyramid. She dismounted then, and came towards me on foot.

'I know that you have decided.' I stopped; glanced back briefly. I caught the bare gaze of her eyes again, and found that they stirred my anger. I turned away; saw Nelson. He was sitting some distance behind us, cross-legged at the foot of one of the huge trees. In his hands he held a split golden fruit. I watched as he took the loose black seeds and ran them through his fingers until they flowed like sand in an hour-glass. He was concentrating on them, and didn't even look at us.

'Whatever your choice is, I respect it,' Thainé said. 'There is no surety, one way or the other. We hang in the balance.'

'I love you,' I heard, as I turned from her and kept walking. I stared at the pyramid – saw faint lines of iridescent light move across its perfect angles. I heard the water of the stream as it travelled over the glittering cobbles.

'I love you, Richard Brett,' I heard again. I stopped, spun round to her; met her eyes with mine. Hers were steady; un-blinking.

'No,' I answered. 'No, you don't. You love the war. That's what you love. You guys don't love! Not people like me, you don't! You love . . . this!' I pointed at the mounted warriors assembled a short distance away. They had not turned, or moved even a fraction to left or right. But their horses still flickered in re-strained restlessness.

'This is what you are!' I shouted; 'nothing else! The war! The army! That's it, period! You love me! Sweet Jesus! You guys don't give up, do you?' She said nothing, but just kept looking straight into me.

'So don't give me that!' I went on. 'You're bred for this! You're an Annihilator! And love isn't part of your schedule, your battle plan, your strategy! That's if you even know what the hell it is! Go out and get your Raiders, and leave me out of it! I'm not part of it, or you, or your war!'

'You are wrong,' she answered quietly. 'It is because of love that we ride. Because of love that we are here. And my words are not pressure. They are truth.'

'Power! Not love! You're hunters! At the most, your love is the love of the chase! Maybe that's closer to the truth!'

She dropped her gaze; then quickly glanced back at me before she turned slowly and moved back to her horse which waited close by. She took the reins lightly in one hand, and mounted up in a swift, graceful movement. I saw her image shift and change as she sat high on the beast's back, watching me. A liquid brilliance flowed over her features; taking them and shaping them subtly into new form. White light crowned her and sank down to envelop her. She smiled; and as she did so, I saw the face of the one who had followed me through these Worlds.

'I love you, Richard Brett.' The voice echoed. 'As I have always done. The pain of your struggling spirit can never weaken my love, but only serve to strengthen it. If, as a warrior, I stand victorious at the time of triumph, I will love you. If I am taken in battle, and vanquished, I will love you. If you run from the blazing Light; or if you turn, to claim it as your Right, I will love you. Through all; from the beginning to the end. From the Alpha to the Omega, my spirit shall be with yours.' Then the face of Thainé returned. The echoes died away, and the crest of brightness around her head drew down; sinking to a place between her breasts, below the sharp angularity of the transparent jewel she wore at the base of her throat. A horn-call broke through the air.

'We ride now,' Thainé said, and gently turned her horse away from me. Its hooves rang lightly on the ground as she rode up to take her position at the point of the arrow of Charos riders. Two more horn-calls followed the first. And as the last note died away, the Gate opened; its symmetry melting into a shining circle through which the thirteen mounted warriors passed, as one single form. And the courtyard became too still; too quiet. It seemed that no-one had ever been in it but Nelson and me. I stood, watching the noiseless light grille of the Gate, which now gave no sign that anything had passed through it. Then Nelson broke the silence. I heard his footsteps as he approached me. But I didn't look at him.

'Your move, boy,' he said.

'What do you mean, my move?' I snapped, turning on him impatiently. He didn't answer. I saw that his eyes sparkled with pooled-up tears. He shook his head, and moved away from me, walking in the direction of the pyramid.

'Gonna get me some dream-space. Why don't you leave me be, awhile, and go chop up some rocks, or something, huh? And while you're at it, maybe you could take a chain-saw to that attitude of yours. That woman is too damn good for you, Hard-Man, and that's the bare-ass truth.'

I stood still; watched him as he reached the entrance of the pyramid. But he didn't go in. Instead, he squatted down by the narrow stream and gazed into it.

'You forgotten the Rose?' he called to me without looking up. 'You forgotten the fire of the blood you drank? You know what they were? Huh? Gifts, that's what they were. You don't get 'em unless they're given to you. You don't take 'em. No, Man! Why were they given to you? 'Cause you could carry 'em, that's why. No other reason.'

'Give it up, Nelson.' I said.

'Huh? Give what up?'

'This crusade! This trip-out! This goddamn idea you've got about me, about what I am! Let the Charos get on with their war their own way!'

'Guess you don't even know what love is,' he said, suddenly looking up and staring at me, hard. 'If you don't know, I can't tell you. Guess you never got any of it. So now it's smiled at you, you got to take to kicking it in the teeth, 'case it might bite off a bit of attitude.' He got up, turned around, and disappeared inside the pyramid. I didn't need to hear any more. So I left him to his dream-space. I went up to the stream, and sat down on the ground.

26: Call to Arms

I DON'T KNOW how long I sat like that, staring into the water. Perhaps it was only moments; or maybe it was much, much longer. But I gradually became aware of a sound of distant drumming. It was a rhythmic, primitive sound, like ancient tribal music; hands beating on skin drums. The pace of the rhythm increased, and yet the strange music seemed to be coming to me over vast distances. A single voice, faint and high, soared up over the drumbeats, hovered, and faded away to nothing. A single, female, wordless voice. Then the sound was pounding into me from the stones beneath, where the stream disappeared. It became one sound, taking me over; vibrating inside my body. One sound; two-syllables. A heartbeat. And it was no longer apart form me. It was me. And it was no longer music. It was terrifying.

Quickly, I stood up; swaying dizzily. I tore my eyes away from the water, and tried to remember where I was; who I was. I staggered; suddenly panicked. I looked up, and saw Nelson. He stood, saying nothing; his eyes boring into mine. His face had a set and steady look; his expression one of pure will. He wasn't laughing. Abruptly, the sounds cut off. He stared at me a moment more; then looked down at the stones. I noticed that we weren't alone in the courtyard. Behind Nelson I saw the Chieftain and three mounted Charos warriors. One by one they dismounted, and, leading their horses, they crossed slowly towards the arches of trees. For a moment, as they crossed my line of sight, I noticed their eyes. And, even from that distance, I was struck by the strange and terrible expressions on their face. Then they passed beneath the high boughs, and were gone. The courtyard was empty again, but for Nelson and me.

'They've come back.' Nelson said. I started; shocked by his words. I didn't understand. I felt his hands gripping my arms; shaking me.

'You hear me?' He whispered, his face close to mine; 'They've come back. All three of them-'

'Three? What do you mean?'

'Three out of thirteen. That's what I mean. You saw them ride out. Did you see them come back . . .?' In a flash I grasped his meaning, and just stared at him; at the seriousness in his dark face. Then I pulled myself out of his grasp, and ran across the courtyard to the place where I had seen the riders pass out of sight between the trees. I felt him catch my arm from behind.

'Where you going, huh?' I didn't answer, and tried to pull away from the restraint of his hand on my arm.

'Ain't no use going after them . . .' But I shook him off me, and ran to the edge of the Labyrinth. I knew that if I went in, it was sure to close up on me. Realizing the futility of going any further, I stopped.

'Where is she?' I spun round. Nelson was right behind me. With one hand I grabbed him by the front of his fringed jacket, and pulled him roughly towards me. 'Where is she?'

'She didn't come back,' he replied quietly. In disbelief, I kept hold of him for a moment; staring close into his pale eyes, but not really seeing him. The courtyard was suddenly too quiet. Through the hollow silence I heard a rushing sound which seemed to come from somewhere inside me.

'She didn't . . .?'

'That's right.' Nelson whispered. 'Now let go of me, 'cause it ain't my fault. Okay?' I dropped him, and he stepped back a couple of feet. I looked into the passageways of the Labyrinth. But there was no-one there now.

'Where . . . is she?' But he had no answer. He shrugged, and just stood there, looking at me.

'Screw you!' I shouted. Then I turned away from him, and, plunging into the maze of tunnels, ran in the same direction as the Charos riders. I kept running, trying to track them; knowing I didn't have a hope, but doing it anyway. I rushed headlong down deserted archways; turning left, right, haphazardly. As I ran, a throbbing haze fell over my mind pounding with every step I took. And when the pounding became intolerable I shouted down the empty arches, and cursed; my voice travelling to nowhere through the dead silence.

Again and again I ran, turned, and plunged forward down the perfect identical passageways. The Labyrinth was closing, opening, turning on its enigmatic axes, to cross-match every move I made. I knew it. But I didn't care, I cared about nothing except the burning anger and desperation I felt. Then I stopped;, slammed the side of my fist against the metallic substance between the trees. The impact was soundless. The criss-cross impenetrable threads sparkled, rainbow-lit, as my hand contacted them. I slammed into it over and over; but nothing gave. And as I withdrew my hand in frustration, glittering fragments of colour clung to it for a brief moment.

I raised my voice again, to wake the sentinel trees; to shatter their inscrutable silence. And my voice passed down the arcades and was gone. Then, out of the unnatural stillness, the Charos came; two of them. I never saw them approach, and they took form in front of me; seemingly out of nowhere. Then when I demanded to be taken out of the Labyrinth; demanded to be taken to the Dome, the two men said nothing. They nodded and moved away, indicating that I should follow. I did so; and under their guard, passed into the blue Dome, and from there, through the axis-shift. I found, when they had gone, that I was alone. Light-rays filtered down from the massive crystal ceiling; dancing reflections over the smooth floor where I stood. I crossed to the centre of the Dome and shouted; challenging the quietness with my anger.

'Where are you? Game's over, Ethamar! It stops here!' I turned, round and round; shouting into the empty glittering hall. There was no sign of the Chieftain. I didn't know if she could even hear me.

'It has only just begun.' Her voice sounded behind me; echoing back from the faceted ceiling. I turned again, and saw her, standing where the two axes met.

'You . . .!' I said, setting her with an angry stare. She moved towards me. Her statuesque form crossed the floor with ease, and the gracefulness which comes with exceptional strength.

'I know what you've done! Exactly what you've done! You sent them in! Didn't you? You knew the score, and you sent them in! You first-class stinking bitch!' She didn't respond. I paced away from her in my rage, and returned; glaring into the coolness of her stare.

'I know! I don't need anyone to tell me! You sent them through the Warps! They can't ride the damn Warps, and you know it! But you sent them in, anyway, for the kick! Okay! Which Warps? Let me guess! The Crossing-Place, am I right? You and your strategy! God damn you to hell. Three, you bitch! Three of them came back So where are the others? Burn-up? Yeah! You burned them up to put the pressure on me!'

'Richard Brett,' she answered. The calmness of her words came as a shock through the echoes of my voice. 'Why are you here?'

'Why am I . . .? I'm here because there's no-one else to give you this! Because everyone else seems to think the rising sun comes up over your ass, woman! Well, not me!'

'You suddenly show concern for the welfare of my people. You show grief for the loss of ten warriors in an attempt to breach Gehina's stronghold. You surprise me, Richard Brett. You appear to show no concern for the rise of darkness, or for the peoples of the Earth, or for the creatures of the Word's creation throughout the Worlds. You show nothing but cynicism and mistrust for the Operations which we mount. You show concern for little but yourself. Yet now you rage at me for the loss of ten. We have lost many thousands; but they were not wasted. You have wasted, and you accuse me.'

'Your stinking tricks! Thainé! She was one of your stinking tricks! Wasn't she? You used her! To get me! But why did you bother? She's gone, burned damn well up! And you still haven't got me! Your strategy's getting old, Ethamar!'

'You are remarkably intelligent. But you are wrong.'

'Wrong? How can I be wrong, for God's sake?'

'Thainé was not destroyed.' I stared, speechless, at her. I knew Thainé hadn't returned. She didn't come back. I heard Nelson's words again; She didn't come back.

'She is inside.' Ethamar said.

I felt a sudden pain; as though something invisible had delivered me a stinging blow. It stifled the flare of my anger. '. . . Inside . . .?'

'In the stronghold. She was taken. Nine were lost to the Warps, but she was not. She was taken in.'

'By the . . . by the Raiders? Taken by the . . . Jesus! The Raiders? The Raiders have got Thainé?' The Chieftain didn't answer. I remembered Weismann's eyes; his voice.

'They're after the Charos . . .' I said. I felt icy cold. Energy seemed to drain out of me. 'They're trying to replicate the Charos . . .'

'No,' Ethamar replied. 'Not the Charos. It is the Great Ones they want. They seek a matrix for the Great Ones.'

'Who . . .? What do you mean?'

'The Great One. She who is joined with Thainé.'

'I can't . . . I can't take this in! They're using her, is that what you mean? To get to the Other One?'

'Exactly. And you are also joined. You are the third principle of the Sacred Three. You know it. But you run from it. And the Raiders learn. Now, with each moment, they slowly learn to conquer even the Innermost, the highest, of the Worlds.'

'Okay! I'm going in.' I answered suddenly. 'Like you said! Like you want! I'm going in! You've got me, Ethamar!'

She drew closer to me. 'Do you truly choose that way?' I

nodded. I felt the weight of my decision. But I had decided.

'I do.' I replied.

'The Way of a Warrior of the Charos? For that is what you will become if you lead us in.'

'I'm going in.'

'Three times I am bound by Law to ask you if your choice is the choice of free will, Richard Brett.'

'Yes . . . It is.'

'Then you shall be taken from this place to a place of execution.' I closed my eyes. As her words hit me, my body began to shake, and I clenched my fists tightly.

'For part of you shall die. And part of you shall rise up. That which you were shall be sacrificed on the point of the Arrow.' She was silent for a moment. Where my fists were tightly clenched, I felt a sharp stab; feeling the rose's thorn still embedded there. I opened my hands; looked down at them. I saw no blood, but only a small light, like the blue-white glint of a distant star. The drumming returned. It seemed to come from far away, but it was inside me, mounting, deafening. I could hardly hear her as she said.

'It has begun. Come with me.'

She turned away, and walked to the place of the dual-axis. I couldn't speak. And all around me were the strange sounds of the ancient music. As I moved forward, the weight of what I had chosen pressed down on me. But I had no desire to turn back, even if I could have done. I was going to a place I had never been; a new World. Its shadow was already breathing on me. I remembered the rose that grew on the iron tree; and the thousands of frosted particles where the Woman of the Rose had stood in Hell. I heard Thainé's voice again as she had mounted up to ride out.

I love you, Richard Brett.

I'd always known love was for fools. It weakened and divided, and took away strength; the strength of *one*. But I couldn't forget the flood of strength which had come into me as I stood, weary on the Outer Plain of Xentha, and she had touched me. It didn't matter. I was going in. I was going to get her out. And nothing was going to stop me. I'll go the way that I decide. She was there, in the scheme of things. And if the Raiders took her, she'd be one of them. Maybe she'd come out of that Warp-zone like Weismann came out of the desert. And she'd be looking for me.

I stared at Ethamar. She stood, impassively, preparing to cross the axis. Now she had got what she wanted. A soldier of fortune.

'What happens now?' I asked.

'You must keep silence. And follow. That is all.'

We passed through the blue Dome; and from there, we moved through the paths of the Labyrinth. As I followed her, I could hear strange cries echoing through the passageways. They seemed to originate from somewhere above the trees; like the hunting calls of eagles circling in forest skies. Then I realized they came from a place inside myself; from a place of remembering.

The Chieftain halted. She reached out towards me, taking my hand in hers. Her grip was cold and firm as she turned me to face the trees.

We both stepped through the glistening latticework between the tree trunks; and as I moved through, I felt its metallic substance drift, cobweb-like over my body. I put up a hand to brush the stuff off my face, but I found there was nothing there. The cries of the eagles drew closer, as we entered a total darkness. And then the sounds were gone; and so was Ethamar.

27: Lord of Gates

THERE WAS ONLY darkness. Unable to see, I lifted my arms, reaching out to feel the air. But a sixth sense told me not to move from where I stood. It told me that I might be balanced on the lip of a precipice. My hands, groping through the blackness, touched nothing. And the silence was total. I waited; then took one careful step forward. I felt my foot slide roughly over stony ground. There was no precipice; but I could still sense one.

To go in; to go through the Warps, she had said that I would become one of them. But that wasn't possible. I was no warrior of the Charos. I was only myself. They were wrong.

For part of you shall die. And part of you shall rise up. That which you were shall be sacrificed on the point of the arrow.

Then I understood. No doubt they intended to put me through some kind of ceremonial. Fine. It didn't mean a thing to me: their customs, their ways, their ceremonies. They could do what they liked. I'd play the game, if that's what I had to do. Because I'd decided to go in; and I was going.

You shall be taken from this place to a place of execution.

Death. What death? Dead men can't die. Then Nelson's words echoed again in my memory.

The way to her is known as the Way of the Arrow. It's a Warrior's Way. It's the Way of Death. But it takes more dying than you know, and more burning to find her. She'd ask you to die, and die, and die again. She's Light, and Man can't live in Pure Light. She'd destroy you like nothing else could.

What death? What did he mean? They couldn't destroy me because they needed me. I was going in; into the Warp-complex. Without me, they had no strategy – not really. I was going in. To the Heart of the Raiders. I was taking Thainé out. They needed me. Or did they? In the silence, the thought struck home with a sickening impact. Abruptly, I turned round in the darkness. Stumbling on loose fragments of rock, I tried to grope my way back; searching for the place I had come in with the Chieftain. But I was unable to locate the metal filaments whose impregnable hardness had strangely dissolved into thin webs as she and I came through.

There was nothing. My hands, grasping desperately at the air could find nothing.

Oh Christ! how could I have been so stupid? This was what they wanted. I'd known it all along. They wanted me; and now they'd got me. The whole business; the manipulation, the tricks they'd used to get me here. I'd fallen for it all; and in the end, played into their hands of my own free will. And why, I thought, why did they want me? I wasn't one of them, and never could be. Nelson was closer. Oh yes, he was close to being one of them. But not me. So they wanted rid of me. Simple.

Frantically, I searched through the blackness for the way which led to the Labyrinth. I knew I'd only taken a few steps when I came in with her; so it had to be somewhere behind me.

But as I felt about, fighting a rising terror, I touched nothing. No walls. No way back. Nelson. He could take them through. They didn't need the two of us. They only needed him. And he wasn't here; he was well out of it. I stopped; screamed into the empty darkness.

'You bastards! Sons of bitches! Okay! You've got me! Okay! Come and get me! Come and . . .'

A whiplash cut through the air. It bit into me, and coiled round my body. My right arm was pinned, and a cold pain ran through me. Another crack opened up the silence, as I felt the agonising bite of a second whiplash. I fell; clutching at the cords which stretched away into the dark. I pulled, hard; but something with tremendous force pulled back. And I was dragged, trying to stand against it, stumbling, going down on to the rough ground. But the speed at which I was dragged along threw me down again and again. I felt the cruel sharpness of rocks against my back, tearing at me; and I screamed, first in anger, then in sheer pain. But whatever pulled didn't hear. Or it didn't want to hear. I heard the breaking of my body on the rock, stones tumbling about me, and the sound of horses at a gallop. And between my shrieks and the raging of the horses' hooves, I heard men's voices. Whoops and cheers rose out of a reddening dust-cloud. I found that I could see. But I saw blood, and dust, flying stones. Through the gritty haze of pain, I glimpsed them, as a blur of leather boots, bright-coloured neckties, brown leather. I heard the crack of a whip, and I was dragged faster. The words they spoke were oddly clear through everything.

'Names, Injun bastard!' I heard, 'Names an' where they're heading to!'

'Kill the filthy punk!'

'Hey, Medicine-Man! Wanna go to Hell? There's a party waitin' for ya!'

'Names! Gettin' the message, son-of-a-bitch? Gettin' it?' I gasped, retching. Pebbles and blood were choking me.

'Send him round a few more times —'

'Dunno if he's strong enough . . .'

'Yeah! He's strong enough! The Devil's in them Red Men, boy, an' he's strong enough for anythin' you like, an' a bit more!'

'What if we take him out?'

'Ain't no chance.'

I couldn't even scream any more. I could make no sound.

'Eat shit, Injun!' They were laughing. Shrieks went up from outside the circle of blood and dust which I was carving with my dying.

'Dog Soldiers! Gimmethenames!' Dog Soldiers. They are my brothers. They ride the wind.

'Dog Soldiers! Or we waste ya!' The red circle was deepening. It made mud of the dust.

'We know 'em! We already know which ones! Kill the punk!' Again, the whip lashed down. Foam from the mouths of the horses flecked me; mingled with my blood.

'I wanna hear him say it!'

'Maybe he dunno . . .'

'He knows an' he knows which trail they hit!'

'Waste him! Give him to the buzzards!'

'Ain't nothin' but scraps left!'

'Buzzards ain't fussy.' But I had no words, any more. No anger. No more pain. But I heard them as they laughed. And I knew the Dogs were far away by now. They'd ridden in the dawn. Then the Woman came; her black hair blowing on the wind. And I couldn't see her brow for the light which shone from it. She held a green snake in one hand; and with the other she touched my face. And I felt love, so strong, as Death took me.

'Brett.'

I spun round. I was standing barefoot on sharp rocks; not lying dead in crimson-soaked prairie-dust.

'Dead men can't die, Brett? That should be so. But it is not. There are so many ways of dying.'

We were surrounded by a circle of red light. It illuminated his face. I recognised him. He was the one who had first taken me into the Dome. His amber eyes shone, through the lurid glow.

'We meet again,' he said, 'as I foresaw.' I became aware of the movement of something loose against my body, and I quickly looked down. The shirt I had worn hung in ragged, bloody fragments. The Dog Soldiers. Who were the Dog Soldiers? The ones whose names the White men murdered for? The names they never got. I gripped the tattered cloth, tearing it from me. Then I stood, half naked, facing the warrior. My feet and chest were lacerated. In the red light, the blood looked tar-black. His eyes and mine met, and fixed on each other's. I knew, by the force; the razor-sharp intention which radiated from him, that his mission was to break me.

'You are our hope. Our Mutation;' he said. 'With you, we evolve, or die. Evolve, or die Brett!'

As he spoke, I heard a wind spring up in the pit of blackness behind him. Then it roared out, breaking through the dark and shattering the air around us. I staggered under its onslaught; but glanced up in an attempt to keep my eyes on him at all costs. He was smiling. His angular, powerful face and the set of his stare did not flinch, even slightly, as the hot dry gale bore down. Below the gold band he wore on his brow, his hair lifted and spread, corona-like round his head.

'My name is Mathon!' he shouted over the howling; 'Fourth tide of the Waning Sun. The tide I serve is the tide of the Lord of Gates! Great One of the Night of Time! The One who Transforms!'

Winged things, birds with wings of flame came screeching out of the dark, flying on the gale. They soared over him, then dived into the circle of red light, rising above me, wheeling about me. As they flew, drops of liquid flame fell from their wings. Where the drops fell to ground, thin fiery rivulets ran across the black rocks. Mathon kept his stare fixed on me. I tried to hold on to that stare, but couldn't . I was moving about rapidly to escape the cascade of burning rain. He raised his arm, and one of the fire-birds flew in towards him, hovered, and settled on his gold-clad forearm. As it settled, its wings spread, and a dazzling flare of reflected light rayed out from the gold arm guard. I threw up my arm to protect my sight, and turned; lurching and stumbling on the uneven ground. One by one, at random, the fire-birds skimmed low all around me, and, stretching their wings widely as they landed, touched down. Where they met ground, pillars of flame shot up into the blackness.

'Shall you rise? From the ashes of the Burning-Ground?' I heard his voice echo. 'Or shall you be taken by the Lord of Gates?'

I slipped, and regained my balance. The birds were flying in, diving, hitting the stones, incinerating the area around me. Streams of molten rock ran between my feet.

'Neither, you bastard!' I screamed. He laughed. The bird on his arm spread its wings again, then folded them back. A flickering scarlet radiation surrounded the warrior and the fire-bird.

'You shall need to call on more force to challenge the Hawk Master! Birds or Gates, dead-man?'

'Me, or you? That's the choice, is it?' Rage burned in me, like acid through my torn and bleeding body. Then I only knew one thing. I needed to destroy him, as surely as I knew he had come to destroy me.

'No contest!' I shouted, across the roar of flame and melting rock. 'If I go down, I take you with me!'

'You have chosen the Path of Death!' he replied. 'Now there is no more choice! You have already chosen!'

'Bullshit!'

He raised his arm again, and the great bird opened its burning wings, and took off, flying up. It rose high above him, pouring light down to illuminate his perfect glittering armour. For a moment it hovered in the black sky; then it swooped down and, flying at terrible speed, close to the ground, moved towards me. I leapt to one side, tumbling over sharp loose fragments of stone. The bird banked, curved, and dived at me again. I jumped over one of the fiery streams, grasped at smoking rock, and hauled myself upwards, over a rise in the stone where the rocks were cooler.

I climbed – my feet slipping and kicking black loose fragments which rolled away into the rivulets below to be engulfed in fire. Scrambling to reach a rough ledge, I flashed a glance back, and looked for the bird. I saw it, skimming the ground, heading in my direction. But there was no sign of Mathon. The creature rose and came at me; its eyes shining luminous-green through the dark fires. Then, when it was only an arms' length away from me, I flung myself to one side, grabbed at the rocks and rolled away. But the fire-bird soared up suddenly, instead of hitting the stone, and spread its wings above. The voice of the warrior sounded all around.

'I am the Shape-Shifter! Prince of trickery!'

I looked up, and saw his form mingle with that of the fire-bird. The golden armour became tongues of flame. Scintillating feathers dropped specks of burning liquid on to the black rock. The Shape-Shifter. I saw the face of Thainé again, as she sat high on her pale horse. And I saw the shape of the Spirit-Woman, the Great One, drawing down into her.

The bird plunged; its tail flaming behind it like a comet's trail. I scrambled desperately to escape its dive. It swerved; hitting the ground, and spreading a track of molten rock just below me. Then it was gone. I stared into the flames; a crescent-shaped searing pathway below me. As I watched, the fire extinguished itself. And I found that I looked into a gaping abyss. The voice of Mathon sounded out of its depths.

'Your destiny is assured. You have no defence.'

'We are all shape-shifters, Mathon! If we choose to be! I promise you, if you take me, I take you with me! I promise you!' I looked down into the emptiness. I remembered the Time-Chasms; the traverse which took us across the very edge of them. At the side of me, a thin ledge of rock traced across the brink of the gulf. And I saw my route; across it, to the other side, where the fires had now gone out, leaving tendrils of oily-grey smoke.

I began to walk; moving sure-footedly. The need to destroy him had taken over. One of us would win. I didn't care how, and I didn't care why. It was going to be me. An arrow whistled out of the empty space, and embedded itself in the rock just behind my head. It shone, silver, through darkness. Then the rock cracked open. Behind me, the ledge disintegrated; falling down into the abyss. From the huge crack, yellow-red burning liquid spewed out; pouring down like a waterfall into the depths. Instinctively, I lunged forward; grabbed at the rock at my shoulder. My foot slipped and I swayed. Then I pulled myself back to the narrow ledge, regained concentration, and continued to move along it.

'You cannot destroy me!' the warrior shouted. 'Do not imagine that you can! I am the bringer-in of the Alpha and the Omega! I am the Opener of the Gate!'

'Stick it! Where the sun doesn't shine, you rat's ass!'

'I am Conflict! For Conflict shall bring forth Mutation!'

I heard his voice echoing up from beneath; but I kept moving, aware that he waited for me to fall. I was aware that he was trying to unbalance me. But whatever shape he took I'd be waiting for him. My anger was single; one-pointed. I had never needed anything more than I needed to destroy him, to survive – and to follow the Woman, as I had chosen to do. I *was* nothing else.

A second arrow plunged into the rock inches in front of me. In a burning torrent, the ledge fell away. I slipped down, grabbing desperately at the lip of rock with my fingertips. Inch by inch, I hauled myself up, and swung back on to the ledge. Another arrow screamed through the darkness, – splitting the stones open on the other side of me. Suddenly I had nowhere to go. Now there was either up, or down. There was no sideways. The bastard was trapping me; slicing through until he got to me. And then my anger turned cold. I stood, my back against the rocks, and didn't make a move. Arrows flew to my left; systematically edging nearer to the place I stood. Rivers of fire poured down into the chasm, one by one. I waited, as a predator waits for the killing time, as the ledge was transformed into a pinnacle of stone, and the last arrow came.

And in one lightning move, I plucked it out of the air. It seared my hand, but I gripped it tightly, twisting its momentum to go with my will.

'I am armed now, Mathon!' I shouted down into the empti-ness. 'I've chosen weapons, and this one's got your name on it! Lord of Gates! That's what's written here! This one's for the Lord of Gates!'

My challenge was met by silence. My voice echoed in the hollowness of the chasm. Then, across the empty space, I saw a line of warriors appear, through swirls of smoke, and mists rising from deep below. They stood on the rocks opposite; their heads helmeted with the skulls of hawks. Their breastplates reflected flame from the burning rivulets which poured ceaselessly into the abyss. Each was armed with a spear, and held a shield of faceted crystal. The line of glittering shields split the light into dazzling rays so blindingly fierce they forced me to turn aside. Raising my left arm to protect my vision, I kept a tight grip on the arrow in my right hand. Mathon's voice crossed the gap between us.

'I am many lies! The Shape-Shifter! My name is Legion! Yet I am but one! Which one?'

Through the blinding rays, I saw the line of hawk-skull masks; their eye sockets glared as black holes in the light.

'*Which one?*' he shouted again. And I heard his laughter.

'Mathon!' I called out. 'I will take you with me!'

'My mission is to put an arrow into your heart!' he replied, across the dark space. 'And do not imagine that you cannot die! The heart of your Soul can die! And thus shall you be destroyed! It is that for which I aim!'

In one movement, the line of warriors raised their spears.

'Choose!' he cried, 'one!' The eyes. The truth would be in the eyes. But the line of skull-holes masked truth. I focused my concentration. And the warriors took aim. I sought my destroyer; hunting down the line for the pattern which was his. Slowly, all but one became indistinct. Their forms shimmered, liquefied, until Mathon – the true one, stood opposite me. His armour and shield shone with light cast by the torrents of fire.

Instantly, I lifted my arrow, and with all the force I had in me, launched it across the chasm, aiming at his throat which was unprotected by armour. In a flash, he raised his shield. I saw the arrow explode as it hit the crystal; and a blazing whiteness lit the smoky air. In the midst of the brilliant flare, a huge winged creature rose up.

The light faded, suddenly. And I saw that Mathon was no longer there. I gazed towards the opposite rocks; straining to see through the semi-darkness. But as I searched the rocks for sight of him, I heard the beat of wings above me. Quickly I looked up to see a great eagle swooping down on me. Balanced on the pinnacle of rock, I had nowhere to go. I had only one move left. And I was going to keep my promise.

The eagle's talons ripped into my arms as I twisted, gripped its neck, and clung on, as together we fell from the rocks into the depths. I heard the roar of the flaming rivulets. I heard moaning winds rush past us as we plummeted downwards, locked together in combat. The eagle's great hooked beak opened and its tongue lashed my neck. Its talons tore into my limbs. But I felt no fear. And I felt no pain. I had kept my promise.

We met fire, and passed through it. Then we plunged deep into murky water, and sank. Through the gloom, I saw Mathon. Our faces drew close together as we grappled to destroy each other. But his amber eyes shone with a triumphant light, even though my unnatural strength began to overpower him.

We rose up; broke surface. Around us, skimming over the dark water, fires drifted, licking around us. I took Mathon by the throat; crashing him down, back underwater. But he came up again, fighting my grip. And I saw that in his hand he held a huge arrowhead, which glinted silver as he lifted it high, then plunged it, once, into my heart.

A pain came, like I had never known; then passed. And I found that I looked down from above; watching in silence as he raised the body of a man high, in both hands, above his head. I watched as slowly, through the still water and the dancing surface-fires, he moved, carrying the man whose torn and lacerated form was lit by a glow of whiteness which spread out from the arrowhead. Step by step he emerged from the waters of the lake; climbing effortlessly over the jagged black rocks of its shore. He moved slowly upwards along a pathway, to a dimly-lit cavern. There, in the centre of the cavern, where a slab of marble stood, he put down his burden. Then he knelt, touching his brow, once; and pulled the arrow from the man's heart. Blue light flooded into the wound.

And I looked up; saw his face above me. His eyes, fixed on mine, glowed, animal-like in the gloom. His proud head, circled with gold, inclined down; and he saluted me with the Charos' sign.

'I destroyed you,' he said, 'as I was called to do. But I did not master you. And I do not stand in triumph. I join you as your brother. I changed nothing but the pale shadow. Such was my mission. That which is risen is base metal.'

28: *Mutagenesis*

SLOWLY, UNSTEADILY I got up from the white slab of marble. I looked down at my body, but could see no trace of wounds, no blackened blood-streaks. Fascinated, I lifted my arms in front of me, gazing at them. Where the eagle's talons had torn and gouged, there were no marks. I remembered the Dog Soldiers. I knew who they were; and that I was one of them. Strange warriors. They were my past, my future, my present. I understood. From a time which was all time, I recalled them and understood. When I looked up, I saw that Mathon stood a short distance away. He watched me.

'They have come for you,' he said. 'They wait in the Labyrinth.'

Without answering him, I turned, and walked away up a dark sloping path which led out of the cavern. I knew that he followed me. I knew where I was going now; and how. And why. But I walked as if I were crossing a dreamscape. We passed along the twilit narrow track, to the metallic filigree between the Labyrinth trees. As we moved through, its once impregnable hardness offered no resistance. Fine, almost invisible weblike substance brushed my arms and face as I stepped out into the tree-lined passageways.

There, on the other side, two of the Charos awaited us. After they had given the signs, we continued in silence along the still arcades to the Blue Dome, where we moved on to the second axis. Then the glittering hemisphere of the Inner Dome confronted us, and I saw Ethamar. She was seated on a large plain blue stone, and she was surrounded by a perfect semi-circle of warriors, who were dressed not in war-dress, but robed in white flowing garments. As we entered, she rose and stepped forward, towards us.

'It is done,' Mathon said. I felt odd as I met her gaze; filled with a sense of great strength and weakness combined. I remembered the Woman of the Rose on the stairway which led from Base Camp; and how, at her touch I had felt the same sensation. Then, Ethamar spoke;

'If it is your will, come forth into the Company of Twelve.' She moved back, retuning to her seat in the centre of the crescent of standing Charos warriors. I walked forward; and heard her speak again.

'You have stepped over the threshold, where the Lord of Gates holds dominion. You have opened the Portals of the Beginning. You have challenged the Night of Time, and you have been born out of it. The Arrow has taken your existence, and given you power.'

A light began to surround the whole gathering. I felt it run through me, and experienced a kind of fear; a quick fear. I glanced behind. Mathon had positioned himself at the open end of the semi-circle. The Chieftain spoke again, and I turned .

'Thus shall you enter within our number. Thus shall you receive the Instruments and the knowledge of their operation. Thus shall you bear arms; neither for the supreme triumph of Light over Darkness, which, in the Dance, can never be, nor for the sole purpose of destruction. But for the restoration of the Law of the Balance, which is before all other Laws.'

Around us, the brightness increased. Two of the blue-robed Charos moved out of the gathering. They came towards me, and I saw that they carried objects which glinted and shone in the spreading whiteness of the air. They positioned themselves on each side of me.

'What say you?' Her voice, clear and strong, broke through the dreamlike strangeness of the scene. She addressed me, but I couldn't speak. I looked at the faces which surrounded me: calm, dispassionate, aware of their own power. But they were of another World; a different scheme of things. They were not even Human. Yet they were my brothers. From now on, I worked with them. Their faces merged into the brilliance, until I could no longer distinguish one from another.

'What say you? Are you ready to serve?' I nodded.

'You must speak.'

With difficulty, I tried to make some sound. Then my voice came through, resonant in the light.

'I am . . .'

In one swift movement, what remained of my clothing was torn away by the two warriors who flanked me. They lifted the

objects they held; then, piece by piece, clothed me in them.
Metallic webbing was placed cross-wise over my shoulders, and
was fixed to a belt of titanium. I watched fascinated, as the lower
part of my body was covered with a dull-grey flowing substance,
which bound itself to me like a loose skin. Over this, on each
thigh, the warriors placed soft webbing, of the same kind that
crossed my shoulders. It wrapped around, angling downwards
on my outer thighs; and on the outer part was studded with
single-terminated crystals. The crystals jutted out, catching the
light; raying clear colours through the white air. On my arms,
the gold arm-guards were placed; and on my feet, boots of the
same colour as the strange material which formed my leg-
covering. The boots were soft and fine; but instead of covering
loosely, they adhered where they touched.

'You have received the dress of war,' the Chieftain said. 'And
the old form is cast off. The skin is shed.'

The two warriors, having completed their task, moved slowly
away to re-join the semi-circle. Then Ethamar left the blue
stone, and approached me. As she drew near, I noticed that she
carried two objects. In her left hand she held a gold circle, and in
her right hand, a black crystal with fine threads attached to it.
The threads hung from her fingers. I felt a sudden flash of
apprehension.

'Receive the Instruments. The knowledge of their operation is
contained within the Circle.'

I saw her raise the circlet of gold. And as she did so, in a
kaleidoscope of visions, I saw the Spirit-Woman, who held the
green snake. I saw the eagle, wheeling high above me. And I
heard the black-haired Spirit-Woman speak.

The serpent devours its tail and is born anew.

Her voice rang through time, and spaces of the darkness, and
through spiked iron trees, where her touch had brought life to
the wasteland. Her voice rang in the voice of the Grandfather,
who pointed a brown, long-nailed finger at the sky. Once more
I saw Thainé, as she reined her horse around, and turned away
from me to take her position at the point of the arrow formation.

*Through all, from the beginning to the end; from the Alpha to the
Omega, my spirit shall be with yours.*

Ethamar placed the gold circle on my head. When it touched

me I saw, not her, but the eagle swooping down towards me through Sequoia branches. I gripped the snake; holding it high on my chest as an intense pain burned on my forehead and my sight reddened. I heard my own voice cry out. And the eagle banked sharply; its powerful wings whipping my face. In my hand, and on my chest, I felt the weight of the black crystal. Where the circle of gold had been placed, a brand burned into my head; and the visions blended together into one agony.

Then Thainé came, riding towards us across the desert of the Outer Plain of Xentha; her horse leaping the fissures which we had found so difficult to cross. But this time, instead of seeing only Weismann, I only saw her. I watched as she rode in on the storm; watched as out of the blackness of that strange jewel high on her breast came an ultra-violet radiation which rendered the crystal transparent.

Then, suddenly in the midst of the raging wind, horse and rider halted; and the radiation spread to form a spherical shield which enveloped them totally. The stark whiteness of its glare didn't blind me. On its surface I saw three reflections: Weismann's, Nelson's and my own. And beyond the reflections, through the whiteness, I saw Thainé, her eyes focussed on us as the storm whipped tendrils of long hair about her face. When I looked again at the images on the surface of the light, I saw that only Weismann's reflection remained. And in Thainé's eyes; in the concentration, the focus of intention, I saw the hunter take aim. Immediately, the light-shield drew in, to a single beam of radiation; and Weismann was struck. But as his replica lit up with an unearthly glow, and the rocks of the Plain melted around us, something left his forehead, slowly drifting into the air. It was a small translucent sphere, clearly defined, like an air-bubble in water. In the very centre of that sphere, was a red spiral form within a transparent six-sided figure. I hardly had time to see it, before a whirlpool of light caught it up, and it was consumed in a tongue of white fire. Then, around us, the Plain twisted, buckled, and froze. My consciousness returned to the Dome at the sound of the Chieftain's words.

'It is given.'

She moved back, giving me the Charos' sign. I stood, unable to move; aware that the crystal had been laid below my throat, and that in its opaque darkness lay the secret of the Annihilators. It felt both heavy, and light; massive, and of no substance whatsoever. I found myself returning the salute. As I touched my forehead, I realized that I felt no trace of pain. The great brilliance had faded from the air of the Dome, and I noticed that Ethamar and I stood alone. The twelve Charos and Mathon were no longer there. If they had ever been.

Then she moved on to the place of the axis, and I followed. Neither she nor I spoke; and as I took the second axis I was filled with a sense of unreality and great energy, combined. I felt sure, deep inside, for the first time, where I was going, and why.

Mathon waited in the Labyrinth beyond the axis-shift. He was mounted and held the reins of a second horse. The creature turned as I drew near to them, gazed at me through the eye-holes of its war-mantle, and touched my hand with its muzzle. Then its proud head lifted again, to stare ahead into the trees. I stood, watching Mathon, who observed me in silence. The faintest trace of a smile crossed his face. Then he bowed his head slowly.

'Forgive me, my brother,' he said, and stretched out the hand that held the reins, offering them to me. I hesitated; then took the threads from him, and mounted up. Once astride the lean grey beast, I knew that not only was I able to ride, and ride well, but that I was a skilled horseman. The graceful creature responded. I felt it thrill beneath me, as something ran through it and me, bonding us. I addressed Mathon.

'Okay. What do we do?'

But the words felt so old. And I felt as though I hadn't spoken for a long time. Then I turned to the warrior. For a moment, our eyes met; but Mathon didn't smile, and neither did I. He pointed down the long arcade ahead of us.

'We ride out,' he answered. 'The time has come.'

With another glance at me, he jerked the reins of his horse, once, and took off through the Labyrinth, riding at a gallop. I followed, feeling the light grace and power of the creature under me.

We rode on; and out of the shining network between the trees, mounted Charos appeared, breaking through the lattice material with ease. Thin, gleaming fibres momentarily clung to them as they rode forward on to the pathway. From somewhere deep in the Labyrinth came the sound of a single horn-call, which soared, and hung, mingling with the thunder of horses' hooves as one after another warriors emerged from the trees to ride behind us. Ahead of me, I saw Mathon raise his horn and answer the call with one drawn-out note. Nine riders, eleven with Mathon and me, entered the courtyard; slowing to a trot as we circled round, preparing to make formation. Mathon rode beside me. He lifted one hand, stretched across the gap between us, and grasped my hand in a tight fist, lifting our arms together. I looked at him, seeing him smile widely. And I accepted the comradeship of his powerful grip. As we passed through the courtyard, I noticed that the pyramid had gone. And by the thin stream, another rider waited. Nelson. Mathon moved away to join up with the war-party on the far side of the courtyard; and I rode up to Nelson. From high on his Charos horse, he gave me his exaggerated left-hand military salute as I approached.

'Birds,' he said. 'It'll always be birds. Guess I could've told you that. Gates ain't your style.'

I looked at him, noticing he wore no battle-dress, but only his usual rainbow outfit and pseudo-Red-Man jacket. He was watching me closely.

'Yeah,' I answered in a low voice, then added: 'It looks like you're planning to ride with us.'

'Sure am,' he replied, and gave an extra twist to the leather headband he wore. 'Can't keep me from where the action is, Man. No way.'

I looked at the same place on his chest where I wore the Disintegrator. But his upper chest was bare, down to the top of his low-necked black shirt. Yet I noticed a thread of leather thonging hanging down, and on it, at the level of his heart, was a thin white bone with a curled dried claw-foot. The claws gripped a piece of amber. Next to it, on the thong, hung the star-shaped plastic ring his woman had made for him. He saw me looking at them and said;

'I ain't no gun-toter. It just ain't my Truth. But I got a number of Bright Spirits hanging round my neck and I'm game to see where they lead me . . .'

He was cut off by three sharp horn-blasts, delivered by

Mathon. I turned, to see that the warriors had already positioned themselves in the arrow formation in front of the Gate. From across the courtyard, Mathon's eyes burned with their yellow fire. I reined my horse around. So did Nelson. And we moved towards them. The point of the arrow was open. Nelson glanced at me and grinned.

'That is some hot spot,' he said. Then Mathon stepped back, indicating that the open space was for me. I felt a flash of caution, but moved into position. I heard Nelson coming forward, laughing as he positioned himself in front of me.

'Man!' he said. 'You ain't even got a clue where we're heading! Figure I'll ride along here a while, huh?'

Then the Gate began to melt and widen. And suddenly, too suddenly, came Mathon's final horn-call. And we were riding, moving out, riding into the wind, on the Plain of Xentha.

29: *Riding Wild*

I COULDN'T RECKON the speed at which we travelled. But as we rode away from the encampment the causeway seemed to lift up, bearing us higher and higher above the Plain. I heard the nine riders and Mathon; heard the thunder of their galloping beasts at the rear. I tried to turn, to look at them, but I couldn't, as the force of the air around me made any movement except riding impossible. I felt the skin of my face draw back, stretched tightly over my bones: The bones of my soul, Nelson had said. The atmosphere was silvery; flecked with ever-changing colour. I watched Nelson riding ahead of me, his long braids swept out behind him. He raised his right arm, to signal.

'The first Ring!' he shouted. I could barely hear him through the sound of the wind. 'Two more!'

There was a dull thump. A sudden rush of air. For a moment Nelson's form, and that of his horse, was covered with something which looked like shining mercury. Then it was gone. And far beneath us, I saw rhythmic waves of shifting desert-dust. We rose up and up, following the line of the causeway, and passed through a second unseen barrier. As we moved through it and headed for the third, the force which drove against me almost made me black out; but I hung on, narrowing my eyes against it, and forcing my concentration on Nelson ahead.

'Mach three!' I heard him shout as we crossed the third with a dull explosion of sound; 'That's it! We can even out now!'

His pace began to slacken, and I matched his speed; turning to glance back at the riders behind us. Gradually, Nelson slowed to a trot, and I rode up to him.

'What the hell was that?'

'The Rings,' he said, as I drew up next to him, 'rising in the spiral. We're in a higher location.'

I viewed the terrain. The causeway had disappeared, and we were in a grey, deserted landscape. Contorted plant-forms stood in a terrain of volcanic ash. But they weren't living. They had no energy, and were twisted into grotesque shapes; frozen, barren.

'Okay. So what's this place?'

'Seriously inhospitable, ain't it?'

I didn't answer. I kept my eyes on the land around us. But I saw no evidence of habitation.

'You won't find no-one here,' he said, reading my thoughts. 'This is a mother of deserts, Man.'

'You can say that again.'

Hearing Mathon approach, I turned. He'd broken away from the formation and rode up to us.

'This area is clear,' Mathon said. 'Beta fifty to Beta seventy-six, clear. We remain on standby, but have worked the margins thoroughly. There can be no re-activation yet.'

'What's he saying?' I asked, turning to Nelson.

'He's saying it's clear. No replicas. No Raiders.'

'There have been mass disintegrations,' Mathon continued. He addressed me. 'From Beta fifty, that is the present location, to sector Beta seventy six. The area is sterile. Nothing can be built, here.'

'Used to be beautiful,' Nelson said quietly; 'that is, till the Raiders came. Used to be like Heaven, Well, sort of like you might imagine Heaven to be. Streams, and lakes with trees

round them. Little slopes, going down, over there, into hollows.'
He pointed, into the distance to the right of us.

'All green,' he went on; 'green with crazy flowers like you've
never seen in all your days. Gentle people. Okay, they weren't no
way perfect, sure, but they were good company. And they didn't
fret themselves over nothing, 'cause life here was sweet. They
were happy. It was sunny, kind of. Pink and blue like the evening.
Oh shit! Makes me want to kick some ass!'

I gazed around, and out to the horizon. The sky was pale grey
– a shade paler than the ashen ground.

'So the people . . .' I began, but stopped in mid-sentence. I
didn't need to ask. I knew what happened to them. They went to
the same hunting-ground Weismann ended up in. Then they
got melted.

'Guess they didn't keep enough Truth to stay immune,' Nelson
said, and added: 'not even in high places, Man.'

Mathon rode abreast of us. I watched him; noticed his expression. He was staring at the far horizon, and his eyes were
narrowed with concentration as he spoke.

'The next sector is an unknown quantity. Beta seventy-six
onwards has not been cleared. I suggest we keep guard.'

'When . . .?' I began.

'We will know when,' Mathon continued, turning to look me
in the eyes. 'We will know.' Then he dropped back, re-joining
the mounted warriors behind us. And we carried on, across the
grey desert. For a long time, Nelson and I, in the lead, rode in
silence together. I felt the featureless sky and the lifeless atmosphere of the terrain as a brooding inside me; clinging
threateningly. I knew what was coming. Sometime soon we
would be finished with this desolate place. Then it was all
going to begin. The reason why we had come this far. The
reason we were riding with the Charos. The purpose, we had
come to fulfil.

'Is this forever?' I suddenly said, breaking the tense silence
between Nelson and me, 'This . . . wasteland . . .? Will it ever
grow again?'

'No,' he replied. 'It ain't forever. This side of the Crossing-
Place, ain't nothing that's forever. But it won't grow again till the
plague's over. Then it'll take a lot of building. Ain't nothing you

could make here right now. Like Mathon said, it's sterile. After disintegrations, the land's like that. 'Cause the land and the people are one. They built this out of what they were.'

'But that wasn't enough.'

'That wasn't enough,' he answered.

As we increased our speed, communication became difficult. I sensed that Nelson didn't want to talk anyway, so I left it and just rode. We crossed the wasteland; finding as we progressed that the ground had become twisted and irregular. The dark ash-like substance gave way to jagged, fantastically shaped rock formations. It was bad riding ground, but I felt the creature beneath me take it with agility and surprising strength. I knew how hard it would have been to cross that landscape on foot; remembering our last desert crossing on the Outer Plain of Xentha.

The land gradually began to incline upwards, until we were travelling continually uphill. After we had climbed for some distance I noticed a faint glow over the horizon, which grew more distinct as we moved towards it. And the ground over which we travelled became greener, lusher. Nelson slowed down, and we matched our speed to his. He raised his arm as a signal to us, then slowed even more until he came to a halt. He dismounted. Ahead of us, the light shone: glowing and gold, like the gleam of a sunset in high summer. I rode up to him, and as I approached I saw that he stood on the crest of a hill which sloped down into a shining crater-like valley below.

'The Valley of the Sun,' he whispered. 'It's always been a sacred place. Maybe it still is. This place has got its correspondence in Old World. It touches the people with high ideals of the Spirit . . .'

I looked down. White-pillared classical buildings stood on the glowing green landscape. In between them, apple trees grew; in full leaf and heavy with fruit. Vines − cascading with purple flowers − clung to the pillars which supported the open-sided buildings. As I watched, I saw white-robed figures moving slowly across the flower-covered lawns. And I saw people meet, greet each other and walk hand-in-hand to sit by small pools of clear blue water. Laughter drifted up to us − light notes through the golden air.

But I felt strange as I looked down on that scene. It was joyful, peaceful, but somehow it sickened me. It was cloying, even after the endless greyness of the wasteland. I noticed that Nelson had turned to me, and was watching me. He had unfastened the plastic ring from the leather thong around his neck. I hadn't seen him do it. Then he reached up, handed the ring to me, and told me to close my eyes.

'What's this?' I asked.

'You tell me.' I held the ring; closed my eyes. I felt better. When I opened my eyes again I saw him nodding slowly, looking serious.

'Medicine,' he said. 'Remember it.' He took the ring back; fastened it back on the thong. Mathon approached us on foot, leading his horse. He addressed us.

'We have just left sector Beta seventy-six. The area ahead has not been worked. We must be watchful.'

Nelson nodded. 'We'll go through. Got to, to get to the Crossing Place.' Then he turned his back on the scene below.

'So we can't tell, from here, if it's okay?' I asked. 'We've definitely got to ride through it?'

'Looks okay. But it feels weird. You know that, Man.'

Mathon had re-mounted. He reined his horse around and headed back to the formation of waiting riders.

'We proceed,' he called to us. Nelson gathered up the reins of his horse and, leading it, moved aside.

'We let them lead. Give 'em a head start. Then we follow. Okay, Man? Keep it tight.'

'Are they . . . Raiders? Down there, those people. Have they been taken?'

'Dunno yet. We'll see.

The Charos, led by Mathon, went out first; going down at a steady pace into the valley. We waited, watched them go, then remounted. Nelson looked at me, nodded. And at his silent signal we followed them down the incline. As we descended, the smooth soft greenery underfoot became washed with light. I watched the riders ahead of us. They had completed their descent, and had begun to cross the valley floor; riding slowly and in tight formation.

Some of the inhabitants had noticed their presence, and

watched in silence as they passed. A few, gathered on the steps, or by the low walls of the white buildings, seemed fascinated by the mounted warriors. And the ten riders travelled on.

Then Nelson's hand jerked out towards me, quickly, sharply. I flashed a glance at him, but he didn't look at me. His gaze was set straight ahead. In front of us, there was a sudden flash of searing light. Between us and the Charos riders the ground lifted and flowed. A roaring sound began, and increased as bright metallic liquid rushed through a channel which cut across the golden landscape.

'Holy shit, Man!' I heard Nelson shout. 'This is it! Go left!'

There was another great flash, and a beam of brilliance lit up the air. Directly in front of us the ground began to swell and push upwards. Immediately I jerked the reins of my horse, lunged sideways, and rode. Nelson followed.

'Go round!' he shouted. 'Keep going left!'

I turned; looked into the blinding lights. I saw glimpses of the Charos; their horses rearing, the reflecting shields springing out around them. Beams of blue-white fire shot across the terrain, finding target after target. I saw Mathon, standing high in the stirrups of his mount. Then he was rushing forward, and was gone, swallowed by the whiteness. The open-sided buildings flared and melted. Their forms liquidised, flowing over the ground. We galloped through. To the left, an open pathway took us round the mayhem, as the rocks beneath us heaved; pushing upwards. Ahead of us I saw buildings half-standing, half-melting on the fringe of the combat zone.

'Okay!' I shouted to Nelson. 'Where?'

'Round the edge! Just ride!'

'Why not in? With the Charos? Take some of them out! Why not?'

'Save it!' he shouted back. 'It's not the jewel! It's you! Your energy! Your energy's what activates it! You're gonna need all you've got and more, yet!'

'Nelson . . .!'

'Let them do it! Let's ride! Move round 'em!'

'Nelson!'

'What?'

'I can hear something!'

'Leave it!'

'Screaming! Nelson! There's someone screaming in there!' I heard it, from one of the melting buildings; a high-pitched scream. Inside what was left of the pillared structure, I caught sight of a figure, darting to escape the up-thrust of the heaving ground. I slowed, pulled away from Nelson, headed towards the building.

'Leave it! Man! Leave it!'

But the screaming didn't stop. As I rode, I shot a glance back at Nelson; saw that between us, the ground had buckled, cutting him off from me. I saw him rein his horse back sharply, and turn amidst a cloud of dust to avoid the jutting rock. As I rode up the white steps, a twisted, charred skeleton of an apple tree snagged against me, hitting my arm-guard with a dull ringing sound. Brittle remnants of a branch caught my neck, pulling at the cords which held the jewel. I flung myself sideways, ducked, still clinging to my horse. The jewel stayed fixed. Then, as I straightened up, I saw the one who screamed. At the far side of a turquoise and silver inlaid floor, part of which remained intact, a woman sat crouched; her knees drawn up, and her head sunk down on her arms.

As I dismounted and approached her, she must have heard me, for she lifted her head. She had stopped screaming, and was now weeping; her eyes tight closed. Tears fell from beneath her long fair eyelashes, and she shook her head from side to side in despair. Then she spoke. Her voice was wracked with sobbing.

'Help me . . . Are you one of the Destroyers . . .?'

'I am.'

'Please . . . I ask you to spare me! I am not one of the New Race! It is the New Race you seek to destroy! I am one of the Enlightened!'

'Open your eyes.'

'I cannot.'

'Open them.'

'I am blinded. By the rays. Help me, please! Our Holy Place is burned, destroyed, and I am afraid to stay here. But I cannot wander, sightless' The woman stood up suddenly with an agility which surprised me. She was naked to the waist, young, so fair her hair was nearly white. The lower part of her body was robed in a flimsy garment. She stretched her hands out in front of her, and moved towards me, unsteadily. The sounds of the battle raging outside seemed further away. Her breasts were shining, golden flesh; whitening where the skin stretched over fullness. Her nipples were pale, pale pink, delicate, almost childlike. Her hands reached to me. I couldn't move. I watched her; watched the cascade of white hair around her flawless features.

'I do not see you, Destroyer,' she whispered. 'I do not see you, but I feel your spirit brushing mine.'

Her fingertips touched my face, feeling, following the line of my brow, my cheekbones, my chin.

'Now I see you,' she said faintly. I watched the dewdrop of a tear on her eyelashes. It sparkled. And her breaths came, steady like waves lapping on a shore. A pink light began to glow around her; crossing the gap between us, swirling round me. And I realized I could hear no warfare any more. The waves of her breath washed away the notion of conflict. Her nipples touched my lower ribs. Then she leaned forward, kissing the jewel high on my chest. The glow deepened.

'I am afraid . . .' she whispered; '. . . of being alone . . . Let me take you with me. Without you, I shall not survive. Let me in. Let me inside you, Destroyer . . .'

She sank down, kissing my body. She stretched my arms out, wide, with hers and sprang up again, imprisoning my fingers in her clasp. Her lips burned down on mine. And I heard a humming, a pulsing in the reddening light. She tore her lips away and whispered:

'I know you, Brett. Now there is nothing I do not know. Because I have entered you.'

Behind my closed eyes I saw red spirals; small, like slowly-flying insects. They moved on pulsing cycles of sound. I watched them rise up, and sink down. My eyes flashed open, and I saw that she and I were cocooned inside a translucent sphere. Delicate, pastel-coloured eddies of light played over its inner surface as she caressed me, and her arms, her hair, her fingers, began to blend with mine in the pink glow.

Get out of there!'

'Who is that?' she whispered. 'Nothing but a dream, Brett. He is nothing but a dream. I shall take you where there are no more dreams.'

'Man! Hot shit! Listen to me!'

'He is deluded. Tell him I am one of the Enlightened.'

'Get out of there! Now! Man! The bitch is raping you! You get that? She's raping your goddamn soul!'

'He lies. You are hungry, Brett. As hungry as I am.'

'You reckon she's a woman? She's not a woman! She's Gehina! She's a virus! Open her goddamn eyes and see for yourself!'

'He lies. He is old, and he is insane. You know that.' 'Her eyes . . .' I whispered. Stroboscopic images of Weismann danced over the surface of the sphere . . . 'Blinded . . . by the radiation . . .'

'. . . You damn fool! Okay! Don't bother! Just get over here.'

'. . . Nelson . . .? Is that you . . .?'

'Remember, Man! That's all I'm asking you to do! Red River Rock! Remember? Duke? You remember him? The Woman! The Rose! The iron tree that grew a rose! Ask her if she can do that! Go on, ask her! The answer's gonna be no! 'Cause all she can make is a copy of you! A copy, that'll take ten steps out of here, and get blown away! Once she screws your soul, you got ten steps of future! Kill her! You can do it! You know how! Do it!'

Her eyes opened. In the pale crimson mist that fused us together, two black holes began to suck my strength away. And she was whispering something I didn't understand. Then I heard a tune. I recognized that tune, and the gravelly voice that screamed the music out. There were no words; just da, da, da, and a beat cracking down, again and again. Red River Rock. Someone was beating time. An old man with long grizzled braids was kneeling, lifting a stone, pounding it down on the ground as he sang, on and on and on. But it wasn't a song any more. It was a war-chant. I saw him leap up when the stone broke in two, and take the two halves, beating them together. He was dancing, bending, jumping. But the ice-cold cutting edge of the light in his eyes was fixed on me. The stones shattered, and he stopped singing. Tiny fragments fell from his fingers; running through his hands like sand in an hour-glass. I'd seen that before. Somewhere before. He stared at me, silently, with tears on his

face. Then he was holding a gleaming object; stretching out his
hand towards me.

'Remember this?' he shouted, his voice harsh, forceful. 'My
woman made it for me! She made me a star with a shining heart!
Out of her love! Here!'

He lifted his hand high, above his head. 'Catch it, Man! I'm
gonna throw it to you, right now! And you're gonna catch it!
You drop it, and I'll break your goddamn ass, you son of a
bitch!'

I saw the star leave his hand, and cross in a great arc through
the air. And as it fell, I needed to touch it again, to remember it.
I needed it. I lifted my arm; felt tendrils of fusion drag at it,
where her arm met mine. They elongated as I reached out to the
edge of the sphere, then suddenly, they snapped; and the sphere
stretched outwards as my fist pushed through it. Liquid light
poured down my hand. My fingers opened; catching the falling
star, And at that moment, raw instinct flung me back; out of her
embrace. As I gripped the ring tightly, and gazed at her form, a
rush of pain cut through me. I became dizzy; staggered backwards, away from her.

'Do it! Now! Or she'll come back for you! She'll try again!
She'll try till either she wins or you destroy her! You got to do it!'

Destroy her. I touched the jewel. My hand seemed to move too
slowly. *It isn't the jewel. It's you. Your energy's what activates it.*
She'll take you with her. She's raping your goddamn soul. That's
how they do it. They rape us. I looked across at the desiring,
ravenous thing that dwelt at the bottom of those pits of darkness
in her eyes. It was nameless, deadly, alien. But more than that;
far more. And I hated it.

'Fire with fire!'

Then, with a tremendous force of my Will, the light-shield
formed. Through it, I saw her; not as a Human shape, but as
fragmented red-black particles swirling, trying to fix a pattern in
their attempt to survive. But it was I who would survive. Not it.
The light-shield contracted instantly; and a great surge of some
essential thing in me rayed it outwards, into the heart of that
obscenity. Then I was watching as Nelson ran, fell, scrambled up
again, as the building dissolved around us, pouring white-hot
substance in rushing torrents. With a roaring sound, the ground

buckled upwards. And then, in a frozen blackened landscape awash with terrible brilliance, I saw Nelson swing himself high on to the back of his horse.

'Get out of there! Come on!' I ran, stumbling on the jagged up-flung rock; grasping at the scabrous surfaces, hauling myself over them. And in my hand, I was aware of the ring. I was vaguely aware that I was clutching it; taking it back to him.

30: *The Crossing*

WE RODE. WE seemed to skim over a landscape which melted, twisted and re-formed into tortured sculptures of steel-grey rock. There was no more golden light; no more buildings; no more people, as our surroundings began to take on the barrenness of another Wasteland. I had barely enough strength to ride. But then I felt that strange bond between me and the creature which carried me. It knew. It allowed me my weakness; and needed nothing from me to control or guide it as it kept steadily abreast of Nelson's horse, matching its speed exactly. I heard Nelson's voice rise over the wind.

'We're going up again soon!' he shouted, 'through another Ring! Just hang on and ride light! Got me? Then we can steady out a bit!'

I held on, but couldn't give him an answer. Then we broke through the invisible barrier; and as I heard the rushing, explosive sound, my strength suddenly returned to me. As we reduced speed, I realized that we had entered a completely new location. The landscape had transformed, becoming a high-altitude World. Around us, glittering white peaks soared up through the misty pale-blue air. Between them, we were moving over a high mountain plateau. The air had a fineness, a rarity. But it wasn't in my breath that I felt it, but in my mind, which became clearer, sharper. As we gradually came to a halt, I noticed the Charos warparty were assembled, waiting at the far side of the plateau. Glints of gold shone from Mathon's arm as he raised it to signal to us.

'Feel better now?' Nelson asked. He gave me a curious look. 'They ain't very nice, 'specially when they're down on your case.'

'I'm fine. Just about,' I replied. 'Nelson . . .?'

'What?'

'Thanks. Okay?'

'Uh-huh.' He nodded. Then he looked away from me, towards the riders in the near distance, and said;

'Yeah. Well, we're their last hope. Divide and rule, ain't that the situation? I know for a fact the Charos got loaded dice while they got us. Not me, not you, but us. And you and me, we've got to do our damn best, or those dice are gonna fall where they don't give no double-sixes. And we got to guard our backs. That is for sure.'

'Let's go.' I said, tightening the reins in my hands.

'They're waiting for us.'

'Hey . . .'

His hand went out, gripping my upper arm, and he looked at me carefully. 'Don't mean to be telling you something if you already know, but you are the hottest target around here. You got some fancy prize on your head. You are Wanted. Get my drift? Cause you ain't one of them.' He pointed at the Charos. 'And you ain't like me, neither. I'd just give the Gehina sons of bitches a bad case of indigestion. They'd break their damn teeth on me, and so they don't try. The Charos? Raiders can't reach 'em. But you. Oh boy. You're different. So I'd pay some attention to that ass of yours, and make sure it's so shiny-clean it squeaks when you walk. Or you're a dead dog.'

'Dead dog, huh?'

He grinned and let go of my arm. As he moved, I saw the silver-star ring glint next to the bird's foot on his chest. I knew that Nelson's woman and her plastic star had held back the bounty.

'Okay. Let's go,' I said. 'A price like that is too high, and I don't like the feeling. So let's keep going.'

'They don't come through the front door, Man' Nelson added as we began to move away. 'And they don't come through the back door, neither. They come in through those little cracks even a bug'd find it hard to get through. But once they get in, they make themselves at home. Then you got no more say, 'cause they get the last word. And remember this, they get through the cracks in something you feel strong about. And always when you least expect it.'

I glanced at him briefly, then moved off, heading towards the riders. Now I knew what he meant. I knew how the Raiders operated. Their hunting was easy for them. And it didn't even feel like being raped. It didn't even hurt. We crossed the light-blue air of the plateau, and came to a halt as we joined the Charos. Mathon drew away from the other riders, approached, and addressed us.

'This sector seems naturally clear. We have encountered nothing here.'

'Ain't that many get this far,' Nelson said. I noticed Mathon watching me. But he said nothing about the battle in the Valley. I wondered if he was aware of what had taken place there; that his last hope had almost vanished without trace. I had a feeling he knew.

'We go that way,' I heard Nelson say. I looked where he pointed. There, the plateau sloped up and in the distance rose almost to the height of the surrounding peaks where, high above us, we could make out a kind of mountain pass shining brilliantly through the misty air. Its whiteness had the appearance of sunlit snow fields. But I knew it wasn't snow up there. It was light.

'Okay, let's move out,' Nelson said, riding forward to take up position in front of the Charos group. I joined him, and we continued, travelling at a steady pace along the plateau. The ground began to angle steeply and we followed it, up towards the shining pass. The smooth, opaque-white surface of that ground reminded me of a high glacier slowly cutting its course across the heights of the Worlds. We continued; and as we rode, I saw no evidence of any person, or any creature, ever having trodden here. It seemed, as Mathon had suggested, naturally clear.

Then I remembered what Nelson had said. I watched him as he pushed on, slightly ahead of me. He had been here before. Once, sometime, he must have travelled this route with her. Together, they must have crossed those high peaks, making for their goal; the destiny that drew her. And all the time, I thought, he knew he was losing her; losing her to the forces which move through everything; the forces which never stand still. I remembered what he had said, about waiting at the Crossing-Place, somewhere beyond that pass. But the sound he had been waiting for never came. He had heard only the crying souls, and had returned, alone, over the same ground we travelled now: over those white pinnacles, across that deserted glacier. Alone, and without the one thing that meant most to him. And I wondered why. A great silence fell over us as we climbed. I could hear nothing; not even the feet of our horses. At the highest point of the pass, glass-like peaks rose up, shot through with rays of spectrum colours, constantly shifting and changing .

I felt a sensation of lightness, of freedom; and the quality and speed of my thoughts seemed to alter, as if thought itself was too slow and had to be replaced with something clearer, finer, faster. Nelson spoke. His voice cracked through the air with the shock and suddenness of ice breaking in spring.

'That's it,' he said, indicating towards lower ground in the distance ahead of us. 'The Crossing-Place.' Brilliance burned my eyes, and I could see nothing at first, as I was forced to shield my sight. But then I dared to look into it. The shining burned less. The pain in my eyes passed.

'That's it,' Nelson said again, whispering now. 'Ain't that some sweet baby? Where it all comes from Where it all goes to. That sure is some River of Jordan, boy!'

I watched him as he stared into that light. I had never seen more happiness, ever, in any man's face.

'Yeah, that's something else . . .' I said, drawing up next to him.

'Okay.' He turned quickly to me, then shot a glance back at the warriors waiting behind us. 'We're moving down. And keep on stand-by. 'Cause this ain't the end of nothing. This baby is just the beginning.' He turned to me again, and his pale blue eyes cut into mine.

'You got your ass tuned in? I hope so. 'Cause you're gonna need all the tunes you ever knew before we're through.' And before I had chance to reply, he was moving away, down into the light-filled valley; riding towards that radiance which I knew was the innermost point of the Levels. But I also knew that this, like he had said, wasn't the end of the journey. It was the beginning. For somewhere out there, the Raiders had their core, their Heart. That, and only that, was what we had come for.

I watched him as he rode; strained to see into the white gleam beyond him, all the time watching for any sign, anything, to betray the Raiders' presence. But I could see nothing but his mounted form, moving down, silhouetted against the light. Then I followed; not looking back, but knowing that the Charos moved with me. I shortened the distance between Nelson and me, and called out to him;

'Nelson!'

'Yeah!' I heard him reply; but he didn't turn round.

'The Warps! They've got to be soon. Like when? I don't know this place, Nelson! I don't have any idea . . .'

'You figure I've forgotten?' he shouted back. 'I don't forget nothing! Feel that breeze?'

'Yeah!' I felt it, coming towards me as I rode; blowing out of the whiteness ahead. 'Yeah! I feel it!'

'Right!' he called out. 'We're okay so long as it blows! When you don't feel it no more, stop. And I mean stop! Right where you are! 'Cause that's where it starts to get interesting! You got me?'

'I've got you!'

'Can you see?' he shouted, 'in this light?'

'It's okay!'

'Fine! You see one weird thing, you let me know!' Then I saw it. The one weird thing. Ahead of Nelson, immediately notice-able in the dazzling air, was one tiny speck. A single pin-point of blackness; no more than that. Almost instantly, the breeze stopped.

'That's it!' I shouted, and pulled back hard on the reins. I saw him pull his horse back, so tightly that the beast reared up. That dark speck stayed motionless – hanging in the air which was now dead-still. Beyond it, I could make out the immense river of light – heard it surging on its course, dividing the Worlds.

'Now, Man, don't move! Not even a little bit!' Nelson's gaze was fixed on the tiny area of blackness, but he lifted his arm, gesturing a signal to the Charos. Slowly, I turned my head; aware of his warning. I saw that the Charos needed no signal. They had already pulled up to a halt behind us.

'The Warp entrance, isn't it?' I said, drawing my gaze from the black spot to Nelson.' That's the way in . . .' I felt something tightening around me; something constricting inside me.

'That's the way in,' he repeated. He was quiet for a moment, staring at it. Then, suddenly, he spoke; raising his voice for the benefit of the Charos. 'Now I want you to listen real well, 'cause we don't get a second shot at this baby! In a minute, we move, and we move right into it! You got that? We don't ride to the right of it, and we don't ride to the left of it, but we go right down the middle!'

Mathon said nothing. I expected him to speak, but he was silent. I turned to look him in the eyes. He caught my stare for a moment, but his face was impassive; his only expression that of concentration.

'Where I go,' Nelson continued, 'we all go! Step by damn step! One by one! And we ride steady. Now you're gonna see all kind of things! You're gonna hear all kind of things! And you're gonna feel those Warps pulling you and pushing you, and stretching you right out! But you ain't gonna even think about it! You're gonna just ride, and follow my damn footprints! And . . .'

He looked at me, then gave a sharp glance to the Charos formation. His voice lowered as he added;

'. . . We'll get through. Every single one of us.'

I stared at him, recalling what he had said about the Warps. *There's always a risk. Don't imagine there ain't.* I steeled myself. We had always got through before. But the past was the past; and to me it never was a Mythical Beast. And there was always a first time to lose; to miss the target.

'Okay,' he said, too suddenly, 'we go.'

Without hesitation, he rode head-on into the spark of darkness; and was sucked away. Something, an old thing in me, wanted to turn then, and ride away. But I went in on his heels. Right in the middle. Rays speared me. Rays of violent light alternating with beams of deep darkness were turning, reeling; fragmenting Nelson's image ahead of me. The powers, moving together were fierce, deafening. My horse reared, twisting its head in raw terror; turning to look at me through the holes in its war-mantle, but I grasped the reins tightly, pressed down hard on its neck. Then I heard it scream as the beams of concentrated force swamped us totally, and I struggled to hang on.

'Nelson!' I shrieked. 'For God's sake! This isn't like the others!

It's nothing like . . .!' The Line. I tried to grip it, to bring it back, as I travelled, out of control. Behind me I heard the thunder of horses at a gallop; the sound magnified out of proportion. There were hundreds, rushing, plunging forward; screaming, frenzied. From somewhere inside the rays I heard shouts, and recognized Mathon's voice. But it came from the left of me, as I strained to retrieve the Line; tried not to hear the terror. My horse rose on its hind legs; shuddering as it pitched forward.

'Nelson!' But through the spears of light and dark, no reply came. The creature reared violently again, its screams echoing on the storm.

'I'm sorry!' I shrieked at the beast beneath me. But the grind and crash of the rays pulled my voice away. 'I'm sorry!! Sorry!!' The silver reins tore through my grasp, as the horse thrashed its head, twisting it round, as once more, and for the last time, its eyes met mine. Then I was thrown downwards, outwards plunging through one of the rays. My body met a resistance. It held me for an instant. Then it gave in, and I lost grip of everything.

31: Ice Heart

I COULD SEE a figure, moving towards me through milky light. Out of deep stillness, an old man came slowly nearer. He was speaking, but what he was saying was not intended for me. His words were in a language I only half understood; the language of the Spirits. He held the hawk's foot to his brow. It gave him power to travel with them in the Dark Spaces. Long hunter's claws, viciously sharp, clasped the shining amber between his eyes as he stood in front of me.

'Man . . .?' A voice whispered. I struggled to see through the light. Then I saw – an old man, not right in front of me, but far away, coming closer; his movements hesitant and weary.

'Can you see me?'

'Nelson?'

'Can you see me?'

'I see you.' But my voice sounded strange, uncertain.

'They didn't make it . . .' he whispered as he came up to me and stopped, an arm's length away.

'They didn't make it across; don't reckon they did . . .'

'They've . . . gone?'

'Saw half of 'em go down at the first crossing. Then I lost 'em, the rest. Dunno what happened . . .'

'The first crossing?' I broke in. 'So how many have we gone through? Where the hell are we, now, Nelson?'

'Never want to see stuff like that again, Man. Not even if I live a thousand times over. Horses screaming, men being burned away, being sucked down . . .'

'Jesus!' I gazed desperately around into the white nothingness.

'I figured they might have made it . . .' he went on; 'might have done. You can't tell till you try . . .'

'Nelson, where the hell are we? Are we through, or what? Is this it? Is this . . . *nothing* what we came for?'

'We ain't. No we ain't through.'

'We're not . . . in there yet?'

'There were four,' he said. 'There's another one.'

'Five Warps? We've got to cross another Warp?'

'Yeah.'

'And we get to the other side! Two of us! And we do what we can! And if we can't, we burn! Like them! Like the Charos! We've got one Disintegrator and a goddamn necklace of bright spirits between us, and we pull the switch on Armageddon! So stinking what?'

'Man, we got to go. We can't go back, and we can't go sideways, not on this bitch.'

'Yeah! We're going! Damn right we are!' My voice dropped, and I turned away from him. 'She's in there, Nelson. And I'm getting her out.'

'That all you got to say?'

'Look, I know what the game is! And I know I'm a piece in it! They wanted us to take them through, so they can carry on with their war! Okay! That's fine with me! They used her to get us! Fine! I don't even care!'

'Man, it's more than that. I don't need to tell you. You know what's riding on this . . .'

'For the first time in my whole damn memory, Nelson, something means something to me! Do you know that? We haven't got a hope in hell, you and me, when we get through! And you know what? I don't give a shit!' Then I heard a horn-call, echoing through the emptiness.

'Nelson' I grabbed his arm; 'You hear?' It sounded again, closer this time.

'Yeah!' he shouted, turning in the direction of the sound. 'Son of a . . .! It's them! It's got to be!'

I saw Mathon; walking out of the whiteness towards us. His face was set; strained. But when he spoke, his voice was clear.

'Three of us came through. Only three. But we are with you.'

Behind him, and on foot, two more warriors of the Charos followed. They didn't speak. I knew that discipline held them in a tight steadiness, but it was obvious that they had been stretched to their limits. I could see it in them.

'Oh boy,' Nelson said. 'We could still make it. If three of you guys make it, there's a future. Just three. It don't matter.'

'We're not there, yet.' I said. Mathon was quiet. His strength was still apparent, but there was a haunted look in his eyes.

'Okay,' I went on. 'So where's the other one? The fifth crossing?' I took a few steps outwards, away from the others. 'Come on, baby, we know you're here somewhere! All we've got to do is get across you!'

'Hold it. Let me go first. We take it cool and slow. And I want you guys with me, all the way.'

'Right. So where do we go?' I asked. He looked around; then pointed in the direction the Charos had come from.

'Let's try there,' he said.

I stared at him. 'You're flying this whole operation off the seat of your pants Nelson! Aren't you? I don't believe this! You don't know any better than I do! Jesus Christ!'

'Man, when you start to get mad at me, I know you're riding! But if I were you, I'd save it. You're gonna need it.' He began to walk into the whiteness.

'We should follow him,' Mathon said, moving in the direction Nelson had taken. 'He knows the route.'

And that was all he said. We had little option. We followed; but had only gone a short distance when the air became filled with streaks of faint colour. And I knew that was it. That was what we were looking for. I came to a halt; on guard for the opening up of the Warp. Then in front of me I saw Nelson and the Charos simply disappear. Behind them a dead silence closed in, with no sign that they had ever even been there. I watched; trying to feel the Warp's pull. But apart from the shifting pale colours in the air, there was nothing to betray its presence. For a moment I held back; then because there was no other way, I moved forward, and stepped into it.

A violent force caught me up, throwing me outward across ice-bound howling Worlds. As I clung desperately to a knife-edge of Will, I knew that we had never made any Warp crossing as treacherous as this. And I knew I was crossing the edge of the birthplace of all coldness; and that the Thread, which came only from myself, was my only hope. Rods of purplish light broke out of the glare. A high whining sound, rising in pitch, soared over the roaring winds, and lifted higher and higher until it faded away. The rods of colour sank low. And the wind gradually became less fierce; eventually dropping away to a steady moan. Around me, grey mist drifted. Then it slowly parted to reveal, an Ice World.

As the mist began to disperse I saw that I stood on the very edge of what seemed to be a vast frozen lake. I scanned it; listening carefully for signs of Nelson and the Charos. But there was no sound except the constant low-level moaning of the wind, which I could hear but not feel. A pale glow spread across the expanse in front of me, illuminating strange ice-sculpture shapes. Their twisted fingers were sharply uneven in places; in other places smoothed, carved by unknown forces. I stared over the ice field, searching for the source of light, and I saw angular structures in the distance, rising into a lead-grey sky. They could have been natural forms but something in me told me that they weren't. I knew, then, that they had been shaped, not by that Mind which carves the Elemental things, but by a different kind of intelligence. The Mind of Gehina.

A sudden movement behind me caused me to whip round

immediately. Through the parting mist, I saw Nelson emerge. And he wasn't alone. Mathon was with him. They had made it. Then I realized there were two men, not four. As Nelson approached me, his expression was tired and tense.

'The others?' I began. But his answer came as no surprise.

'They didn't make it. But Mathon did. So we got three now. Three against the New Order. It ain't much but it's better than nothing, and it's gonna have to be enough.'

We stood at the fringe of the frozen waste; staring out and taking stock of those strange shapes in the distance.

'Raiders' homeland,' Nelson said, narrowing his eyes as he gazed at them. 'There you are. That's what they build for themselves when they're nesting. Neat, but it ain't sweet.'

I glanced at Mathon. He was silent; looking at the structures ahead of us. I didn't know how he got through, when nine, the whole Charos war-party hadn't. But he had made it. And I knew what that meant. Just Nelson and I would never have been enough. One of the Charos had to do it; had to learn how to.

'You seen anything out there?' Nelson asked.

'No,' I replied. 'If you mean Creatures, people, replicas, no.'

'Well you can bet your ass they know we're here. We stirred enough stuff up getting here.'

'They went into Burn-up; the Charos. They're all burned up for the Cause, aren't they?' I said.

'Nine of them! All gone . . .!'

'Look, Man. They knew the risks. They did it anyway. That's what they're like!'

'Yeah,' I replied, unconvinced. The loss of the nine warriors suddenly hit me. But there was nothing I could do about it. They were gone. 'Yeah! Now with one of them, we've got one hope more than a snowball's chance!'

Then Mathon approached me; and without warning he gripped me hard, by the shoulders, looked directly into my eyes and said: 'We are trained for conflict. And its consequences. And never do we operate out of blindness or misjudgement. We are not here to mourn the passing of nine, but to prevent the taking of the Countless. We are here to lay a counter-weight upon the Scales; to restore the Law. However many of us there may be, that is what we have come to do. That is what we shall do. Are you ready?'

'Okay,' I whispered. 'Sure.' I turned away from his eyes and gazed towards the far buildings which loomed sinister and glittering.

'They know we're here . . .' I said quietly. 'That's what you said isn't it? Well maybe we'd better give them something a bit less boring to do than just look at us. That's where we're heading?' I pointed across the great stretch of frozen ground. Nelson nodded.

'Let's go.' Slowly we moved out; treading over that smooth hard substance. It was semi-translucent like ice, but when I tried to look into it, it revealed nothing but layer upon layer of the same material. As we progressed I felt obvious, exposed; knowing as well as Nelson did that the Mind which created those buildings on the other side was an intelligence which would not have omitted to notice trespassers on its patch. But all the time we moved forward, shortening the distance between ourselves and the structures I heard nothing, saw nothing, to show me that anything had registered our presence. Yet I knew for certain, that what lay ahead of us was no crumbling neon-city, abandoned and decaying. It was in a different league.

'That wind's a bitch,' I heard Nelson say. 'Goddamn bitch! Groaning and howling fit to make your Spirit freeze over.'

'Tough shit.' I replied.

'Hey, Hard-Man,' he whispered. 'Where'd you go to finishing school, huh? Sure taught you some fancy phrasing.'

I laughed. But my laugh sounded hollow and empty. I caught sight of Mathon scanning the area ahead. His expression was concentrated and he didn't even seem to hear us. Step by step we drew closer to the buildings. They stood, too-silently, too-perfectly ahead, and gave me the feeling of cold power; being itself for the sake of itself, nothing else. There was something about the approach, the wide flat empty plain we crossed, and the ordered structures which somehow reminded me of the entry into Xentha. Different in atmosphere; but at the point of the axis of difference, strangely similar.

There was no evidence of habitation. No sounds, except the nerve-wearing notes of the wind. No signs of life, or of anything which seemed aware of our presence. We kept moving. And the three of us fell into a tight silence. As we approached the buildings, they took on more definite shapes. Then I saw that they weren't buildings, but were complex crystal forms; some glassy, transparent, some grey, almost black. As I looked at the groups of forms, I knew for certain that they had been positioned exactly for a purpose; and I wondered what that purpose was.

Huge odd-shaped blocks of streaked rock rose above us; their conflicting angles and deep fissures, sharp spurs and huge grainy masses positioned in a way that could have been random. But as I looked at those shapes I felt oppressed, smothered by something cold drawing down into me. And as we reached a gigantic archway of elongated grey crystals I realized there was nothing random about the place. We were at the gateway of a citadel; and I felt myself recoil.

'Titanium Oxide . . . Antimony . . .' I heard Mathon say . 'These formations . . . are exact replicas of minerals.' He pointed to the arch above us. 'Elongated, prismatic, crossing at sixty degrees . . . It has the metallic lustre of Titanium Oxide. And there . . .' He touched the sharp filaments of a darker formation at the base of the arch. 'Antimony, acicular crystals . . .'

'He's right,' Nelson said. 'That's a fact. Look, there. And he moved under the archway, pointing at a mass of something which could have been quartz or ice. 'Strontianite. That's what this is.'

I gazed at him, puzzled. 'So what? So damn what? Rocks are rocks! Why? Why all this? That's all I want to know, right now. Why?'

'Dunno.' Nelson shrugged.

'It's irrelevant!' I snapped. 'Strontium, Titanium, whatever else! I just know it! It's about as relevant as ice-cream!'

'Man, don't yell at me. I get the same feeling.'

'But there's a reason, damn it, there's a reason for all these shapes, being put together like this! But it's like what they're *made of* doesn't matter!'

'We should continue,' Mathon said, passing under the massive archway; 'It appears to be uninhabited. I have made a scan of the area ahead, sufficient to see that we are alone.'

'But we're not, are we? Alone?' I called after him. 'We're in the

Raiders' heart, and we're alone? I don't believe that for a second!
Those guys want to survive, and we are not part of their survival
pack!'

'I know,' Nelson replied, and indicated towards the open
ground on the other side of the arch. There, the ice-smooth
ground was flanked by walls of crystal forms. 'But I don't see
anyone, and that's the best we've got. And that's the way we got
to go, so we go.'

'Dead man's gulch. That's what it looks like to me. It's classic,
Nelson, classic ambush set-up. Those high rocks, up there; us,
down here.'

'We move through at good speed' Mathon said, 'and aim for
the heart of the citadel. It would be wise to remain vigilant, but
I can see no evidence of any Creatures.'

'Okay,' I said quietly. I could see for myself that what he said
appeared to be right. But instinct told me that we were not alone.
Far from it. 'Okay. We keep going.'

I made the first move, and entered the courtyard; for that was
what it seemed to be, a vast courtyard of a bizarre city. I gazed at
the varied shapes in the walls around us. I noticed that ahead of
us, a short distance away, the entrance area narrowed, forming a
street-like walkway between the blocks. Obviously that was to
be our route.

'There are Creatures all right . . .' I muttered as we worked our
way across the open space.' They're here all right. But we just
can't see them. They've ducked the radar . . . somehow . . .'

With Nelson and Mathon behind me I pushed on; finding
that the first walkway joined another which intersected it. There
appeared to be a systematic network of wide pathways like
street-systems, leading deeper and deeper in. Looming above us
were colours, textures, sea-greens, sparkling blues, icy transparent needles, great curves of streaked rock, white chalky deposits.
I glanced down and saw my reflection. It stared dully back from
the ice beneath me.

'The centre . . .' I half turned, addressing Mathon. 'You said
the centre . . .? How much further?'

'We will know when we reach it,' he replied. 'But we must
reach it.'

'Thainé . . .? That's where she is, isn't it? In the centre.'

Mathon nodded. 'Yes I am certain of it. They will hold her there.'

'They!' I suddenly shouted, no longer caring if the silent invisible threat heard me or not. 'They! Goddamn it! Who are they? You can't see them! You can't look into their eyes! Not till they take someone! Then you can! Then it's too damn late!'

I spun round; turned to Nelson. 'Thainé . . .' I didn't shout any more but my half-whisper echoed back from the richly-patterned walls. 'They can't take her! I know it! They just can't! She's Charos! She's immune! She's armed, for God's sake! . . . Nelson!'

Then I began to feel the shape of things. The Spirit-Woman, myself, Thainé the warrior. Three, linked somehow together oddly, powerfully. And I knew that somehow, because of me, Thainé and the Spirit-Woman I had followed *had become the same Being*. And I remembered what Ethamar had told me; that Gehina had taken Thainé to reach the Other One. I felt the great weight of what I was beginning to understand; and its meaning was almost too much to take in.

'Listen, Man.' Nelson caught hold of my upper arm, gripping it tightly. 'I know you're seeing it, the Plan. I know.'

He paused, but his eyes locked on to mine. 'You're part of her Truth. Hers, and the Spirit-Woman's, the One who's with her. You're seeing it. There's no immunity without Truth. There's no immunity till all the lost pieces fit together, work together; not split off, or half-hidden, or denied, but all there, making a complete shape. You are a working part of that Spirit. You. Even though she seems far beyond you, beyond your kind, more powerful, wonderful, untouchable. You're a working part, like a little wheel's part of a big machine, or one star's part of a Universe. Without that part, the other parts don't work.'

I stared back at him. 'She's not immune . . .? Thainé? And the . . . Other One? I can't believe what you're saying! Without what I've got to do?'

'We must make progress,' I heard Mathon say, and saw him move on. Nelson said nothing but dropped his grip on my arm and followed Mathon.

'And you?' I called after him. 'You, Nelson. What about you? Are you immune?'

He didn't answer. He just kept moving.

'Jesus! I can't take this in! You kept saying you . . .! And what about him, Mathon?'

'It don't make no difference.'

'Sure it makes a difference! I'm carrying the can! That's the difference! For the whole damn lot! It's unbelievable! It's . . .'

'Don't you punk out on this! Don't even think about it! We've come too far, and your ass is on the line . . .!'

I fell silent – shocked by the realization. We moved on; didn't speak. I daren't think. All I had to do was keep going, keep it tight, do the job, take it to the limit. Anything else was unthinkable.

We became shrouded in a moving silence as we drew closer to the centre with every step we took. I turned within myself and gazed at the looming walls as we passed underneath them. I stared at the dark and light, the shadows and bulges, the curves and angles. And I felt afraid; of the weight of responsibility, and of the unseen enemy, so quiet, so hidden. A face leered suddenly from just above me. On the edge of my sight, its stretched mouth grinned, too big for its viciously pointed face. Instantly I spun round to it; and saw it melt back to blend with green-grey stone. I stared at the place on the wall. There I saw light and shadow. Nothing else.

'Oh, Christ,' I whispered. 'Pictures in the fire . . .' Nelson and Mathon had pressed on, putting distance between us. I turned and, increasing my speed, continued. I could still hear the moan of the wind and its effect was mind-chilling. Ahead of me the two men turned a corner, passing out of sight down an intersection. I approached the corner. A horribly emaciated child hung from a coal-black wall. One of its arms and one foot were missing and the stumps were blackened. Its tongue hung out, beginning to snake towards me.

'Dear Jee . . .!' I fell back hard against the opposite wall. The impact threw me forward again and I was swamped by horror as I stared at what was now living rock.

32: *Enemy Within*

THE SIGHT LOST its solidity. And the tongue became only a shadow on jet-crystals, cast by the eerie glow in the walkways. Suddenly weak with relief, I bent forward and gripped my knees; letting the shock of what I'd seen pass. Then I lifted my head to look back at the place in the wall where it had been. There was nothing. Nothing but raised areas and hollows. I watched. Slowly, the image took form again; just an illusion in flat dimensions, created by light and shade on the stones' texture. But the effect of what I'd seen wouldn't leave me. It followed as I walked unsteadily towards the next intersection.

At the junction of two paths, I paused; hearing the voices of Nelson and Mathon nearby. As I began to move towards them, I glimpsed a soundless thing at the fringe of sight, edging nearer. I whipped round to see the jet-black child creeping over the crystal wall; its eyes set on me. I froze; stared at it as a feeling of mounting horror washed over me. Its too-prominent ribs glistened. Its mouth hung open, and its tongue, covered in white growths, flickered out, snake-like. Segment by segment, it pulled itself free from the rock wall; moving slowly, but with intent. And for not one second did its eyes leave mine.

A rapid movement above tore my attention away. High up, fanged moths emerged from beneath an overhang of green rock; flexing wings covered with hundreds of needle-like shards. One by one they peeled their grossly-swollen bodies from the green stone, and, spreading their monstrous wings, dropped to land on the ice between the black creature and me. In a reflex move, I turned; seeing that my escape wasn't blocked. Then I tried to run, but ploughed desperately, trying to fight the too-slow dragging of my body.

A bristling weight settled on the back of my neck. I felt needle-wings wrap over my shoulders. The creature's touch freed me from stupor, and I flung myself forward, only to fall to my knees. But hardly had I touched ground than I sprang up again; trying to gain a footing on ice which had now become treacherous. I sprawled, slid, to crash against sparkling crystal. I caught sight of one of the huge moths taking off; skirting an outcrop above me, and coming to rest on a ledge of granite. Beneath the ledge, half-lit grainy rock slowly parted, forced open by the contorted movements of a man, hanging by the neck. He raised his head, silently screamed; and in a flash, his hand flew up to grip the rope above him. He tugged at it, and the rope snapped. Then he leapt down; his hands clawing at the ice as he came towards me on all fours.

I scrambled up, stumbling away across the slippery ground; trying uselessly to get a hold on the rock wall.

'Nelson!' I shouted. 'For Chrissakes!' My hand touched the Disintegrator at my neck. I struggled to focus. *Wipe them out. Now. They're Creatures. Gehina's Creatures.* But it wouldn't work. The Disintegrator was inert. I heard a faint voice.

'Hey . . .! Come on! Get your ass together!' I could hear him, but not see him.

'For Chrissakes, where are you?'

'Man . . .! What's hitching you up back there?' Another shape oozed underneath the layers of ice at my feet. A long, dark, heavy form slipped forward, aiming for me. I watched it come. Then it erupted through the frozen surface; rising up high, its sharp-toothed jaws slamming shut, missing me. The ground began to crack and, along its entire length, the walkway split apart.

My mind was racing. I tried to form the Light-shield as the hanged man straddled the widening crack. His voice was chanting:

One, two, three, four . . . someone's knocking at my door . . . four, five, six, seven . . . must be an angel come from Heaven . . .

But the crocodile was coming back. As I twisted round, I saw it turn, change course, start to break through the gash in the ice. As it came for me, I leapt, lightning-fast, feeling my feet touch its stony hide just before I landed behind it. Then I ran.

It's the walls . . . Just like you thought . . . There's something about the shape of them . . . The way they're built . . . Somehow that's forming the Creatures.

I skidded and was thrown hard against a wall. Clinging to a cruelly-sharp stone, I looked up. The hanged man and the child were drawing closer to me, their lurching walk slow and silent.

'Nelson! Can you hear me?'

But this time there was no answer. Only the moaning wind.

'Oh dear God . . .!'

Behind me I felt a new bristling; felt the crystals move. Instantly I threw myself sideways, sprawling full-length. Skidding, grasping at the sheer surface, I found myself turning helplessly to gaze up at a dark form. Approaching me was a cloaked man; his back hunched with growths of wavering porcupine spines. He had no mouth; only eyes, set at each side of his head. Those spherical eyes were split into hundreds of minute lenses, insect-like. His bare, skeletal feet of greenish iridescent metal, lifted one by one, delicately, as he crept closer to me. Frantically, I tried to scramble up; slipped back and tried again. And he kept coming. The giant moths swept down to flutter round his spined shoulders.

'Mathon!' I screamed; twisting my head back to glance into the empty pathway behind me. Then as I whipped back again, I caught sight of the crocodile making its way over the rock face above me. On its back, membranous wings, pulsing with fine green veins, flexed, spreading and folding back as it trod, sure-footed amongst the rough crystals. I saw it was moving past me, heading towards the clear area on the other side of the path. Then it changed course, and I knew, as I saw it begin to climb down, that it would block off my escape.

I slid quickly across to the rocks on the opposite side, and began to climb; pulling myself over sharp juttings of brittle stone, which partially crumbled as I grasped at them. I knew that if I could find Nelson and Mathon, there was some hope. Mathon could destroy them. Then a sickening thought hit me.

It was possible there was something about this place which was jamming the Matrix-Disintegrators.

Why carry the creatures of your nightmares to another? He has his own dreams of black roads, and has no need of yours . . .

I listened; gripping cubes of red transparent stone. *That is the voice of your power*, the Grandfather had said. I remembered. *When the Vision touches your feet, then you will hear the voice of your power from beyond the Thunder Place. And that is your own voice.*

I clambered up the rocks, grasping, slipping, scrambling up again; aiming for the top of the wall. Once, I glanced down to see the Creatures climbing behind me. Overhead, the spine-winged moths hovered; their fangs bared, glistening. But I kept going, knowing that if I could reach the top of the wall, I could move along it, to keep parallel to the walkways below. *Pictures in the fire . . .*

I almost stopped. A moth-wing grazed my shoulder. As I twisted my head, I saw the Creature pass by me, and rise. But the voice within me came again. *Pictures in the fire. You dreamed them into existence . . .* I struggled on, faster, higher; reached above me to claw my hand round an outcrop of shining stone. I hauled myself up. *Listen to the voice Bird-Man. Listen . . .*

'Nelson . . .?' As I gained the top of the wall, I thought I heard him. For a second, I stopped. Again I called out to him; but there was no reply. I could only hear the constant howl of the wind. I glanced down; saw the Creatures climbing quietly. *You have to listen.* I heard again. *It is time to listen, or you will create hundreds of them.*

A rough, narrow area of stone ran ahead of me, glowing with a faint yellow light. I got to my feet and ran; searching below me for sign of either Nelson or Mathon on the icy paths. Then the wall crossed another at a sharp angle. The intersecting rock sloped downwards in a long, sweeping causeway. But as I reached it, I was faced with a gap between the rocks. It was about twelve feet across, maybe more, and the next section of rock was much lower. Beneath me, I saw sharp points of gleaming purple crystal. I leapt. Their sharp angles snagged at me as I landed, and I fell; clawing at them. As I dragged myself up, blue, jagged features grinned at me, toothlessly.

No. As soon as you see it, you give it life . . .

But the face was already seen. Through the layers and facets, it began to rise, floating upwards soundlessly. Blue long fingers, black fingernails, twisted into corkscrew shape, began to haul its grotesque form through. I leapt up; threw myself over it, and looked back in fascination and horror as the Creature birthed itself out of the stone. It turned to me; still grinning. Blue-green glistening vertebrae jutted out along its back as it began to crawl towards me. Then I knew; I knew what the voice was saying. It was telling me that I was father to these monsters; that I had created them.

I spun away from the newly-emerged form, scanned the length of the slope ahead of me, and ran; leaping and stumbling over shards of amethyst.

Now you know how it works . . . They use your mind . . . your imagination. Whatever dreams you dream; whatever fragile shapes you have in the shadows inside you, they take them. They give them reality . . . You are the father. They are the mother. Gehina is giving birth to the seed which came from you.

I gained distance. But when I glanced back, I saw the Creatures coming. Trembling and sickened, I tried frantically to operate the light-shield. To see them as they really were. Then to burn them. But the Disintegrator remained inert; and the distance between me and them narrowed. I stopped trying, turned, and continued down the rough slope. I saw that it led back to another walkway. But there was no choice. Calculating my leap, I balanced and jumped. I touched down on ice and slid, struggling to keep upright on the slippery surface.

It's not the jewel. It's you . . . your power. Your energy is what activates it.

I collided with the opposite wall; groping on its smooth surface for anything to grip.

Swirling striated patterns met my eyes. I saw them, then twisted my head, instantly dragging my sight away from them. Then I realized that something had changed about the ice, too. Since the manifestation of the Creatures, it had changed; become more slippery. And now I could barely stand on it. Suddenly, I knew what the key was. Fear. The Raiders were using my fear. My imagination and my fear.

'Okay!' I shouted. 'Okay, I've got it! I've got the way you operate. I know, now!'

My voice returned to me on the moaning wind.

'You want me to be afraid? That's what you're after? You want my terror, and the pictures of my scared-rabbit mind? '

My sight flashed to the opposite wall, where the Creatures were slipping down; moving towards me. *They can't harm you. Not yet. Only your fear can do that. There'll be nothing left of you soon. Then . . . they'll move in and conquer.*

I focused; aware that I still couldn't grip the ice beneath my feet. I could try to run, slide, get up and try again; but they would keep coming. They would never give up. They were born from me, and Gehina. I pushed against the weight of terror. It was them, or me. Them, or the mission, and Thainé.

With a sudden flare, the light-shield shot out around me, capturing the twisted, mutilated images and analyzing them in its brilliance. And in it, they were what they were; not what they seemed to be. Thousands of tiny particles, spirals, moving randomly, yet searching frantically for shape to cling to.

Destroy them. You have entered the Kill Zone now.

By force of will, I gathered in the sheet of light; concentrated it. And as it centred between my forehead and the jewel, I saw them for the last time. In a burning flash of brightness, they melted. Miniature spheres rose into the blaze of light; then, speared by blinding rays, they ignited. I spun away from the wall as it began to disintegrate, and streams of flowing silver fire coursed down the length of the passage. I turned; glanced back at the liquidizing crystal masses; then ran headlong as walls of malachite and quartz, granite and topaz melted around me. I kept moving; vaguely aware that the ice underfoot had lost its sheerness. I ran through wide pathways which narrowed, joined intersections and continued; taking me deeper in towards the Heart of Gehina. Behind me, I heard the roaring sounds of my strike blotting out the moan of the wind. And as I raced forward, I saw that the walls were becoming lower, the paths narrower.

Then I saw it. The centre of the citadel.

33: *Kill Zone*

WHERE THE WALLS ended, it began. A vast sheer surface stretched out in front of me. From the perfect straightness of the edge of it, I guessed that the huge clearing could have been a geometric shape; but I wasn't certain. Just ahead of me in the pearly light I caught sight of the two men. They stood very still, facing away from me; and as I watched I saw why they were motionless. Moving in towards them, across the wide flat area was a line of gleaming Creatures; gigantic warriors, helmeted with shining visors of white metal, led by monstrous hyenas in perfect formation.

You have entered the Kill Zone now.

'Dear God . . .!' I whispered, as I gazed at the advancing lines.

Nelson turned, whiplash-quick. His eyes met mine. 'You heard it', he said. 'The Voice from beyond the Place of the Thunder.' His voice was steady and clear, and he had his back to the advance.

'Nelson . . .!'

'I know.' Then he turned away from me; pointed to the Creatures as they moved in.

'See them?' he said. 'Gehina's armies.' He began to move forward towards them.

'For Chrissakes! Nelson!!' I screamed. Mathon turned to me, his eyes grave. 'My brother . . .' he said. 'The armies. Look. They advance.'

'Mathon! Burn them! Do it!'

'I cannot. The power . . . is gone from me. I am disarmed . . .!' I stared, unable to believe what I heard. His voice was weak; and in his eyes was something hollow, beyond pain.

'No!!' I shouted; 'No! It's not true! This place is using something in you – for God's sake! Something in you to drain your power! To turn you against yourself! They did it with me!'

Nelson kept walking. He was already half way between us and the lines.

'You created them!' I screamed again at Mathon. You dreamed them into life. Gehina's using you to destroy yourself!'

Mathon stared at me; right into me. But the expression in his eyes hadn't changed.

'That's what's happening here!' I yelled. 'The rocks, the different shapes – they're designed to make you create those Creatures! The Raiders take them from your mind, Goddamn it! This is their home, Mathon, their Heart! This is where it all begins! They can do what they damn well like, here!'

'My brother . . .' he whispered. 'My people are not gods . . .'

'Yeah? Well never say die!'

I turned away from him, and ran for Nelson who was drawing

nearer to the helmeted line. He was walking steadily, slowly, towards them. He didn't look back.

'Nelson! Get your ass back here, you crazy son of a bitch!' He didn't respond; gave no sign he had even heard me. From closer range, I could see glistening chains leading from the necks of the hyena Creatures to the hands of the giants. I threw myself at Nelson; grabbed hold of him roughly, and tried to turn him back; but he didn't move one inch from his course. He just kept on walking.

'Screw you, old man! Can't you hear me? For Chrissakes, move it! Get out of there!' Intrepid, the line came on; a shining haze around them. Their visors shone in the light.

'No!' I shouted. 'This . . . damn you to hell. This isn't going to happen!'

I stood; watched Nelson. He had moved away from me, and was now only yards from the silent advance.

'No-o-o-o!'

As I screamed, the light-shield sprang up; a dazzling sheet between me and them. In it, I saw the shape of Nelson; and in front of him, the hundreds became thousands, scattered in the shield into the many tiny fragments of their existence.

'Nelson!' I shrieked, not knowing if he could even hear. 'Get out of the way!'

Then they were upon him. His form seemed to blend with them. But I couldn't wait. I drew in the light; rayed it out in a single beam. Then I saw only whiteness, as the ground began to heave and dissolve into the flare. In waves it rolled forward. And the roaring began. I dived sideways as bright rivers poured across the open space; and ran, twisting my head to throw a glance back. There, in the lightstorm, I thought saw him, but I couldn't be sure. A dark shape seemed to raise its arms in the unearthly glow, and I thought I heard a wild, joyful cry of triumph, or of pain. And I seemed to see a figure, dancing. But then I saw nothing but the glassy surface as it pushed upwards and froze into solidity. Great angular lumps protruded from the glowing ground.

'Nelson!' I screamed hopelessly. I got no answer; and plunged forward to where the surface of the huge clearing was still intact. Shielding my eyes against the aftermath of the strike, I stared desperately back; but could see no sign of him. And then, beyond the buckled ground, I saw another line, advancing.

'You stinking bastards!' I shrieked. 'Stinking bastards!'

You have to go back in. They're not finished yet. You have to do it. You're the only one left.

'Okay!' I cried, maddened. And I ran back again, leaping over angles of glass, my feet sinking between them into grey deadness;

'Okay! You'll get it till there's nothing left to give.'

Lingering radiation lit their helmets; played on the chains of the leading beasts. And I ran towards them, needing closer range, needing to be nearer. Instantly, a sheet of light went up and a narrow beam crossed, over me. I watched it as it broke out, cut through the air, found its target. The line of advance disintegrated. The roaring began. But I couldn't run. I fell; rolling out of control on the violent heavings of the ground. I tried to get to my feet; but was thrust down again, clinging to shining, moving fragments as the battleground changed shape. A hand gripped me; throwing me roughly aside. Then something with tremendous strength dragged me.

'It is not finished yet . . .' The harsh whisper came over the sounds of disintegration.

'Mathon!'

'It is I.'

'Where is he? Nelson? Where is he?'

At first he made no answer; but dragged me to the fringe of the battle-zone and pulled me down beyond the broken ground. Then he spoke;

'The old man;' he said. 'I saw him dance upon the fires; moving between the advance. And I saw a hawk-bird and a young wolf with him. Then I saw him no more.'

I twisted away and staggered up. Then, unable to move and unable to reply, I stared out into the flare which was now fading.

'Well you ain't been looking hard enough, boy . . .'

I turned quickly, to see Nelson moving up behind us.

'Jesus! Nelson . . .'

'I don't deal no grief, Man. They ain't the cards I like.'

He looked weary, but the light in his eyes was burning.

'I like bigger things than that. And we gotta move on, 'cause if those mothers are the last, I'd be damn surprised . . .'

'Why did you do that? What the hell were you playing at?'

'Hah!' he answered. And that was all he said.

'We must move on. As he suggests,' Mathon said. 'We are here; the centre.'

'Let's go.' Nelson began to walk away.

'Where to?' I began.

'Like he said, this is it. See this ground?'

He waved his arms, pointing from edge to edge of the wide area. Where we stood the terrain was flat. But where we had waged war, it was tortured and broken.

'This is where she is . . . Somewhere here. Keep going.'

We said no more, but crossed the glassy surface, passing the torn area of destruction. We moved fast. But the silence was ominous. They were waiting, watching, holding fire. And I didn't know why. The radiating glow slowly began to dim over the strike zone. We skirted round it; keeping constant watch across the torn and melted area we had blown. We saw no signs of anything; but a creeping mist was moving over the landscape making vision difficult. Yet at the edge, we trod on glass, opaque and perfectly smooth. I noticed we were following a straight course; walking a distinct line. Then the line veered off at another angle.

As we passed the angle, Mathon dropped back, studying it.

'Mathon!' I called out to him. 'Let's keep on the move! Come on!'

'It is as I thought,' he replied. 'A system characterized by three equal co-planar axes, intersecting at angles of sixty degrees . . . There will be a fourth, perpendicular . . .'

'Okay! What does that mean?' I said impatiently.

'It means . . .' he whispered; 'they are like us.'

I halted; caught Nelson by the arm. 'They are like . . . like who?'

'The Charos,' Mathon replied. 'They use an identical system.'

'They like sixes,' Nelson said. 'That's what he means. It figures.'

Mathon was watching the mist. He had turned away from us to stare into it.

'We are following the outer angles of a hexagonal form,' he continued.' And must move on to the perpendicular, take ninety degrees, a straight line, inward. But it will lead us on to a new plane. We must not deviate from that course, as I believe to do so would be hazardous.'

'We go in?' I asked.

'Yes. Like us, they have a type of axis-shift protection. It is simple, pure. In its simplicity it is near-inscrutable. Except to a mind which knows it.'

'What? Back in towards the war-zone? You know what it's like there! We've wiped it . . .'

'No. If we take a perfect line, an accurate perpendicular, there will be no trace of the strike-area. We shall transcend it and enter . . . the Source.'

'Okay,' Nelson said. 'Got the picture. Find the line.'

Mathon walked away, searching along the length of the hexagon's side. The straight edge extended for some distance. In the thickening air, I couldn't see where it met the other side; and realized that Mathon had only been able to tell that we were on a huge hexagon by observing the angle we had just passed. I hadn't even noticed it. We waited; watching him merge into the mist. Then he slowly re-appeared, coming back towards us.

'I have located it,' he said as he drew near. 'The exact mid-point. That is what we must use to find the line.'

I nodded. 'Right,' I said to him, 'you take us through.'

He walked back a short way along the edge. Nelson and I followed. Then Mathon stopped suddenly, made a half turn, and pointed inward across the flat space which was now covered in thick mist. He said no more, but watched us for a moment. Then he began to walk, away from the straight edge into the clouded air. In silence, we progressed in single-file; and as we went, I noticed that I could no longer hear the low moan of the wind. We kept on going; then Mathon spoke and his voice broke the total silence.

'Hold course. We are going in.'

A light cut through the mist. Ahead I could see only Mathon. But I heard a low throbbing.

'Oh . . . my God,' I whispered. Formations of dark riders came at us, gleaming black as they swept in.

'Move!' Mathon called out. 'Pass me. Keep going! Do not lose course!'

I held my ground; prepared to activate the Light-shield.

'No!' he shouted. 'Follow my instructions!'

'Where are they coming from? Where?' I shouted back. The riders bore down on us, cloaked in silver, their cloaks billowing behind them as they came.

'Move on!' Mathon ordered. 'You and the old man, go before me.'

Then he whipped round; and I saw the focus of his eyes change as the great burning flare went out from him, reflecting the swarmings in it. Nelson forced his way past me. I felt the weight of his hand in my back, and the violent jerk of his pull on me.

'Okay, do as he says. Gogogo!'

'I will hold off the advance.' I heard Mathon say as we stumbled forward. 'Now go!'

I looked back; saw the expanse of whiteness draw in, concentrate about Mathon and fire out in a focused beam. Then the roaring came; and around us, drops of rain, like mercury, sliced through the air. Then it was gone. Mathon was gone. I spun round, feeling that we had lost our course. I turned quickly to Nelson.

'We got it.' I heard him say.

34: *Source*

I LOOKED PAST him to what now lay around us. Another hexagon, a perfectly flat shining area of glass stretched out, but this time no more than thirty feet or so in breadth. The angles of its edges glinted in a pale glow given off by a small sphere which stood at the very centre of the clearing. I stared at the sphere. Barely four feet in diameter, it seemed fine, paper-thin, delicate, like a glass bubble.

'Look . . .' Nelson whispered, and pointed to the right of it where a silent, formless mass stood, almost twice its height, glittering with reflected light on countless tiny fibres. Thin, light-violet rays danced over the surface of the mass; passing backwards and forwards from the spherical object.

'What . . . is that?' I whispered. He hesitated; and I began to move towards it. But he grabbed my arm, halting me.

'The birth place', he replied. 'Genesis, Man. Where it all begins.'

The transparent sphere was alive with impulses, crossing and darting silently; rising from its core, spreading across its surface.

'It's . . . alive . . .?' I could hardly speak; couldn't take my eyes from it. '. . . Alive, communicating . . .? With that . . .'

'This is them', Nelson broke in. 'This is what they are.'

I remembered the miniature bubble-like forms which had risen into the air after every disintegration. And how one strike was never enough for them. I watched, staring into the rhythmic violet rays. Then I caught sight of an inner form beneath them; a red shape slowly twisting round itself, twining in a double spiral as it floated suspended in colourless substance. A delicate frosted network bound the spirals together; knitting them into a curving ladder of fragile sparkling rods.

'That's it' I whispered, almost to myself. 'The red spirals . . . in the Disintegrations. The same thing . . .'

'You see that?' His voice sounded far away; and I broke my gaze to watch him for a second. But his eyes didn't leave the sphere. 'You know what it is? Basic data. The essence of them. Their D.N.A.'

'D.N.A . . .?' I could hardly hear my voice as I spoke to him. 'But it can't be . . . here? That's science, physical . . . Old World . . .'

'No. It ain't. It's the blueprint for all existence. All things come from Inner Space, remember? The double helix, the intention. It's the first principle, Man. This is theirs.'

I turned back to see it: graceful, pure, silent. An embryo of Gehina's existence. Knowing that made it terrible. I felt myself weakened as the red shape writhed quietly. Then my eyes were drawn to the shining fibrous mass. I gazed at it; not understanding.

'That . . . thing' I whispered. 'What the hell is it . . .?'

He turned to me; looked closely at me.

'Her,' he replied. 'Thainé.' As the full impact of his words hit me, I jumped forward, but I felt the powerful restraint of his grip.

'No, Man! Don't go near it!'

'Nelson! What are you saying? Don't go near it? That . . . is her? Thainé? In there? In those . . . webs? *Jesus*!' I struggled to get out of his grasp; strained to see into the shapeless mass. But Nelson's arm was too strong on mine.

'Not yet', he said. 'You go near it, you try to take her and it'll turn on you.'

Then, between the shimmering fibres and lilac rays I saw her; a vague outline of her form. 'She can't . . . see us . . .? Know we're here?'

'Yeah', he replied. 'She can see us. But she can't do nothing about it. She's immobilized. See those rays? From the sphere? They're taking data from her, for the Matrix of the Great One.'

'Dear God! Let go of me, Nelson!'

'You blow this and you blow everything. The whole lot. You get that? You blow the whole show!'

'That's just what I intend to do! Blow it!'

'No!' He gripped me, harder; tugged me back. 'No! You ain't, Man!'

'Let . . . go of me!' I wrenched myself with sudden force and broke free of his grip. He lunged at me.

'Man! It ain't gonna work! Listen to me, will you?'

'I'm not damn listening! Back off for Chrissakes!'

'We can't smash this one. Not like the others! It's a whole different ball-game. We're not looking at what they've created here; at something they get inside. We're looking at their *Creator*!'

'Let go of me, Nelson! You see that . . . that webbed-up thing? That's what I came to get! That's her, inside of there.' He grabbed at me again, and I swung round; twisting out of his hands.

'I blow it! Now! I pull the switch on the whole damn thing!'

I activated the light-shield. It spread in a great white blaze between me and the sphere.

'Shooting into the light! Drag your ass sideways, Nelson, if you don't like it!'

'You can't . . .

'Watch me!'

'. . . destroy it, Man! Listen! *You can't destroy it!*'

I searched the shield; but I knew she wouldn't reflect in it. Only the enemy, a million tiny fragments of Gehina's Genesis, spirals like a swarm of mayflies dancing; that was all I saw. Then I sent the ray. Straight, clean, quick, the concentrated beam struck target. Incandescent, the sphere seemed to expand as the bolt I had sent to destroy it split over its surface; coursing round to fly out again in bright fingers of lightning. I felt Nelson pull me to the ground.

'Damn your ass!'

The glassy hexagon rolled; broke open. A thunderous roaring moved everything apart around us. I twisted with Nelson and together we tumbled to the edge of a fast widening crack.

'Damn it, I told you. You hot-headed dumb shit-brained son of a . . .!'

Molten glass poured past us as I rolled again, pulling Nelson with me. We rose up on a wave of heaving ground, and I caught a glimpse of the sphere, and the cocoon. Both were untouched; perfect. Then suddenly, the heaving stopped. The ground froze into contorted forms. Floating particles of purple dust fell about us like snow.

'Got to get her out.' I stumbled forward, clinging to angles of solidified melted glass; crawled to the edge of the broken area and staggered up. Immediately around the sphere, the glass was smooth, unaffected. I stood, so close to the small object that had resisted my attack.

'It ain't possible to destroy it!' I heard Nelson shout. Then I saw him moving towards me. 'Any more than it's possible to destroy the night. Night and day. Dark and light. You gotta have both. Not just one. Not just the other. Both! It's the Law.'

'Screw the Law!'

'Man! You don't know. But you got to know. You'll burn your power, again and again, fighting the Law you can't change. And Gehina waits; just waits, for you to destroy yourself. Take her.

Yeah, maybe you can. But you can't touch the sphere. Let the Charos keep the Balance. They'll do that if we don't blow this! They'll take over where we leave off.'

'Screw the stinking Law!'

'Goddamn it, I'm asking you!'

Then I lunged forward; grasping at the webs which concealed her. My hand touched their substance and seemed to pass through it. I felt a searing heat. Coloured light cut across my field of vision. Above a throbbing sound, I heard Nelson's voice, and saw him moving towards me through the haze of colour. I touched her hand, only for a second before I lost it again. But I could feel her Self, struggling to survive. In that touch, memory of the Rose flooded to me, and the memory of many deaths. I tasted the blood of the power of the Great Ones, as I would forever. And I saw the pale warrior woman who rode into the wind. Webs brushed lightly against me. I glanced down. Fine threads were forming over my arms. I lifted my hand to brush them off my face, and I saw her eyes, set on mine, fighting to reach me. Her mouth was moving, trying to shape words. But I heard nothing.

There was an old man coming, through the sparkling patterns that wove around me. Slowly, like movements in a dream, he bore down on us, and turned suddenly, his arms stretched out in front of him. As the shining tendrils began to block off my sight, I saw fragments of him, plunging forward towards the Sphere, reaching out to embrace it with both arms. And as he touched it, the webs were falling from my eyes; and I heard a cry. Animal-like, defiant, like the cry of a beast in a trap, its sound began to cut the threads which were building up on my body. A screaming came to me. Words cracked into many parts.

'Go! . . . out! . . . take her . . . now!'

The webs split; sparking as they fell away.

'Do it . . .' I heard. And then there was the reality of Thainé's hand, gripping mine. Instantly I could move. And together we pushed outwards; staggering to the fringe of the torn ground. Twisting round as we escaped, I caught sight of Nelson, enclosed in glistening web; his hands stretching its substance as they reached out. His scream changed, from one of pain to one of victory as the mass of fibres meshed round him. Then he began to push; forcing against them, until his shape was moulded in lines of light which resisted his attempts to be free. I watched as his fingers finally broke through. Charges from the Sphere flickered along his arms, to re-build what he had torn. But his upper body ripped free, and he turned, straining backwards, shrieking words I could not understand. The webs clung. Then one by one they snapped, to float silently upwards as they eventually lost their grip on him.

'Okay!' he cried as he rushed towards us. 'Move it. Get out of here. Go!' His voice was desperate, weak. But his eyes burned.

I turned to Thainé. She could move, but seemed unable to speak. Then, without looking back we stumbled over the twisted ground, plunging through up-thrust forms of now-solid melted glass.

'I'm right behind you.' From behind us I heard his cracked whisper. 'Right here. Now go, Man, go!'

I couldn't see the outer edge of the hexagon any more; couldn't see where we had come in when we had entered the centre. Gripping Thainé, I turned frantically, to scan the area.

'Where?' I shouted. 'The place we got through. Where the damn hell is it?' Quickly I glanced at Thainé. Her expression was glazed, exhausted. Her eyes were pinned on mine, as if she were trying with all her strength to reach something in me, and couldn't. A flash of strength rose up in her, then passed, faded, and rose up again.

'Come on!' I half-whispered, half-screamed at her. 'I can't drag you through. I need you! You come back, or we're not going to make it. There's just two of you now, just two Charos! You and Mathon. And if he's gone down out there, and who knows? he might have done, then you're the only one left. Do you get that? You have got to make it. Goddamn! You've got to!' I saw her eyes flare, and her mouth move, in her struggle to speak. Then I heard Nelson cry out.

'Here!' Rays crackled through the air; pale purple lines, seeking, probing. As I spun round, I saw that they came from the Sphere.

'Jesus!' I yelled. 'It's trying to *find* us!'

'Get over here. I've got the place,' he screamed. 'Just do it!'

Hanging on to Thainé, I crossed the buckled surface of the hexagon. Her strength responded, then ebbed away again as I struggled forward, dragging her behind me. The rays grazed her hair. I saw them, and pulled hard on her arms, jerking her away. She stumbled and fell; but immediately was on her feet again; swaying as her eyes narrowed with effort, and locked on to mine.

'I am with you' she whispered. 'I hear you . . .' And when we reached Nelson, I heard the wind rise, roaring about us as we threw ourselves forward to cross the axis. Then we broke through to the outer hexagon, and I saw Mathon, holding off line after line of attacking forces. He had fallen to his knees; and when he turned to us, his face was wracked. Tears poured down his cheeks.

'Take them . . .!' he cried out. 'Take them from me! My brother!'

Melting torrents flowed. The walls of the citadel had fallen, becoming rivers of melted crystal which rolled over the landscape. Great sheets of ice heaved up on waves of blinding light, to slowly turn and crash back into the turmoil. And above, on the grey air, metal-winged reptile-Creatures advanced.

'They did live from my visions!' Mathon gasped. 'Until I mastered those visions. Then they came forth from my contempt!'

He staggered back. 'Now they rise from my weakness . . . my despair!'

'No!' I shouted to him. 'No, Mathon. They're more than that. I know, now. More, much more!'

I activated the sheet of light; didn't wait to see the thousands swarming, but sent out the beam. The first line incinerated. But behind that line, another came, in perfect formation. I struck again; and in the flash of the strike, I could no longer see where the ground met the sky. Then, through a storm of fire-hail, I saw a third line winging down.

'We need to move!' Nelson shouted. 'Find the way outa here!'

I blew the third line away. The immediate deafening roar blotted out Nelson's voice; but I caught sight of him, pushing ahead in the brilliance.

'C'mon! We fight as we run!' I heard him shout to me. I glanced back; saw Mathon rising again. In the set of his face, I could see steely determination. But his exhaustion was obvious. Then his gaze swept past me, and I turned in time to see a fourth line bearing down on us. As I focused, ready to attack, I felt suddenly overcome, drained of energy. In that moment I knew what Mathon had done in holding off the advance.

'Brett!' I heard her voice. 'Go, now! We will take them!'

'No! I'll stay with you!'

'No! Gather your force. You are weakened. Go!'

A wide sheet of blinding light spread out. But before she activated the strike, she shouted to me.

'Go!'

I hesitated; but saw that her strength had returned. And so I ran, weaving in and out as the war-zone changed shape.

'Nelson!'

'Okay!' I heard, and saw his dark form leaping and plunging ahead of me. 'Make it fast, boy!'

I turned on the run; straining to keep sight of her, and Mathon.

'They'll be okay,' Nelson cried out. 'We just got to keep moving.' Then I saw the two of them, racing towards us across the brilliantly-lit ground. Fire and ice rained down as I turned back, to follow where Nelson led. Another light-storm flared. I was unable to even see the attacking forces; but knew that either she or Mathon must have disintegrated them. The landscape heaved again, re-forming. Suddenly, ahead of us stood the ice-field. Under rolling mists it lifted and buckled, as masses of ice pushed up out of its flowing. I could see no possible way to cross it.

'The Warps!'

'Right here. You ready?'

'Thainé! Mathon! They're still in there.' But as I spun round, the two of them emerged behind us from the melting citadel.

'We are ready,' Mathon said.

'Okay.' Nelson's eyes held mine for a second as he said 'We ride! Make this good!' He stepped away; disappeared. I stood still; watched him go. Then I turned immediately to the oth-

ers. I saw her face, lit by the fires from the Heart of Gehina.
And there was power and love in those eyes as they met
mine.

'We ride' I said. 'Let's go.' Together, the three of us entered the
Warps. I caught fleeting glimpses of Nelson; but then he was
gone. And one after the other we traversed the Chasms of Time
and the howling gales from the Outer Reaches; and all the way,
I held on to her Spirit, because it was all I had, or could ever have,
to take me home. And I hoped, for Mathon. I hoped.

There was no more howling; only a great brightness flooding
across my sight. A tremendous light burned into me, making me
never want to look away from it. And then, over strange and
beautiful sounds, I heard a voice, faint at first, then strong.

'We done it! . . . Yee-hah! Oh boy! We done it!' I felt stunned;
could hardly move. But he gripped my arm from behind, and
swung me around, then lifted his hand, slapping our palms
together, once, twice, three times.

'We really done it Man! We done it!'

But I turned suddenly, searching for Thainé and Mathon. I
saw only high peaks of the white mountains, shining above the
dazzling light of the Crossing Place.

'Where are they?' I whispered, unable to share his excitement.
'Nelson . . . Did they make it?' Searching for sight of them, I
spun round, breaking away from him. Then I heard him say
'Yeah. They made it.' And when I looked back, they were there,
standing next to Nelson in the glowing air. I gazed at Mathon,
then at Thainé. She smiled, touching her forehead with both
hands in the Charos salute. When she looked up, there was joy
in her eyes.

'Hope,' I whispered. 'Okay, now there's hope . . .' The strange
music returned, drifting out of the light.

'You hear that?' Nelson said. 'Ain't that the sweetest thing you
ever heard?' He came up to me, stood eye-to-eye, and took me
by the shoulders. 'Know what it is, Man? That's the sound of
Angels dancing . . .'

I watched as he unfastened the silver star ring and the hawk's
foot from the thong around his neck, and handed them to me.
Not understanding, I took them from him; held them.

'Nelson . . .?'

'That's it,' he replied. 'That's the sound.. It's time for my crossing over. You take those Bright Spirits that hung round my neck a while. 'Cause I don't have need of 'em no more.'

He stepped back; saluted me left-handed.

'Nelson . . .!'

A breeze caught him, blowing his long braids back as he stood for a moment, his eyes fixed on mine one last time. Then he said no more, but turned and walked into the River of Light.

'No!' I ran towards him, seeing the outline of his form silhouetted against the flowing torrent. Then slowly, gradually, it blended, melting away as the sounds rose up, filling the white air. I felt the touch of a hand on my arm.

'Let him go,' she said. 'For his work is done, and in the End is the Beginning.'

But I kept watch; straining to see into that great Light until I saw nothing but the waves of its course, that I knew would be there forever, at the Crossing-Place. And Nelson was gone. After a long time I turned to her; saw that she held out the reins of a horse, mantled for war. As her hand touched mine I took those reins from her. But when I did, I heard his words again, echoing in the brilliance;

'And I'll tell you another thing. One day I'll go there and find her. One day'll come when it'll be time to go over. And I won't be back no more.'

And he brought many things to me, that man.

He brought the tides of crazy winds, in which I learned to grow wings.

He brought me the storms, with fears riding bare-backed on them.

He brought me recall of what I was.

He laughed at me. He laughed, even at Armageddon.

But he cried when I said I wouldn't take up arms against the spreading darkness.

And in the silver star of his love, and in the hawk's foot of his power,

I salute him.